T0208213

THE ISLE OF

FIRE

AND

ICE

BOOK 1

THE ISLE OF

FIRE AND ICE

PJ THOMPSON

WESTBOW
PRESS®
A DIVISION OF THOMAS NELSON
& ZONDERVAN

WestBow Press books may be ordered through booksellers or by contacting:

WestBow Press
A Division of Thomas Nelson & Zondervan
1663 Liberty Drive
Bloomington, IN 47403
www.westbowpress.com
1 (866) 928-1240

ISBN: 978-1-9736-5902-0 (sc)
ISBN: 978-1-9736-5904-4 (hc)
ISBN: 978-1-9736-5903-7 (e)

Library of Congress Control Number: 2019904049

Print information available on the last page.

WestBow Press rev. date: 4/19/2019

Artist and Illustrator are titles spoken over me to describe what I do, but who I am is an image bearer of the Master Creator. I truly delight in bringing empty paper to life with truths written in the deeper places of my soul. As a child it looked like swirly lines, and silly characters of the familiar, but now, joy abounds as I sit with The Creator and surrender every word lettered, image drawn and color chosen to what He enlightens, which feels inadequate at best with my limited knowledge and skill.

Carla Autrey, *Artist and Illustrator*

Once, long ago, on an isle of fire and ice, there lived
a prophecy of hope in a land darkened with despair:
"In that time when wickedness holds full sway,
two shall stand in evil's way.
Uriisis- and wolf-marked, this pair,
shining, like-marked swords will bear.
Their appearance will display
the Maker's mercy in that day."

CONTENTS

THE RUNAWAY

DARE SHIVERED WITH COLD IN HIS SHORT tunic as he fled down Rave's back stairs. The frigid stone of the ancient keep was slippery from last night's storm. He tried to be careful.

From the portal at the top of the stairs, Ursul screamed, "Dare, return at once! Do you hear me? At once!" The fleeing serf heard both disbelief and fury in his master's voice. Startled, he stumbled on the slick stone and crashed down hard on his right hip and elbow. Panic flooded through him. He ignored the sickening jolt of pain, pushed himself up, and raced down the remaining steps.

I won't turn back! I won't! Still, he was sick with fear at his brash, foolhardy act. *I've decided to run, and now I must escape. The alternative is … unthinkable.*

Perspiration trickled down Dare's face and body as he dashed toward the outer ward. It lay outside the keep but remained within the confines of thick stone walls. Yet it was closer, much closer to freedom. His breath came in quick, short gasps. Pain from his fall pulsed in sharp agony through his arm and hip, causing him to limp.

If I starve in the forest, it will be better than the misery I've endured these last few years. He held tightly to this idea and made an effort to think ahead. *Will Ursul send someone after me, or will he continue the chase?* Dare decided Ursul would do neither. Josata, the overseer, would be waiting for him. The old servant was extremely irritable because important guests of the duke's were coming. Dare knew Ursul could not spare any of the other drudges from the frantic preparations for their visitors' arrival. *Anyway, not many of them are big enough to bring me back,* he thought with a grin. His face brightened, and for a moment, his spirits lifted.

This is a good time to run, what with the swarm of activity all through the keep. I did not plan this. Bore's bow, I wish I had. However, the preparations for important folk coming will keep Ursul busy—for a time at least. Another possibility occurred to him as he threaded his way through a maze of stacked goods, barrels, and lumber. *Will he send a messenger telling the guards at the main gate to be on watch and take me prisoner? Will he go to all that trouble for one clumsy, insignificant drudge?* The prospect made his stomach cramp. The main gate was his only chance to get free of the fortress. All the others were locked.

He forced himself to stop and think clearly. *It will not occur to Ursul that I'm leaving for good. He'll think I am running from a beating. Chances are good that he has not called a general alarm. Why should he? Where can I go? Drudges are not allowed out of the keep.* These thoughts calmed him.

There were no sounds of pursuit as Dare broke into the bright sunshine and the bustling commerce of the outer ward. He needed to stop to rest and plan. But where? A small stable was close by, dark and out of the milling traffic and noise. He slowed his pace and casually grabbed an armload of hay from a deserted wagon. He carried it, with a shuffle and a half-witted expression, to the small stable. Under Ursul's brutal apprenticeship, Dare had learned to feign slowness and ignorance. He hid his quick mind and wit behind a fabricated dullness that had become second nature. The young drudge had found that when he played the half-wit, Ursul and others didn't suspect him of thinking, much less planning. Often they didn't even notice his existence. He became invisible.

He smelled the distinct odors of horse and hay as he entered the stable's cool shadows. Once inside, he tried to devise some kind of a workable plan. First, he needed different clothing. The gray drudge's tunic identified him as a castle servant. Going outside the keep was one of the many things drudges weren't allowed to do. Then he must find food, water, and, if possible, a knife. Once he reached the forest, he would need them to survive. Dare began to search the small structure.

A sound outside the stable door suspended his thoughts and made his heart race again. With a new cunning born of desperation, Dare quickly found a place to hide.

"Bring the healer's horse over here, Raff. That's right—this be his stable, him leaving at all hours and not wanting a stable hand."

Dare scooted back into the dark corner of the first stall. He quickly covered himself with armloads of hay. *Don't put him in here!*

"Put him in the far stall. And do get some fresh hay from that wagon out there," the kindly old stable hand ordered as he puttered and muttered to himself. He and Raff rubbed the horse down and finally left.

Dare breathed grateful thanks to the Maker. For a time he did not move, but when all seemed quiet, the anxious runaway quickly searched the stall he was in. He found nothing.

He decided to chance disturbing Ollif, as Raff had called the horse, and search the rest of the small stable. As he softly talked to the animal, Dare went through the saddlebags on the rail of the stall. He hoped his voice would reassure the animal. No need to worry; Ollif snorted softly and then ignored Dare as he munched his hay.

Why did the healer leave these bags here? Is he going out again soon? Maker, grant me time. Some food wrapped in a cloth—cheese and two small apples—lay in the bottom of one bag, and a leather case lay in the other. He took the food but decided not to search the case. *Interesting it might be, but I've no time.*

Dust motes danced in the sunshine that poured through cracks in the boards of the old barn. In this faint light, Dare found a small knife on a shelf among some hair-filled brushes. The pegs on the wall bore rags and tools but no clothes. He quickly wrapped the food and knife in one of the rags and tied it tightly in a knot.

Wait, what's that? Piled in the corner was a brown wool garment with a hood. *Much too long,* Dare thought as he tried it on. *Perhaps I can cut it off. No, it will take too much time.* He found a piece of rope, tied it around his waist, and pulled the extra fabric up and over it. *Aye, that'll do.* Dare listened at the door and then carefully looked out at the yard.

It was still busy with merchants, farmers, soldiers, and the nobility who were buying and selling. Servants and drudges hurried about, talking and arguing with each other. There was little laughter; the tension in the castle seemed to have spread out here. Dare wondered again who could be coming.

The sun was sinking in the west, which created many shadows among the tents and outbuildings, shadows where he could hide. *At sunset the gate will close. I must be out before then, if possible with more food and something to carry water. Maybe even boots. I am crazy. I will be favored to get out with my skin.* However, a reckless sense of adventure that astonished and frightened him was growing in the young drudge. *You have made it this far, haven't you?*

A crew of outside drudges armed with twig brooms, rakes, and shovels worked feverishly to clean the grounds. Many merchant tents and booths still dotted the grassy areas. As Dare walked to the shadow of one of the tents, he heard a low groan behind him. He turned quickly and looked for the source of the miserable sound. A lump of darker shadow moved and groaned again. Cautiously approaching whomever it was, Dare smelled the reek of sour wine. Someone who had indulged beyond his limit was sleeping it off in the shade. Dare hoped he was his size and wore boots.

The young nobleman was almost as tall as Dare but not as heavy. After carefully relieving him of his cloak and boots, Dare searched him for anything else he could use. His fumbling hand touched something smooth. A wineskin! There was very little in it, but it was just what he needed to carry water.

Dare slipped close to the tent and put the boots on. They were far too fine for a monk. He covered them with mud and hoped no one would look closely. The cloak was also too fine. He rolled it into a bundle and carried it under his arm. A stab of fear made him close his eyes and clench his fists; the duke severely punished drudges caught stealing. Gruesome images flashed through his mind. He pushed them firmly aside as he searched the courtyard for the safest path to the gate, which was looking farther away every second.

Dare stepped out and moved purposefully toward a merchant's booth near the gate. The sun was very low now, and he throttled a desire to pick up his robe and run. Someone bumped into Dare hard, causing him to stumble.

"I'm sorry, sir! That's what comes of being in such a hurry. Are you hurt?" It was Lfdau, the baker's apprentice.

Dare kept his head down, for he knew Lfdau well from his days in the kitchens. He assured him in a low voice, "I'm fine. I'm fine." Lfdau hurried off with a heavy bag of flour on his shoulder. The distracted baker did not recognize his old friend. Dare steadied himself and went on.

Just ahead of him, a large farming family was following a lumbering wagon, now empty, out of the gate. The wagon driver was talking to a big fellow dressed in green who sat beside him, and the others in the group chatted happily as they walked. Dare slipped in with the group as the sun's last rays shone on their weathered, merry faces and dark hair. The group passed the tired, disinterested guards and went through the huge gatehouse. Dare strolled with them out of the deep shadow of the gatehouse and into the golden sunlight on the other side.

I can't believe it was that easy. I am free!

Suddenly, the old man driving the farm wagon pointed down the road and yelled something. *What's wrong?* From Dare's vantage point in the middle of the group, he could see nothing but his fellow travelers.

Quickly, the large man next to the driver grabbed the reins and forced the horses, with much yelling and slapping of leather, into the ditch next to the highway. At his shouted command, those around the wagon piled into the weed-choked gully also. Someone tackled Dare, and together they fell on the hard ground at the bottom of the ditch.

Hard-pressed horses with riders dressed in gray-and-gold livery thundered past them and through the gate. It closed behind them with a crash. Dare went cold inside. The supreme ruler of all Ree or his emissary must be visiting Ravensperch, for gray and gold were the colors of the intensely hated monarch King Bardock. The kindly people around Dare cursed their king, very quietly of course, under their breath. They quickly sorted out the mess his arrogant soldiers had made of them and their possessions. Thanks to the large man in green, both the wagon and people were safe.

A sudden, powerful sense of urgency pushed Dare to his feet. Without stopping to thank his rescuer, he turned and walked rapidly toward the deepening shadows under the trees. He hoped that no one noticed his departure. Once hidden among the fragrant pines, he leaned gratefully against a tree for a few moments' rest and then pushed on. *I have really done it. I have run away! Have I lost my mind? Marth will worry.*

He stayed on the edge of the great forest, going in only deeply enough to remain hidden from the road. In the morning, someone might start putting things together … reports of a stolen cloak, wineskin, and boots and a missing brown robe—and a missing drudge.

The darkness around him became so complete that he knew he must stop and wait for the moon to rise and give him light. Dare crouched behind some bushes that grew closely against a rock. He untied the cloth he had tied on his rope belt and ate one of the apples and drank a few swallows of wine. *No more*, he told himself firmly. *You'll be hungrier than this before it's over.* He pulled the fine woolen cloak over him. Though sitting, he soon fell asleep.

Dreams of food and a crackling fire lingered in his mind when he woke with a start. For a moment, he could not think where he was. Cold, hungry, tired, and sore from both Ursul's switch and his fall, he pushed on.

At first, the ache in his hip brought tears to his eyes, but as he walked, it grew easier. Fear of capture forced him to keep going in spite of growing pain in his arm and on his scored back. He walked and rested and then walked again until the darkness turned to gray in the eastern sky. Dare realized with surprise that he had walked all night. *Now, I have no choice. With daylight, I must go deeper into the forest or risk capture.*

He gritted his teeth at the thought. *We drudges, poor souls, do not receive training in woodcraft. How am I to find my way to the province of Ohsay? I don't know, but I don't have time to worry about it now.*

Dare's directions, at best, were sketchy and vague. The terrible reality of a vast and rugged mountain range stretched out in untold acres before him. It mocked his simple plan. Until today, the plan had been only a dream. Dare wanted to find his parents' home. *The duke's hunting dogs will make short work of finding me, a keep-bred drudge with no skills, in this … this wilderness.* His ignorance struck him a harsher blow than any Ursul could give.

Added to his lack of skills, he found true terror in the memories that came unbidden to his mind. He had heard, like all the other drudges and servants, the terrible stories about Glodwin and the mastiffs. Mounted on strong, swift horses, dogs at their side, Glodwin and his soldiers tracked down any thief, murderer, enemy, or runaway. They rarely failed to catch the fugitive and return him or her to the duke for punishment. At least that was what the storytellers said.

Remembering the tales, Dare searched his mind for every trick he had heard around the evening fire. After taking a deep drink and filling his wineskin at a swiftly running brook, he waded up stream in the hope that the water would drown his scent. When the little stream no longer went his way—what he hoped was east—he scrambled up some rocks and rested for a moment in the sunshine. He searched the beautiful, lonely landscape around him and listened but heard only the muted sounds of the forest and his own hard breathing.

To the east, the birches and pines climbed up a slope to the edge of barren rock slides and cliffs that ended in towering, snow-covered peaks. In that direction, the terrain grew rougher. There were tremendous boulders scattered everywhere and deep cracks in the earth; yet east was the direction he must go to find a pass named Uriel-on.

The golden sunshine poured its radiance over everything, and in spite of his fear, Dare enjoyed the beauty that surrounded him. With his whole being he pled silently, *Maker, help me. I have no knowledge of anything outside of Rave. Your world is beautiful beyond belief but vast!*

Feeling calmer, he walked on the rocks as long as they were available, but very soon he found himself hiking on the pine needle–covered ground again, leaving a trail that would be easy to follow. The climb was gradually getting steeper, and Dare felt the strain. In a moment of rest, he heard the chilling sound he feared—the howling of hunting dogs. His walk in the stream and on the rocks might fool them for a time, but they would surely find his trail again.

What can I do? Up! Perhaps there will be a place to hide among the rocks … a cave the dogs can't reach or find. Dare scrambled and fought his way up, slipping on loose rock and twisted roots. His side burned, his breath came in gasps, and his muscles trembled.

Suddenly, a frightened forest creature crashed through the bushes right in front of him. At the same moment, Dare felt a stunning blow to his right shoulder that knocked him to the ground, and then, terrible pain.

He stifled a cry. Over the ragged pounding of his heart, he heard something coming up the hill behind him. Willing his head to clear, he pushed himself up to one knee, but his vision went black and a roaring filled his ears. *Don't faint, you stupid drudge!* He waited for his vision to clear, for some strength to return. The footsteps were very close now. *I must get to my feet and run!*

"Don't run! I'm a friend. My arrow was meant for the deer, not for you. You frightened her—when she shied, you were hit."

Dare hoped the man was telling the truth, because he could not hold his body upright; he felt himself slipping to the ground. Firm hands laid him carefully on his stomach. "My young friend, I hear the duke's hunting dogs behind us, and I think neither of us wants to stay and play. I'll break the arrow off and deal with the rest of it later. We have no time now! You must not cry out—it will be over in a minute."

An arrow? Dare thought through a haze of pain. "Be still now," his unknown attacker commanded. Fire blazed through his shoulder, and the threatening darkness fell.

It's better this way, the young hunter thought. *I've no time to even deal with the bleeding.* The baying grew confused, and the dogs howled their frustration; they had lost the scent.

Gods, grant me time. The young hunter struggled straight up the mountainside with Dare slung over his shoulder. Gasping, Sher headed straight for a sheer cliff of solid granite. *This boy is no lightweight!* Dare moaned and started struggling in Sher's arms.

"Be still, friend," he ordered, his breath coming in gasps now. "We're almost there."

Where? Dare wondered hazily.

Sher slipped into a crack in the wall that some upheaval had created long ago and ran down its narrow length for about thirty feet. He laid Dare down gratefully, and looking into the boy's eyes, he said forcefully, "I'll be back—I must cover our tracks. Be very quiet."

Dare nodded his understanding—all he had the strength to do.

Sher sped back down the path to cover their trail. Finding a fallen pine limb, he used it to erase their tracks in the damp soil on a ledge. Then he dusted the ledge with a powder he carried in a pouch. It would drive the dogs crazy, for a time. *Not much, but it will have to do.*

The winded hunter raced to the spot where he'd left the young man.

Breathing hard, he picked Dare up again and continued deeper into the cut. Outside, the hounds started to howl triumphantly.

Noting Dare's anxious look, the man said, "They've found the scent, young friend, but don't worry. Old Sher has many a trick up his sleeve yet." Gazing at Dare with sudden exasperation, he added, "Why couldn't I have shot someone lighter? How much do you weigh, young giant?"

Dare grinned weakly.

HAVEN

ALTHOUGH THE POWERFUL CANINES HAD found the lost scent, Sher was standing in front of a concealed entrance to their refuge. "Sorry, Glodwin, old friend—we don't have time for this game today," Sher said with a merry grin.

He winked at Dare as he rolled a large, flat boulder sideways, exposing a three-by-four-foot entrance to a cave. After placing Dare on the ground about ten feet into the hidden cave, Sher quickly returned to the opening. He rolled the large boulder back into place by putting his hands in carved holes around the edge and pulling down. Total darkness fell.

Sher fumbled around and then let out a muffled outcry as he bumped into something. A spark of light caught a tar-smeared torch on fire. Sher stuck the torch in a crack between two rocks in order to get a better look at Dare's wound.

"Only a slow trickle of blood is seeping down your back, lad," he assured Dare. *When the arrow comes out, it'll be another story,* Sher thought grimly.

Bright blue eyes in a handsome face smiled reassurance at Dare. "My name is Sher, and believe it or not, I usually hit what I aim at. We've still a way to go, but we'll be safe now for sure. The duke's men will never find us in here."

Dare nodded thankfully through growing waves of agony. Sher lifted Dare up on his shoulder with a groan, which made Dare smile. The man was slight, and the young drudge outweighed him by many pounds. However, Sher somehow managed to trot down the inky tunnel with his burden. The flickering light of the torch he held barely dented the darkness, yet the man moved with confidence and speed. Each jolt brought Dare searing pain and then darkness.

He woke to soft voices and glowing firelight. He lay on his side on a cloak. *I escaped the duke's hounds ... but where am I now? Who is the man who shot and then rescued me?*

A soft, husky voice murmured, "It must come out now, Sher. I'm thinking we can bind him up and take him to Lock, who will not be pleased, but at least the lad will have a better chance."

A black leather kettle filled with water simmered on the fire. Sher took the kettle off with a stick and with the same simple tool scooped a knife out of the boiling water and onto a waiting cloth.

"So, you're awake are you?" Sher searched the pale, young face. *What kind of game have I bagged this day? Are you worth the trouble I'm going to be in? Yet I couldn't leave you behind, now could I? No, no—he'll understand, though he'll scorch my ears and half my hide for bringing you in the mountain without a blindfold.*

Dare's blue eyes were fierce in his pale face. "Must ... you cut it out?"

"Aye, lad, and it's going to hurt like fire for a time. I've nothing to deaden your pain here, but we'll carry you deeper into the mountain to a place where my people live. We have some medicines and a healer there."

Deeper into the mountain! His people! What is he talking about? What have I gotten myself into?

All questions vanished as Sher rolled Dare gently on his stomach. "Josen will hold you, lad."

Dare could hear the pounding of his heart as the young hunter placed leather between his teeth. Dare closed his eyes, bit down on the leather, and sought the Maker for courage. Sher quickly removed the broken arrow and arrowhead, which thankfully were not very deep. He washed the wound with warm water and bound it tightly with torn strips of cloth. Then he carefully lifted his young charge onto Josen's back.

Taking turns carrying him, the two men again moved deeper into the mountain down a tortuous tunnel. Somewhere along the way, blessed insensibility released Dare from pain.

The dogs had him. Their teeth were sinking into his shoulder. In torment, he cried for help, but no one could hear him.

"Lad, wake up! You are all right; you're with friends."

Dare slowly came out of awful dreams to a cool liquid dripping onto his lips. Greedily he opened his mouth. Someone lifted his head and said, "Slowly." Coolness slid down his throat.

"Thank you," he croaked. "Where—"

"Lad, wait—listen. You're safe in the mountain. Sher and Josen brought you to me, and I will care for you till you are well. Later I'll answer all your questions. Now rest and do as I tell you, agreed?"

Dare could barely see the man who was talking to him. They were in a darkened room lit by a small fire in a brazier. He shook his head desperately and tried to think, but he could bring nothing into focus.

"Lad, trust me," the voice urged.

"I have no choice, I think."

"That is true. Now drink this, all of it. It is very bitter, but it will make you sleep and take away the pain."

Dare drank and slept. When he woke up, the same man was carefully bathing his face with a cool, wet cloth. The healer gently washed his arms, legs, and torso. Abnormal tears filled Dare's eyes. Though this display of emotion embarrassed him, he could not seem to stop it. It had been a long time since anyone had touched him with respect, much less gentleness. He scrubbed the tears away with his left hand and tried to regain his fever-weakened composure.

The young drudge remembered Marth's small, comfortable sitting room. His earliest memories were of her and that room. He'd played on brightly woven mats on the floor while Marth had sewn in her moving chair. A fire had seemed to always burn merrily in the stone fireplace, and the yellow cat would pounce on her yarn ball or sleep in the sun on the windowsill. He'd stayed with Marth during the day and slept in a large alcove in her room at night until he was twelve.

At six he'd started helping Sybil in the kitchens. Even then Marth had been old and crippled. Her useless legs made it impossible for her to do any work that was not done sitting. Marth's beautiful embroidery and needlework had earned her a small room of her own and an even smaller stipend. Yet he'd never heard her complain of pain or her state in life. She'd been Dare's only mother; he knew little of his own parents.

Marth trained many of the castle's servingwomen who showed an aptitude for needlework. They'd become his family of sorts and played with, teased, cuddled, and taught him. Laughter and lively conversation would fill the small room as the women, their tongues as busy as their needles, sat around Marth's table. He'd felt safe, loved, and had known no want.

As he'd grown older, he'd helped Marth by becoming her legs. He'd grumbled about it in front of the other boys, but in his heart he was grateful for her care and had served her gladly. He'd also served her well, and for that reason, the overseer had allowed him to remain with her much longer than was normal. In the afternoon he'd also helped in the kitchens.

On Dare's twelfth birthday, because he was unusually large and strong, Ursul had claimed him for heavier service—his service. Marth and the other seamstresses had wept, but there had been nothing they could do. Josata was not a cruel master, but he was a weak one. Ursul barged and pushed his way through life like a large, surly bear. He'd intimidated and bullied the old retainer until Josata let him have his way.

When Dare had entered Ursul's service, the door to his old life had slammed firmly closed, and all joy had remained on the other side. Dare had slept with the other drudges in a dorm room with little heat and no comfort. Fear and exhaustion had inhibited conversation, yet out of aching loneliness and shared misery, Dare had found a few friends among the other unfortunates. These friends and his three yearly visits to Marth had been his only light.

Ursul had hated him from the beginning. Dare had learned to hide his intelligence and humor—in fact, as much as possible of himself—from the fierce man. Ursul liked no one, and the drudges stayed out of his way when they could. It was an oppressive and fearful service.

These flashes of memory took only a few moments. The man who bathed Dare was old. He had wrinkled nut-brown skin. His snow-white hair was shoulder length and bound with a strip of leather around his head. He wore a light, soft tunic and leather breeches. His blue eyes twinkled.

"Be still—no questions yet."

Dare obediently stilled his aching, hot body and held back the questions tumbling in his mind. A tall shadow swept back the skin that covered the opening to the small alcove.

"Shonar, when will the boy be ready to talk to the council?"

"Not for a few days, at least."

The tall man nodded curtly. "Two days then, but that is all."

Shonar bowed acceptance.

What council, and where am I?

Shonar knelt by the brazier and removed a cloth sack from a clay bowl. He brought the bowl to Dare, and the young man drank its bitter, warm contents without question.

Again Dare woke struggling to separate dreams from reality. Shonar's firm hand held him still as the old man urged him to quietness. "Be still—all is well. Your fever is down, though you will be weak and sore for days yet. Now, let's see if you can sit up." Dare tried with Shonar's help, and once sitting, he felt dizzy and sick. Shonar smiled, his old face cracking into a thousand wrinkles, and said sympathetically, "It will pass." It did, and Dare was able to drink and eat a little.

"Soon they will come to take you to the council." At Dare's startled look, Shonar said, "I have kept you asleep for two days." Vaguely Dare remembered waking and drinking the bitter brew again and again. He realized his anxiety must be visible, because Shonar advised, "Speak only the truth and as simply as you can. All will be well."

Dare's heart lurched—the truth! *Will they return me to Rave if they know the truth? No! Sher saved me from Glodwin. Surely they would not send me back. It seems they might be fugitives too, or else why stay hidden in this mountain?*

The tall man reappeared and, bowing slightly, requested, "Come." Dare followed him, noting that he wore soft leather boots, leather breeches, and a white tunic belted with a brightly embroidered sash. A leather thong tied back his raven hair. Shonar was dressed much the same as this silent man. Dare had gladly shed his drudge's tunic to put on clothes like theirs. The healer must have borrowed them from someone for him. He felt a new man.

The caverns were amazingly warm; he knew there must be a source of subterranean heat somewhere. Suddenly, Dare reached shakily for the wall to steady himself, but his trembling legs crumpled under him. *I am as weak as a newborn kitten.* His guide picked him up gently and carried him to the council room without word or expression.

The council of four sat on skins around a small fire. Armed men guarded both entrances to the cavern. Dare sat nervously where his silent bearer placed him. He faced the four serious men and bowed formally. Marth *had* taught him manners after all. They bowed back but remained impassive. A dark-haired man with brown skin and piercing black eyes spoke. "Welcome in the Maker's name to Glidden Mountain."

Surprised, Dare responded correctly, "May his name be praised. I thank you for your welcome and for my life." Only Marth and a very few others used this ancient greeting and only when no one was listening.

The man's eyes twinkled for a moment. "It seems one of our hunters did as much to endanger it as he did to save it—for that, I apologize."

Dare nodded his acceptance.

With no more small talk, the man began questioning. "Why were Glodwin and his dogs chasing you?" Dare took a deep breath and sought the right words and strength. Taking Shonar's advice, he answered simply, "I am—was—a serf in Ravensperch. I ran away, and they sought to catch me."

"Where did you serve in the keep?"

"In the castle itself. I worked in Ursul's service under Third Master Josata. We carried coal baskets, laundry, things like that all over the castle, as well as cleaning the lower rooms, storage areas, and the like."

"Would you say you know the castle well?"

"Only some parts of it, sir."

The cave was quiet except for the crackling fire. Dare's nervousness increased.

"Why did you run?" a man with dark hair, a hooknose, and fierce eyes asked.

"Ursul, my master, is a difficult man to work for—he hates me especially. I do not know why. The day I ran, he thrashed me for a mistake I made. When the third master interrupted him, I twisted loose and ran. I did not plan it, but I won't go back."

A slender man dressed all in leather asked, "Did you deserve the beating?"

Dare flushed with anger. "Aye, if dropping a basket of coal is reason enough."

"Who are your parents?" the oldest asked.

"My parents died when I was very young, from the black plague. Marth—a friend of theirs from Ohsay, where they had once lived—took me to live with her in the castle. Their names, my parents', were Sean and Zarie. That is all I know of them." This was not entirely true, but it was all Dare intended to say. They asked many questions about Marth and seemed amazed when he mentioned that she'd taught him to read and write.

What did he know about the duke? Dare had never so much as seen him. Well, he had seen him but at a great distance. Duke Roth was very careful about whom he allowed close to him or his rooms. Only carefully picked servants served him or entered his private quarters. Dare could certainly understand why; he was a despised ruler.

Dare had never realized how much there was to know about him and his life. *I am a much more interesting person than I imagined.*

The council then turned to his escape. He'd been found wearing a noble's boots and cloak and the king's own healer's robe. Why? Having their measure now, Dare went through the whole escape, leaving nothing out. If he did, he was sure they would point it out and make him explain it. Shonar had advised him to keep it simple. *Right!*

Sher, looking very uncomfortable, entered the cavern. He winked at Dare but was obviously feeling stressed. Gradually, as the questioning went on, Dare realized that Sher had breached security by bringing a stranger into the mountain, especially without a blindfold.

It was becoming harder and harder for Dare to concentrate; sweat drenched his tunic, and he felt light-headed. His shoulder ached abominably.

"Lock," Sher said, "the lad's done." Lock looked quickly at Dare and then ordered, "Molis, carry him back to Shonar."

"No, thank you. I can walk," Dare declined irritably. *I am not a child.* Getting to his feet, he swayed unsteadily. *Though, truth to tell, right now I wouldn't mind lying down.*

Sher chuckled, though he quickly turned his amusement into a cough after receiving a cold stare from his chief. Rarely did anyone refuse to obey one of Lock's commands. Lock smiled slightly, and it changed his whole face. He ordered softly, "Yet you will allow this. Shonar will have our hides if we make you ill."

Dare started to argue the point, but after looking into those stern jet eyes, he changed his mind. Soft voice aside, Lock expected obedience. The guard lifted Dare with a grunt at his weight, which salvaged Dare's pride a little. He considered demanding the man put him down once out of Lock's sight, but he felt so weak that he said nothing.

"I would say that at one time the boy has had gentle care," Shonar told the council later that day. "He has pride, spirit, and, I suspect, a temper, but he has learned to hide them." While Dare slept, Shonar reported to the council what he had learned about the young serf.

"He has unusual coloring for Haviland. Could he be from Ohsay as he thinks?" Lock asked.

"It is very possible. There are few fair heads in this area," Shonar replied.

After deliberating, the leaders came to a decision. "Well," Lock said, glancing at his council, "we have decided that Sher did the best he could under the circumstances, though it has put us in a dangerous position. We have also agreed that Dare's story appears to be true, but we will check it with our people in the castle.

"My father"—Lock looked at Shonar—"will keep an eye on Dare until we hear from our people. When we are sure he is not a spy, we can decide what to do with him. However, if he is a spy, we have a difficult decision to make."

JUDGMENT

Dare paced Shonar's herbal room restlessly. His only escape from this room and his little alcove was going to the bathing pools once a day. He had never been so clean. A hot spring in the mountain overflowed its basin and created a small stream that wound down to the lower caverns. Glidden's residents dammed it up here and there along its course, to form pools for bathing and washing clothes. Water for drinking and cooking came from a cool waterfall.

At first, Dare was content to rest and help Shonar with his plants and herbs. The large cavern contained rows and rows of gourds and jars. Rope, thickly hung with drying leaves, flowers, and plants, stretched back and forth across the high ceiling. Their aroma filled the air with a pungent fragrance that sometimes made Dare's eyes water.

Dare learned much herbal lore. He could now recognize many plants with healing properties, but he found it hard to be grateful for Shonar's patient teaching. Sick of rock walls and inactivity, the young fugitive longed for sunshine, fresh air—action! He was in prison, a kind prison, but one he longed to escape.

Shonar watched him intently as he worked. "Today the council should decide what to do with you. Reports from Ravensperch came in yesterday. They were much delayed."

Dare's heart lurched. He knew he was suspect. The men who lived in these caves were fugitives, just as he was, and their lives depended on keeping their existence and their hiding place a secret. Never while in Rave had he heard the slightest whisper or hint that this group existed.

In my ten days of captivity, I have seen only my small cave, this larger one, the tunnels, the council room, and the bathing pools. I have met only seven men: the council of four, two guards, and Shonar. No, wait, I forgot Sher and Josen, which makes nine. He knew, without quite knowing how he knew, that there was much more to Glidden Mountain than they were allowing him to see.

Shonar watched Dare's restless pacing and speculated on how much longer they could keep this young lion caged. Dare's years of carrying heavy loads up and down the keep's stairs had given him muscle and endurance. He glowed with health from the rest and good food in Glidden. A band of leather tied around his forehead restrained wild tawny curls. Widely spaced blue eyes gazed calmly from a pale face with a wide mouth and a high forehead. His moods changed quickly, swinging from merry to depressed in a moment. Shonar found no meanness in Dare, but he did sense a full measure of anger and hurt from painful memories.

At first, Dare was a good patient, grateful for the smallest kindness and touched by Shonar's gentle care, sometimes to the point of tears. But returning health had brought restlessness, then irritability, and then limited rebellion, which was very normal with any patient but especially normal in a growing boy. Having raised three sons, Shonar experienced no trouble dealing with Dare's occasional revolts.

Their first struggle was about binding Dare's right arm to his body. Shonar did this to keep movement from reopening the wound in his back as he became more active. "My arm will lose its strength. Shonar, I will be careful—I promise," he pleaded, his large eyes dark with intensity.

"No," Shonar explained patiently, "it is too soon."

Dare tried pouting and being sullen. When this tactic did not work, he tried disobedience, which, as it turned out, did not work either.

He unwound his bindings and exercised his arm at the pools, then wound the long strips of cloth back again, but it was difficult to do one-handed. He did his best, but it was a sorry mess. He hoped Shonar would not notice the lumps under his tunic.

Of course the old healer noticed immediately, and he ordered Dare to the bench by his worktable. "Sit," he said and took off Dare's tunic.

19

At this very inopportune moment Lock entered. "Father, would you come talk to me when you have a minute?"

Shonar nodded. "I'll be there shortly."

Lock's quick, bright eyes took in the scene. "Good." He left without further comment.

Dare felt sure Lock had noticed the tangled, soggy bandages. *Great, now he knows too.* He did not know why he cared, but he did.

"Dare, I want your word you'll not touch these bindings again till I tell you it's safe. Your wound has opened and is bleeding."

Dare opened his mouth to argue, then shut it again. Ruefully he acknowledged, only to himself of course, that he was being hill-mule stubborn. *Later I will work extra hard to build the arm up.* "Aye, sir, I will not. You have my word."

Shonar put something that stung like fire on his injury and bandaged it again. "You will miss your dinner tonight, to help you remember."

"Aye, sir." It was really too bad; dinner was the biggest event of his day.

They crossed wills a few more times. Sometimes Dare capitulated; sometimes they compromised. After Shonar praised him enthusiastically one day, for a lesson well learned—something that rarely happened to serfs, who were frequently disciplined but almost never praised—Dare realized that his respect for Shonar was deepening into affection.

Carefully, with pen and ink, Dare marked reed baskets with the names that Shonar called out to him. Yesterday, Shonar had escaped into the sunshine with two guards to protect and assist him. Dare envied them with his whole heart. They'd gathered herbs, nuts, seeds, and all the necessary ingredients of Shonar's craft. It was late summer, and the harvest was bountiful; it would take two days to store all that they'd brought back from wood and meadow.

The council had not called him yesterday as they'd hoped; perhaps they would today. He was afraid of their verdict, but anything would be better than not knowing. Molis—the tall and very silent guard who had carried him to and from the last council meeting—came into the herbal room. He requested that Dare follow him to the meeting chamber.

Shonar stated his intention of coming also, and they left together. His presence was a great comfort. Now that the time was near, Dare felt nervous. There were many more people around the fire this time than last. He stopped for a moment, panic flooding his body, before he could force himself to enter the cavern.

Lock greeted Dare and the healer courteously and asked them to sit in the places he appointed in the circle. The firelight flickered on the cave walls; the room was very quiet. As Dare waited for Lock to speak, he tried to settle his nerves and quiet his mind. *Help me, Maker.*

"Lavel, give us your report." Lock nodded to a large man dressed in green. His dark hair and beard glistened with moisture in the firelight; his clothing, too, was damp. The man looked vaguely familiar. Dare remembered the evening of his escape from Rave. Could this be the man on the wagon seat, who had forced the wagon off the road just in time?

Amusement shone in Lavel's eyes. He smiled and nodded at Dare. "The mysterious young man in a brown robe who disappeared suddenly, I assume."

"Aye," Dare said in wonder. "How did you know?"

"By putting this and that together."

"Lavel," Lock reminded.

"Ah, the report," he said. "I contacted our friends at the castle on my last trip to market with Meyer and his family. They have confirmed that Dare is a serf in Ursul's service, that he worked in the kitchens before that for Sybil, and also that he served Marth."

He shook glistening drops from his short hair as he ran his fingers through it. "Nothing is known of his parents or background. Marth took care of him from the time he was one year old till he was put with Ursul at twelve. There is general agreement that Ursul is a harsh master. I can confirm that someone dressed in a brown woolen robe joined Meyer's family eleven days ago and passed through the gatehouse with them. Sorel knocked him into a ditch to keep the king's men from trampling him. Glodwin is furious that he lost a mere boy … He speaks of sorcery!"

Up until this point, everyone had been listening seriously, even intently to Lavel, but the picture of Glodwin's discomfort and his ridiculous excuse made them laugh.

Lavel chuckled also and continued, "The duke and his court were amazed at Glodwin's failure and have done some mild chiding, but the servants are secretly delighted." He added, looking at Dare, "And Marth and your other friends in the keep are praising the Maker for your safety. They have not ceased to speak for you. I could not tell them where you are of course. I did tell them you left the keep with the Meyer family. I told them that I was with the Meyers also, realized you were a runaway, and helped you find a safe place with a family a great distance from here. It is at least partially true. I asked them not to speak of what I told them in order to keep you safe."

Dare felt a burden lift from his heart. *They know I'm safe!* He looked down for a moment to hide his emotion and then back at Lavel with a grateful smile.

Do they believe me now?

Lock gazed into the fire, frowning. "I have other reports that confirm what Lavel has told us. Are there any questions anyone would like to ask Dare before he leaves?"

There were none, and Dare bowed to the council and left in hope and fear. He paced Shonar's workroom and besieged the Maker as he waited with what patience he could muster.

Shonar came to get Dare; he smiled encouragingly but would say nothing. Only Lock and three other council members awaited Dare. He still did not know their names. He and Shonar sat down. Dare's hands and knees were trembling.

Lock said, "Dare, our friends in the castle have confirmed what you told us, and we believe it to be true. We see no evidence that you are a spy. If you will speak a pledge of silence, by whatever god you believe in, we can discuss your future."

Dare grinned shakily, his relief apparent. "Thank you. I will gladly promise by the ancient god of our people."

"Aye, I thought as much," Lock said. "He has many believers here also. All of the council and most of the others with us follow the Maker."

Dare was amazed. He'd thought Marth and a few others in the keep were among a minority who even remembered the Maker. Dare spoke a simple but solemn pledge that he would not reveal the hiding place in Glidden Mountain or the names or existence of the fugitives who were hiding there.

"My name is Verona," the dark man with the narrow face told him.

The slender man in leathers said, "My name is Wirth."

The ancient one smiled and said, "I am called Shils."

Dare bowed to each politely. "I thank you for the honor you show me by trusting me with your names. I shall not abuse your confidence."

Though his amazement did not show, Lock felt puzzled by Dare's behavior. Where had this unusual young man gotten his poise and polite speech? This was no ordinary serf.

"Tell us where you were headed and your plan, if you had one," Lock said.

Dare replied eagerly, "I want to return to my parents' birthplace in Ohsay and discover if there are any folk there who remember them or if I have any kin."

"Young man," Verona said, "do you have any idea how far it is to Ohsay?"

"No, sir," Dare replied truthfully. "I know it is over the mountains in the east, and I know there is a pass called Uriel-on that I must find. Marth told me that much when we talked of her home, but that is all I know."

"It is far, a month's journey on horseback at least, and it is already the last month of harvest. Snow flies early in the mountains, and the way is rough and little traveled now, especially at this time of year," Wirth said.

Dare looked down for a moment, trying to untangle his thoughts. How could he explain to them what he really did not understand himself? Perplexed, he looked up. "I cannot explain how I know I must do this. I cannot even explain why. But I know that I must. Marth taught me that the Maker leads his children; I believe he urges me to go. Can you understand?"

"There are many voices, child. Darkness also seeks to lead us, and sometimes our own secret desires masquerade as the Maker's voice," Wirth said.

"Marth has explained this to me. Still, I think I must go to Ohsay."

"Then we will see what we can do to help you on your way," Lock replied.

Dare felt relieved. Strange his explanation might be, but he didn't have a better one.

"You are not yet healed, but to wait any longer is to risk winter weather," Shonar said with a frown.

Lock said thoughtfully, "Sher, Josen, and I will teach you how to survive in the wilderness. Shonar will continue to teach you healing, and perhaps we can induce Wasatch to help you learn to ride. You will need warm clothes, weapons, a horse, and a winter pack. Do you know how to use a bow?"

"No, sir." Gratitude swelled in Dare's heart as he listened to these plans that would help him on his journey, but doubt rose as well. "Lock, I have nothing to trade—no goods of any kind. I cannot pay for such valuable things."

"We seek to compensate you for the injury Sher inadvertently caused. To repay an injury is part of our law. Also, the folk of Glidden always help those fugitives we can to escape the duke's justice—or injustice, to our way of thinking. After you find what you are looking for, come back to us. If it seems good to you, join and help us," Lock answered.

Dare was tempted to stay. He would like to belong to this group of men, but not yet. First, he must find his birthplace and kin, if any.

The next morning Josen and Sher taught Dare to make a fire, under even the worst conditions, and to shoot with his new bow. Josen pretended to be terribly afraid of Sher when he picked up his bow. "Sher, be careful! Dare already has one hole in him, and I'm a father. My children need me, so for the sake of my poor family, be careful where you aim that arrow!" He teased the handsome young hunter all morning about his poor aim, to which Sher took understandable exception.

They argued good-naturedly, and Dare thought that they probably were very good friends. Of course, they teased him also and called him many unflattering names: clumsy ox, bungler, and bird arm among the best, none of which offended him.

At midday, they sat down in the shade of a twisted old piñon pine to eat midmeal. As Dare looked up through the branches into the azure sky, he felt at peace—with the forest, with archery, with his fellow men … with life.

That afternoon he met the gruff Wasatch, who taught him to ride and a hundred things more about the care of horses, all of which he feared he would forget. Wasatch was a slim, dark man with long black hair. He moved with confident grace and rode his horse as if he and the animal were one. Dare sighed. How long would it be before he could do the same?

The next two days duplicated the first. Dare fell into bed each night too exhausted to eat more than a few bites of food. His wound continued to heal, although it ached at night, but then, the rest of him ached too.

On the fourth day, Lock waited for him in the grove instead of Sher and Josen. Sunlight streamed through the trees, the birds were singing to one another, and the fragrant smell of pine filled the air. It was a beautiful, warm summer day. Dare bowed respectfully and waited for Lock to speak. "Let's see what those two worthless woodsmen have taught you," he said with a twinkle in his eye.

Dare started to defend them before he realized the man was teasing. "They have worked very hard, but they say I am still bird armed and clumsy," Dare said, laughing.

"Let's see your progress with the bow."

Dare quickly strung his bow and took an arrow from the quiver on his back. Aiming carefully, he shot a low-hanging pine cone on a tree only thirty feet away. He'd chosen a close target because he knew his limits. Even at that distance he often missed.

"Good," Lock said. He pointed at another pine cone higher in the same tree. Dare shot again and again, sometimes hitting, sometimes missing. He shot with such force that his arrows shattered whatever they hit. Lock gave him advice in his quiet voice. "Your arm is strong, but you must focus your eye and your mind on the target, holding the rest of your body still. Be totally quiet inside. Think only of the pine cone." Dare's improvement was slow but steady.

"Tomorrow you must start to work on a moving target."

As they walked to the meadow, Lock talked of many things: weather signs, geysers, and the animals Dare might encounter on his trip. Flag, Dare's pony, and Wasatch were waiting for them. Dare had taken to riding like a duck to water. He could saddle and unsaddle his pony and had gained at least head knowledge of feeding and caring for him.

Wasatch suggested that Dare and Flag spend the night in the meadow so that Dare could practice his new trail skills. Lock frowned over this at first but decided after a few minutes that it was a good idea. He warned Dare that he must be very quiet and make no fire this close to Ravensperch. Glidden lookouts watched the woods and the roads both day and night, but the Glidden folk took care to do nothing that might attract the duke's patrols. Dare agreed readily.

I can't believe this is happening to me! I came into these woods an ignorant runaway, knowing nothing of woodcraft or anything else—except cleaning and carrying heavy loads. Now, I have the best teachers. Because a Glidden hunter wounded me, that same hunter saved me from certain capture by Glodwin, and now a hidden people are helping me on my way! The Maker's ways are mysterious—wonderful but mysterious.

The next few days sped by as Dare tried to make what he was learning second nature and a part of him. At the end of the week, he stood ready to depart in the rosy light of early dawn. A pack, saddlebags, blanket, and warm cloak were strapped behind Flag's light saddle. Dare carried his bow and quiver on his back and a short knife at his side in a leather scabbard. As he looked at the group around him, his eagerness to be on his way blended with sorrow at the need to leave such good friends.

Sher grabbed his forearm. "Good journey, bird arm. The gods be with you." He gave Dare a quick smile and wink. Josen too shook his arm and told him to keep his eye on his target—Dare's worst failing in archery.

Wasatch said, "Good journey, young friend. You and Flag will do well together."

Dare turned to Lock and shook his arm. "Watch the weather and come back to us if you can. Sher has told you what to do?" Lock asked.

"Aye, sir."

Dare next looked at Shonar, and an unexpected lump blocked his throat. Shonar embraced him. "You will do well, young lion. The Maker is with you."

He thanked each of them as best he could and mounted Flag. As he rode into the early-morning mist that clung to the forest floor, he turned to wave, but his friends had disappeared in the rising fog.

ALONE

TREES ARCHED OVER THE PATH TO NORDIK Brook; some of the leaves were already tinged with yellow and gold. Many had lost their leaves completely. The rising sun was warming the cool air. A hawk overhead hung motionless on the currents, watching for his morn meal. While their feathered brothers sang overhead, forest creatures chattered and rustled about in the pine, birch, and oak trees. It was a bright beginning.

Maker, may it continue. It could not all be like this, he knew, but while it lasted, this was good. He did not have to look at his map that day or for the next two. The weather remained beautiful and the trail easy to remember and follow.

Among the towering trees, his lonely campfire was a small circle of comfort at night. Castle bred and unaccustomed to nature's sounds, he slept fitfully, but satisfaction with his new ability to take care of himself made loss of sleep seem unimportant.

On the fourth day, angry, low, roiling clouds, moving fast, appeared on the horizon where the sun was rising. A cool, sporadic wind buffeted him and Flag and roared in the trees.

Dare took a quick look at the map Shonar had drawn for him, then put it back safely in a saddlebag. He untied his cloak and struggled into it as the wind tried to whip it away. Flag snorted uneasily. Dare patted his neck. "Easy, boy, easy. The good weather couldn't last forever."

He crossed a mountain meadow and searched ahead for a standing stone. It would mark his passage through a steep canyon and into another large valley. Lock had warned him not to travel the canyon's narrow length in hard rain; the swollen river at the bottom could make the narrow path treacherous. The valley would take many days to cross.

There it is—a huge, reddish-brown column in the eastern sky!

Rain, coming harder and faster every minute, splattered down around him. The wind grew increasingly strong and made it difficult for Flag to hold a southern course. Thunder rolled in the distance, and Dare could see faint lightning strikes on the horizon.

I should stop and hole up, but where?

The level valley possessed flourishing piñon and aspen groves, but he could see no refuge. He decided to push on to the standing stone. The land there mounted into high cliffs; perhaps there would be an overhang or a cave there that would give him shelter.

Dare could barely see the stone through sheets of horizontal rain as the intensity of the storm rolled over him and Flag. The noise was deafening. He quickly got off Flag, leading him as best he could, and struggled forward. After hours of slogging over wet grass, slippery mud, and uneven rock, they reached the stone. It gave them fair protection from wind and water while Dare decided what to do next.

Early fall storms could last for a long time in the mountains, and night would be coming soon. He had traveled all day with only morn meal. Both he and Flag needed food, rest, and a fire. His teeth were chattering from the cold. Resolutely, Dare stepped out into the blast and fury in order to search the cliff face in front of him. He tugged on the reins, forcing Flag to come with him. They were again surrounded by the storm's fury.

"I'm not sure I could see shelter, even if it were right in front of me," Dare mumbled with dismay. As cold water ran down the inside of his clothes and into his boots, he noticed with apprehension that it was growing darker with each passing minute. The ground was gradually getting higher, yet even here the water was getting deeper. Deafening thunder shook the ground, and suddenly, Dare's foot slipped on a rock, and he crashed down on his back. Grinding pain from his injury made him gasp as water pelted his face.

As he lay there resting a moment, he spotted something in the darkness above him. In the illumination from a lightning flash, he saw what looked like a ledge with an overhang. *But is there a way to get up there?*

It was steep, but he thought he saw a track. He and Flag struggled up, sometimes waiting for a lightning strike to find their way. Gasping and trembling, Dare fell into a small cave. He pulled his distressed horse in behind him. It was not very deep, but it was large enough for them both. For a few minutes they rested; it was enough just to be out of the storm's fury. Dare ate some flatbread and dried meat with fingers numb from cold. He unsaddled his sturdy animal and rubbed him down. "What a fine companion you are, Flag." Flag nodded his head and whinnied; evidently he agreed. Dare gave him some oats from a saddlebag. Moving around warmed Dare up a little, but he remembered Shonar's warning about being wet and cold: lowering the body's temperature too much affected the mind.

I must get warm, but there is no way to make a fire! This cave has a scattering of leaves, pine needles, and twigs but no real wood. Anything out in this weather is soaked by now, and truthfully, I've no energy to look.

He stripped off his wet cloak and all his clothes. Hoping his blanket would be dry, Dare unrolled the protective tarp. With relief, he discovered that it was and wrapped it around his cold body, grateful for its warmth. After he persuaded Flag to lie down, Dare lay next to him and pulled the tarp over both of them. Perhaps the horse's body heat would help warm him, and he could sleep for a time. As Flag's warmth surrounded him, his eyes became heavy. Soon, both he and the horse slept.

Sunlight and birdsong woke them the next morning. Dare stretched and looked out over the valley from his narrow perch. The storm had washed everything clean, leaving gleaming puddles here and there. The view was astounding: massive, snowcapped peaks surrounded the lonely valley. Aspen, birch, and pine clung to the edges of a swift stream that flung up glittering sprays of water when it struck boulders. He watched a small herd of deer disappear into a dense copse of trees. They probably drank at the stream at dawn and then grazed before returning to the protection of the trees.

"How late we've slept Flag—and no wonder after yesterday. Thank the Maker for this cave and a dry blanket. We'll have a late start today." He thought it looked to be the third hour after dawn. Cheerfully, Dare wrung out his clothes and laid them in the sun to dry. With only his blanket around him, he took Flag down to the meadow and hobbled him in knee-high grass to graze. He searched for dry twigs in sheltered places and found a few. Then he climbed back up to the cave and made a small fire to brew tea.

"I hope no one comes to visit, since I'm hardly dressed for it." He grinned at the thought. He felt contented and mindless in the warm sun. He thanked the Maker for his safety and that the storm had not lasted any longer. The standing stone stood silent, brooding in the bright sunshine.

Flag neighed nervously down below, and Dare woke up with a start. *I must have fallen asleep again!* Horses with silent riders streamed into the valley from the canyon—the canyon that Dare would have to travel to go south. Heart pounding, he gathered his clothes and threw them into the cave. Then he crept down the cliff to retrieve Flag.

"Quiet, boy," he whispered soothingly as he fumbled with his hobble rope. It finally came free, and crouching by Flag's side, he urged him closer to the cliff wall. Frantically, he searched for some kind of cover. Leading Flag up the cliff to their ledge would not only make noise but also put them in plain sight, so that plan was out of the question.

There were some scraggly pine trees and dense attleberry bushes just ahead—not much, but they would have to do. Dare could now hear hoofbeats; they were faint but coming closer. Horse and boy concealed themselves behind the sparse cover, and Dare kept his hand over Flag's velvet nose, urging him to be quiet. He counted twelve men on horseback. They rode large, beautiful animals that could outrun Flag easily. The men traveled in a loose formation behind their leader and certainly had the look of soldiers, yet they wore no uniform or insignia, no crest or emblem. Their clothes were brown and sturdy with no other color showing anywhere; it gave them a menacing look. They were all well armed with bows and swords.

As they pounded past him, intent on the other end of the valley, they looked resolute and grim. They rode as men with a firm purpose, and Dare shivered as he thought of his narrow escape. "Not a merry group," he whispered to Flag.

Suddenly, they pulled up in the center of the valley and circled their leader to converse. It was an animated discussion. As the leader pointed around the valley, panic shook Dare. *They are going to search this area! Who or what are they looking for?* The discussion went on a few minutes longer, and then, much to Dare's relief, they regrouped and rode again toward the northern pass.

He remembered Lock's warning to go quietly and stay out of sight, avoiding people whenever possible. There were many desperate people on the Isle of Fire, and some turned to robbery to survive. If meeting with people was unavoidable, he must be careful and say little. His Glidden advisors had decided that his reason for being on the road must be the true one, with one notable exception: they told him to say that his master had given him *permission* to travel back to his homeland.

Everyone in Ree was in service to someone, and no one could travel without sanction. Shonar had written a letter of permit for Dare, supposedly from Josata, that should satisfy any official who might stop him. The goal, of course, was not to be stopped. These men had not looked like robbers or fugitives or officials, but they also had not looked understanding. Whoever they were, he felt relief that they were gone.

Dare's clothing had dried in the sun while he slept. He dressed and carefully packed his gear. If anyone were to enter the steep canyon while he was there, it would be hard to hide. He felt exposed as he rode Flag across the meadow and started the descent into the canyon. Massive gray-black walls towered on either side of a rough-and-tumble river whose roaring filled his ears. The narrow, rocky trail lay in deep shadow. Only the noonday sun would reach down into this place. Dare was glad for his warm, dry clothes because the air was full of water spray and cold. As he rounded a sharp corner, he heard a muffled sound that was neither the river nor him. Perhaps a small animal of some kind?

He stopped Flag to gaze in awe at the view. A monstrous peak in a group with many others filled the sky above him and glowed with fire; smoke drifted from its blown-off top. It was one of the reeomos, the fire mountains that Lock had warned him to avoid. Sometimes rivers of melted rock flowed from them, destroying everything in their path. No description he had ever heard prepared him for the sight of a real one. It was terrifying and made him feel both insignificant and helpless. From these reeomos and the huge fields of snow and ice often found around them, called gallos, his island had received its name—Isle Reeigal. The reeomos was menacing, but Dare forced himself to go forward.

Again Dare heard a scuffing sound behind him. Flag's ears swiveled back, and he snorted. Holding tightly to the reins, Dare threw his right leg over the saddle horn and slid silently to the ground. As he searched the rocky trail behind him and the cliff wall, he unsheathed his knife. Nothing was there—he heard only the roar of water. He could not go on without knowing whether something was tracking him. "Is anyone there?" he called. *What a foolish thing to do*, he thought angrily.

Finally, he decided to lead Flag forward along the trail while keeping his knife ready. A hard, clear voice from somewhere above him asked derisively, "Do you always talk to those who stalk you?"

Dare looked up. On the ledge above him, a young man stood in the dim light. He was dressed in tattered black leathers and held a glittering long knife. Straight, dark hair hung to his shoulders; his skin was brown, and his eyes were fierce.

Ignoring the sarcastic question, Dare asked, "Why do you follow me?"

The proud young man in black looked unwell, and the knife he held trembled. "I have need—of your horse, peasant," he replied with disdain, but the hand in which he held the knife dropped to the rock in front of him, and he slumped forward. He was still conscious and clinging to his weapon but barely.

"I think, my arrogant friend, that you ought to be careful how you speak to strangers. You might stay healthier that way." Looking for a way up, Dare dropped Flag's reins and climbed toward the stranger cautiously. Because he did not trust the man, he remained ready to defend himself.

"I don't need advice from the likes of you! Though, it seems I am the captured, not the capturer," Dare's tracker said weakly as his long knife clattered to the ground. Dare retrieved it, keeping his eye on the young man. Then he searched him and discovered a knife in his boot and another on his belt. These he carefully put in his own belt with a disbelieving shake of his head.

"Do you think you have enough weapons?" He relieved the fainting man of his quiver and bow as well. "What is your name, *captive?*" Dare taunted.

"Bardon," the man answered faintly. "Everyone calls me Bar."

Dare half carried him down to the trail and laid him down on it. "Are you injured?" he asked, concerned in spite of his anger.

With closed eyes and a weak voice, Bar said, "I fell from my horse … in the canyon … and have been … long without food. My left arm is bruised and has a long gash from … I don't know … perhaps a sharp rock. Do you have water?"

In spite of himself, Dare felt compassion for this stranger and admiration for his courage. "Aye, just a minute."

Dare gave him a drink and then carefully lifted his cloak back to see his injured arm. Dare cut the sleeve of Bar's kard shirt and uttered a sharp cry. There was a long, ragged cut on Bar's lower arm, and a bruise was already spreading. Dare carefully felt the bone but could not feel a break. *What pain he must be in! No wonder he couldn't stand.*

Dare washed away the blood as gently as he could. Bar clenched his jaw but then forced himself to speak. "There is something … I *must* tell you, boy—"

"Do not call me boy if you want me to listen!" Dare interrupted with rekindled wrath.

"What shall I call you then, boy?" Bar asked with a pale grin and a less fierce look in his eyes.

"Try Dare," the former serf said. "Well, what is it?"

But Bar could not answer; he closed his eyes and groaned as pain engulfed him. When it passed a little, he said urgently, "Men are chasing me … will come back looking … when they find my horse."

Foreboding caused Dare's heart to pound. "Men dressed in dark brown, about twelve on horseback?" he asked.

"Aye."

"Why? Who are they? Who are *you?*" Dare asked, seething.

"I cannot answer that, but I am not a criminal or bandit. I am a runaway, and they want to return me to my … to where I came from. They are efficient—ruthless. They *must not* find you. Me, they will return to my home, but they will kill you, just for knowing about this." Black eyes searched Dare's face. "Leave me here and hide; you will be safe. I'll not tell them about you."

"Do you want to go back?"

"No, never!" His eyes were shadowed with trouble.

"Then let's fix your arm and get out of here." *Fool*, Dare called himself, but not too long ago, he had been in much the same place. "Fortunately, I know something of healing; unfortunately, I have never stitched up a cut this deep ... well, any cut. This experience will enlarge my education." Bardon grunted and closed his eyes again.

No time. Dare couldn't stop himself from listening for hoofbeats. *Over the roaring water, I might not hear them in time!* He made a decision, right or wrong, to bind the wound and strap Bar's arm to his body. They needed to move to a safer place before trying to deal with the injury. He put one of Shonar's herbal concoctions in water and made Bar drink it. "It will ease your pain." Bar bore this stoically but had no strength to stand when Dare finished. Dare offered him some cheese and bread, but he could not eat.

"Thanks, friend Dare. Now with your help, perhaps I can mount." Somehow they got Bar in the saddle, and Dare led Flag down the trail.

"Do they have a good tracker?" he asked Bar. Though the path was granite, they were still leaving a trail that could be followed by someone good.

"No, they trust to speed and numbers. They did not bring any of the Basca with them."

Dare shivered with dread at the mention of the Basca'. Who was this fugitive that the king's famous trackers would be used to find him? Dare pushed the question to the back of his mind; there was no time to worry about it now.

The sky overhead was clear blue, and the sun shone brightly. It was well past noon. Because the canyon curved to the left, Dare could no longer see the reeomos. Surely they would come out into the meadow soon. Lock had said it should take about six hours to get through the canyon. Dare tried to think how long he had been on the trail. It was now about the eighth hour; he had been traveling for about four hours, leaving two more to go. He hoped that Bar could stay on Flag that long and that the searchers would not find them in this canyon where there was no place to hide.

At first Dare walked, but Bar was getting too weak to stay in the saddle, so he got on behind and held him. Their weight would be hard for Flag to bear if this went on too long. The ground started to rise, and they finally broke out into another beautiful valley. The reeomos filled the southern sky; it seemed frighteningly close. Caves honeycombed the cliff walls. There were also woods, canyons, and a meadow. All were possible refuges, but Dare didn't know how much time he could spend looking for a safe retreat.

Maker, help me find a good hiding place, fast! He forced himself to rest a few minutes and take a drink. He knew from the tension in Bar's body that he was conscious and just trying to stay in the saddle. While Bar took a drink, Dare decided to seek a cave, one that was close so they would be settled before nightfall. There were so many—the men in brown could not search them all.

He reined Flag toward the cliff on the east side of the valley. They crossed a river that was shallow and swift but not dangerous. Dare examined the cliff face. As he rode parallel to the craggy wall of granite, he searched, but nothing seemed right. He feared to use the caves that were too easily accessible, but the others were either too shallow or too hard to reach. As the sun sank in the western sky, the fiery radiance from the reeomos became more visible and filled the valley with a pulsing orange glow.

Dare entered a copse of aspen. Their yellow leaves shimmered in the light breeze, and the gentle sounds of birds and insects filled the air. Flag would be easier to track on this softer ground, but Dare went on. A small rivulet flowed from the rock wall, and Dare stopped to let Flag drink. He looked up but saw nothing. Sighing in disgust, he started moving again. Out of the corner of his eye, he saw movement and quietly turned to watch a small brown lampet disappear beneath the ground at the cliff's edge. Lampets, creatures much like ground squirrels often made nests in the recesses of dark caves. He dismounted and lowered Bardon carefully to the ground. As Dare searched for the spot where the small animal had disappeared, Bar lay down gratefully.

Dare found a cave with an entrance well hidden behind a tangle of bushes and undergrowth. Because the opening was partially below ground level, he feared it might flood in a rainstorm. The floor of the cave appeared to rise toward the back; he could not tell how deep it was. Perhaps they could go back far enough that it wouldn't matter if it rained.

Cautiously, Dare walked in, looking for any sign of large animals. He earnestly hoped not to find any, especially not any belonging to the black bears that inhabited these mountains. He saw signs of small scurriers but nothing else. Quickly, he decided that this was the place and carried Bar into the cool darkness. Then he led Flag to the back. Hurrying to the edge of the trees, he searched for the soldiers; no troop was visible yet. He covered their trail and then refilled the water bag at the rivulet.

Dare cared for Flag first and then turned to Bar. "You look terrible."

Bar laughed a little. "I feel worse." He looked seriously at Dare. "Can you fix this thing?"

"I don't know, but we can't leave it as it is, so I must try." The young healer mixed more of the pain-killing herbs in water, and Bar drank. While Dare waited for the herbs to take effect, he ate but would let Bar have nothing. It would be better for Bar to have as little in his stomach as possible when Dare stitched and bound his wound.

"How do you feel?"

"Limp and slightly numb," the runaway said softly, his eyes glazed.

Dare mixed cleansing powder in water and cleaned the area carefully. Feeling extremely nervous, he asked the Maker to guide his hands. He quickly stitched and smoothed salve on the wound. Then he bound it with rolls of cloth Shonar had put in his pack along with the herbal medicines. He elevated Bar's arm on Flag's saddle and threw the blanket over him. Then the young healer wrapped his cloak around his aching body and joined his patient in sleep.

He woke in total darkness during the night. Listening, he heard only normal sounds: the breeze in the trees, insects humming, and an occasional birdcall. Flag seemed relaxed, and Bar was sleeping. Dare had given him as much pain medicine as he dared, hoping Bar would sleep much of the night. He lay down again and slept dreamlessly until morning light brightened the cave. When he woke up, it took many minutes for him to remember where he was and why.

Bar's gaze was on him; his eyes were full of pain. Dare moved quickly to his side and examined the arm. It was swollen, but that was to be expected. Otherwise, it looked good. He saw no sign of blood poisoning or infection. Looking Bar in the eyes, he assured him that it was doing well. "I am going to put your arm in a sling to keep it still. It will help it heal. Try not to move it."

"It hurts like hot coals, and I'm thirsty," Bar said bitterly. His irritability was understandable and, in a way, a good sign.

Dare grinned. "I'll bet it does. I'm going to take a look around. Then I'll see if I can help you feel better." Dare left the cave cautiously, listening for any unusual sounds. He really did not expect the men in brown until later in the day. *Surely no one would travel that canyon at night.*

He searched the valley and saw nothing suspicious. However, as he turned to leave, he saw movement in some attleberry bushes near the stream they'd crossed yesterday. Perhaps it was an animal getting a drink? Then a shape stood up and stretched, shortly followed by others. The whole troop was rising out of their blankets!

How badly they must want Bardon to have taken such a risk! As he refilled the waterskin and returned to the cave, his mind raced. "They are here," he told Bar calmly, more calmly than he felt. "Any noise we make needs to be made now." He could not let Flag outside, so he gave him the best drink he could from his cupped hands and moved him farther back into the cave. He gave Bar medicine and food. "You must keep Flag quiet. I'm going to watch them."

"Dare, be careful. They are very good at what they do, even without expert trackers." Bar's expression betrayed anger and worry. "Boer's bow, why did I let you get into this!" he said, angrily slamming his good fist into the dirt. "Dare, I'm sorry! I wanted to get away so badly that—"

"Forget it!" Dare interrupted him firmly. "We aren't caught yet." The despair on Bar's face frightened him deeply but not as deeply as his apology.

He tried to count the moving shapes that were men; all twelve seemed to be there, but he couldn't be sure. As he settled to watch, the troop ate and then mounted. Their leader gave directions, gesturing around the valley, and they began to search. Dare forced himself to watch until the last minute. *Two men are definitely coming this way!* He went quickly back to the cave. Holding his finger to his lips, Dare sat near Flag and Bar to wait. Soon they could hear voices and horses.

Dare stood up and talked softly to Flag. His and Bardon's eyes met; they were both pale but still hopeful. Time passed slowly, and still they could hear the men talking to each other as they moved section by section through their little woods. They were very close now.

"Here, by this small stream—someone has washed over what looks like a hoofprint!" one cried out to the other. They heard someone crash through brush and then search the area right in front of the cave.

Bar's head was sunk on his knees. He looked up and whispered intensely, "Dare, we must convince them that I am sicker than I am. It is the only chance I can think of to keep you alive. Tell them you are an apprentice healer and that I need you. It is your only hope." His eyes were pleading. Dare nodded assent. Bar lay down, trying to appear really sick. It didn't take much pretense; he looked awful.

It seems Bar is more human than I thought. Dare's heart was pounding so hard its sound filled his ears. *Maker, grant me courage,* he thought as the men entered the cave.

In Enemy Hands

Two veterans, sunburned, weathered, and strong, stood looking at Bar and Dare triumphantly. "Your Grace," the oldest said as he bowed mockingly.

The heavyset one asked with menace, "And who is this?"

Bar answered weakly, "His name is Dare, Truel. He is a competent healer. He has bandaged my arm—and kept me alive. He found me on the trail after I fell."

Dare was now confused as well as frightened. *Your Grace?* He tried to appear calm and confident, but his mind was spinning.

"How did you injure your arm?" Truel asked suspiciously. Bardon explained, and the men listened carefully. Then Truel said to the other man, "Let's take them both to the captain. Bardon really does look awful sick to me. I want no part in makin' the captain any more bad-tempered than he already is."

"Aye! I agree with that," his companion said.

They put Bar on Flag and mounted Dare behind him. Dare knew the runaway was in pain and tried to move carefully, but Bar cried out at the pony's first move, and then his rigid form went limp. Dare held him tightly. The soldiers frowned over this development and returned to their camp at a slow walk. They kept a sharp eye on Bardon, as if they were expecting a trick of some kind.

At the camp, the two soldiers lit a signal fire, and the other members of the troop began to return. Truel and his friend—Fox, based on what the

39

others called him—gladly answered the same questions over and over again about how and where they'd found Dare and Bardon. When a stocky man with short-cropped gray hair and dark skin got off his brown stallion, the troop became quiet and respectful.

The man, obviously their leader, bowed slightly to Bar, who was now awake, and said, "Bardon."

As if they were meeting on the street, Bar bowed in return. "Captain Ganshof."

"Who brought him in?" the captain demanded, looking his men over. Truel and Fox stepped forward and gave their account in short, factual sentences; none of their former triumph was visible. The soldiers' behavior in the presence of their captain gave Dare some measure of the man.

His hard eyes looked Dare over. Without a word to Dare, he glanced furiously at Bardon, who looked as if he were barely able to remain on the horse. "Much trouble you have given us. I would not be in your boots when we return you to your father," he said harshly. Bar swallowed hard but kept his tongue between his teeth for Dare's sake. The captain looked at Dare and ordered him to get Bar down. Dare quickly helped Bar out of the saddle and helped him walk to a fallen log and sit down.

"Take this peasant over in those aspens and kill him," the captain ordered two of the men as he walked toward the troop's supplies. Dare gasped in shock. He didn't know whether he was more stunned by his imminent death or by the captain's casual attitude toward it. *As if I were a rabbit or snake!*

"Captain," Bar said swiftly, lifting his pale face, "will my father thank you for returning me dead or crippled for life? My arm is badly hurt. Who in this group knows anything of healing? Who will take care of me on the way home?"

The captain turned and strode back to Bardon with suppressed fury. "Injured are you?" Concern flickered for a moment in his dark eyes. He knelt beside Bar and motioned for Dare to remove the bandages. Dare did so quickly, and Bar went white to the lips and groaned. The wound spoke for itself. It was fiery red, swollen, and looked infected.

"All right, we will keep your healer alive till we get you back to Feisan." The captain stared a long moment at Dare. "As long as he gives us no trouble." Dare felt the impact of his gaze like a blow. Though the man did not touch him, he was trembling.

Bar, looking truly ill, lay down on the ground and cradled his arm. No sound escaped his lips, but they were pressed firmly together, and sweat dampened his dark hair.

Dare quickly asked the soldier closest to him for permission to get medicines out of his pack. "Aye, you can get him something, but make it quick," the soldier said in a bored voice. Dare was surprised at his callous attitude. He glanced at the faces of the men around the fire as they began to prepare a meal. They showed no interest in or compassion for Bar at all.

Strange—these men are in service to Bar's father, yet they treat their liege's son with scant respect and no affection. Perhaps they are sick of chasing him … *Still, it is strange.*

He mixed herbs for fever and pain. As he helped Bar drink, he mouthed, "Thank you. Close call."

Bar nodded. "Be careful!" he mouthed back. His arm was swelling badly, and Dare elevated it on his rolled-up cloak.

The captain allowed them all to rest that day, having decided, with no one to urge him, that his runaway needed to rest and get stronger. Dare could see no affection for Bar in the captain, though. In fact, he and Bar seemed to hate each other. He evidently did not want to return Bar to his lord maimed or ill.

They broke camp before dawn the next morning and left without breakfast to get an early start. Captain Ganshof decided to put Bar on one of their horses with Dare behind him to keep him from falling and injuring himself. The horse was powerful, but Dare had no trouble controlling him. Thank the Maker the horse was a good-natured beast. Dare wondered if the captain would be interested to know that he had never ridden a full-sized horse before. As he looked at the captain's angry expression, he decided, *Probably not.*

They traveled steadily the first few days through beautiful spruce country. Under other circumstances Dare would have enjoyed the fantastic sights, but Bardon suffered miserably, and the taciturn men around them seemed strained and jumpy. Perhaps their captain's vicious temper and taut nerves were causing their edginess; perhaps there was some reason unknown to Dare. Whatever the reason, the captain's scathing tongue raked anyone who made a mistake or was slow. Dare tried to keep Bardon and himself out of the captain's way. Among the men, Dare was encouraged to discover two who were sympathetic to them—Enzig and Foner. Each one tried to help when no one was watching.

Enzig helped Bar down at the end of the exhausting first day when Dare could hardly stand. His arms ached badly from holding Bar in the saddle. The protesting muscles of his shoulders and back were burning and trembling. He smiled gratefully at the tall, wiry soldier but said nothing, knowing the man would not appreciate any attention his thanks might draw to him.

The second evening on the trail, Dare walked to a shallow brook through dense aspen and pine to refill his waterskin. He followed a faint game trail that turned sharply. Before he saw Ganshof, he ran full into the man. The captain slipped back on damp rocks into the stream and barely kept his balance.

His sword was out in an instant. "You clumsy, stupid peasant," he said, his face red with fury. He smashed Dare in the arm with the flat of his sword and then strode rapidly down the trail, grumbling to himself. Dare crumpled to the ground holding his right arm and trying to bite back a scream. Foner found him a few moments later huddled on his knees, waiting for his reeling senses to clear. The huge, young soldier filled Dare's waterskin for him and, when the pain lessened, helped him back to camp. In the deepening darkness, no one noticed. Dare's arm ached for days.

Each morning, Dare gazed in wonder at the beautiful region they were passing through. They climbed steadily for at least a month through wild country filled with craggy ravines and deep timber. Eventually, the trail they were following split, and Captain Ganshof, after a moment of indecision, decided to take the higher path. The snow was about a foot deep, and the path looked slippery in places. Though it was still harvest season, snow often fell in the high country at this season, or any other.

When his first officer remonstrated with him, he struck the competent man with his quirt and shouted for everyone to follow him. Both the first officer and the rest of the men were astounded. Evidently, even for Captain

Ganshof, this was an unusual display of temper. After a few minutes, they stopped staring and followed their fierce captain up the rough trail.

Dare asked Bardon quietly if he knew why the captain was so desperate and irritable. "The—" Bardon cut off and started over. "My father is without doubt holding something over his head, and then … there are the braith," he said thoughtfully.

At Dare's questioning look, he explained, "There is a strange man, some say a sage, who lives up near the timberline on Fairgrieve Mountain. He has bred and raised some fell beasts called braith. They are like mountain cats yet larger and all white except their eyes, which are pink or red. The braith are reputed to be extremely cunning. The men don't want to go into their territory, but, for whatever reason, Ganshof is in a terrible hurry. He wants to use the pass near Fairgrieve instead of going through the valley. It takes much longer to travel the valley, but it is safer."

They were at the end of the troop, which was snaking its way up the trail. Enzig was behind them. There had been little chance to talk before without being overheard, so they had spoken little, but the roaring mountain stream on their right and a high wind in the trees on the left gave them some privacy.

"How old are you?" Bar asked abruptly.

Dare started to lie and then changed his mind. "I'm fourteen." Bar was amazed, just as Dare thought he would be. People always thought he was older because he was big for his age.

"You look much older."

"How old and *who* are you, *Your Grace?*" Dare asked pointedly in return.

Bar stiffened, and after a slight pause, he said harshly, "Don't ask. You don't want to know."

"Great Gant save us! I may die at any minute, and you tell me not to ask? Remember who picked you up and fixed your arm, *Your Grace*. I could have left you. Ganshof fingers his sword every time he looks at me. It's obvious he still wants me dead. Help me understand what I've gotten into; *perhaps* it will help me to stay alive."

Unrelenting, Bar said stiffly, "Some knowledge is dangerous." He refused to listen to any of Dare's arguments. After riding many minutes in silence, some of the rigidity went out of Bar's back. "What right have I to keep it from you? For that matter, what good will it do? You will find out sooner or later anyway. Perhaps sooner is best." Then he said bitterly, "I am sixteen. I am Bardock's son."

King Bardock's son? Prince Bardon! Dare could not speak. He had reasoned that Bar must be some noble's son, perhaps even the heir of a provincial ruler, but never had he expected to hear that he was His Royal Majesty Bardock's only heir. Bardock was reputed to be cold, cunning, ambitious, and cruel. He was certainly despised, in secret of course, by most of the common people.

Bar remained silent for a few minutes to give Dare time to absorb what had to be a frightening revelation. Then he said grimly, "My father and I have little love for one another. He wanted nothing to do with a child and set up my mother and me in a separate establishment. She resented me because she felt my father sent her away from Casterray because of my birth. From court talk, I gather he was tired of her, and my birth gave him an excuse to be rid of an unwanted alliance. She left me solely in the care of my nurse and tutor. They were good people. If not for them, I'm not sure I'd have survived my childhood. There are many people who would like to see Bardock's son dead. I can't say that I blame them.

"They, my nurse and tutor, protected me as well as they could until I was seven. My father's councillors reminded him of my existence at that time, and he set up a program of training for me with his weapons master, battle chief, horse master, and many others. At the end of each day I returned home to Durie and Feller, my nurse and tutor, but I saw less and less of them.

"Because I learned quickly and became skilled with weapons, my father was proud of me and came to watch me more and more often. He was a cold man. I'd overheard stories of his cruelty of course, but I was pleased by his attention. Because of the stories, though, I kept my distance, and that seemed to please him. He thought I was aloof, cold and uncaring just like him, but nothing could have been further from the truth. Durie and Feller follow the Maker and raised me to revere him too. Because my mother took no interest in me, she never realized what was going on under her own roof. You follow him too, do you not?"

"Aye," Dare whispered. It was not an admission one made lightly.

They stopped on a wider ledge to rest and eat. Above them they heard the scream of a cat, somewhere near the timberline. The horses whinnied and reared nervously. The men became even more uneasy, and the captain paced restlessly till they mounted and were on their way again. A cold wind howled through canyon and tree. It smelled of pine and snow.

Bardon's arm ached, and he moved restlessly on the blanket behind Dare. They were trying a new approach to riding double. Bar now rode behind instead of in front. It was much easier on Dare, and he truly had better control of the horse.

"Did you never live in Casterray with the king?" Dare asked softly.

"When I was twelve, the king commanded that I come live in the palace." There was a long pause before Bar took up the story again. "I continued with my usual lessons but also sat in on trade meetings and that kind of thing. I saw much—the greed and double-dealing. No one who disagreed with Bardock lasted long in his regime; some didn't live long. He saw my disappointment in him and resented it. Before the year was out, the court knew of our animosity. Many treated me with barely hidden rudeness. A few, very few, remained my friend: the horse master, the elong master, a few of the house guards, and one of the Basca'.

"The king must have gathered information about my childhood and realized that it was not my mother who raised me but Durie and Feller. He then understood where I had learned about the Maker, studied his scrolls, and gotten my strange ideas, like honesty. When I refused to worship his evil god, Choack, or learn from his prelate, Durie and Feller disappeared. I still don't know if they are alive or dead; he would answer none of my questions."

There was a long silence before Bar began again. His voice was hard and emotionless. "I ... I became very careful. I showed affection for no one—not admiration, not approval, not anything. I was afraid that he would make others disappear also. As it was, when he wanted to discipline or control me, my punishment fell on someone else—someone I cared for or even someone I barely knew."

Dare felt the pain under Bar's harsh tone. He almost told Bar to stop sharing these things that were obviously very difficult to talk about, but he hardened his resolve. He wanted to live; to do that, he had to understand.

"I became, on the surface at least, just as cold and aloof as he was, to protect those around me. Yet I did not truly understand him fully until last year. He sent me to Alberi, a southern province, to lead some of his special troops. A major dispute was disrupting trade, and the troops and I were to put down the insurrection. He sent a capable young captain named Roethive with me. He was really in charge. It was a test, I think. Believe it or not, I still hoped for his approval." Self-loathing was in Bar's voice.

"I settled the dispute my way: by listening and negotiating. In fact, I completely disobeyed his orders. Not one life was lost." He shook his head at his own naivete. "He was furious. He insisted that the people would think he was getting soft on rebellion and it would spread and ... a lot of other things. I should have realized, I guess, but I was shocked—dismayed—at his anger. He would not listen to my explanation.

"Later that day, the mask of indifference I so carefully kept in place broke when I realized what he was planning. I begged and pleaded with him not to discipline another for my actions, to no avail. He called up the captain of our troop and had him whipped in front of the men ... and me. I will never forget the look Roethive gave me. He was paying for my youth and inexperience—my stupidity. They were all reduced in rank. I remember shouting, 'How could the men refuse to obey me? I am your son—Bardock's son!' In his eyes, I saw a look of satisfaction and realized what he was doing. It had never been his intention to punish the captain. He wanted to punish me and, more importantly, to control me in the future. It was very effective." There was still grief in his voice.

"He did nothing to you?" Dare said in astonishment.

"The king has never laid a hand on me, nor has he allowed anyone else to do so. He is fully aware that it is more effective to make someone else suffer for what I do, because it creates distance between that person and me. It isolates me, which serves his purpose. Dare, please understand—I had to escape! The Maker alone knew what he would demand of me next and who would suffer if I refused. I started planning my escape that night, and I almost made it." Bar's right hand formed a tight fist.

The story of Dare's own life seemed to pale in comparison with what Bar had been through. Ursul was cruel but stupid, and Marth—Marth was safe in her small, sunny room. He felt anger toward the cold monarch and pity for this somber young man who was being returned to a life that was little better than that of a drudge. After a few minutes of thought, Dare realized that he was now part of the sticky web that entangled Bar.

"You fear he will use *me* against you?" Dare said with sudden insight.

"Aye, he will use anyone against me. We *must* escape." His voice was calm, but Dare heard the desperation in it.

Captain Ganshof called a halt near the timberline. They set up camp in near darkness, close to a boulder as large as a cottage. He posted two sentries, bows ready, on top of it and four others around the camp's perimeter. Placing the horses near the boulder for protection, he then ordered the men to build two large fires and start preparing their eve meal. Half of the men slept that night with their weapons ready beside them, and half remained on guard. At the fifteenth hour they changed, and Dare and Bardon finally fell asleep.

"Braith! Braith!"

Dare and Bardon awoke with the sentries' cries in their ears. The captain had a burning brand in his hand and was shouting orders over the screaming, roaring chaos created by the five huge braith bounding out of the darkness. After only a few seconds, the animals were too close for bow and arrow, so the men threw their bows down and drew their swords.

Many arrows had found their mark and stuck out from the cats' bodies like quills, but the embedded bolts did not seem to even slow the beasts. The captain was everywhere. He kicked up both the fires so the men could see better and shouted an order to fight in groups to prevent being overcome. Dare and Bardon were in the middle of the camp with the horses and safe for the time being. They watched as a braith slammed a young soldier against a huge boulder with a massive paw. The soldier crumpled to the ground, and then the same cat pounced on a man who came to his aid. The huge feline held him pinned helplessly, unable to use his knife.

Dare came out of shock and opened a small pouch on his belt. He poured some of the powder into his hand; ran up to the monstrous cat, which was roaring in triumph over the man; and threw the stuff in its face. The cat snarled fiendishly at him, shook its head, and swiped at its nose with first one paw and then the other.

To Dare's delight, the braith staggered off the soldier and ran, sometimes falling, back into the dark forest. *Thank the Maker for Shonar!* Dare quickly poured more powder into his hand and threw it in the face of another cat that three of the men were holding at bay with swords. Bar had taken the injured soldier's sword and was helping some of the men with yet another braith. He screamed a warning at Dare. "Behind you!"

Dare spun around but too late. He crashed to the earth under a huge, furry body. Terrible yellow fangs were only inches from his neck; the cat's stinking breath poured over him. The beast's eyes blazed red with hatred and intelligence. It threw back its massive head and roared proudly, as if it had singled Dare out because of the terrible powder he held. Dare struggled wildly, but his arms were pinned by the great paws. There was nothing he could do!

The three men he had helped attacked the braith holding him down. They hoped the huge cat would leave Dare alone so someone could get the stunning powder from the young healer. Their plan worked. Suddenly the braith snarled at the soldiers and left Dare to attack them. Dare shakily stood and tossed the powder to a soldier named Sel, who quickly threw a handful at the cat. Like the other braith, it was dazed and began stumbling. It soon left for the shelter of the forest. Sel then used the powder on the fourth cat, which had wounded two men before the others could help them. The captain and four of his men killed the fifth. There were only five braith, yet it seemed that they'd fought many more.

As suddenly as it had begun, it was over, and the night around them became unnaturally quiet. Captain Ganshof put the uninjured men on watch. He asked Dare how long the effects of the powder lasted. "I … I really don't know, sir. It was meant for the great black mountain bears, but with cats that large, perhaps four hours, maybe less."

"Will you help the injured?" he asked gruffly, looking at Dare intently.

"Aye, sir. I'll get my medicines." *A request from Captain Ganshof? Next the sun will rise in the west.*

The horses had made a disaster of their tether lines. Flag was trembling but fine, and Dare took a moment to soothe him before he got his saddlebags. The captain ordered the men to place the injured near the fires. "Dare, is there any more of that powder?" he asked distractedly.

"Here, sir," Dare said as he handed him the pouch.

"Sel and Dunn will help you. Just ask them to do whatever you need," he ordered as he hurried toward the horses.

Tell grown men what to do? That will be a new experience! "Sel, put water on to boil. Dunn, please get my medicine pack out of my saddlebags. They are over by the closest fire."

Amazing. They're actually doing it! He examined the four injured men quickly. One was bleeding where a cat had clawed his arm. A friend had wrapped his shirt tightly around the injury and stopped the bleeding. He went on to the next man, who was conscious and talking. All he could find was a large lump and cut on the back of the man's head. Next he greeted a hardy old veteran who was bleeding badly from claw marks down his back. These he could handle. The last man—Chin—was middle-aged and unconscious. He'd been badly clawed on both arms and had a deep cut on the back of his head. He was cold, white as the snow, and unresponsive. Dare appealed to the Maker as he examined him. *This head injury is beyond my skill. What should I do?* He knew the answer clearly, but he hesitated. *Captain Ganshof holds the power of life or death over me. If I admit my lack of knowledge and ask the captain for help, I could lose his confidence! The man is longing to get rid of me anyway!* Before he could talk himself out of it, he called to the captain.

Ganshof stopped untangling the horses and came at once. Dare told him he could help three of the wounded but one of the men had a head injury that was beyond his skill.

The captain examined Chin and shook his head gravely. "Do what you can for him. Keep him warm; see if he will take some liquid. Perhaps he will waken in the morning."

When he was finished cleaning and stitching cuts, Dare rose and ran as far into the darkness as he dared. He heaved till he was weak. He was no longer sure he wanted to be a healer.

A strong hand gripped his shoulder. "Boer's bow! That was ... hard," Bar choked out. For a few minutes, they gulped cold air and didn't speak.

"Dare, there are two more men who need your help."

"Enough! I can't do it—I just can't."

Bar held a steaming cup in his right hand; his left arm was back in a sling. "Drink this tea; it will make you feel better." When Dare pulled away from him, Bar shook him and commanded, "Drink. Will two brave men go unaided because you feel sick?"

Tears came to Dare's eyes. He took a deep breath and said, "Great Gant, Bar …"

"I know … I know. But you are helping them. The wounds made by the braith's claws would become infected without your cleaning powders and stitching to close them. What would the men do without your medicines and aid?"

Dare's eyes focused and became less wild. They gazed at each other for several long seconds. Dare swallowed the sour bile in his mouth and reached for the mug. "You're right." The tea and a piece of bread took some of his exhaustion away. He and Bar walked firmly back toward the fire.

With Bar's help, Dare did what he could for the other two men. They covered all the injured warmly as big, feathery flakes of snow began drifting down. Dare didn't think it was cold enough for the flakes to stick to the ground.

"Dare, turn around for a minute," Bar said softly. He examined the back of Dare's head in the firelight. "You are bleeding—from that crashing fall you took, I bet. You must have hit a rock. Tell me what to do."

Dare groaned. As inexperienced as he was, Bar was even more so. He did not like the idea of his new friend working on him, especially with his bandaged left arm out of the sling … again.

"Come on, coward—have some faith in me." Bar's long, slender fingers were gentle, and the lump was still numb enough that Dare felt only stinging as Bar worked. He wound a roll of cloth around Dare's head to protect the injury. Then he gathered some of the thickly falling snow and held it to the back of Dare's head. It hurt, but Dare clenched his jaw and kept quiet. He knew using the snow was the right thing to do; it would reduce the swelling.

"Boer's bow! I don't believe this! I'm bleeding too, I think," Bar said indignantly. "I didn't even feel the cut or whatever it is. I thought it was your blood. Now you will have to bandage me!" There was a note of hilarity in his voice.

For some reason the situation seemed extremely funny. They choked down laughter as they searched for Bar's injury and found a cut on his upper arm. Many of the men around them were asleep, and the others were on guard. They tried to be quiet, to be serious and manly, but the harder they tried, the more comical the situation became. "At least it's not the *injured* arm," Bar gasped. He really tried to smother his laughter, but it burst out of his clenched lips.

The captain came over, thinking something was terribly wrong because of the strange, stifled sounds the two were making. Having been a captain some twenty years, he understood immediately that the two exhausted young men had been stretched too far and were letting off steam.

He looked each sternly in the eye and said severely, "Would you like to do after-meal cleanup for the rest of the trip?" The thought of this awful, dreaded chore sobered them almost immediately.

"What brought this on?" he asked.

Dare pointed with quivering lips to Bardon's arm.

"Lie down. I'll take care of it," Ganshof ordered Dare, eyes narrowing dangerously.

Dare obeyed meekly, biting his lip to keep from laughing again. *I am crazy!* The emerging pain in his head helped him to gain control.

The captain quickly cleaned and bandaged Bardon's arm. Bar carefully avoided looking at Dare; he really did not want to wash stacks of pots and plates until they reached Feisan. Ganshof mixed some of the herbs for pain in water and made them both drink, knowing it would help them sleep, which was what they both really needed. *Youth!* he thought—but with a smile.

Dare wondered, as sleep took him, what had become of the "cruel" captain.

Journey to Casterray

DARE AND BAR AWOKE LATER THAT MORNING in soggy, frigid blankets. Snow was still falling lazily from a gray sky. Captain Ganshof, looking haggard in the predawn light, roused everyone out of their blankets. The men on the last watch prepared hot tea and laid out a cold breakfast on a blanket. Dare smelled woodsmoke and the damp coldness of falling snow.

They all huddled around the fires, eating their flatbread and cheese, drinking the steaming tea, and trying to get warm. Their eyes continually strayed to the forest where the braith had disappeared last night. Everyone was edgy and quiet.

Dare and the captain checked the injured men. Five were doing well and were even able, with the help of their comrades, to get some breakfast. The last man, Chin, was alive but still unconscious. The captain gave orders to break camp and lash together a litter to carry Chin.

"Men," the captain called out, "we are going back down the mountain and into the valley. It will take us much longer, but we cannot chance the braith again. We owe much to Dare and his stunning powder, but there is little of it left. We would never last another assault, and the next time the cats' master might be with them."

The men looked relieved. "I hoped that the stories of the braith were exaggerated tales told by simple folk," he said grimly. "We can attest to the fact that they are quite true. Let's get moving, but quietly."

It took them all day to get back down the mountain, partially because of Chin's litter. The weather remained overcast, damp, and cold. Snow fell fitfully. It was a thoroughly miserable day for everyone but especially for the wounded.

Dare ran out of medicine the next day. The captain sorted through his stores and gave the young healer what herbs he had and directions for using them.

The valley they were passing through teemed with wildlife. The creatures were so unfamiliar with people that they did not always run from the troop but stood and watched their passage curiously. On the third day, two wonderful events occurred. The sun came out, and they came to a small hot spring bubbling from a cliff wall into a basin of rock.

The captain set a guard and let the men bathe and wash clothes and blankets. They brushed the horses; cleaned their hooves, checking them for rocks; and worked on their gear. It was a warm, restful afternoon, and everyone felt much better for it.

They feasted under the trees that night on deer and rabbit that Wise and Foner shot. The captain, amazingly, allowed both Bar and Dare to keep the weapons he had given them in case of another braith attack. He also gave Bar Chin's horse to ride.

It was hard to imagine the heavy Foner being able to move his huge bulk quietly enough to hunt, but Wise insisted he was as good a stalker as he had ever seen. There was much ribbing and laughter around the fire that night. Dare remembered the tension of the troop before the braith attack and wondered at the change.

A fiery dawn the next morning spread rosy light across the valley. The troop, in a much better frame of mind, started down the trail clean, rested, and well fed. Chin, Dare's most troubling patient, opened his eyes and started talking, hesitantly at first and then normally. For the first time, Dare believed that Chin would live and be in his right mind.

Later that day, as they were riding two by two through thick doro pines on a very narrow trail, they heard a ferocious roaring and crashing in the woods on their right. The troop pulled up and wheeled their mounts toward the sound.

Something very big and angry was rapidly coming their way. The captain and Enzig were in the lead. Before they could draw their swords, an enormous black bear barreled out of the trees and right at them. Rising up on its hind legs, the huge beast roared its fury at their intrusion into its territory.

The leaders' terrified horses shied, reared, and plunged. Neither veteran was unseated, but they had their hands full controlling their terrified mounts. They had no chance to defend themselves.

Dare saw Bar move out of the corner of his eye. In one fluid movement, Bar bent to his boot, grabbed his knife, and threw it, all while his horse danced with nervous fear. The bear's roar turned to a gurgle as his neck sprouted a knife.

"Give me your knife, Dare!" Bar hissed. Dare grabbed his knife and handed it to him. Quicker than the eye could see, Bar threw the second knife into the crazed animal's chest. The bear was batting at the knife in its throat when the second blade plunged into its flesh. The creature dropped to all fours and began to shake furiously in an attempt to dislodge the blades.

On the narrow trail, it was difficult to get a clear shot, but a few of the soldiers shot arrows at the raging animal. In spite of this, the weakened bear was able to turn and run into the forest, leaving a path of broken branches. The huge creature also left the knifte lodged in its neck, which it had managed to dislodge, on the ground. Dare quickly retrieved it and got back in the saddle.

The captain and Enzig were finally able to settle their frightened horses. Ganshof, panting from exertion, managed to shout an order quickly. "Do not go after the creature! Ride!" Quickly they followed the captain down the trail and, hopefully, out of the bear's territory.

In a few hours, they broke out of the trees into a rocky meadow and were able to relax their vigilance a little. Black bears, even badly injured ones, had been know to follow people for days and inflict injury and death on those who wounded them. They moved slowly across the rocky ground as the sun began to set over lofty peaks in the west. The captain called a halt beside an ice-crusted stream. They ate creegal, a type of mountain trout, that night. In the back of their minds lurked the thought that creegal was the black bears' favorite food.

After their meal, while the men were still gathered around the fire, the captain came over to Bar and asked him to stand. Fear shot through him as he obeyed. Desperately, he tried to think what he had done wrong.

"Enzig and I owe our lives to Bar's quick thinking this afternoon," the captain announced to the men. The troop murmured agreement and approval. He reached out his hand to clasp the prince's arm. "I thank you," he said with simple sincerity. "Where did you learn to throw a knife like that? I have rarely seen anyone so fast."

"My weapons master is a Basca'. I have been practicing almost every day since I was seven," Bardon explained with a grin.

"A Basca'! That would explain it," the captain exclaimed, slapping him on the back. Enzig thanked him also, and many of the other men complimented his skill. The captain gave Bar one of his knives to replace the one lost in the bear attack.

Bar rarely showed any emotion or lost his poise, but Dare knew by the red flush creeping up Bar's neck that he was both pleased and embarrassed. There were a few men around the fire who did not look pleased. Dare wondered if King Bardock could have soldiers loyal to him in this troop. Perhaps they were just withholding judgment until they knew the king's son better.

It was the end of Ree's short winter and the beginning of planting season in the lowlands. In the mountains snow could happen at any time. "Bar," Dare asked while they were riding the next day, "how far is it to Feisan?"

Bar calculated for a minute and said, "We have maybe forty-five to fifty-five horse-travel days at least before we reach the city. It will be almost the end of the second month of planting season before I am ... home."

Dare found this hard to believe. "Do you mean that you had been on the run for almost two months?"

"Aye," he said. "If my horse hadn't stumbled in the canyon, I might have made it." He shook his head wearily. "No, that's not true. I was exhausted and hungry, which is probably why I was thrown from my horse. Ganshof was so close behind me that I could not take time to hunt or rest. On bright nights when the moon was full, he would continue to track me, which meant I couldn't stop. I had a good start on them, but once they found my trail, they pushed relentlessly."

"Where were you headed?"

"My plans after getting out of the castle and then the city … were sketchy," Bar admitted with a grin. "I had been on many trips with my father's soldiers, so I knew my way around a little. I thought I would try to hire myself to some large landowner as a soldier. I'd hoped that the search for me would have died down after a month or so, but Ganshof … well, you know the rest." He sighed.

"I have told you much about me, certainly more than anyone else knows. Now tell me about your life, before you came to my rescue and became a … a prisoner." At this last word, guilt shadowed his mood, which had been merry, and he became serious. Dare shook his head; the prince had a definite problem with seriousness. Of course, being Bardock's son was enough to make anyone sober—gloomy even.

Dare told Bar as much of his story as he could without mentioning the folk of Glidden Mountain. He told him that a local healer and hunter had helped him hide from Glodwin and taught him about herbs and healing. They had already talked about why he was traveling to Ohsay.

Bardon listened attentively and did not comment for many minutes. "You would be halfway there by now," he said regretfully. With his forehead wrinkled in thought, he gazed at the distant mountains and sighed. "Snow can catch us up here anytime now. I think it would be best to stay with the troop until we are over the high passes and in the foothills, but then we must try to escape."

That night after they ate venison around a crackling fire, the captain gave them new orders. "Our wounded are doing well now, but they are slowing us. Tomorrow Enzig will take Fox, Chin, Dirk, and Junson, and they will follow us as quickly as they can to Feisan. Truel, Foner, Sel, Dunn, and I will take Dare and Bar to Feisan and make better time."

Avoiding Bar's eyes, he continued, "His Majesty wanted Bar in Feisan for the Merchant Festival. That was weeks ago. It is my hope that we can return him before Summer Fest."

The next two weeks were a blur of exhaustion. They rode hard from first light to dark, stopping only for short periods of rest. They often ate and drank in the saddle. On the fourteenth day, the beautiful, sunny weather was broken by a howling wind that roared out of the north. Heavy clouds covered the sun, and the air grew colder and colder; it smelled of snow.

About noon the storm hit them. Both men and horses suffered from the frigid temperatures and blinding snow as they struggled to keep the rigorous pace the captain set.

Ganshof was again a man possessed, driving them all to their limits, yet his temper was even, not vicious as it had been before Fairgrieve. When the storm finally blew over after three days, they pushed south through knee-deep snow. After winding through the High Pass of Anor, they started a slow decent into Soles. The storm had greatly slowed them.

When they reached the foothills, the captain regretfully took Dare's and Bar's weapons, bound their hands, and put a guard on each at all times. At night he also bound their feet and kept them separated. All hope of escape evaporated.

Bar could not dispel visions of future coercion and torment. Dare would be used in the king's game! Guilt for the young healer's future bondage and suffering gnawed at him continually. He moaned at night while in the grip of terrible nightmares, and he grew pale and distracted.

The next day, after morn meal, Bar put out his hands to be untied. He said in a low, desperate voice, "Ganshof, let Dare ride out of here. You know what Bardock is capable of doing!"

The captain's eyes were steady, but they mirrored Bar's guilt. "I can't. All the men have seen him. The price is too high, my prince; I can't pay it."

"We return evil for good."

"Aye," the captain said. Motioning to the men, he ordered, "Move out."

Both young men had earned the soldiers' respect. The men valued their courage and considered them comrades. In their hearts they hated to turn them over to Bardock, yet each man was too afraid, for the sake of his position and family, to help them.

Because Bar had dropped his stiff attitude of indifference, for the first time since Durie and Feller's disappearance, he had, unbeknownst to him, made many new friends who felt great loyalty to him. This was no small thing when one considered how they felt about the king.

The closer they came to Feisan, the heavier Bar's heart became. When he saw the great city rise out of the distant plain, despair and bitterness flooded his mind. He searched frantically for a means of escape, any idea to keep Dare safe, but nothing came to him. In the mountains, he had been able to forget who he was. For the first time since age six, he had felt free. Trusting the Maker was easier there, and he'd known true peace. Now he felt sick with fear as terrible thoughts of what Bardock might do to Dare assailed him. He knew his fear showed. He could not control his nightmares or force himself to eat much beyond a few bites.

On their last night on the road before they would reach the royal city, Ganshof allowed Dare and Bar to sit next to each other and talk. Bar's attempt at a smile was stiff and crooked; his bound hands trembled in the fire's flickering light. Dare realized his prince was feeling guilty and far too serious—again.

"Look, Bar, the Maker sent me and my newly learned skills, such as they are"—he grinned—"just in time to pick you up and put you back together. He has a plan and will not desert us, so relax, will you!"

"Dare, you cannot possibly understand," Bar began with a spark of anger.

"I have a really good imagination."

Eyes snapping, Bar started to speak but changed his mind. After a few seconds, he grinned ruefully at Dare. "I suppose I'm being 'unheroic' again—not 'merry in the face of danger' and all that."

Dare nodded sadly; it was very disappointing. Bar had not learned this lesson very well. Dare had explained to Bar, in great detail, that in the best stories, the heroes laughed in the face of danger and made jokes. In spite of his paralyzing fear, Bar chuckled a little, and Dare joined him.

After that, strangely, they spoke of inconsequential but pleasant memories of their trip. When the fire died to a few glowing embers, Captain Ganshof separated them again. By the Maker's gift, both boys slept, Bar for the first time in many restless nights.

The road into Feisan was crowded with traffic the next morning. Farmers, merchants, and landowners were traveling into the city for Spring Fest, which was only two days away.

The captain and company had made the long trip as fast as they possibly could, yet Ganshof knew he was in deep trouble. Bardock would blame him for not returning the prince for the all-important Merchant Festival. The king had made it plain that the consequences for failure would be severe. Ganshof had lost almost all honor in his desperate attempt to return Bar in time, but the shock of having his men wounded in the braith attack had returned him to his senses. No matter the consequences, he would not risk others' lives again to save his position or even his family from Bardock's wrath.

The captain hid Dare's and Bardon's bonds under their cloaks and instructed his men to act as an honor guard for the prince. It was his hope that they could travel through the city without being recognized, but if they were, he did not want the people to see Bar bound. It would cause a great deal of talk and that would displease the king greatly. Because of the crowds, their small group received no attention at all and arrived at Casterray without incident.

Bardon was pale but calm, his fear tightly caged. Dare was dazed by the city, the crowds, and the cold beauty of the castle he was entering. Ganshof took them through checkpoint after checkpoint, and they finally came to the inner court. The troop dismounted wearily. As unobtrusively as possible, the captain cut Bar's and Dare's bonds. Each boy walked into the keep between two guards.

"Captain Ganshof! Your Highness! Welcome," a tall older man dressed in severe black said as he quickly ushered the troop into a private chamber. "I will inform the king that you are here, immediately. He has anxiously awaited your arrival."

What an understatement. Bar's mouth was dry, and it seemed his fear would not stay caged. Dare was in no better shape, nor was the captain, though neither young man suspected it.

Quickly, the king's chamberlain returned and took Ganshof, Dare, and Bar by a back passage to Bardock's study. The cold corridor was filled with golden light from the setting sun, which flooded through high windows.

The soldiers who had traveled with them were ordered, under penalty of death, to speak of their "journey" to no one and to return to their barracks.

After the chamberlain guided Ganshof, Dare, and Bar into the study he quietly left. *Bar looks like his father,* Dare thought numbly, *though Bar's build is much slighter and, someday, he will be taller.* He felt a distant pleasure in the fact that he *could* think.

The king kept himself tightly controlled, but his displeasure showed in his glittering eyes and jerky movements. He was a darkly handsome man, richly dressed in green robes trimmed with the black fur of a mountain bear. Beside him, dressed in the black robes of a prelate, was a small, round man of perhaps fifty years. Dare had heard tales of the king's prelate whose coldness was said to rival that of the king's. His smile chilled Dare to the bone. *He must be Draville.*

The two very different but supremely powerful men stood before a beautiful stonework fireplace that filled the room with light and warmth … yet Dare shivered.

A numbing sense of the hopelessness of resistance was stealing over Bar—a feeling that his father's presence always brought. Nothing he had ever done to stand up to his father had succeeded. Always the king bent him to his will with ease—while noting, enjoying, and cataloguing, for future reference, Bardon's reactions. Seething anger almost choked Bar.

"Captain Ganshof, you have finally returned. Perhaps you can explain why it has taken so long to return my son to me," the king said softly but with menace.

Dare admired the captain's calm, controlled answer. "It took us many days to find his trail, Your Majesty, and forty days of tracking to catch him."

In an impetuous change of subject, the king asked, "Who is this peasant?"

"This is Dare. He found Bar after the prince had been thrown from his horse. He bound up a terrible gash in Bar's arm and helped him to hide from us. He has had some training as a healer but served at Ravensperch as a drudge. His skill as a healer saved us time and saved Bardon, and many of my men as well, much pain and perhaps permanent injury or death. He was on his way to visit his parents' home in Ohsay when he found the prince," the captain answered.

The king's glacial stare froze the captain for a long minute. "You failed to meet my requirement that Bardon be home by the Merchant Festival— yet you have returned him in one piece. He is evidently a skilled woodsman to have evaded you so long."

"His excellent training was not wasted, Your Majesty. He planned well, and if we had not pushed day and night, he might well have escaped us, but exhaustion finally caught up with him." Ganshof's voice betrayed his nervousness. He knew how close he was to disaster.

"You are dismissed, Captain Ganshof. I will talk with you again later," the king said coldly, gesturing toward the door with his hand. Ganshof was visibly startled and left, unsure what the consequences for his failure would be.

King Bardock paced softly to where his son stood and stopped a close twelve inches in front of him. "You left because I disciplined your troop, in particular that sniveling Captain Roethive?" the king asked with contempt.

"Aye, sir," Bar said, his voice hoarse from thirst and other things. He would have given much for a cup of water.

"So you thought to escape me. Absurd, Bardon—no one escapes me," the king said with indifference as he held out his hand for his wine cup. Draville smoothly placed the desired vessel in his hand. "You will pay dearly for your … trip, shall we call it? We have spread a story that you've been visiting your uncle Alsase in Possan. See that you support it."

For Dare's sake, Bardon held his tongue in check and said softly, "Aye, sire."

Dare felt sick. The king's conversational tone was laced with sarcasm, which was much worse than shouting. The young healer easily understood Bar's bitter hatred for his father.

"You have interfered with our plans and caused us much trouble—much embarrassment too, I might add—for the last time, my son. Is that clear?" Bardock's face was just a few inches from Bar's; his dark eyes glittered dangerously. Bar nodded.

The king seemed satisfied for the moment. "I can see that you are near exhaustion. Go to your room and rest. It has been prepared for you. Take Dare with you. We will talk again later." He called two guards to escort them.

When they left, Draville said curiously, "You let him keep this … this … drudge?"

"Aye, he will have his uses, I'm sure."

"Ah." The enlightened prelate smiled. They discussed their plans in low voices by the fire. Both looked content.

Just in Time

THE GUARDS CLOSED THE DOOR FIRMLY BEHIND Dare and Bar, leaving them alone in a large room filled with fur rugs and massive but plain wooden furniture. Weapons, scrolls, and a variety of treasures, among them a large wasp nest, a saddle, and a fish skeleton, were stacked on chairs and shelves. A huge, steaming cask for bathing sat comfortably near the crackling fire.

"I'm sure the guards are still there," Bar said wearily, with a gesture toward the door. "I don't know if I am more hungry or thirsty or tired."

They found a table spread with a snowy-white mat and laden with cheese, meat, fruit, and drink. They both grabbed a pitcher and drank thirstily. Then they ate till they could eat no more. Grinning with anticipation, they stripped off their crusted, filthy clothing and gratefully sank into the hot water.

"This is heaven," Dare sighed.

"More likely Hades," Bardon said bitterly.

Too tired to talk, worry, plan, or even use the cleansing leaves, they gave up all effort, fell into the soft bed, and knew no more till the next morning.

A manservant softly opened the door at dawn. He motioned two servingwomen inside to clear the dishes from the night before and place morn meal on the table. He got a small fire going, opened the heavy drapes, and then withdrew without speaking to his waking prince.

Dare yawned, stretched, and rolled out of bed. "There's much to be said for being a prince," he said while selecting a roll from the bountiful selection.

"Aye, it's a well-appointed prison, and the service is good." There was only a trace of bitterness in his voice. He checked the windows and discovered they were tightly shuttered. The shutters could not be opened, but he knew the windows looked out over Fishhead Bay. Directly below them was a stone seawall that protected the castle's foundation from the crashing waves. Sticking his head out the door, he noted the two guards in the hall. "We are definitely not going anywhere."

Bar used hand signals to explain to Dare that they were being watched from the next room through spy holes in the wall. While doing this, he was careful to turn his back to the wall in question, where a large chest was located. Dare felt his already enormous anger growing again; he did his best to hide it from Bar. The prince apparently took being spied on for granted.

Though Bardon had found a measure of peace from food, rest, and his faith, he ate little. He was restless, pacing the room with quick strides and thinking something over. Dare was sure he knew what. Bardock's threat— "You will pay dearly …"—hung over them this morning and robbed even the food of its flavor. This, however, didn't stop Dare from eating heartily.

Suddenly, Bar stopped his pacing and looked at the young healer with disbelief. "How can you eat at a time like this?" Dare shrugged. He was one of those people who woke with a hearty appetite, alert and ready for the day.

"No! Don't even think about whistling!" Bar said as Dare started a merry tune. "I don't even like to talk till I've been up for hours."

"Don't I know it! It would be a sad thing if Your Royal Highness ever had to fight an enemy or make a decision before noon!"

Enraged, Bar spluttered indignantly, "You, you—"

"Evidently your tongue doesn't work well in the morning either," Dare said smugly. The frustrated, tongue-tied prince hurled a pillow at Dare with all his might. Dare ducked it easily, and the large missile landed in the middle of their morn meal table, sending dishes flying and spilling milk.

"Your aim, I see, is also adversely affected. This problem is a serious deficiency in a prince. Perhaps I should mention that you need some early morning, *really* early morning, practices added to your sched—"

"Dare, stop! Please," Bar said helplessly, a smile tugging at the corners of his mouth. He also hated to laugh in the morning.

"Cry uncle!'"

"Uncle! Aunt! Anything you like. Just be quiet!"

Always good-natured, Dare stopped harassing Bar and attempted to clean up some of the mess. The less somber prince found clean clothes in his large wardrobe. As they were pulling on soft leather boots, they heard a scratching sound. They looked at each other questioningly. The sound did not come from the door but from the outside wall!

Puzzled, Bar walked quietly to that section of the wall. Dare followed him, but he said nothing, conscious of unfriendly eyes and ears in the next room. The scratching sound was repeated, this time more insistently. The area the sound came from was out of the view of the spy holes. They began searching for they knew not what. Perhaps there was a trapdoor or secret entrance that opened by a lever of some kind.

A soft voice startled them both. "Look under the broken tile for a lever, and please, talk to each other normally, or the servant who is listening will become suspicious!"

They looked at each other in wonder, too amazed to respond. Dare's eyes blazed with excitement while Bar's were wary with distrust. Thinking hard, they were finally able to design some small talk as they searched for the broken tile.

It was far to the right of the place where they'd heard the voice but still out of the vision of the watcher. Lifting the tile carefully, they saw a dusty lever and pulled it, while talking loudly to cover any noise. Two of the large stone blocks that made up the turret slowly moved into the room. As they watched numbly, a dark head and massive shoulders pushed through the opening.

The man urgently motioned them to keep talking, and they stuttered into what had to be a very strange conversation. Dare recognized Lavel, the man who had reported to the Glidden council about him. Whatever else he might be, he was definitely a friend. Lavel shook Dare's arm in recognition and smiled reassuringly. He held a finger up to his lips, warning them not to talk to him, and then he handed them a note:

> You are watched at all times. You must come with me now, or it will be too late. Do not stop to get *anything*! You have been out of the watching servant's sight for many minutes.

He will soon make an excuse to enter the room. We have learned that you are in great danger.

When they had read the note, Lavel whispered urgently, "Come!"

Bar's eyes were dark and skeptical. Dare grabbed his hand and mouthed, "Trust me. Come."

Looking from Dare to Lavel with a hard, searching gaze, Bar finally nodded. After he replaced the broken tile and threw some of his dirty clothes over it, Bar followed Dare through the opening.

They were in a tight, dark stairwell that must be between the round turret and the castle wall. Lavel's huge shoulders barely fit. He pulled the two stones back in place and motioned them down the stairs. They went as quickly as they could in the dark, sensing Lavel's huge bulk behind them. The sound of crashing waves became louder and louder.

Dare, in the lead, caught a breath of fresh, cool air and saw dim light ahead of him. It grew brighter, and as he rounded a turn in the spiral stair, he was blinded by sunshine pouring through an open door.

"Come quickly, lad," a dark figure said softly. Someone took his arm and led him down some roughly cut rock stairs that were slippery with sea spray to a waiting boat. The small craft was tugging on its rope in the pounding surf. *An escape in broad daylight! I hope these folk know what they are doing.*

Bar and Lavel were right behind him. Dare knew Bar must be feeling terribly anxious and confused. The prince had shown much confidence in Dare to leave with a total stranger. He had no idea where he was going or what the man's intentions were. Dare knew Bar did not trust easily—for good reason.

The sea was bright in the morning sunshine, and waves tossed the small sailboat about roughly. Two men helped Bar and Dare get aboard, and then Lavel got in, almost swamping the boat with his great weight. The two men untied a rope, quickly jumped in, and rowed against the incoming waves while Lavel raised the sail. It instantly caught the wind, and they moved out into the bay, crashing down hard in the valley of each wave. Dare had never seen the sea till this day. He watched his companions uneasily, wondering if this pounding up and down was normal. They looked grim but calm. As soon as they got into smoother water, Lavel guided their vessel north along the coast. They passed Fishhead Bay and were finally out of sight of Casterray's watchtowers and windows. Everyone relaxed a little.

Lavel gave the tiller to one of the men with him and moved carefully in the small craft to Bardon's side. "You have trusted this far, and now, I must ask you to trust again," he shouted over wind and sea. "We cannot stay on the open water. The alarm will be quickly raised, and they will be searching for you soon, if they are not already. Where I take you … the people are understandably cautious. I must blindfold you both. Will you allow this?"

Bardon gave Dare a haunted glance. "If he says aye, I will also."

Dare smiled stiffly at Lavel. "Aye, do it. The less I know the better."

Lavel placed thick cloth over their eyes. After a time, they felt the boat change direction and move in toward shore.

Near the castle the shoreline of Ree was rocky and indented with many narrow bays and inlets surrounded by high cliffs. There were boulders in the water that had to be carefully avoided. The waves pushed them into shore with great heaves. Suddenly, they felt the warmth of sunshine leave their skin. The air turned cold and damp, and sounds became muffled and full of echoes. They heard the men take the sail down and begin to row on water that was smooth. Still the men were silent and did not talk to each other at all.

Dare and Bar kept still also. They waited with patience to know more. Dare realized that Lavel must have many spies in the king's castle. He had learned in Glidden that there were many spies in Ravensperch, the castle he'd served in. He was amazed that there were people who were willing to risk their lives to help Lavel. A chilling thought struck him as it probably had Bar. What if Lavel was part of some plot of the king's, or what if he was part of some rebel movement that wanted to kill the young prince? Dare shook his head and tried to clear his thoughts. *Shonar and Lock trust Lavel. For now I will too. It is too late to do anything else.*

Dare realized they were in some kind of cave, and he was amazed that they continued to travel underground for what must surely have been an hour. Finally, Lavel and the other two men started talking softly with one another, so the need for silence must be less urgent. Dare ventured a question. "Lavel, how much longer?"

"We have hours to travel yet. Lie down and get some rest if you can," Lavel whispered. He was clearly distracted.

"Are there any blankets or warmer clothing?" Dare asked. He and Bar wore lightweight wool tunics, breeches, and their boots, and that was all. They had both been cold the minute they'd entered the cave and even before that, but the sun had helped when they were outside.

"What an idiot! Forgive me," Lavel said softly. "Aye, we brought you clothing, not knowing if you'd have anything on when we came for you. And here I'm so busy getting us through that I forgot all about giving it to you." He handed them warm fur-lined cloaks and woolen blankets.

The two sailors hissed, warning them to silence, and they all froze. The men did not even put oars in the water. Above them, they could faintly hear voices and the sounds of carts and horses. The boat glided for a space, and then the men started rowing again—very quietly. They went on and on until finally Lavel whispered, "Rest, hishua, young warriors, rest. We have far to go." Warmth from their cloaks and blankets was stealing over them. They gladly lay in the damp bottom of the boat and were soon asleep.

Dare struggled out of dreams to wake in total darkness. He had been fleeing some terrible, slimy monster that had risen out of a cave's dark waters. The dark shape next to him was Bar, who appeared to be still sleeping.

"Lavel."

"Hush, Dare," he said urgently. "We have seen light ahead where no light should be. We pulled the boat against the wall and are waiting to find out what it is."

The inky-black water slapped gently against the subterranean tunnel's walls; there was no other sound. Then Dare heard the subtle sound of oars or something moving in the water. Lavel put out their light; he had seen its glow, even through the blindfold. Time passed slowly in complete darkness. Suddenly a light glowed again; it flashed once, twice … There was a pause, and it flashed once more. One of the men on Dare's boat removed something from their light and returned the familiar signal with relief.

"Something must have gone wrong," Lavel whispered. "They will come to meet us now, and we'll see what has happened."

Both boats allowed their lights to show and approached each other quietly. An angry, frightened voice came across the water. "The king's guard, soldiers, and even the Basca' are swarming all over the city like angry hornets! They are watching the docks closely. That demon Urskal is sittin' on our goods from Garamon, just as if he knew what we was planning."

"Captain Watson," Lavel greeted with a nod. He then asked anxiously, "Do you think they have discovered the lungala?"

"No, no, but Urskal has never liked nor trusted me, so he assumes, I'm thinking, that I might have a part in this … this escape," Captain Watson said bitterly. "Our sources say that every possible exit to Feisan is bein' watched. With the festival goin' on, the city is full o' all kinds and sorts; not an inn has any space. The whole population is in an entire uproar, it is. There's no way he'll keep it quiet *this* time."

Bar had woken up while the lights were flashing, and he was sitting next to Dare listening. He shook his head from side to side as if he were saying to himself, *No, no.*

"We need a new plan, Captain; we surely do," another, younger voice said from the other boat.

Watson sighed. "Well, Lavel, let us think this one through. We'll put our heads together and come up with a new plan to rescue the youngsters."

"I understand, Captain," Lavel assured him.

Lavel gave the "youngsters" food and water and explained a little of their situation. "The waterway we are using is a well-guarded secret and, hopefully, unknown to any of the king's men. The lungala are underground caves and fissures that are natural for the most part. In places they have been joined to make a secret canal system under the city. There are places where natural fissures in the rock above us make it possible to hear sounds of the city; they are also why we must always be so quiet. Some of these fissures we have sealed, but some we keep open for our own use. We were going to get you out of Possan by boat. I fear that option is gone, so we will have to think of another way."

Lavel joined Watson on the other boat, and they talked quietly for several minutes. Lavel returned, and then Bar an Dare could hear the skiff leaving.

"Here is the new plan," Lavel said. "We are going to climb up a fissure, sort of a chimney in the rock, that will put us in a secret room aboveground.

There will be men above holding two ropes, one for me and one for Dare. I will be behind you, Dare, to steady you if you need help. Dare, do you know what queal is?"

"No," he answered.

"Bar has a condition that makes him very sick if he is suspended over a space without his feet on solid ground. I will come back down and carry Bar up on my back." At Bar's frown, he said, "It takes two strong arms to climb up a rope, and that you do not have yet. Also, we don't want to trigger your queal. You can put one arm around my neck and your legs around my waist and then be carried. One of the captain's men will get things ready above us in an old warehouse. We will wait for their signal at the bottom of the chimney, and then we will start the climb. It is too far to simply haul you up, and there are outcroppings of rock that would make it impossible." There was a note of humor in his voice. "Also, at my weight, there's probably no man alive who *could* pull me up." Bar smiled at his humor and relaxed a little.

They waited quietly for the signal. Finally a light flashed above them, and a man said, "Come! Quickly now!" Two thick ropes dropped down to them. Lavel removed Dare's and Bar's blindfolds.

With a rope tied securely around his waist, Dare climbed with Lavel behind him, moving steadily from one foothold to the next. The climb took patience and endurance, but they accomplished it without any problems. The men above pulled Dare into the room. Lavel climbed back down for Bar and carried him up easily. Blindfolds were put back on Bar and Dare the minute they climbed out of the chimney. They stood on the rough wooden planking of the dark room at the top. The short glimpse Dare got of Bar made him wonder if his friend's arm was hurting. His face was pale and damp with sweat, his eyes strained. Dare felt irritation at the blindfold, but he counseled himself to patience. These people were taking a terrible risk to help them at all. If he or Bar were caught, the less they knew the better.

Strange and spicy smells filled the air, and Dare could hear muffled voices. He guessed they were in a warehouse filled with goods from all over Ree. Lavel startled them when he put a hand on each of their shoulders. "I must leave you now, but you are in safe hands with Morin. Do as he says, and all should go well. Bar, I've heard good reports of your conduct when you were on the trail back to Feisan; so I'll say only this: the men you'll be with are rough and uneducated but worthy of your respect. Treat them fairly, learn their ways, and they'll honor you for it."

Dare thought Bar might be offended, but he answered courteously, "I understand. I will speak to the Maker concerning your safety. Thank you for all you have done."

"I'll send for you or come get you myself when the uproar settles a bit," Lavel said. Dare thanked him also, and Lavel squeezed their shoulders. "The Maker be with you."

Before they could feel forlorn, a cheery voice said in a hearty whisper, "Well, sirs, well! You're not going to like this next part a bit, but what can we do, I ask you? What can we do?" Apprehension filled them both as the man with the hearty voice pumped their arms up and down vigorously. "I am Morin. Good to meet you! Good to meet you! Now, lads, we're going to take you aboard my ship with the supplies. Since it's a fishing ship, we go out into the Ag'nuo Current for spineys and such and then come back when we have a good catch. We're hoping those searching for you won't be watching us, as they certainly will be watching all the merchant ships who leave for ports around the island. We chop up bluefins for bait, so we always buy and take lots aboard with us. They're a big fish, you see, and we're going to slip you each inside one. It'll be a bit cold and smelly, but I don't think even that wily Urskal will think to look for you in there."

I'll bet he won't either, Dare thought. He hated tight places and rigidly controlled his emotional reaction to this plan.

Bar said, "Lavel told us we would not be taken out of Feisan on a ship. Are you saying that we will go fishing with you and come back in a couple weeks' time?"

"Aye, lad. That's it. We're hopin' the uproar will have settled a bit and we can get you out by land," he answered.

Two of Morin's men wrapped them in furs first and then did indeed fit each inside a gutted bluefin. The only consolation was that the men removed the blindfolds. The men then placed them on a wagon and stacked a pile of the fish on top of them. The wagon jolted and bounced over a cobblestoned street on its way to the docks. They could hear Morin's booming voice as he yelled to friends and merchants in the noisy streets. He had exactly the kind of voice you would expect a ship's captain to have—one that could be heard over gales and would reach to the highest rigging.

The wagon stopped, and Dare concentrated on staying calm and not gagging. He was trembling, but not from the cold. He had never … *never* been able to handle small, dark, confining places. "Maker, make it short!" he whispered incoherently.

Bardon did not have trouble with small places, but he too was afraid. He knew the king well. This was a clever hiding place, but the Basca' were cleverer, and visions of Dare's capture haunted him again. He too spoke to the Maker in simple terms. *Hide us!*

The men had begun unloading the fish. Dare and Bar could hear the sea crashing against the docks and the scream of gulls; then they heard the sound they dreaded.

"Hey there, Captain Morin! I've been waiting for you, I have. We've searched every dock, every ship, and every warehouse in the whole Gilpin district. I wouldn't want to leave you out, you and your crew being so loyal to the king and all. Got a load of bluefin, I see. I might want to take one of those home for supper. They're good eatin' I've heard."

They were not good eating, which was why they were used for bait. It was a veiled threat. Bar's stomach turned over. Dare had problems of his own to deal with; he wanted out—out! He was beyond caring that any sound now meant capture—well, almost. Some part of him still knew that his outcry would mean Bar's capture too. That must not happen.

Captain Morin shouted jovially, "Well, take one for your dinner, if you really need it, Tar Urskal. We can surely spare it, bein' well-fed men who *work* hard for their living, but these fish will be cut up as bait for the spiney, as you well know."

Bar grinned, in spite of his fear, at the captain's barbed comment; the man surely had courage. The rumble of more wagons arriving could be heard. Tar Urskal shouted, "Search every wagon, men, but remember—we want them alive. Be careful."

"Kukul, get these fish loaded," the captain ordered his first mate.

"Aye, sir. Here, men, let's get on with our work and let the king's men get on with theirs," a familiar voice yelled. Bar could not remember where he had heard it. He could tell from the men's conversation that two soldiers were searching every fish; it was messy work, and they sounded thoroughly disgusted.

Maker, Bar pleaded. A growing riot of noise somewhere down the street broke into his thoughts. "Tar Urskal! Two boys was seen running down the street and into that warehouse by the old washing fountain. Captain Grashar thinks it's them! Come quick," an out-of-breath man shouted.

"You men there, stop that and come with me," Tar Urskal ordered tersely. Neither boy could see which men accompanied Tar Urskal, but it was not the ones searching bluefin. However, the soldiers near them apparently lost interest in searching the cold, stinking fish when their master's eye was no longer on them. They quit the project with much complaining and went on to help their fellows search the other wagons. The sailors quickly moved all the bluefin into the hold of the ship and closed the trapdoor.

The sailors on the deck now had hope that their valuable cargo would go undiscovered and the *Karras* would be allowed to sail. Captain Morin had planned the diversion, but even so, the timing had been so close that he was deeply shaken. Tar Urskal would find no boys if their plan worked. Even if the wily soldier did catch the decoys, they would be youngsters who lived on the wharf and could, he hoped, be able to act their way out of a tight spot by feigning innocence.

In the hold, Dare squirmed and fought his way out of the fish, no matter the consequences. If the soldiers searched the ship again, he would have time to get back in—he hoped. The hold was dark, cold, and wet and smelled so strongly of fish that he gagged.

"What if they come back?" Bardon hissed angrily, looking ridiculous with his head swaddled in fur sticking out of an opening in the bluefin's throat. Too sick to laugh or even smile, Dare lay on the rough planking taking deep breaths and willing his reeling senses back to normal.

"Are you ill?"

"Aye. I cannot abide being in small, dark places. It makes me feel sick, as if I can't breathe. I want to scream until I can break or claw my way out."

"I've heard of that but never felt it myself. It sounds really wonderful. Well, since you're out, help me get out too."

"And what if they come back, Your Highness?"

"I don't care! This has to be one of the most miserable and … and … *unique* things we've done."

Bardon wiggled the whole time he talked, but he was evidently hung up on some inner part of the fish. Dare moved across the floor to help him and, with still-trembling hands, reached inside the fish's body cavity. He loosened Bardon's fur wrap from a rib bone and hauled him out.

"It must be well past mid meal. I'm starving, thirsty, and cold," Bar said. "Hopefully, it will be time to eat soon."

"Do you think of nothing but your stomach? It's very unprincely—unheroic too!"

"Quiet, you commoner."

The ship lurched and then started to move. Someone must have permitted them to leave the harbor! The boys looked at the trapdoor hopefully, and after about fifteen minutes it did open. The captain shouted, "Grab the ladder and climb up." They found it and climbed out into a cold, bright night, well lit by the new moon. The ship raced gracefully across the waves, a light breeze filling its sails.

FIRST MARKING

SEAGULLS SCREAMED OVERHEAD, AND sunlight danced on the waves as the crew of the *Karras* shouted excitedly. The spiney were running! Crewmen lined up along the rail with long poles and longer lines and jerked the huge fish into the boat. The prickly fish madly flopped everywhere on the deck. As soon as the sailors swung a fish on board, Dare, Bardon, and two new crewmen were to stun it with a club. This chore Bar could do even with his left arm still bandaged, but not the next step. Then Dare and his new crewmates were supposed to remove the hook, bait it with a piece of bluefin, and rush on to the next fish. Two men with stout poles would push the stunned fish into the hold. That was the way it was supposed to work. After the first day of chaos, the new crew got into the rhythm of their particular jobs, and it did work—usually.

However, at first Dare, Bar, and the new sailors often failed to get their fish completely stunned. Dare and his mates also had trouble getting the fishhooks out of the strange places they managed to get stuck in the fish's bodies. The young men slipped on the slimy, wet deck and were spiked and slapped by the frantic spineys. Fishlines got tangled around legs, arms, and once in the rigging. Hooks embedded in clothing, human flesh, and even the captain's hat. The experienced crew laughed till tears ran down their faces at the often wild scene before them.

Kukul, over and over again, straightened out difficulties and got the system running again, only to have it break down somewhere else. He cajoled, threatened, and yelled at everyone in order to restore order.

On the second day of fishing, their tasks went more smoothly. Both Dare and Bar ached from head to toe and were barely able to work until sunset. The spiney continued to run for the next three days. Every time the crew threw out chopped-up bluefin, the water roiled with large schools of the fish, and another full day of fishing would begin. After a few days, Bar's and Dare's muscles became accustomed to the work, and they began to enjoy themselves. The days were bright and beautiful with temperatures between fifty and sixty degrees, as long as they stayed in the Ag'nuo Current.

On the fifth day, the current grew even warmer, and the spineys suddenly disappeared. The captain and Kukul were concerned, yet they could not say exactly why. Spiney were notoriously fickle. While trying to decide whether to give it another day or head for port, they paced the deck and talked to old hands. The hold was almost full of fish; it would be a profitable catch.

"Captain, Captain, there's a terrible turbulence aft!" a sailor up in the rigging yelled, panic in his voice. The men ran to look and saw the water boiling like soup in a pot. Steam or fog rose and drifted up in a huge pillar that covered over a hundred-foot-wide circle of ocean.

"What in blazes!" the captain exclaimed. His blue eyes, squinted almost shut against the bright sunlight, were intent on the roiling water. He grabbed the rail so hard that his knuckles turned white as he searched the sea for some explanation for what was causing the phenomenon.

Suddenly, the water boiled more fiercely, and out of the sea two enormous blue-black horns appeared followed by two more and then a gigantic wedge-shaped head. The men screamed in amazement and fear, yet everyone remained frozen in place, eyes glued to the creature rising slowly out of the frantic, hissing sea. The creature had spikes down his nose and the sides of his head. He unfurled his enormous, thick blue-green wings, and his heavily scaled chest, blue-black in color, glinted in the sunshine. Bright obsidian eyes observed them majestically. Each man heard within his mind a gentle reassurance. No one moved a muscle. The creature's immensity filled their vision, as if a mountain had risen out of the sea.

Within his mind Bardon heard a gentle, slightly perplexed voice. *"Bardon, my Lord has sent me to you. Will you come into my ... er ... hand and speak with me? I will not harm you."*

Bar did not know if the others could hear this or not. The creature, who towered above him, held out one of his front feet. His talons were at least four feet long and as thick as Bar's arm at their base. The pointed, dart-sharp tips gleamed in the sun. Bardon's heart was pounding like storm-driven surf, loud to his own ears. His body trembled with shock and excitement. He tried to speak two times before he was able to ask, "Who … who is your Lord?"

With his voice sounding like a many-toned harp, the creature said, "He who is, who always was, and always will be and will always remain the same. He whom you call Maker!" The waters responded to this exclamation by vaulting, surging, and swirling around the creature. The way the creature spoke was a hymn of praise, and Bar's whole being answered with a burst of trust. As he stepped onto the creature's palm, the talons snapped together over his head to form a sort of cage, and the creature lifted him closer to his great jet eyes.

Trust dissolved and apprehension overwhelmed Bar at his own brash step and at the enormity of the being who held him in his power. The creature seemed to sense this and said, "Do not be afraid, for I have good news. Now listen to me closely."

Bar interrupted with dreadful necessity. "Who are you?" He spoke out loud, yet he heard the creature's voice not with his ears but within his mind.

The creature seemed amused and answered, "I am E Clue of the Uriisis!"

As E Clue spoke, a strange thing happened. Bardon's mind was filled with images of creatures like E Clue, though none so large, living in a mountainous, sun-dappled land beneath the sea. For a moment, he could feel the swirling warm waters, their living currents tugging at him, urging him to come with them. He could smell strange fragrances and beheld waters of fantastic beauty, shaded from light green to darkest purple. Overhead was a distorted, bright ball that was the sun. A powerful longing swept over Bar with the force of terrible homesickness. "May I come to your realm with you?"

Pity filled E Clue's eyes. "No, child of the land. You have work of great importance to do. Perhaps one day the Maker will allow it, but not this day. Now listen to me carefully. I will mark you today, just as the prophecy foretold. Listen!" E Clue began to recite:

Born of a house become prostitute,
yet he shall be raised up in undying truth.
One wolf-marked, the spirit shall recruit,
to heal, to stand with, and to be his sure proof.
Tsurtne he shall become to the hidden man,
he who has lost all, except his family and new clan.
He shall have a council with four advisors:
one who knows secrets, a fighter of evil,
a truthful trader, and a leader of men.
And six companions who are helpers:
a marked healer, a rock carver, a deer hunter,
a horse warrior, a cavern dweller, and a water seeker—
that makes ten.
If he remains loyal and speaks the truth,
the crown he will surely win.

Once finished, E Clue said, "*Repeat what I have spoken.*" Bardon's numb mind was splintered into a hundred different thoughts. He stumbled badly over the words, but he finally was able to focus and repeat them to his teacher's satisfaction.

"*Now, little one, remove your … er … coverings from your right shoulder, and I will place his mark on you,*" E Clue said. His voice was infinitely gentle and as patient as living rock.

As Bardon unlaced his tunic, anxiety hit him and cramped his stomach. As he took the garment off, he asked, trying to keep his voice steady, "E Clue, is this going to hurt?"

"*Aye, small one, but not for long!*" E Clue said joyfully. Bar thought that joy had little to do with pain, but he relaxed somewhat. If E Clue wasn't worried, perhaps he shouldn't be either. E Clue's attention seemed to be elsewhere for a moment, and then he said, "*I have asked your friend to prepare some herbs for a poultice that will stop the pain and help the mark to heal cleanly. This pain … is not ordinary to man. I cannot explain it better than that.*" E Clue placed one talon in his cavernous mouth, revealing rows of sharp teeth, and breathed on it till it glowed with blue fire. Then the Uriisis gently reached through the cage his other talons had created and touched the glowing tip to Bar's right shoulder.

Burning flared through Bar. He did not know if he screamed out loud or only in his mind, but his body was suffused with fire, and he slumped to his knees, blind, deaf, and numb to all but the raging blaze. It was not a fire that burned up but one that burned in. It was like nothing he had ever experienced.

"Remember the words. We will meet again!"

E Clue laid Bar on the cool deck. Bar could respond to none of the men crowded around him. He heard Dare calling his name and felt something cool on his shoulder. At once the burning started to recede, and soon he could speak and feel his own body again.

"Has he gone?" Bardon asked weakly.

The captain said fiercely, "Aye. He sank back into the water, but the cloud of steam or fog or whatever it is is still there. Who or what is he?"

"He said he is E Clue of the Uriisis."

"E Clue! I always thought he and the Uriisis were just a fireside tale for children," the captain exclaimed. "Why did he burn you?" Bar heard both anger and confusion in the captain's voice. Before he could answer, Morin's puzzled expression changed to wonder, and he said softly, "The prophecy! Of course." He quoted, "Two shall stand in evil's way. Uriisis- and wolf-marked, this pair, shining, like-marked swords will bear. Their appearance will display the Maker's mercy in that day."

"Aye, E Clue said the Maker sent him. He gave me some instructions."

Dare's eyes were bright with awe and laughter. "Never, never did I imagine that day I picked you up on the trail that I would become involved in such an adventure!"

Bar grimaced. "In fact, you enjoy being hidden in stinky fish, clawed by evil cats, chased, bound, and taken prisoner and having no say whatsoever about your own life."

"Meeting E Clue was worth it all!" Dare said reverently, his blue eyes blazing. "Did he ... show you his land?" he asked hesitantly.

"Aye," Bardon said, and it was enough; no other words were necessary.

"Well, this creature did not speak to me," the captain said plaintively, "and I would like to be knowing the purpose of his visit, other than that mark on your shoulder."

Captain Morin was a small, round man full of energy and toughness. His love of laughter and tendency to joke made him an easy captain to work for, but there was never any question that he was the captain. He ran a tight ship, and discipline was firm. Right now his eyes were alight with excitement. *The fulfillment of the prophecy on my ship is grand but a bit too important for the likes of me.*

Bar groaned in spite of himself; the burning was flaring through him again. Dare picked him up as if he were a sack of otet leaves and carried him to the captain's cabin. "It's time to change that poultice. And perhaps this conversation should be private," Dare said softly to Morin.

The captain put Kukul in charge and ordered him to sail for the royal city. Bar's pain receded again immediately when Dare put a fresh herbal mixture on his shoulder. Bar repeated his message from E Clue for Morin and Dare, and all three felt more than a little overwhelmed by the situation. They spoke to the Maker, asking for strength and wisdom. After talking for a short while, Morin went topside, and Bar fell into an exhausted sleep. Dare watched over his patient, changing the poultice when Bar became restless. He pondered all that had happened since he'd met the prince and wondered where this latest event would lead them.

<hr />

Bardon woke the next morning feeling light-headed. Something strange was on the edge of his memory. E Clue! The mark! He checked his shoulder immediately to see if it was really there or if the experience had been only a dream. The mark was there: tender, burning slightly, and blue.

Dare watched him over his morning cup of tea. "Hard to believe, isn't it?" He grinned.

"Aye." Bar nodded wearily. "I feel as if I've had the aching sickness for a month."

"I imagine it will take time to feel yourself again after that experience. We're just a few hours from Feisan, and the captain wants us both to stay below from now on so that we'll not be seen by anyone. They have a plan to get us off during the night."

Bardon nodded his understanding.

"Now you need something to eat, and then I'll put a fresh poultice on your burn."

Bar scowled. The thought of food made him sick, but his healer was likely to insist, being very stubborn in certain areas. Dare held out the tray. The prince swallowed a wave of nausea and then reached for the tray and ate some of the food. He received a stern look, so he finished it. The poultice stopped the faint burning, and he fell asleep again.

When he woke from his dreams, in which he seemed to be continually struggling to get somewhere, it was dark, and the ship rocked gently. They had docked! He must have slept all day. Bar still felt strangely weary and burdened by his newly revealed destiny. He decided that food would make him feel better and started for the galley.

As he passed the open hatchway, he heard the men on watch discussing the fate of two young wharvers in animated whispers. He stopped in the shadows to listen.

"They was the very ones the captain hired to pull the search off our two hatchlings," one man said, using the crew's nickname for Dare and Bar. "Urskal, being smart as a whip, caught them. When he realized they were not who he was seeking, he had them whipped. But they said they didn't know what he was talking about. Well, actually they *didn't* know anything. They just did what they were asked to do. Then he threw them in prison as a lesson to anyone who thought about helping Bar and Dare. It's a shame, it is. They didn't even know what it was all about."

"That man's cruel," the other said angrily. "The men the king surrounds himself with are terrible to his own people—even to his son!"

Bar heard nothing else. His stunned mind reeled, and he felt physically sick. His hand trembled as he reached out to steady himself against a rough timber. *No, not again!*

Durie and Feller's disappearance, Captain Roethieve's bleeding back, thrashings others had received in his place, dismissals, and demotions passed through his mind in a familiar, dark litany that became a whirlpool. It pulled him under.

When the guards' backs were turned, he quietly slipped past them and ran off the ship to lose himself in the night.

ABDUCTED

BARDON DID NOT SEE THE DARK FIGURES watching the *Karras* from their hiding place behind some bales of leronar fiber. They followed swiftly as he strode, head down, among the thinning crowds that were still on Fryes Lane. Dazed, he looked at the inns, taverns, and shops as if he wondered how they'd gotten there. Light, laughter, and conversation flooded from their doors and shuttered windows, but he did not enter any of them. He seemed to lose his way as he simply wandered, a fierce expression on his face, with the crowds.

One of the men deployed the other four to a dark alley. The man, young and burly, lounged against a wall, and as Bardon passed by, he asked him for directions. When Bar turned to reply, the man grabbed him and dragged him into the alley. Bar realized with shock that he was in terrible danger. He came out of his paralyzing dark thoughts and put up a ferocious fight. The prince used every kuni trick the Basca' had taught him.

Someone smashed him in the face, snapping his head back, and he furiously returned the blow through a haze of pain. All his locked-up anger and frustration came to his aid as he laid about him like an avenging wildcat. His attackers, however, soon had enough of this, and at their leader's signal, one of them hit Bar on the back of the head with a ton-in, a weapon made of hardened leather. He went down like a dropped stone.

Bar woke to flickering torchlight in what looked like a warehouse storage room that was not often used. Bales, barrels, and chests were all thickly covered with dust. "Tol-ruf, he's wakin' up," someone whispered.

His captors gathered around him. He scanned them quickly, trying to figure out who had captured him. *Not Urskal! Surely not even king's men. Then who?* Bardon desperately struggled to identify these scruffy young men but could not place them. The back of his skull felt as if it were splitting in two. As he attempted to sit up and see more clearly, his stomach revolted. He was not far from heaving.

There were five of them, young and warmly dressed in worn, nondescript clothes that could belong to any profession. They stared at him with fierce anger and hatred. "You'll not hurt long, my lord," their apparent leader said. "We've lost two of our best because of you. They were whipped and put in prison because Urskal thought they were helping you, and helping you is not a healthy thing to do these days."

Understanding penetrated Bardon's dazed brain and brought with it both renewed despair and relief—despair because the price for his escape from his father had been the suffering of two innocent young men and relief that the king had not caught him.

"Those who caused the diversion—so Dare and I wouldn't be caught—are your friends?"

"Aye."

"You intend to kill me."

They nodded curtly.

"I know how you feel," he said softly, gingerly feeling the lump on the back of his head. "My life has been mostly a burden to me. I would thank you for relieving me of it." At the moment, he meant every word.

This, to their way of thinking, was a very unnatural view of things, and they looked at him in disbelief.

"I have been the cause of grief to any who have tried to help or befriend me since I was seven. Kill me, and Bardock can no longer use me."

"If you are so ready to die, why have you not done it yourself?" Their leader was angry—suspicious.

"The Maker … does not allow it." Bar bowed his pounding head on his knees, no longer able to hold it up. The mention of the Maker brought some unwelcome guilt. *I have not been marked a day, and here I am—wherever this is—running away.*

"Since when does Bardock's son follow the Maker?" the young man asked with disbelief.

Bar lifted his head and, with a weak smile at their astonishment, said, "Since … always. My nurse and tutor follow—followed—him and taught me."

"Not possible! The king would never allow it. With him it's all about Choack." They were perplexed but interested. He told them what he could without revealing any secrets or betraying people who trusted him. His captors were very young, and their curiosity, for the moment, overrode their anger.

Bar spoke a little of his childhood and why he ran away. He told them about Dare, their capture, and most of the events that had happened since. At his mention of the prelate Draville, Tol-ruf said, "Followers of Choack are everywhere with their evil new order and sick practices. They promise people power, high positions, and favor with the king, so many listen. I think few really believe in the dark god—at least at first." He looked away for a moment.

Bardon was shocked that his father's strange new creed was being actively spread among the people. He'd thought it a private, elite religion for the king and some of the aristocracy. *I must tell Morin and Lavel.*

They gave him water and left him to discuss his strange story. In spite of the headache or perhaps because of it, his terrible despair fled, and common sense returned. *Mighty Maker, help me. I must get back to the ship in one piece and out of this mess.* He tried to plan but found he wanted only to lie down and rest.

"We have heard that E Clue marked you," their leader said when they returned. "Is it true?"

Bardon looked at them in astonishment. "You heard what!" He groaned at the pain his emphatic remark caused. *Are there no secrets in this land?*

"A small ship named *Romer* came back with the tale a few hours before the *Karras* docked," Tol'ruf said. "Everyone thinks they've had too much ale, but they insist they saw E Clue or some Uriisis mark someone who looked like Bardock's son. With all the uproar over your escape, the soldiers have given everyone a good description of you and your friend."

Bardon was stunned. Would the *Romer*'s crew be believed? Would Urskal believe the tale, and if so, what would he do? He tried to force his muddled brain to think; the effort made him sicker.

Tol-ruf was watching him closely. "Bar," he asked in growing amazement, "is it true?"

"Aye," he replied distractedly as he untied the lacing at his neck and pulled the tunic off his right shoulder. He showed them the strange triangular blue scar. Even in the quarter they had heard of the prophecy. They gasped to see it and spoke to each other in awed whispers.

Tol-ruf said, his eyes wide with dismay, "We will take you back to the *Karras* when it is dark."

Relief washed over Bardon. That relief made him angry with himself. Evidently he wanted to live after all. He needed to tell Morin about the *Romer*. Morin! He closed his eyes and groaned again. The thieves looked at each other in concern. "What's wrong now?"

"Captain Morin will have my hide for this. I was not to even show my head above deck."

Tol-ruf grinned in sympathy. "We understand. If our head finds out what we've done … we will be doing a lot of extra hard work."

"You are not the head?"

"Me! No. I'm way too young. The young men who tricked the soldiers are my friends. I wanted revenge, but our head absolutely forbade it. The Basca' are too skilled at tracing blame. He was afraid our whole quarter would suffer for it and told me to leave it alone."

"Which I can see had little visible effect on you," a well-built man said grimly as he entered the room like a king. Armed men filed into the room behind him, tough and capable looking. The leronar cloth bands they wore around their foreheads bore strange symbols burned into them.

Tol and his cohorts stood, dismay on their faces, and bowed their heads respectfully. A cold, uncomfortable silence descended on the room. The young men did not move a muscle. The leader's hard, fierce eyes looked into Bardon's own until he felt the man was searching his soul. He fought to hold his gaze.

"You are Bardock's son." It was more of a statement than a question.

"Aye," Bardon whispered, feeling ashamed of his weak reply, yet he could do no better. The man had a powerful presence. He did not envy Tol-ruf and his friends.

"Tol," the head said, still looking at Bardon.

"Aye," Tol replied, raising his eyes to the head for the first time since the man had entered the room. Tol's face was pale and his look stormy: part guilt and part defiance. The head finally shifted his gaze to Tol, and Bardon felt as if he had been released from bondage. He allowed himself to close his eyes and slump a little. He wanted to lie down, give in to his injuries, and rest, but he must listen.

The head's voice was like a whip. "Is revenge worth what your foolishness will cost us?"

"Sir," Tol said shakily, "we no longer want revenge." The head's eyebrows shot up in question. "Will you listen?" Tol asked.

"Aye," the head said bleakly, and they all sat down.

The young men shared with their leader what they had done and why they had not killed Bardon. The subject of their story heard it all through a haze of pain and exhaustion.

"Bardon, Bardon," the head said quietly.

Shaking his head, Bar forced himself out of his stupor. "Aye, sir," he answered, looking at the man.

"Tol and two others will return you to the ship. I want your word that you will forget all of us."

"You have my word, sir, but if my—the king catches me, he has ways of getting the information he wants."

"We'll take our chances. May we see the mark?"

Bardon again showed his scar and saw wonder fill their eyes. The head touched and rubbed the mark to make sure it was real. "A perfect blue triangle," he said, shaking his head in amazement. "Tol, give him some food and otet and let him rest until it is time. He is ready to pass out." Bardon was grateful. "When you have returned him to his ship, report to me immediately, you and all that were with you."

"Aye, sir," Tol replied with resignation.

Bar and Tol waited in the deep shadow of a tumbled-down, old warehouse for the guard to change at the other end of the lane. "Though I'm going to pay for it, I'm glad we've met," Tol whispered to Bar.

"I am glad also. It was worth this headache—I think. May we meet again." They clasped arms in mutual friendship, feeling fairly pleased with the end of their misadventure.

Some of Tol's friends created a distraction, and while both guards were looking the other way, Bardon slipped from shadow to shadow and across the gangplank onto the *Karras*. The night watchman on the ship, following strict orders, went immediately to the captain and then guided Bardon to his cabin. *I would rather have the aching sickness than face this lecture.* The satisfaction of a few minutes before fled.

Captain Morin had passed a terrible night and day wondering why and where Bardon had gone and what to do about it. He'd decided to wait and see if anyone could pick up some news of him before they started a search that would most certainly attract attention. Dare was both anxious and angry and had no clue what might have happened. Now, the runaway was back, and Morin wanted to wring his neck for frightening them all and for endangering the whole underground.

The door opened, and his crewman held it for the bedraggled young man. Bardon's clothing was covered with mud and dust. His nose was swollen, and his face was scratched and pale with dark circles under his eyes—eyes that were filled with pain. He was in obvious need of rest. His gaze was steady, but Morin saw his knees trembling. Bar walked in, and the door closed behind him.

The captain's stare was so stern and angry that Bardon wanted to sink through the floor. *Worse than I anticipated.* Striding to the door, Morin jerked it open and ordered with suppressed fury, "Wes, get otet and some food. Then tell Dare he's safe and have Kukul come to me."

"Aye, sir." Wes ran to do the captain's bidding; rarely had he seen him in such a taking.

The captain forced himself to close the cabin door quietly. "Tell me quickly where you've been and what happened. Your life may depend on it."

"Sir, may I sit down?" Bardon asked uncertainly. "I … my head is pounding." He had known Morin would be angry, but he was not prepared for how angry. He received a curt nod. As he sat near a small, round table, there was a knock on the door. Wes, having striven mightily, brought in a tray with a steaming brown pot of tea laced with otet and bread with cheese. He laid the tray on the table and left quickly.

"I heard," Bardon began, taking a sip of the scalding tea, which stayed down and comforted him greatly, "some men on deck, who had been ashore for the afternoon, talking about ... about ... what happened to the two young wharvers who drew Urskal off ... that day Dare and I came aboard." His face was bleak.

Ah, the captain thought with frustration, *that's why.*

Bardon closed his eyes. "I was sick ... Guilt and despair filled me, and I ran, but I didn't know where to go. I had no plan. A young man named Tol-ruf and some other young wharvers who wanted revenge recognized me. You see, sir, they were watching the ship for us, for Dare or me. They put two and two together ... the big search for Dare and me and the mission you gave their friends. They knocked me out and took me with them to somewhere in the quarter. They decided not to kill me, though that was their original intention. I met their head, and he sent me back." Bar tried to organize his thoughts.

"Sir, they heard about E Clue from men aboard a ship called the *Romer* who watched us that day. The sailors on the *Romer* didn't know which fishing vessel I was on, but they thought it was me. They were too far away and totally focused on the Uriisis. My captors wanted to see the scar; I think it is why they let me live. They too have heard of the prophecy. There was something else I wanted to tell you, but I can't remember ... Oh! Did you know that the king is spreading his new religion everywhere? Even the wharvers have heard about it. That's all." Bar knew his tale was a jumble, but at least he had been quick.

The captain was astonished and speechless for a moment, and then he ran to the door. "Kukul!" he yelled.

"Aye, sir, I'm coming," the first mate answered, huffing and out of breath. They conferred in the passageway in urgent whispers, and then the captain came back into the cabin.

"I would like to hear the details of your story, but there's no time now.

Your Maker has protected you, it seems, even in your stupidity." Bar winced at the word and the harsh tone.

"Do you realize what you've done?" Morin asked with suppressed passion. "Urskal has spies everywhere! If wharvers have heard the story of E Clue, so has Urskal. You can bet spies among the wharvers have already told him that you were on a fishing vessel. Even if they don't know which ship this young person—Tol, was it?—returned you to, they'll search every vessel in the harbor if they have to."

Morin started pacing. "If they question those aboard the *Romer*, the crew will give Urskal a description of our ship. We've lost precious time while you were gone—time we needed to get you away from here and to get us away also. They will even try to capture your friend Tol'ruf to get information from him about which ship you're on." He paused with a frown. "I don't think even Urskal could get to the head; he's well protected from what I've heard."

At the frozen, sick look on Bar's face, he relented a little. The head is ruputed to be a shrewd old wolf. He'll hide Tol-ruf, never fear."

As Bar saw clearly the picture the captain's words painted, he whispered huskily, "Dear Maker, what have I done? The *Karras*, your crew—"

"You have endangered this ship, the underground, and the quarter!" the captain said ruthlessly. *Bar might be only sixteen, but enough is enough. The lad carries heavy responsibility, and he has to stop running from it.*

"You do not have the privilege of thinking only of yourself. Every time you do something, it affects the lives of others drastically. It was terrible that those two young men suffered for helping you, but they are not the first, and they will not be the last to suffer or die in the battle that is ahead of us. Is it right to endanger many lives in your grief over the suffering of two?"

Morin started pacing again. "You cannot run away from who you are, no matter how much you might like to. We need you. E Clue has marked you, and we have risked our lives to save you. You cannot afford depression or despair if they cause you to act without thinking of all the lives you can hurt. Do you understand?"

Bar could not answer him. Fear for his new friends and shipmates created a huge lump in his throat. With terrible clarity, he saw the ripples his actions caused in the lives of others, precisely.

"Do you understand?" the captain repeated.

"Aye," Bar said, and he did understand, perhaps for the first time, how totally centered in self even his grief had been. Morin was showing him a reflection of himself he did not like.

"Look at me," Morin commanded. Bar raised his eyes. "You can no more change that mark you allowed E Clue to burn into your flesh than a Nom cat can change its spots."

Bar rose, turned, and crossed the small room to stare out a high window at the choppy waves. He was stunned at the number of terrible possibilities. He wanted to plead for understanding, to defend himself, but he kept silent. After a few minutes of reflection, Bar turned to Captain Morin. He said more calmly but with conviction, "I'll not run again, I promise you. I didn't think beyond the overwhelming guilt. I am sorry, sir. I've put your splendid ship … your crew … in danger … have I not?" He wiped fiercely at sudden tears with his muddy sleeve, which made an even worse mess of his face.

Even tears Morin could not allow him; there was no time. "You've been pitchforked into this with no proper training, lad, and you're young yet." He lifted his captain's hat off his head and closed his eyes. In an attempt to relax, he ran his fingers through his short white hair. "You've made a mistake, lad, a bad one, but if you've learned something, it'll be worth it. Who knows? Perhaps someday you'll need friends in the wharvers' quarter. Drink your tea, quickly now. We've got to get you out of here." *Then we've got to get us out of here.*

The captain opened the door and almost knocked Kukul over. "Everything's ready, sir," the first mate said. "I'll get the lad dressed and painted up. And captain, I've heard the sailors on the dock talkin of a snow storm coming out of the North."

"Good. It will help hide them." The captain hurried away. After washing the blood and mud from Bar's face, Kukul painted it black without comment on the prince's stricken look. He helped him dress from head to toe in dark, warm clothing. He kept up a gentle stream of explanation and instruction that he hoped the lad was hearing.

Kukul had listened at the door, not wanting to interrupt, and had heard most of the captain's lecture. He thought the captain had been too hard on Bar, and he tried, in his own rough way, to help ease the lad over the tongue-lashing, which was much worse than the other kind of lashing, in his opinion. *Not that he didn't need to hear it,* he thought. That he would think even one negative thought of his captain was proof of his affection for Bar.

The captain had arranged to have the hatchlings rowed in a small dory to one of the merchant ships farther down the dock. The hatchlings would be moved from there back into the city with a shipment of goods for an important customer who also was a supporter of the underground. Hopefully, the young fugitives could be smuggled out of Feisan quickly and moved to a safe place in the countryside. The underground's spies were out listening; they had one very close to Urskal. The *Karras* was ready to run and then disappear into the lungala if need be.

Kukul insisted that Bar eat some of the food on the tray. Who knew how long it would be before he could eat again? Bar forced it down, knowing the man was right but not wanting it. They hurried to the deck where the captain and Dare stood talking. Dare gripped his shoulder without a word, but a hard light in his eye told Bardon he had more explaining to do. Bar turned to Captain Morin and said as he shook his arm, "Thank you, sir, for … everything."

"Off with you now. Tekoma will take good care of you."

Bar and Dare climbed down a sturdy rope ladder into the small waiting scull. The captain waved them off as the first snowflakes fell. The snow came thicker and faster every minute, making their trip to the merchant ship nearly invisible.

A Humble Disguise

THE SAILOR ROWING THEIR SMALL CRAFT warned Bar and Dare to silence. They slipped quietly past ship after ship. Bars of golden light pouring through the ships' shuttered windows onto the ebony waves. Muffled sounds echoed strangely across the water: voices, laughter, singing, and the waves gently slapping against the ships. The scent of cooking mixed with the salt tang of the sea and the pungent odors of the merchants' wares.

The pain in Bardon's head was dulled a little by the otet, but the medicinal leaves had done nothing to calm the storm in his mind. Morin's words ran through his thoughts over and over again. Finally, the storm within wore itself out. In its wake, he felt cold and empty. He spoke with what little energy he had left to the one he followed. *Maker, my confidence is in you. It had better be*, he thought wryly. *I'm fairly unreliable.*

Bar focused on his surroundings and found Dare looking at him questioningly. He forced a stiff grin and whispered, "I'm all right."

The next few hours on the merchant ship *Vigilant* passed in a weary blur. The ship's healer put something on the egg-size lump on the back of Bardon's head. Whatever it was reduced the swelling and stopped most of the pain. Bar and Dare had been taken aboard secretly, as the captain did not trust all his crew. Captain Whit, his healer, two crewmen, and two women who'd been brought aboard to help were the only ones who knew of Bar and Dare's presence.

After the women worked on the boys' appearance, not even Captain

Morin would have recognized them. Dare's blond curls were now black and short. His fair skin had been darkened to a light brown, and he had a scar across his left cheek that distorted his face. He wore the worn, patched brown wool of the lowest order in Ree's society, the curna, who were little more than slaves.

Ree had no beggars. Anyone with no way to make a living—man, woman, or child—was indentured to someone for two years. This practice was a well-intentioned way to train those with no skills or provide for the orphaned, but it was universally abused. Desire to escape being a curna had caused many a desperate adult or child to seek refuge in the wharvers' quarter. They became part of the guild that supplied laborers of all kinds to the fishing and merchant ships. For this reason, the quarter housed twice the number of people claimed on its rolls and kept strictly to itself.

Bar's hair was cut short and his skin darkened. He also wore the clothing of a curna—a brown wool scarf around his head, a long brown tunic, and breeches. The women created a lump on his right shoulder and back with padding sewn in his tunic. By altering one of his scruffy boots, they also gave him a slight limp. When they finally finished, the boys were allowed to rest until morning. Dare wanted badly to know about Bar's adventure, but he knew that his friend was too exhausted to speak of it now. He would have to wait.

During the night the snow turned to sparce intermitant rain, and deep mud clogged the streets the next morning. The boys slogged along with three other curna behind the merchant's groaning wagons. They were miserably cold and grumbled as other vehicles splashed them with mud spray.

With a loud crack, their wagon lurched into a huge pothole. The curna gathered at the back right wheel to push it out. Standing in deep, dirty water and straining every muscle, Dare whispered sarcastically to Bar, "Traveling with you is really … interesting. This, of course, doesn't compare to being stuffed in a gutted bluefin, but it's right up near the top of the list."

Gasping for air, Bar said severely, "I've been told by a friend that it's very 'unheroic' to complain about personal discomfort." With a final heave, they freed the wheel.

Captain Whit's curna continued to guide the horses of the lead wagon through the confused maze of Feisan's merchant quarter. Covered from head to toe with mud and other disgusting things, they screamed and yelled insults at the other curna, who returned the barrage vigorously. Dare removed a rotten cabbage leaf from his face with disgust.

Their misery was soon over. They arrived at the merchant's warehouse in less than an hour. It was a large, sprawling building made of beautifully cut, dark stone. It was bustling with orderly chaos and noise. The curna were allowed to go around to the back entrance and get warm by the kitchen fire. They placed their wet boots and socks on the hearth to dry, though that would take a long time; they were thoroughly soaked. The servants gave them mugs of hot tea to drink, and they began to feel more human. The wonderful fragrance of cooking food made their mouths water.

The lively activity of the large kitchen staff flowed around them. They dozed contentedly on a bench near the blazing logs. After a short time, Captain Whit came for them and took them to meet their benefactor, Tar Andrew. The boys realized, as they walked in borrowed socks through the halls, that this merchant lived in his warehouse. The whole back of the building seemed to be living quarters. They passed dining rooms, bedrooms, studies, and sitting rooms, all comfortable and neat looking but not lavish. Captain Whit knocked on a polished oak door.

"Come in," a deep voice said. They walked into a large, comfortable room that contained goods of all kinds. Colorful rugs were rolled and stacked in one corner, and bolts of cloth spilled warm hues over a large, battered table. Behind a massive desk piled high with scrolls sat a delicate ancient that might have come out of a child's fireside tale. He had a flowing white beard and snowy hair that fell to his shoulders. The sky blue of his long woolen robes matched his merry eyes. He wore a black band around his forehead with intricate symbols burned into the leather. When he smiled, his fair skin cracked into a thousand wrinkles.

Both boys and the captain bowed respectfully. They waited for his voice before they looked up, as was correct. "So these are the hishua, or should I say hatchlings, that need safe conduct out of Feisan," he said in a deep voice that did not fit his diminutive person.

"Aye, sir, that they do," the captain replied.

Tar Andrew observed them with keen eyes for long minutes, but he gazed at them so kindly that both boys forgot their manners and stared back with curiosity, which was not at all polite in Possany society. "So you find me interesting, do you?" he asked in amusement. Dare and Bar dropped their eyes to the floor immediately, embarrassed at their rudeness.

"They are of great size, Captain Whit," he said, laughter in his voice, as he rose and walked toward the fire. He was taller than he looked but so slender that it seemed a strong breeze might blow him away.

"That they are, sir," the captain answered.

"Well, my children, look up, look up. Let us sit and talk."

As he failed to smother another yawn, Dare thought, *Hopefully he is not as thorough as the council in Glidden Mountain.* They sat around the firepit on soft cushions and rugs, except for Tar Andrew, who said his old body needed support. He sat in a beautifully carved camp chair that was upholstered with rich red fabric and fit his slight form perfectly.

Morin had instructed Dare and Bardon to answer all Tar Andrew's and Captain Whit's questions completely and without fear. They were both trusted members of the underground and would not betray them. Each young man recounted his part in their adventures, but only up to the return of the *Karras* to port. Tar Andrew and Captain Whit listened attentively. They even laughed here and there and in no way were critical, yet Bar found it hard to go on.

He looked at Dare with regret in his eyes and said, "I'm not proud of what happened next, yet it is probably important for you to know—unless you already do?"

"Aye, child. We know all we need to know. It came in the report from Morin—unless perhaps you would like to speak of it?" Tar Andrew replied.

Blue blazes! I'm never going to find out what happened! Dare thought in frustration.

Looking down at his hands, Bar said hesitantly, "I would certainly like to forget it, but"—he looked up with a slight smile—"I will speak of it if you wish."

Tar Andrew nodded and asked, "Child, when you had time to think about what E Clue had done and what it meant, how did you feel?" He watched Bardon intently from under his bushy white eyebrows, as an owl might watch its chick.

Bar sighed, closed his eyes, and ran his fingers through his short hair.

"Trapped, burdened, afraid—afraid I would mess up, fail. I should have felt honored or had a sense of purpose—been excited, something like that. And at first I did feel it was good to know there was something I could do—a plan for my future—and that was exciting. Yet after a time I just wanted to be free—to run." Startled at his own words, he opened his eyes and looked at Tar Andrew in amazement.

The ancient nodded his head gently, pleased. "You are not alone in these feelings. Whenever anyone is given great responsibility or a difficult mission, they can feel overwhelmed, unworthy, and aye, trapped. I do not think it was the unfortunate suffering of the young wharvers alone that made you run into the night."

"I think you have great insight, Tar Andrew." Bar gazed thoughtfully into the fire.

"The Maker's army is made up completely of volunteers, child. You may resign at any time. Only the enemy uses conscription." He paused and then said, "You have had no time for reflection, but we must know, Bardon, if you are committed."

Bar looked into his eyes. "I am," he said firmly.

The captain and Tar Andrew looked at each other and nodded slightly, as if something of importance were settled between them. "Good," the old merchant replied softly. "In time, your burden will grow more familiar and easier to bear. You will lean more on the Maker and less on yourself."

The sharp old eyes turned to Dare. "You have been a faithful friend. Do you go on with him or choose a path of your own? We will help you find a new life and a new identity if you wish. You have only to ask."

Dare considered this option carefully for a minute. Two weeks ago, perhaps he would have taken their offer. No, even then I would have stayed. He said simply, "I have not had much time to think since that day I picked Bar up on the trail." He grinned at the memory. "But whether I have time to think it over or not, the answer will be the same. I'll stay. I've started this, and I want to see it through, not just because of Bardon, but because I believe in what you're doing, even though I don't quite know what it is."

"Good enough—for now." Tar Andrew laughed. "Honest men are hard to find. We will treasure you."

Bar felt deep, profound relief. "Thank the Maker." Not until this moment had he considered facing the future without Dare's friendship.

"Now, hishua—" A gentle knock at the door interrupted Tar Andrew. "Come in," he said.

A charming vision in pale-blue wool entered the room with quiet confidence. "Grandfather, it is time for your medicine," she said, a hint of reproach in her voice.

"So it is," he answered, smiling his welcome as if she were his only joy. "Well, bring it here, and I will introduce you to two new friends." She gave him a steaming mug. Not even the intriguing subject of healing draughts could dispel Dare's absorption in the young woman.

She was as slender as her grandfather and had his fine bones, but her eyes were large and gray. Long golden hair hung to her waist; it was swept back from her delicate face on each side with shell combs. Dare and Bar were both held speechless by her fair beauty.

She greeted Captain Whit warmly and smiled at each hishua when her grandfather introduced them to her. They managed to nod but said nothing. Both became suddenly conscious of their soggy, mud-spattered clothing and changed appearance. Tantisongel, the vision's name, said something about the mid meal and left them.

"Let's talk of the next stage of your trip," the captain suggested. He and Tar Andrew grinned as they paused before they began explaining. It took a long time for the hatchlings to bring their suspended thoughts back to reality and really listen.

Dare and Bar left Tar Andrew's home the next day. Getting past the gates of Feisan would probably be the most dangerous part of their journey. They planned to travel with the merchant's wagons to a monastery in the foothills of the Blackdeer Range. All exits to the royal city were guarded and carefully watched by the king's special spies and the Basca'.

The weather remained overcast, and rain continued to fall. This created even deeper water in the busy streets. A wicked wind blew, whipping cloaks and reddening faces and hands. All arteries in and out of the city were clogged with short-tempered, cold tradesmen, soldiers, craftsmen, farmers, and travelers. They all wanted nothing more than to get in out of the miserable weather.

Dare and Bar were halfway to the gate, wet to the waist from wrestling the wagons through heavy traffic, when they saw troopers approaching. The soldiers yelled, forced, and intimidated their way through the middle of the street, pushing traffic to the sides and even up on the wooden walkways. Anyone who got in their way was in danger from whips and hooves.

The rowdiness of the crowds quieted, and the arrogant cry "Make way for the king's business!" rang out over and over again. Waiting for the soldiers to pass, Bar and Dare shivered in the cold wind that howled through the streets.

Bar's face turned pale beneath the dye. "I know the first officer!" he whispered to Dare as he turned his back to the approaching soldiers. He pretended to calm the black horse he was leading. *How many hundreds of soldiers does my father have? And this one happens to be on the street now!*

Dare glanced at the man but did not recognize him. He too turned his back to the troop and tended the other lead horse. They urged the horses as far over as possible and waited in the comparative hush for the soldiers to pass. Dare glanced at the driver of their wagon. Anger was apparent in his expression but no fear. The man did not know that the two curna who were helping him were the most wanted men in the royal city. Captain Whit, the only one who knew their identities, rode beside the lead wagon, which was many vehicles ahead of them.

They heard screams, curses, and hooves clattering on the slate paving stones. These stones buckled terribly when it rained or snowed, leaving great holes in the road. They also sank in the water and mud. Horses neighed in fear or impatience and moved restlessly in their harnesses. Men and women seethed inside but kept their lips tightly shut.

As the elite troop passed their wagon, one of the horses slipped on the uneven stones, and his rider tumbled into a huge, muddy puddle. The sergeant screamed, "You, curna, help that soldier get to his feet!" Bar's heart pounded when he realized that the sergeant was pointing his whip at him. Hiding his face as best he could, he quickly limped over to help the furious, drenched trooper.

Bar tried to remember Dare's lessons in humility and dullness. The former drudge kept warning him that he would destroy the humble curna disguise with his unconscious pride and regal bearing.

Dare felt suspended in time as he watched. *Good, he's remembering to limp and bow. The sergeant has turned his attention to that wagon full of grain that's in the way. Bar's gotten the man on his feet … No!* Dare's eyes widened in horror. As Bar bowed and turned to leave, the soldier he had just helped pushed him flat on his face into the cold, almost-liquid mud. Perhaps it made the soldier feel better to make someone else look as foolish as he felt.

He and his friends roared with laughter as the bedraggled, ugly curna raised his face from the muck and wiped it out of his eyes. When the disguised prince rose, his movements were fluid, as years of Kuni training instinctively took over. His arms and legs automatically formed a fighting stance. Dare silently screamed, *No!*

Before Bar could whirl to face his adversary, fire exploded along his back. The shock of stinging pain broke his automatic response and made him pause.

The soldier had struck Bar with his whip to add to the insult. In doing so, he had probably saved both his life and Bar's. In that moment, Bar remembered who he was and where he was. He regained control and forced his limbs to relax. Trembling with humiliation and anger, he stumbled blindly back toward the wagon.

One of the laughing soldiers paused to watch Bar intently. He had noticed the Kuni stance and tensed muscles. Not believing his eyes, he shrugged and rode on with the troop. After all, the boy was just a curna. The soldiers continued to vent their frustrations on the cold throng.

Dare ordered his stiff muscles to relax and rested his pounding head on the patient gray horse. "Sincere thanks, Maker," he said very softly. Bar went from wanting to slug the man to feeling sick with cold and pain.

"Are you all right, lad?" the wagon driver called out. Bar nodded.

Slowly the snarled crowds of animals, wagons, and people untangled and lumbered on their way. Folk began to talk again, and the noise in the streets returned to its usual ear-deafening pitch, but this time, there was an undertone of anger.

Bar looked at Dare and almost smiled at the fading terror on his face. His friend knew clearly what he had almost done. Captain Whit came riding back to check on the wagons and casually ordered Dare to bandage Bar. All three knew that nothing must draw attention to him at the gate. Dare took the time to wrap his wool head scarf around the slash on Bar's back; that was all he could do for now. It made an itchy bandage. There was nothing he could do about the cut in the tunic. Bar was able to grin by this time and said softly, "Scared you, didn't I?"

Dare grabbed the front of Bar's tunic in one huge fist, jerking him almost off his feet, and hissed fiercely, "It's not funny, you idiot." His face was white, and his blue eyes were blazing. He let go suddenly, fearful of attracting attention.

As Bar walked to his horse, he muttered, "No sense of humor." Muddy and soaked, Bar shook his head sadly.

At the gate, hard-eyed soldiers swarmed through every wagon. They opened barrels, tested for false bottoms, and investigated every corner. Before anyone could pass through the checkpoint, he or she was made to run the gauntlet of two Basca'. Bar hoped he did not know them and shuffled forward in the line of waiting curna, tradesmen, and merchants.

His lips were blue with cold from wet clothing and hair. He was plastered with mud stains and other disgusting stuff. The gusting wind was sheer misery to him, and he shivered uncontrollably. "It is doubtful my own mother would know me," he mumbled reassuringly to Dare through chattering teeth. His eyes lit with sudden laughter. "However, come to think of it, that's not saying much." Dare choked down a laugh, then glared. The expressionless Basca' looked Bar over hastily and motioned him on, as they did Dare, who was behind him.

When the caravan cleared the gate and wound its way around a hill, Captain Whit called a halt for a quick meal. He hated to stop so close to the city, but he feared Bar and Dare would get really sick if they did not get some dry clothes. One of the wagons contained supplies, and he took Dare and Bar there. The young fugitives stripped out of their soggy clothing and wrapped a blanket around their cold bodies while the captain searched for dry clothes. Dare found cleansing herbs, mixed them in water, and washed the horizontal cut on Bardon's back. It was not very deep thanks to the padding that had created his hunched back. Bardon squirmed at the sting. "Easy, you clumsy novice."

Dare ignored him as he poured more of the liquid on the wound and said angrily, over Bardon's yelp, "That's a wicked weapon, Captain, that could do this with one blow."

"Aye." The captain nodded absently as he rifled through piles of clothing. "The king's special bodyguards carry those. They can wrap their whips around a man and jerk him out of the saddle or pull a weapon from his grasp in a second. Comes in very handy sometimes, I'm sure. They are a cocky group and much hated by the people for their needless cruelty. The king often sends them on special errands, with important messages—that kind of thing."

"I knew the first officer," Bardon said quietly as Dare wrapped a swath of fabric around his body and tied it.

The captain stared at him in dismay. "Thank the Maker he did not recognize you!"

In agreement, the boys touched their hearts with their right hands. It was a common gesture among the citizens of Ree that meant "thank the Creator." Even those who did not believe in him anymore universally used the gesture.

Rest at Saint Fauver's

DARE AND BAR RODE HIGH ON THE PLANK SEAT of the lead wagon. As they bounced roughly up and down, the disguised fugitives stared in wonder at the massive jagged peaks that filled the eastern sky. The mountain range looked as if the Creator had hacked it out of black granite with a giant ax. Snow-covered peaks topped a deep and ancient forest that had suffered little exploration by man. Strange mists hung here and there from geysers and hot springs guessed at but not seen.

Even though it was summer, the air was cold, and the hishua stamped their feet to warm themselves. So far, it had been a quiet, uneventful trip. It took them many days to reach the trail to their destination.

Saint Fauver's Monastery lay in the foothills, just at the edge of deep forest. They left the main road on the rolling plains and traveled on a rocky, winding trail for half a day to reach the rambling stone structure. People said that the ancient building had been made by the Mooor ha Chi, a people who lived only in legend. Dare and Bardon glowed with health. Rest, outdoor exercise, good food, and relative freedom from fear had worked a wonderful change in their appearance. They talked as the wagon bumped along. Dare finally heard what had happened the night his friend ran from the ship. Bar hoped that now he was free of that night and would never have to discuss it again.

"Why is this monastery still allowed when all others have been destroyed?" Dare asked.

"This one is unique," Bar said. "It is the only place travelers on the road to Gander can find shelter. There is not another inn or town along the way, and the trip can easily take a caravan three weeks. More importantly, they make leather goods here that are like no other in the land. The brothers have developed a special method of tanning and then working leather. Ree's prosperous citizens would be sorry to do without the good brothers' beautiful work, so the king allows them to exist."

He shifted his position to keep the sun out of his eyes and continued, "However, they are not allowed to add to their numbers. When someone dies, they may replace him—that is all. They are so isolated here that they cannot spread their faith or encourage other believers, so they are left alone. The only people the good brothers see are travelers. Tar Andrew sells their goods. This caravan will pick up their leather and take it to Gander. On the way back they will pick up more and take it back to Feisan."

As they approached the monastery in the golden light of the late afternoon, men in long gray robes came out to greet them. In less time than seemed possible, the men moved wagons and horses across the courtyard and into a large barn. Then they hurried their guests inside to sit beside a warm fire.

The great room had a low and heavily beamed ceiling, whitewashed walls, and a floor paved with slabs of black stone that had been sanded smooth. A trestle table beside the fire offered heavy mugs and a steaming kettle of tea. Pitchers of heavy cream, golden honey, white cheese, and crunchy flatbread, hot from the oven, were set before them. The travelers gratefully warmed themselves with fire and food.

Captain Whit was talking to Brother Devon, a brother who was very unmonkish in appearance. He was not just tall but also as thick of body and limb as an oak tree, and he possessed the confident attitude of one used to command. His skin was fair, but his hair, eyes, and beard were dark. The boys stared at him in amazement.

"He is the image of the Kuni warrior god—dressed all wrong of course," Bardon whispered through a large bite of white cheese.

"We shall have to give him a hint that he's in the wrong profession," Dare said as he munched his third piece of flatbread.

"I'll bet we're not the first to mention it!" They continued to stuff themselves as long as there was food to eat.

Captain Whit started giving orders, and everyone hurried to unload the wagons, which carried supplies for the monastery. Then the monks loaded their leather goods on the empty wagons. The hishua worked till suppertime. In spite of their snack, they were still able to eat two large bowls of thick stew and many slices of brown bread at the evening meal. The food was very, very good.

Brother Devon invited the men to evening devotions in the chapel, if they wished to come. With gentle courtesy, he made it clear that after devotions everyone was expected to be in bed. "I'll bet no one argues with him," Dare whispered. "Who would dare? Let's go and hear what Big Brother has to say."

Very few of the men accepted Brother Devon's invitation to attend devotions. Dare and Bar noted carefully those who did; it might come in handy later. Dare tripped on a woven mat in the hallway and fell to one knee. Bar, who was not looking, stumbled over him. They both fell to the floor laughing, then tried hard to stifle their mirth. Brother Devon just turned, winked at them, and continued walking. He was very young to be an abbot.

Oil lamps, hanging from the ceiling by chains, burned in the spacious chapel. Their golden light flickered on the bare white walls, polished floors, and leather-covered benches and chairs. Two fireplaces, one on either side of the room, burned quietly. Brother Devon stepped behind a simple table that held only a few scrolls. A triangle, the symbol that stood for Creator, Maker, and Spirit, was carved on the beautiful oak wall behind the table. A holy presence in the room quieted Dare and Bardon's merry mood into something deeper. They felt awed and strangely comforted.

Old hymns of praise were sung to the accompaniment of a harp and two flutes. When they knew the words, the boys joined in heartily. Then Brother Devon read from one of the scrolls. Both hishua listened intently. Their faith in the Maker was built on memories of teaching from loved ones, but those teachings had been shaped for young minds. They were older and ready for more—much more. Life had grown difficult.

Brother Devon's theme was love for enemies and forgiveness. Bar and Dare shared a perplexed look. To their way of thinking, these ideas did not go well together. To forgive a cruel and hateful person who did not even ask for forgiveness, seemed strange—even impossible. Brother Devon explained that this teaching came from a letter that had been written long ago and copied down through the years over and over again. "We treasure the few writings we still have that share the Maker's teachings, for the sacred scrolls were burned in the persecutions. We know some were hidden, and we hope they will be found someday. This teaching says we are to love our enemies and even speak for them to the Maker!" There were some audible groans, and he smiled. "I know! It's hard to do … however, the next one may be harder. We are to forgive others when they hurt or hate us, and then the Maker will forgive us. If we truly follow the Maker, we will forgive others. But if we don't forgive and instead carry anger and resentment in our hearts, he won't forgive us. Simply confess your faith breaking and ask the Maker to forgive you. The teachings tell us he will forgive you and make you clean.

Hatred in the heart poisons the whole person. It is not the person we hate who suffers the most but we ourselves. We suffer because we have allowed darkness within us. Who would want darkness inside his mind and heart? It drains us of all peace and joy. The holy writings tell us that there is no darkness in the Maker at all—only light." Brother Devon spoke to the Maker earnestly for a few minutes. He asked him for protection and peace for all their guests and for the brothers too. Then everyone filed out quietly and went to their beds.

At least two of those who heard Big Brother's talk were having trouble sleeping. "How is it that I have never heard this teaching before?" Dare whispered in the darkness of the sleeping room.

Bar, who was on the hard cot next to him, said, "I do not remember hearing it either. Perhaps as children we were not given this teaching. However it happened, I wish I had not heard it now! Dare, I … I can't do it … No, the truth is I don't want to do it! Yet I don't doubt Big Brother has given us a true teaching."

"It would mean forgiving Ursul," Dare said indignantly.

"And the king," Bar added bitterly. Some of the others trying to sleep told them, rather forcefully, to be quiet, and their conversation came to an end.

The caravan left the next morning minus two curna. The hishua were now in the care of large Brother Devon, who, not surprisingly, was also part of the underground. In their new disguise, they were novitiates, student monks, who could try the monastery life before they committed themselves to it or took their final vows. Only the lighter gray color of their robes distinguished them from the other monks. It was a singularly inappropriate color for active young men. In all ways, they participated in the life of the quiet community. Prayer, work, study, eating, sleeping, all in an orderly flow, filled their days.

Brother Mavas, whom they immediately dubbed "Brother Scarecrow," taught their old writ class. He was a tall, stick-thin man who gestured with his arms in wild, jerky movements when he became excited. His mostly bald head had a ruff of white hair that stuck out stiffly above large ears. Hidden behind mild blue eyes was a lively sense of humor. He seemed to accept his awkward appearance with the same loving warmth and kindness that he accepted others.

Dare and Bar peppered him with questions that he answered thoroughly and in the order they were asked. This precise, logical approach drove the impatient hishua to the point of screaming, but they were at first too polite and then too fond of Brother Scarecrow to say anything. Slowly, they gained a deeper knowledge of the Maker's teachings.

"Novitiates," Brother Mavas said with exasperation one dreary afternoon, "stop asking so many questions and let me teach." The oil lamp shed golden light on his shiny, bald head and the hishua's eager faces. "I do not know who will be allowed into the blessed land; the Creator knows. Now—"

Suddenly Lavel, larger than life and full of vitality, strode into the room with Big Brother. His eyes sparkled, his cheeks were red from riding in the cold, and he smelled of horses and fragrant pine.

"It is time to get you two out of here," he said softly, looking at the novitiates with an understanding twinkle in his eye. He had a good idea of how much this quiet life would appeal to them.

"Right!" they said with delight, both glad to see him and excited to be on their way. They jumped up, spilling scrolls onto the floor, and ran across the room to grip his arm. They started asking questions immediately.

Brother Scarecrow interrupted their enthusiasm with a sigh and said sadly, "One would think they did not like the monastic life."

Big Brother replied heartily, "Nonsense! They would like to stay much longer, I'm sure. We have just started their education."

Lavel laughed at the hishua's obvious dismay. They were embarrassed by their eagerness to leave, which seemed impolite and ungrateful. However, Brother Devon and Brother Scarecrow laughed too. The hishua were relieved and grinned cautiously. The brothers had been wonderful, but they were ready to move on.

"Will you use the, er, special route?" Devon asked.

"Aye," Lavel said. "I want to leave when the moon rises, tonight. I don't want Dare and Bar to be here when the caravan returns from Gander. Those helping me to hide them are anxious to get to a safer place."

"I would like to anoint and bless them both before you leave—tonight after evening devotions, perhaps?"

Lavel agreed. "A good idea. We will come to your room afterward."

Dare and Bar fidgeted all through dinner, excited and anxious to be on their way. During evening devotions, Bar felt an uncomfortable weight on his heart that would not go away. He could not concentrate on what Big Brother was saying, and finally, he stopped trying and closed his eyes. While searching for the cause of his trouble, he remembered vividly the first talk he'd heard Big Brother give, the talk on forgiveness, and his uncomfortable feelings about it. The abbot's words had come back to him many times after that, yet each time he'd rejected them.

Mighty Maker, I have ignored this teaching as too hard, yet I cannot get it out of my mind. Help me!

Bar slowly unpacked his heart. He gave up his hatred for his father and others who had wronged him; then he forgave them, each one, and let go of his desire for revenge. He stumbled forward, retraced his steps often, and struggled for words, but he kept going. Then he went the difficult extra mile and prayed for them. In this, he followed the example of Brother Scarecrow. One could not spend time with the monk and remain unchanged by the experience. Bar found that once he began, it was not as hard as he'd thought it would be, but the beginning was truly difficult.

Feeling tired but relieved, he again took notice of what was happening around him. The brothers were singing the last hymn, and the chapel was filled with a sweet peace. When all left, Bar and Dare went to Brother Devon's room. Bar felt a steady assurance that he had done what was right, yet something still weighed on him.

Lavel and Scarecrow joined them after a few minutes. Dare realized that Lavel had not attended the evening meal or devotions. His presence in the monastery was probably unknown to the other brothers. The less they knew the better. As he watched Lavel and Brother Devon talking quietly, he realized what he should have seen earlier. They were either brothers or closely related. Lavel's skin was darker, probably from being outside most of the time, and Devon was certainly larger, but there was a strong family resemblance. Big Brother noticed Dare's close scrutiny; he smiled and nodded acknowledgment of Dare's discovery.

Then Devon looked at Bar thoughtfully. Walking slowly across the room to him, he said gently, "Come," and led him back to the chapel. The three left in Devon's study looked at each other and shrugged. They sat down to wait with what patience they could muster.

Bar sat in a chair opposite Brother Devon in the deserted room. "Now, tell me about it," the large monk said. He had noticed Bar's distraction, then thoughtful attitude during devotions. Afterward, he'd observed his apparent perplexity.

Bar looked at him in surprise. "How … do you know something is wrong?" he asked.

"We have little time now, but I know a troubled sheep when I see one," he said with a kind grin. "If you'll let me, I'll try to help you out of your difficulty."

Bardon unburdened himself gladly. He told Devon of his prayer in the chapel and said with confusion, "Why do I still feel … unfinished?"

Devon squeezed his shoulder reassuringly. "What a victory over darkness! What you have done is right. I suspect, from your own words, that you have left something out." He paused to consider. "Bardon, you realize that hatred and refusing to forgive are faith breaking?"

"Aye," the young man answered.

"Did you confess them as such and ask the Maker's forgiveness and cleansing?"

"No, but I didn't know they were wrong! Not till you talked about those passages in the scroll at devotions that night, and later Scare—Brother Mavas talked about them too," Bar said with confusion and a touch of stubbornness.

"Ask him to forgive you—to cleanse your soul of this stain, for it is stained, whether you knew it would be or not—and see what happens. I'll be in my room; come in when you're ready," he said quietly and left.

Bar did not have to think long. He wanted peace and a return to comfort with the Maker. He bowed his head. *Well, Maker, I have forgiven. Now I seek your forgiveness—for hatred.* His memory displayed clear pictures, and he continued, *For plotting revenge, for meanness and spite—for not forgiving and for allowing bitterness and grudges to take root in my heart.* A part of his mind marveled at the words he was speaking. *Make me clean again.*

Emotion, a thing Bar was not comfortable with, flooded him. He wept quiet tears of relief and regret for time wasted in seething hatred and thoughts of revenge. Then inexplicably, the tears turned to joy because he understood he was free—free from a dark bondage and cleansed from a creeping blight. "My thanks, Maker," he whispered gratefully and touched his heart.

After a few minutes, he returned to Brother Devon's room. The others were talking quietly. Devon took one look at Bardon's face and knew all was well.

"Come," he said, joy in his dark eyes. He placed one large hand on each of the hishua's bowed heads and said, "Limitless Maker, be with and go before Dare and Bar as they follow your path. Fill them with peace. Give them wisdom and discernment." He poured a small amount of oil on each of their heads and continued, "I commit you, Bar, and you, Dare, to his service and place you in his care in the name of the three that are one: Creator, Maker, and Spirit. May you serve with courage, love, and truth."

A quiet accord filled the room. Lavel reluctantly broke the silence. "Bless me too, Devon, and then we must go." Big Brother placed his hand on Lavel's bowed head and spoke to the Maker concerning him also. Bar and Dare thanked Brothers Scarecrow and Devon for all their kindness and help.

As the hishua changed into different clothes, Dare filled Bar in on the plan. With the new clothing, they acquired new identities. This time, they were dressed as Bani hunters—perhaps their most comfortable disguise yet. Impatiently, they waited in a small storage room at the back of the main building for the night to grow darker.

The Second Marking

JN THE MIDST OF THE RUGGED FOOTHILLS, AN immense, winding canyon blocked the fugitives' path. The newly risen moon poured light over vertical cliff walls that dropped hundreds of feet. At the bottom lay a tiny, winding ribbon, the Adon River. Over their heads, the velvet blackness glittered with thousands of stars. It was a glorious night, cold and clear.

Bar had not spoken of his queal problem when Dare told him the strategy for getting through the massive and far-reaching Blackdeer Range. He should have, though, because what now lay ahead of him was worse, much worse, than anything he'd imagined.

Etched in black and glowing pale silver in the moon's light, an intricate bridge spanned the fantastic gorge. Bridge! It was a delicate spiderweb of a walkway woven from elong vine. Swaying gently in the breeze, it was no more than two feet wide with a rail of vine on each side. The vine railings were connected by elong every few feet to the walkway, but this gave no sense of enclosure. He'd never thought the bridge would be made of vine or would be so long and insubstantial. His whole body was responding negatively to the *thought* of such a crossing; he knew the reality would incapacitate him.

Talking softly, Lavel, Dare, and their three guides walked to the bridge. Occasionally, the hunting cry of an animal or night bird could be heard, but for the most part, the night was solemnly quiet.

Bar's queal was shortening his breath and causing him to break out in a cold sweat, and this was only from the anticipation. The reaction would get worse, and he knew of no way to stop it.

In a mountainous land, queal was a serious disadvantage. It affected many people, from all races and both sexes, with varying degrees of inconvenience. Bar could handle heights well if he was on a trail of solid rock or a sturdy bridge made of wood. To be suspended over space by a rope or even to sit on a high tree limb, though, caused a distressing reaction.

As a child, he'd scrambled up a bilbo tree with other boys in training. His reactions had been normal until he'd sat on a high branch swaying in the wind. Then his excitement had turned to fear as the strong reaction of queal slammed through him. He'd lost his grip in the shock and fallen. Faithful Tnavres, one of his tutors, had caught him easily and tried to console him. "Queal can be much worse than this. There are those who cannot ride high, narrow trails or climb at all. It appears you must avoid being suspended over heights. That's not as bad as it might be," he'd told the young prince. Bar was able to control and hide his symptoms under some conditions. *But this—never! I must tell Lavel.*

He walked down from the granite overlook toward the outcrop of rock where the others were waiting for him. One of the guides was leaning against the huge pole that anchored the vines to the right side of the bridge. Bar's stomach turned over at the sight. How could anyone stand that close to the drop-off? He clenched his fists and appealed to the Maker for control as guilt overwhelmed him. What a mess this was going to make of Lavel's careful planning! Dare watched Bar as he approached; he knew something was wrong.

"Lavel, I did not think the bridge would be like this," Bar said. "I'll never make it across with my queal."

Lavel looked at the pale hishua, who was trembling slightly. Bar's body was rigid with the effort it was taking to control his reactions. "How bad is it?"

"Over empty space with no solid footing? Very bad," Bar said, fighting a powerful desire to run back into the woods.

Lavel squeezed Bar's shoulder in sympathy, then slammed his fist into his other hand and turned to talk to the guides. They were a trio of medium height: dark, agile, and slight. Dressed in beautiful black leathers that were lined with fur, the Bani warriors carried quivers, bows, and sheathed hunting knives. Their dark hair hung free to their shoulders and was held in place by a band around the forehead. Speaking little and using hand signals among themselves, the men had led them through the forest with stealth and skill.

Abruptly, Amray, the eldest Bani, raised a hand and pointed west urgently, shock and dismay on his face. They all turned and gasped. "What …?" Lavel said softly. The sky was filled with white smoke where the monastery lay. "Devon!" he cried in anguish and started back up the trail.

Suddenly, screeching yelps and tortured howling filled the quiet night and prickled the hearers with horror. Lavel stopped in his tracks, hesitated, and turned back. This was no time to desert the prince and his friend. He must leave Devon and the monks in the Maker's hands.

"Is that the foul animal you spoke of? The tipeeke?" he asked. The guides nodded affirmation, their faces grim. "What do you advise?" he whispered urgently.

"You, him," Amray said, pointing to Dare, "go now—quickly. We will bring the one with queal. My son suffers from this also. If we cannot bring him, we will hide him. Do not fear. Now, go!"

Lavel agreed. "Dare, follow me and do as I do, but wait till I am past the halfway point to start. The bridge is weighted with huge rocks, but the middle is the most dangerous point. Do not look down. Look at the other side and walk quickly and lightly straight across." He gripped Dare's shoulder. "Do you understand? Can you do it?"

"Aye, sir," Dare said, with much more assurance than he felt. His mind reeled at the thought of stepping out on that thing, but they had enough problems; he would have to make it. "What are tipeeke, anyway?"

"You don't want to know," Lavel said with a stiff grimace that included Bar. He trotted lightly out into nothingness on the delicate structure that swayed gently over the deeply shadowed gorge.

The unearthly discordance of the tipeeke, whatever they were, was getting closer and louder. The guides did not watch Lavel or Dare. Amray turned to Bar, his dark eyes fierce, and said urgently, "You will obey?"

Through the whirlwind of his abused senses, he answered, "Aye!" He felt like a millstone about their necks.

"Sit," Amray said. Bar sat and gagged. His stomach threatened to throw up its contents. They blindfolded him and gave him something to drink that was bitter, but he swallowed it without question and held it down.

"You will remain still no matter what happens. Do you understand? No matter what happens. We will carry you. If you move at all, you will unbalance us, and we will all go into the gorge. Clear?"

"Aye," Bar said, but his mind was full of questions that he attempted to push down. He knew there was no time; he would have to trust.

Amray heard his hesitation and was not satisfied. "Clear?" he asked again.

"Aye, sir, aye," Bar replied reassuringly. His senses were narrowing and turning inward. *What have they given me?* His vision, his hearing, and even his sense of touch all dimmed, and everything in the outside world became very far away. He became conscious of the beating of his heart, his breathing.

They rolled him in a blanket and lashed him to a pole that one of the guides had cut. He hung from wide strips of blanket as if he were in a sling. In spite of the drug, the indignity made him flush with embarrassment. *Thank the Maker I may be long but not very heavy.* Bar probably didn't weigh 140 pounds, but to the slight Bani he was a heavy burden.

The Bani knew that the drug, di'ak, would have him well under its control in minutes. Amray and Balful trotted lightly out on the bridge, with the pole on their shoulders, and Bar swung between them. Akeel protected their backs and carried their gear as well as his own.

In spite of the drug, the blindfold, and his promise, Bar panicked when he felt the swaying of the elong bridge. Amray's voice, stern now, cut through the threatening disorientation. "Be still, very still. Remember all our lives depend on it." Amray talked continuously, and by concentrating on the Bani's voice, Bar kept himself under control.

A vicious growling and uproar of yelping seemed very close. Bar heard a scream; it had to be Akeel! Amray's voice in his ear ordered stillness, and with an effort beyond anything he considered himself capable of, he did remain utterly still. It was a more difficult task than any physical feat he had ever attempted.

The growling grew louder and more frantic. Amray continued to order Bar to stillness, but the hishua lost his focus and started to struggle. His carriers stopped. The bridge was swaying dangerously. Amray's stern command to "Be still" brought Bar back to control. *I cannot help. I can only hurt. Be still—be still*, he told himself over and over. They started forward again. As the swaying grew much worse, Bar heard almost continual baying and screeching from the tipeeke. His heart pounded like a wild drum. Finally, he sensed that they were on firm ground. Someone laid him down, still wrapped in the blanket, and removed the blindfold. Bright white moonlight blinded him for a moment. He managed to get free and watch what was happening.

From Lavel and Dare's point of view, the scene on the swaying bridge was unnerving. Unlike Bar, who could only hear what was happening, Lavel and Dare were forced to watch. Having crossed the terrible bridge and arrived on the other side of the gorge, they looked on helplessly. Snarling tipeeke swarmed onto the outcrop of rock on the west side. Teeth flashing and saliva dripping, the monstrous creatures made a horrendous uproar.

The tipeeke were an unnatural animal with back legs shorter than the bowed front ones, strong barrel chests, pointed faces, and mouths full of gleaming teeth. Their yellow eyes and stiff gray fur shone in the moonlight.

The leader of the pack stepped cautiously out onto the swaying bridge. Crawling forward with greater confidence with each step, he howled triumphantly. Akeel drew his long hunting knife. Looking over his shoulder continually, he tried to keep his eye on the approaching animal.

Seeing the danger, Lavel quickly strung his bow and shot arrow after arrow at the creeping animal. The creature's concentration did not falter, and he moved steadily closer to the Bani, snarling in anticipation. One of Lavel's arrows struck the leader in the chest, and he slumped to the mat.

However, the cunning animal behind him simply jumped over the dead leader. His leap caused the bridge to sway dangerously, and then the foolhardy tipeeke leaped, with insane abandon, straight for Akeel's throat! The creature's wild shriek caused even his brothers to cringe. Akeel's knife gleamed in the moonlight as he slashed at the animal. The injured tipeeke fell to the mat and then tumbled over the edge into the gorge. The daring Bani had injured the vicious animal, but not before it had clawed his right arm. Though the walkway was swaying wildly, he kept moving, staggering more than walking along the bridge.

The next tipeeke crawled quickly over the leader's body. Akeel looked back desperately, his right arm hanging limply at his side. He took his weapon in the other hand, threatened the animal with it, and kept backing.

Lavel and Dare continued shooting desperately at the animals who were strung out, single file, on the narrow bridge, but they were difficult targets because of the swaying and the angle. Also, Lavel and Dare did not want to accidentally injure Bar or the Bani. They prayed that the Bani carrying Bar and the injured Akeel would be able to keep their balance on the increasingly unsteady bridge. As Akeel backed steadily, Dare's arrow took the lead animal in the throat with such force that the missile went all the way through its neck. Akeel was able to turn and catch up with the others. Dare couldn't believe he'd actually hit his target. *Sher and Josen would be proud. I wonder if I will ever see them again.*

Lavel threw down his bow and stretched out his hand to help Amray off the violently swaying bridge. He took Bar, still tangled in blankets and pole, and laid him down in a safe place. He also removed Bar's blindfold before he left him. Amray and his companions immediately turned with drawn knives and hacked at the vines that supported the bridge. Lavel and Dare kept shooting at the advancing tipeeke, who were easier shots now that their friends were not in the way. Finally the thick vines gave way. The elong bridge sprang free and whipped down into the canyon. Howling tipeeke plunged to their death hundreds of feet below.

The animals still on the other side shrieked their fury. Their prey had escaped across the gorge! They ran howling up to the edge and back to the path, frothing in rage, sometimes leaping into the air savagely. The small company watched their frenzy in mesmerized horror.

The immediate danger was over. Each slumped down where he was to rest a few minutes. Dare slipped off his backpack with trembling hands and went to Akeel, whose arm was stained black in the moonlight. "I have some skill, if you will let me help you."

The young Bani nodded, eyes closed against the pain. "Aye, *alati*," he said, thanking Dare.

"We must leave here quickly and get into the woods where we will be hidden from view," Amray said firmly. The Bani chief seemed calm and relaxed. *Does the man have no nerves?* Dare wondered. "Take time for nothing but bandaging."

"Aye," Dare said, though it went against the grain to bandage a dirty wound. He understood. In the bright moonlight, they were visible to anyone who might be searching for them. The others wearily gathered their gear and took time for a drink from their waterskins.

Amray went to Bar, who managed to remain sitting but who was pale and still experiencing di'ak-induced distance from them. Bending to look into Bar's dazed eyes, he said softly, "You did well, my friend, very well under difficult circumstances. It was close there for a minute. Aye?"

Bar nodded, swallowing hard at a surge of distant emotion. He reached for Amray's arm, gripping it hard to assure himself he was really touching him. Through stiff lips, he said, "Thank you."

Amray nodded courteously. "Now you must drink much water to flush the di'ak out of your system. We will carry you to the woods. Then you must try to walk." Bar nodded.

They hurried up a rough, rocky slope to an overhang, and from there they fled into the forest. Lavel carried Bar easily over his shoulder, as if he were no heavier than a sack of grain. Looking back at the other side of the gorge, he saw a few die-hard tipeeke milling around watching them and howling.

Unexpectedly, shadowy figures, armed with bows and knives, joined the tipeeke, who did not seem to mind their presence at all. Stunned, Lavel called Amray softly.

From the hidden safety of the trees, they gazed at the newcomers in consternation. They could only guess what might be happening. All the answers were on the other side of the gorge—they hoped. Amray looked around him uneasily. "We must find cover for the rest of the night. Akeel and Bar need rest. We can scout the woods and see if the enemy is also on this side."

"Agreed," Lavel said quietly. "Do you have a place in mind?"

Amray looked questioningly at Balful. "Aye, Lord, I can find it," Balful replied confidently, in answer to the unspoken question.

"Quickly, then—we go." Amray set off at a fast trot.

They followed him as quietly as they could, but he motioned "silence" over and over again. His frustration at their crashing and thrashing noises was apparent. Dare supported the weakening Akeel. There was no question of Bar walking now; Lavel carried him. The large man was panting when Balful finally signaled a halt.

They stood catching their breath in the darkness under huge pines, darkness that was definitely growing lighter. Balful moved tree branches and then slid a small rock, which looked like part of a huge boulder, aside. He motioned them into a hollowed-out cave in the earth under the boulder. They filed in quickly and were glad for the rest, even if they were in complete darkness.

"Be patient," Balful said. "This hole is kept stocked. Soon I will find the torches." He struck two firestones together, and an oil-soaked rag on the end of a torch glowed softly, filling the earthen cave with light. The air was good, so there must be cracks somewhere for ventilation. Dare began to wash Akeel's wound. Amray climbed up a chimney-type crack to look out of a spy hole hidden in the craggy rocks on top of their boulder. He parted the tough, sweet-smelling grass and searched the direction they'd come from—nothing.

He and Balful left to scout the woods for sign of intruders. They needed no surprises when they started out again. Bar was drinking water steadily with the inevitable result. They moved the rock so that he could go outside. Fragrant with the smell of pine, chill air flooded their hole, and they could all hear the distant howling frenzy of tipeeke. Amray and Balful materialized out of the shadows.

"So far, we see no sign of them in this area, but I think we should move on. I fear for Akeel's health, but it would not be good to be trapped in this hiding place or to have them ahead of us. The tipeeke and their masters, whoever they may be, could find another way to cross the gorge. It would be better to be as far ahead of them as possible."

Lavel said, "We are all tired and hungry. We have gone the whole night without sleep. Do we have a safe place to hide ahead?"

"Aye," Amray answered.

"How far?"

"Ten hours," the Bani chief replied.

They all groaned and stared at him, trying to understand. Why would Amray advocate such a plan when they had a safe hiding place? After a few minutes of consideration, Lavel said, "You are our guides. You risked your lives for us and have brought us safe this far. I will trust your judgment on this; though I must tell you, I am worried about being caught in the open."

Amray just considered him quietly, not responding to his concern. Then Lavel nodded and said, "Lead on."

Amray, a man of few words, said, "Follow me." They gathered their gear from the cave and trotted after him into the trees. The forest was growing more visible in the bright light of dawn.

They stopped for rest and food only four times in the long day that followed. Each time, Dare gave Akeel medicine for pain and fever, but by evening, the warrior could barely stand much less run. At their last stop, the young Bani rested on his haunches, looking pale and sick.

Amray came to him and, squatting beside him, put a hand on his shoulder. He said, "You have done well through a difficult day. Now you will let us carry you."

"No, Lord, I can make it. I will lean on this young giant when I grow tired," he said quickly, glancing at Dare, who had helped him all day.

Unaccustomed to argument, Amray raised one eyebrow, a danger signal to those who knew him. "You will do as I say."

Akeel flushed, dismayed at his words. "Aye, Lord. Forgive me." Amray gave a curt nod, and they continued through the valley.

Lavel and Dare took turns carrying Akeel. The Bani warrior's conflicting emotions were visible in his expression; being carried was an indignity, yet he was grateful. He thanked them stiffly.

The sun went down in a spectacular display of color, and the forest suddenly grew ominous and full of shadows. Still, the tireless Amray and Balful kept going and encouraging the others. "It is not much farther now," Amray said. "We will soon be there."

"Right," Dare whispered to Bardon bitterly. "He's been saying that for the last hour." Bar, who had done well once the di'ak wore off, was strangely quiet.

In the distance, very far away, they heard the howling and screeching of the tipeeke. They looked at each other in apprehension and quickened their pace.

A dark cliff face, featureless in the blackness, suddenly rose out of the valley they were crossing. It looked like the end of the road, but Balful turned south confidently. They followed, wondering where he would lead them. The night was clear and cold; it was never far from cold in the high country. The moon had not risen yet, and it was very dark. Balful splashed into a shallow brook and followed its narrow, winding course. The water was frigid, but the first few steps were the worst; then their feet grew numb. Suddenly Balful and the stream entered a dark crack in the cliff face. Dare groaned with dismay. *No … not another dark, tight space. I was not made for adventuring.* However, he followed his companions into the inky blackness of the crack.

Bar groaned, and Lavel, who was in front of him, stopped. "Are you all right, Bar?"

"Aye," he said abruptly, and they moved forward again. The narrow, twisting tunnel they shared with the stream was difficult to navigate, even crouched and single file, especially for Lavel. Dare was sure the man must feel as if much skin was being scraped off his wide shoulders.

They were all relieved when they came out of the winding tunnel into a small valley. The brook welled into a small pond. It must have an outlet somewhere, or it would have flooded the whole area. Balful, with Amray's help, pushed a rock across the tunnel's exit. The rock rested on the banks of the small stream and allowed the water to bubble on its way underneath. Then their guide led them through the trees to a cabin built against the cliff wall. They filed in gratefully, too cold and tired to speak.

Amray and Balful got a small fire going and prepared hot soup from dried venison and vegetables. Meanwhile, the others searched their packs for dry socks and breeches. With this change and warm food, they all began to feel less miserable. Dare gave the grateful Akeel as much otet as he thought safe. The man was soon asleep in a thick hammock of woven elong.

Bardon held his head in his hands and moaned softly. Lavel asked him with foreboding what was wrong. His answer made them all stare in disbelief. "I think—I am fairly sure—I have the aching sickness."

"No!" Dare said, reaching for Bar's hand and then his forehead. Both were burning. "I don't believe this! How could you get sick now?" he asked indignantly.

"I'm sorry," Bardon said, "but I didn't plan it. Many of the brothers at Saint Fauver's were ill. I must have caught it from them."

Amray and Lavel looked at each other in speechless shock and finally grinned. "He is a constant challenge, is he not?" Lavel asked, and Amray and Balful nodded.

A miserable prince tossed in his hammock, in spite of everything Dare poured into him. "Dare, do something," he ordered. "This is unbearable."

"Haven't you read any of our history? Our champions never get the aching sickness or any other sickness. It just isn't done. Sure, you can suffer from wounds, but this—this is unheroic."

Bar gazed at him bitterly. "Dare, this is not funny. Please, please do something." In spite of their weariness and anxiety, the men smiled at Dare's teasing.

"Amray, I don't have the herb I really need to help him. I would like to go into the woods and search for it."

When Lavel and Balful rose to go with Dare, Amray ordered them to rest. "I will take the first watch. Come, Dare, we will look for this healing herb." It was difficult to go back out into the cold when what they both wanted, and their bodies were crying out for, was warmth and sleep.

Amray climbed a large boulder with a view of the valley and settled uncomfortably in his cloak to watch. Dare searched first the wood and then the meadow floor, but he found nothing. He squatted by the brook to check out yet another plant, but it was not thful. Looking up, he started in fear.

Not ten paces from him sat a beautiful smoke-colored wolf. The wolf's ears were perked up, and its eyes were bright with curiosity, as if it wondered who this strange creature might be. The longer Dare looked, the less afraid he felt, and he relaxed, in spite of every instinct that told him to flee or draw his knife.

Suddenly, a strange mist full of light seemed to stand near him. Dare froze, his heart thudding in fear. He heard, *"This is Starfire."* Dare trembled, for he felt the presence of something powerful pressing against him. *Surely I am dreaming!*

"Will you let my servant mark you for the Maker's service, in order that

119

another part of the prophesy may be fulfilled?" an unearthly voice asked. Dare did not know if he heard it out loud or in his mind.

"Who are you?" he asked somehow. Afterward, he did not know where he had found the courage.

"I serve the Maker also," it answered. The bright fog or whatever it was faded and was gone. Starfire slowly approached him and sat again, directly in front of him. Dare reached out his hand and touched the beautiful, warm fur.

"May I?" the wolf asked. Dare heard this question in his mind.

"Aye." Somehow Dare knew that his mark would be where Bar's was, and he fumbled with cold, stiff fingers to untie his cloak and unlace his shirt. Lost in Starfire's gaze, he finally managed to bare his shoulder. Starfire reached out a paw with claws extended and left four scratches on Dare's skin. The top two scratches were highter than the bottom two.

He knew there would be pain, and there was—a searing fire. He closed his eyes and gasped but did not cry out. When he opened them, the wolf was gone. But the animal had left clear prints on the soft, wet ground. Dare touched one. *A real wolf then …*

At his feet lay a plant that surely had not been there before—or had he been too exhausted to see it? "Thful! Alati, Maker," he said with a dazed gratitude that filled and overflowed his heart.

He turned to go back to the hidden cabin and saw Amray watching from the edge of the clearing. He tried to imagine what his experience would have looked like from Amray's point of view, but his mind couldn't focus on the problem.

"I am all right," Dare assured him.

Amray said with wonder, "This night we will let the noble Starfire guard us, I think, and we will all sleep safely."

"You know him?" Dare asked in surprise.

Amray laughed and paused a moment, trying to remember something. Whatever it was, it wouldn't come back to him, and he shook his head. "Aye. Tomorrow we will share our knowledge. Tonight, it is enough to know that Starfire is here."

They walked back to the cabin in quiet trust. Dare ground the thful, mixed it in water, and used some of it to wash his scratches. The fiery pain stopped immediately.

Bar drank the rest gratefully, too sick to notice Dare's unusual excitement. Both Dare and Amray climbed into their hammocks. They slept until the sun poured into the deep canyon. Light filled the small valley, as tea fills a cup.

SEPARATE PATHS

THE SUNLIGHT SHONE THROUGH THE CRACKS in the shutters, awakening first Amray and then Balful. They stretched and got up slowly, enjoying their relative safety. Soon a merry fire crackled on the hearth. The appetizing smell of cooking food woke the others.

To one of their number, the smell was anything but appetizing. Bar groaned and turned his face to the wall. Dare quickly mixed more thful. Bar drank it thirstily and tried not to moan or complain, realizing it would be very unheroic. Dare forced cold water from the stream down him until he cried, "Dare, let me be. No more!" His healer decided he had drunk enough and went back to the fire to eat his own breakfast of hot tea, porridge, dried fruit, and smoked venison.

After a sip of tea, Amray said quietly, "Dare had an unusual experience last night."

With an obvious effort to suppress irritation and alarm, Lavel asked, "What has happened now?"

Dare looked at Amray, who nodded encouragingly. "I'm not sure you'll believe it." He grinning ruefully and shook his head. "I'm not sure I believe it."

"Try us," Lavel said with apprehension.

Hesitantly at first and then with greater confidence as everyone listened respectfully, Dare traced the events of the previous evening. "When I opened my eyes, Starfire was gone, but he left prints on the ground, so I think he is a real wolf."

Amray said, "I saw the wolf from my high place while on watch and came down quickly to warn Dare. When I got to the edge of the clearing, neither of them had moved, and I too saw a light-filled mist close to Dare. I was both awed and curious and waited to see what would happen. As the wolf moved closer to Dare, I recognized *her*"—he grinned at Dare's shock— "as Starfire, who is known to my people. I was no longer worried about her harming Dare, but I was filled with a sense of wonder. There are many legends among my people about this wolf. She has been the Bani's special protector for hundreds of years, and there are many who have glimpsed or touched her through the years. I had never seen her till last night.

"There is an old tale of a child lost in the deep woods whom she led back to our village. The child said that Starfire had a thorn in her paw that he removed. So, aye, I think she is very real but ancient nonetheless. The light-filled mist is also in our legends but only a few times. Long ago, we were in great danger from a fanatical group of Losigh, who wished to exterminate us for our belief in the Maker. We lived on the edge of Blackwood then and had much commerce with Feisan and other cities. We supplied the leather they needed from the blackdeer, whom we hunted carefully, to preserve their numbers. The mist filled with light told our leader, Lord Epsilon, to flee and hide in a special place that none of our people knew existed. We believe this light is a special being appointed by the Maker to guard us, and we believe Starfire is his servant. There are many other such stories in our scrolls." Again a chord of memory troubled Amray, but he could not recall what was just on the edge of his thoughts.

"How good the Creator is," Lavel said softly, his face full of awe. His gaze was distant. He was remembering the day that he'd rescued the prince and a drudge from Casterray, with no thought except to help two of the Maker's children. Many members of the underground had reproached him for embroiling them in an altercation between Bardock and his heir. They thought abducting the king's son suicidal and no way to keep a covert organization a secret. Then, much to the underground's astonishment, E Clue had marked Bar and given him prophetic words—or instructions, as Bar called them. His critics had been not only silenced but overwhelmed by the implications of the first marking. Now, right on top of the first marking, was the second! The second line of Bar's prophetic instructions was complete. Dare, one of the common people, was the wolf-marked. In the midst of his wonder, Lavel felt the almost unbearable weight of having these two marked young men, children really, in his care.

Rising from his hammock, Bar said in a soft voice, "One wolf-marked, the spirit shall recruit, to heal, to stand with, and to be his sure proof." Though Bar rarely mentioned the words of the prophecy, they were never far from his thoughts. He was grateful beyond measure that Dare was confirmed in his role. Perhaps more importantly, the meaning of the mark on his own shoulder—of the words themselves—was now confirmed in his spirit. Bar would never be the same.

Amray finally knew what it was he had been trying to remember. The Bani knew of the prophecy also.

Bar stared at Dare, who rose to face him. The young prince walked to his friend and touched the puckered red marks that already had a blue-gray cast. "I am so glad," he said simply.

Dare's attempt at a smile cracked, and he admitted, "So am I, but I'm also frightened."

"Aye," Bar agreed with sympathy, "so am I."

A fugitive prince and a fugitive drudge, they were now the marked ones spoken of in the prophecy. It had begun.

The Bani, who were still unaware of Bar's true identity or marking, realized that there were gaps in their knowledge of the three fugitives they were guiding. They were puzzled but unwilling to ask questions until there was time for answers. The small group did take time to thank and praise the Maker together, and then they discussed what to do next.

Lavel said gratefully, "Dare's experience has assured me that we are on the right path. Yet I question going forward when we do not know what has happened at Saint Fauver's or who sends the tipeeke and their masters against us." He bowed his head for a moment in thought. "I have committed Devon to the Maker, but I feel I cannot leave him—perhaps a prisoner or dead—and I seek your council on this. Should I go back and find out what has happened, or should I go on? Dare is an important part of the prophesy, and he is in my care. Bar is a fugitive. Lavel had not told the Bani about Bar's true identity. Should I leave them? If I am injured or caught, who will take them on the rest of their journey? We have all waited so long for this day, yet I don't know what to do next." Lavel's expression revealed his indecision.

Amray said, after a few minutes of quiet, "Bar is too sick to travel, and Akeel needs rest also. Let us take the time this morning to seek the Maker's will and think this over. Balful and I will climb to a place we know and observe the valley we traveled through yesterday. We will look for signs of the enemy. I am also concerned for my people. They are well hidden, and guards are always on watch, but I also must consider what to do." They all agreed to this.

Dare changed Akeel's bandages and sent him back to his hammock. He nodded gratefully. "Alati, my young friend." Then Dare went to Bar, who was resting but not asleep, and they talked quietly.

Lavel sat in the sunshine polishing his beautiful keat bow. It was made of cherry wood and very large. He soon fell asleep, and the morning passed quietly. Amray and Balful did not return at midday, so Dare started preparations for midmeal. They ate quietly; even Bar ate a little. Each was worried but not willing to admit it. Finally, at the eighth hour after dawn, the door opened. They looked up anxiously. Amray and Balful entered, looking grim and tired.

"First eat. Then tell us what you have seen," Lavel said. From their faces, he knew the news was not good. He and Dare laid out food for them, and they waited until the two Bani finished eating to talk.

Amray quickly swallowed his tea, then said, "Tipeeke are all over this end of the valley and their masters with them. These men are dressed in long black robes with a red crest on the front. They drive the tipeeke with special sticks; we think there is some poisonous substance on the end, but I am not sure of that. We did not wish to get close enough to find out. They have tracked us to the stream, but they lost the scent there. I pray they do not follow the watercourse and figure out where we are, but it is possible they may. It would be very difficult, if not impossible, to move away the stone from the other side."

Bar said from his hammock, "Tell me what the red crest looks like."

Balful, who rarely spoke, answered, "It is a circle with a large C in the middle."

"The symbol of Choack," Bar said. "The king, his spiritual advisor, or both seek our lives."

"The king?" Amray questioned harshly, eyebrows raised.

Dismayed at his slip, Bar flushed red and looked quickly at Lavel. "I'm sorry, sir."

Lavel shook his head. "It's all right. They already know about Dare. I considered telling them the rest; this just settles it."

They gave the Bani a short version of the hishua's story, and Bar showed them the mark E Clue had made on his shoulder. They also explained that the men in charge of the tipeeke were called Blackrobes and served not only the king but an evil god named Choack. The cabin remained completely quiet for a few minutes as the stunned Bani tried to absorb this new information. Conversations they had not understood now made sense.

Finally, Amray said with great feeling, "We have waited long for this day. We welcome your coming and have hoped for your reign." Balful and Akeel nodded agreement, eyes sparkling with excitement. Almost to himself, the Bani chief quoted softly, "One shall come who will have burned in his flesh a triangle of blue. Beside him shall stand the wolf-marked, and together they herald the beginning of defeat for a great evil." This was another ancient prophecy that had now been fulfilled! They were all awed.

Shaking off his mood of wonder, Amray looked at Lavel with some anger. "It would have been better if I had known who I was helping to escape."

"How was I to know—" Lavel started to answer sharply but closed his mouth and bowed his head in acknowledgment of Amray's anger. "Please understand, Amray, it is better sometimes not to know too much. We have left a trail of destruction and death behind us because the king seeks them, and for no good reason. I thought it better you not know. But I did *not* anticipate the tipeeke and their masters *or* what happened at Saint Fauver's. Perhaps I was wrong to keep it from you. If so, I am sorry. It was a difficult choice—I bear a heavy trust."

Amray's face softened. "Aye, that you do. I am a cross old man with a heavy trust of my own. I should not fault you, for I would probably have made the same decision." He sighed and shifted his position to ease tense muscles. "This journey has had too many surprises, and I am fretting over not being where I feel I should be—with my people. I usually do not accept such assignments as this one myself. In this case, I am glad I did."

"Has anyone come to a decision about our next step?" Bar asked.

"If you would be willing to take the hishua for a time," Lavel said, looking at Amray, "I would go back with one of your men and find out what is happening at St. Fauvers."

Amray stared at him for many minutes. He was thinking of the heavy responsibility and the enormous danger these two marked young men would bring to his people. For years they had lived in relative safety. The Bani helped save many fugitives, through the well-developed underground. Yet it had never been their intention to remain a hidden people forever. They had eagerly waited through long centuries for the prophecy to be fulfilled. He had looked forward to its fulfillment—but sometime in the distant future! Because he'd assumed the event was years from unfolding, he had not considered the danger. Amray chided himself. *Will I hesitate now, when the time has come, even though it is in my time?*

"I will take your 'responsibilities' with me and keep them as safe as I am able. I will also send Bani warriors with you to Saint Fauver's, if you will take the time to return to our home."

Lavel's face relaxed a little, and he shifted his shoulders as if a great weight had fallen from them. He nodded his acceptance of Amray's offer and turned to Balful. "Balful, would you come with me? I think the two of us would be enough, and I don't want to waste time going back to your people for more warriors."

Balful grinned. "Gladly, sir, if my lord allows?" He looked hopefully at Amray, his eyes bright and eager, but he was by no means sure that Amray would give his permission.

Balful was a sure guide to his people. He knew the Blackdeer Range and all its natural and created hiding places, as a child knew his or her own village. His people depended on him, and he would be missed, but at twenty-three he was not yet married and felt free to go.

Amray finally nodded decisively. "Aye, Balful may go with you. I do not think numbers will help on this mission of stealth, and his talents will aid you."

"Alati ma, old friend," Lavel said huskily.

They all cleared their throats and started talking. Amray sent Balful and Dare to watch the Blackrobes. He and Lavel discussed the best plan and route for finding out what had happened at Saint Fauver's. Before leaving, Dare gave his patients permission to go for a short walk.

The next morning as Lavel and Balful watched their enemy, one of the robed figures gave two of the tipeeke strict orders and motioned them to the stream. The beasts were being left to watch. Then he and the rest of the tipeeke and Blackrobes disappeared into the forest. They were headed back toward the monastery.

Lavel and Balful moved the rock that blocked the stream and walked stealthily to the entrance. They quickly killed the two massive tipeeke with arrows shot from their long keat bows. The two animals died quickly. The warriors threw the carcasses into a nearby ditch. How the animals could smell anything over their own stench was a mystery. The men followed their enemies' trail but not too closely. They did not want the tipeeke ahead of them to catch their scent.

Amray waited until the next morning; then he took his party up the trail to a ledge that overlooked the whole valley. This was where he and Balful had watched the Blackrobes and tipeeke. In the predawn light, the valley was quiet. Amray led them north over a rugged trail that stayed high above the valley. He wanted to be in Glimmervale by nightfall. Both Bar and Akeel felt good and easily kept the pace Amray set. Slowly, the sky lightened, revealing heavy gray clouds that moved sluggishly over the peaks. The air smelled of snow. Even in summer it could snow in the mountains. Amray scanned the clouds with a practiced eye, then told them to put on all the clothing they had. He placed Dare and Bar between himself, in the lead, and Akeel, at the rear.

It didn't start to really snow hard until after midday. Dare had no idea how Amray knew where he was going. The scraggly piñon, rock, and cliff all looked the same to him, especially covered with a blanket of snow. There was no wind to speak of, just silently falling snow and the sound of their breathing. Occasionally an unseen bird would chirp. Bar and Akeel were breathing hard and slowing. Dare hoped it was not much farther.

In the dim light of the hidden setting sun, they came to a vast field of strangely twisted depressions in the rock. A high cliff wall protected these holes from the snow. They could be seen clearly, but what they were was a mystery to Dare and Bar. Amray counted, and after taking a quick look around him, he led them to a specific one in the middle. He slipped over the edge and fell out of sight.

Akeel grinned and motioned the hishua to follow Amray. He held a finger to his lips, to warn them not to speak. Bar slipped over the edge, and Dare followed him. They landed on a sandy floor, perhaps nine feet down.

Amray grabbed their arms and led them into a tunnel that was pitch black. They heard Akeel land softly behind them. Amray had to be leading them by feel, for surely no one could see in the darkness. They each walked, hands trailing the rough-hewn walls, for what seemed an hour but was truly only a few minutes. The ground was level and smooth but appeared to be going steadily down. An occasional air current or lack of a wall on one hand or the other indicated other passages, branching off the one they were following. Either Amray had memorized this maze, or there were markings of some kind that neither Dare nor Bar could feel.

They heard a low growl, and a voice somewhere ahead ordered, "Identify yourself."

"Your father, Akeel, and two guests," Amray answered softly.

"Welcome, Father!" the voice said with relief. "You have been gone longer than we thought you would be. It is good to have you home." They heard rather than saw an embrace.

"Come to me when you are off duty." Amray bent to pat a large shadow they knew had to be a dog when it whined a friendly greeting.

"There is a ledge in front of you that overlooks Glimmervale; stay close to the wall. We will go down stairs into the valley. It is very dark, so watch your footing," Amray said.

There was no need to ask where the valley had gotten its name; hundreds of pinpoints of light glittered far below them. They went down and down for a very long time. Dare wondered if this was the haven that the Bani's guardian had given them long ago.

Dare and Bar were so tired when they arrived at the guesthouse that they dropped into elong hammocks, fully clothed except for their boots, and slept till morning.

At daybreak they hurried out of their hammocks to see Glimmervale in the daylight. Their guesthouse was really a small cave located high above the valley floor. Comfortably fitted with the necessities, the cave had a twelve-foot-wide entrance that had been walled in with wooden logs. The door was a small opening snugly covered with a deerskin. There were no windows. Outside their door, they stood on a solid rock ledge that wound downward.

They gazed in wonder at the high cliffs that surrounded the valley known as Glimmervale. Many of the Bani lived in the caves that honeycombed the cliff walls. Those cliff walls totally encircled the valley. Bar and Dare could see no break in them anywhere. What a refuge! The Bani had woven a complicated system of elong walkways that branched here and there like a spiderweb gone wild. "No wonder they had no trouble with the bridge that spanned the gorge!" Bardon said as he gazed at children running on walkways many feet over his head.

"Do you think this was once the inside of a volcano?" Dare asked as he gazed around him at the towering walls.

"It would have to have been a huge one. This place must be ten, maybe twenty miles wide."

The valley floor was covered with pine, aspen, oak, and some umbrella trees. They could see stone buildings hidden among the trees. It was beautiful in whichever direction they looked.

They met a bewildering number of people that first day, among them Amray's family. He had two sons, Tierray and Kostan, and a daughter, who was not home. She was working with those who crafted in elong. Tierray and Kostan looked much like their father, slim and of medium height with dark hair. Tierray was eighteen, and Kostan was fifteen. They offered to show Dare and Bardon the valley, and the hishua readily agreed. Kostan and Bar declined exploring the tosga—the high, swaying walkways.

TROUBLE ON THE TOSGA

A HORRIBLE STORM HOWLED AND SCREAMED among the peaks and crags high above Glimmervale. High winds and heavy snow, mixed with freezing temperatures, were making the world outside the valley impassable. The winds occasionally whipped a swirling funnel of snow down into the valley, but for the most part, the storm stayed high above them. Bar and Dare were snug and warm in Tierray's cave and dreaded going out into the fierce cold. They'd moved in with Tier after spending a few days in the guest cave. The move seemed a good idea to everyone but Kostan. He thought it was extremely unfair that Dare, who was the same age as he, could live there and he could not. Amray told his youngest son that he was not ready to lose him quite yet. He would not be moved on the subject, though Kostan continually tried to change his mind.

Both Dare and Bar were given a daily schedule of training and duties, similar to any Bani of their age. They fit smoothly into the daily life of the industrious community. Both spent time with Lorox, who taught them Bani history and customs, and with Ourit, who trained them in crafting with elong. Elong was the name of both the vine and the fiber which came from it. The people of Ree had found hundreds of uses for elong. Haner helped Dare improve his skill with the bow. Sureese taught them both healing at Amray's insistence. Amray felt strongly that everyone should have knowledge of healing and insisted that all his people know at least the basics.

The hishua were not allowed to hunt or ride. This was difficult for them both, but these activities were done outside the vale. Amray could not bring

131

himself to risk them when Blackrobes, tipeeke, and who knew what else were roaming the meadows and forest. This did not discourage the two, and they were almost as bad as Kostan at pestering the chief to let them go with the warriors. They also helped dig fire rock, which the Bani used for fuel, and did many other chores.

Calley, Amray's wife, invited them often to dinner, knowing what kind of meals they cooked for themselves. Her name, which meant "cricket," fit her perfectly. She was merry and full of mischief, a perfect balance to Amray's serious, even temperament. Kostan had inherited his mother's personality and kept them all laughing at his antics.

Dare, Bar, and Tier braved the cold to go to Amray's sentaque, or ground house, so called because it was located on the valley floor, for the evening meal. A gustaque was a home in the cliff wall. They stomped on the porch to remove the snow clinging to their boots and then entered the single room that was warm and full of appetizing smells.

Calley and Amray greeted them warmly, and they all sat to talk until Kostan arrived. After thirty minutes, Tier looked aggravated. "Where is that brat? I'm hungry!"

Calley looked anxious and went to the door. A cold draft filled the room as she cracked it to look out. "I see no one; perhaps we should go look for him."

Amray nodded in agreement. "He has probably just lost track of the time, but it is too cold out to take a chance."

They all bundled up warmly and went out into the dark night. Amray lit a torch, and they started knocking on doors. From Kostan's friends, they found out where he had been about an hour before they started searching. Amray looked really worried for the first time.

Kostan's friends disclosed that he had been watching them swing from vine to walkway, near the stone stairway. He'd cheered them on as they'd tried more and more dangerous feats. Because he had queal, he did not participate in their games, except to make up names for their tricks and for them. Tier knew what his father was thinking, because he was thinking the same thing. *Kostan has never accepted his problem with queal, and he keeps hoping he will outgrow it. Perhaps he tried to walk the tosga again. The last time he tried, when he was twelve, he ended up with only a broken arm and bruises. If he has tried again, in this cold …*

They all hurried to the stairs and searched the tosga above them. There was something dangling from one high over their heads.

Tier cried, "Kostan!" and started up.

His father grabbed his arm. "Careful! You might cause him to fall."

Bar's pulse raced as he looked at the limp form high above them. Nausea washed over him. Reaching out to Amray, he said thickly, "Wait, Lord! Tier, if he has been there an hour or longer, he can no longer see correctly or move his limbs. His vision is shattered into a hundred pieces that do not fit together. Believe me, I know. He can do nothing for himself, especially hang on if the tosga lurch and sway."

Amray nodded calmly. "What do you suggest?"

"Let me go get help. We need men to hold blankets to catch him if he falls. Do nothing till they are in place. Then light this area with many torches and send your best climber up there with a rope. He can tie it around Kostan and lower him to the ground. Now, you must be ready with your cloaks to catch him if he should fall before I get back. And talk to him. The one sense he has left is hearing." Amray sent an unwilling Tier with Bar to alert the healer and the others they needed.

Soon a fourth of the vale's population was below the elong walkways, silently watching and seeking the Maker for their chief's son. Saer, a twelve-year-old who was the vale's best climber, worked his way up the tosga without causing the slightest movement. The walkways were all interconnected, and a movement on the first level would cause one on the second and even a small vibration on the third.

"How did he get so far?" Calley asked her eldest son, her anger mixed with wonder.

"I don't know," Tier said with suppressed violence, "but when I get my hands on him, he will wish he hadn't."

Everyone held his or her breath as Saer swung on a vine around an outcropping of rock. He carried a rope over his shoulder and held a torch in one hand. He landed as gently as a bird on the section Kostan occupied. Amray's youngest son hung, wedged between two vertical vines, at an odd angle. Everyone realized, with the added light from Saer's torch, that only

133

Kostan's head, left arm, and shoulder were on the tosga. His upper body was wedged between the vines; the rest of him dangled over nothing! The crowd's gasps and cries were audible to Saer and surely Kostan too.

Saer wedged the torch in a crack in the rock wall, took the noose he had made while on the ground in his hands, and, lying flat, moved forward an inch at a time toward Kostan. The two boys were talking, but no one could understand their words. Suddenly, Kostan's body slipped a few inches. Everyone gasped, and the men holding the blankets got ready. As they gazed up in hope and horror, Amray put his arms around his wife and eldest son. Kostan's body started to slip farther. Before the limp body could fall, little Saer darted as quickly as a snake. He clung to Kostan's left arm with all his strength and both his hands. The Bani watching below groaned in unison.

"Father!" Tier said softly, his eyes never leaving the two so high above them.

"Aye, go quickly," Amray answered faintly, his face very pale.

Tier went as lightly as he could up the tosga until he was on the third level. He swung around an outcrop of rock and landed gently. After climbing over the straining Saer, he took the abandoned noose and got it around his brother and under both his arms with the twelve-year-old's help. Saer gladly let go and rested his trembling muscles.

"Tier, is that you?" Kostan asked faintly.

"Aye, you crazy loon, now shut up! I'll lower you to the ground."

"I did well, didn't I? Got to the third level!" he crowed.

"Did well?" Tier stared at his young brother, speechless with indignation.

"Tier, my vision is scrambled, and I can't move anything, not even my head. Do you … do you think …" he said fearfully. His speech was soft and slurred.

"No! Bar says it will pass, but it will take time. You will be fine," he assured his young brother.

"Is father very … angry?" he asked as Tier started lowering him.

"Aye. If I were you, I'd act very sick."

Bar and Dare too had watched, frozen with horror, as Kostan's body had slipped. Bar had left bruises on Dare's arm where he'd gripped it as he'd stifled a cry. Swallowing hard, the fugitive prince tried to banish the memory of a like experience.

The clan sighed with relief when Kostan's completely limp body slumped on the solid ground. Calley and Amray, much to Tier's disgust, were not angry but so thankful that Kostan was safe that they hugged and fussed over him.

"Parents," he said, shaking his head.

The forgotten Saer agreed fervently. "Aye!"

Tier started at the sound of Saer's voice. He was embarrassed that he had forgotten, even for a moment, this boy who saved his brother's life. "Saer, you did it! He'd have fallen if it had not been for your quick thinking." He reached out his hand and shook Saer's arm till the boy's whole body shook. "Alati. You have served your clan well this day. Let's get off this freezing cliff and get in where it's warm."

Saer flushed with pleasure at praise from his idol, and they quickly trotted down three levels. The clan patted and praised Saer so effusively that he ran home, pleased but embarrassed.

Amray wrapped Kostan warmly in blankets and carried him to one of the hot springs to warm his cold body. Calley and Sureese went with him.

Dare, Tier, and Bar ran to Amray's sentaque, and sat around the firepit eating Calley's venison stew. Now that the danger was over, they were very hungry. "Thank the Maker Saer acted so quickly and was able to hang on till I got there!" Tier said. "Even if those below had caught him on the stretched blanket, he could have broken something or been injured." They continued to talk and stuff themselves until they were too full to eat another bite.

Later, the door burst open, and Amray, followed by Calley and Sureese, carried Kostan, who was very limp and quiet, to his hammock. They shrugged out of their heavy cloaks and came to the fire to warm themselves. Tier ladled bubbling-hot stew into wooden bowls and served each of them. "Is he better, Mother?" Tier asked gruffly.

"He is warmer and very sleepy, but he still can't see properly or move anything."

Bardon went quietly to Kostan's hammock and talked softly to him for a few minutes. When he returned to the fire, Sureese said, shaking his head, "This reaction is entirely new to me—I have never seen anything like it. How did you know what to expect?" he asked Bar.

"I had a like experience."

"Ah." Sureese rubbed his hands together over the fire to warm them. "Would you share your experience with us? Our ignorance today could have caused Kostan's death."

The ruddy firelight flickered across Bar's face as he gazed at Sureese. "It's not easy telling, sir," he responded with cold courtesy.

Surprised by his reticence, Sureese explained, "We have many people who suffer from queal. It is my duty to learn all I can about this strange illness. We have found many ways to help those who suffer its effects, such as the herbal mixture that Amray used to get you across Hagare Canyon. Bar, we live in these mountains; we must have answers—solutions. There is nothing in any of my scrolls exactly like Kostan's reaction—just some similar reactions here and there. Will you tell me what happened to you?"

Watching Bar closely, Amray said, "We know so little about queal. *Anything* you tell us will help. I will not forget, nor will my people, what you have done for the Bani this day."

Bardon bowed his head in reluctant agreement. How could he deny Amray anything after all he had done? He would never forget Hagare Canyon. *Maker, help me. I hate this—I truly hate it.*

Staring into the fire, Bar began, "My father was very proud of my physical abilities, but he could never accept the fact that I had queal. There were so many things I could do without much trouble: climb rocks, ride a horse, or walk a narrow mountain trail—anything where solid ground was under my feet or I was seated on a horse or even riding in a wagon. He was sure if I just pushed myself, tried harder, I could overcome my reaction to heights where there was no solid footing."

He paused to organize his thoughts and then continued, "One day, a few other boys and our Bas—our weapons master were in the training hall, running through a series of exercises." Bar caught his slip, remembering that Amray had decided not to reveal his and Dare's real identities to the Bani community. They thought the hishua were ordinary fugitives. "I skipped one of the exercises routinely because of queal. It involved climbing a long elong vine attached to the ceiling through a wooden ring, switching to another one, and climbing down. Father was watching. He insisted I try to do it. I was twelve and wanted to please him very badly, but I knew what would happen and refused.

"He is … a proud man. He became very angry, and he ordered our master to tie one of the vines under my arms, then hoist me up perhaps twenty-five feet off the floor. He said that all I needed to do was climb up the vine in front of me and switch to the other vine and climb down that vine—something all the other boys could have done easily. The other boys all left at his order and closed the doors. What sounded so easy for them was impossible for me."

Bardon looked at Sureese for the first time. "I managed not to throw up until after they left—the only dignity I managed that long night. I threw up again and again, and then my body became unresponsive. First, I couldn't move my hands, then my arms. I tried to move my feet and couldn't. Then I couldn't move my legs. Later, my vision started to change. I thought at first it was only the growing darkness in the room, but I soon realized that I could not focus on any one thing. Everything I saw splintered and broke apart. I could see, but not what I wished to see and not how things really were. The pain around my upper body from the vine was growing, and forgetting pride, I tried to call for help. I could talk but only very faintly."

He sighed and rubbed his temples. "For the first time, I faced the fact that I might hang there all night. It grew darker and colder, and I asked the Maker desperately for help. After a time—I do not know how long—I heard soft noises. Someone released the vine from its bracket on the wall and slowly lowered me to the floor. I crumpled in a heap on the cold stone, unable to move or straighten my limbs. I waited, hoping whoever had released me would come help me, but I realized later that she—I think it was a woman—had no way of knowing I couldn't move. She was probably very afraid of getting caught, and she probably expected that I would stand up and walk away. I grew colder and colder, and my muscles started to cramp from the strange position I was in.

"She must have been waiting in the shadows, and when she heard my groans and saw that I was not moving, she came and straightened my limbs for me and put something soft under my head. I whispered thank you, and she was gone. At that moment, I felt very … alone. I did not know if the symptoms would pass or if they were permanent." His listeners were utterly silent, too appalled to speak. "The cold became intense, and my body tried to shiver but seemed to have difficulty doing so. Someone came, still in total darkness, and lifted me and carried me to my room. I think the woman had gone for help; there was no way she could have lifted me. The man who carried me alerted my servants. They got me warm but could do nothing for my other problems. They were very fearful that they would be blamed for my condition, so they called for a healer, who ordered them to massage me and keep me warm. All they could do was wait and hope."

Bar came out of his reverie, and his voice became brisk. "My ability to move came back slowly, first feet and legs and finally hands and arms. It was not until morning that my sight returned to normal and sometime after that, my voice. I suffered no permanent damage, but if I had hung there longer, I suppose it is possible I might have. I don't know. I cannot tell you exact times; I can only guess. I was very sick for the next two weeks with a chest cold and cough—from getting so cold, I think." Bar stopped and looked down at his clenched fists. He forced his hands to relax while fighting down the feelings the memory had resurrected.

Bardon's audience stared at him in shocked silence. Manifold emotions were written plainly on their faces. Sureese failed to write anything on his scroll; his features were rigid with anger. Amray, Calley, Dare, and Tier reflected various feelings ranging from anger to compassion, depending on their natures. They realized much of what he hadn't said—the fear of paralysis or permanent injury, the humiliation, and the hurt. Bar felt embarrassed and wished someone would change the subject.

"Well, that is enough storytelling for this night," Calley said gently, as if Bar had related a much-heard fireside tale. "We are all tired. Off with you three hishua. We will see you in the morning." She helped them into their cloaks and pushed them toward the door. Calley hugged each, Bar with particular tenderness.

Out in the cold night air, the young men walked to Tier's gustaque. "I would like to take your father to the wrestling floor," Tier said fiercely.

"He would pin you in two minutes. He is in superb condition and outweighs you by fifty pounds, but alati anyway."

Unable to say what he was feeling, Tier punched Bar hard on the shoulder.

Dare remembered the tall, dark-haired, handsome monarch and

understood, even more clearly, what Bardon's childhood had been. "Did he ever say anything about it?" Dare asked, his voice stiff with anger.

"Not one word," Bar replied, "but he never asked me to climb the vines again, and no one that I heard of was punished for helping me—and he would have made sure I heard. To this day, I do not know who the woman or the man were who came to my aid—no one ever saw their faces. But I thank the Maker for them both."

His friends touched their hearts in agreement.

ATTACK!

THE SHORT MOUNTAIN SUMMER PASSED pleasantly into fall. Bar and Dare grew stronger and healthier. They became part of the Bani tribe and enjoyed the beauty, serenity, and security of Glimmervale. For each young man the time in the vale was like no other season in his life. They gained new skills and felt respected and appreciated by the Bani folk who taught them. It was a rare experience for both. They also learned to laugh and play, which were also new experiences. Tier became a valued friend, and the three were often together. Harvest-season weather was good, and the tribe worked to store provisions for the winter.

Winter decended on the vale with cold temperatures and much snow. One frigid day, Bardon sat cross-legged at Amray's firepit waiting for him to return. The Bani chief and his lieutenants were in the council lodge discussing changes in their defenses.

How did I get in trouble, serious trouble so easily? He remembered Morin's reprimand on the *Karras*—he had followed an impulse again and again endangered others' lives! Bar's thoughts flashed back to the morning hunt.

That morning, he and Dare had followed Amray and his hunting band through the twisted labyrinth of tunnels, passing several sentinels, until finally emerging in to the outside world. The Valley of the Cracked Rock was a wonderland of strange drifts and snow-frosted trees formed by a blizzard. Everything sparkled in the golden light of the rising sun. The snow was powder fine and dry; they moved through it easily except where there were deep drifts. It was good to be out of the vale, away from lessons and chores, and in the bright forest with his knives and his bow.

Amray, with a Bani named Aeech and their two guards, directed two groups with nine hunters in each. Two Bani lookouts watched the eastern end of the valley from high vantage points on the cliffs. As an extra precaution, Amray placed his two best lookouts on the valley floor: one in a high and ancient pine and one on a craggy slab of rock that towered over the eastern valley.

Decker, the lookout in the tree, found blackdeer feeding on grass in a large meadow a storm had swept clean the night before. The meadow was surrounded by lofty pine, and the winds had created drifts taller than a man's height under the trees. Decker directed them with hand signals when they could see him and birdcalls when they could not to the easiest path to the meadow. They waded through the snow quietly, their breath frosty white in the cold air.

Tier, Dare, and Bar were in the group circling the north side of the meadow. The other group was circling to the south. The deer—doe, buck, and adolescent alike—looked strained and thin, yet winter had just started. No one knew why the deer appeared to be struggling, but they suspected that packs of tipeeke might sometimes be allowed to hunt in the area on their own.

The hunters in their group crouched down in the snow at their leader, Vas's, signal. The blackdeer were suddenly edgy. Their leader, a fine stag with a huge rack, lifted his nose, scenting the air. For a moment he was frozen in place. Then in an explosion of speed, he leaped across the meadow into the trees. His whole herd followed him. Before they could figure out what had frightened him, both sentries gave frantic warnings, using both hand gestures and birdcalls.

"Tipeeke! Closing in from the north and west with Blackrobes on horses!" Vas interpreted for his group in astonishment.

Immediately, Amray called both bands back to him. They reached his side quickly. "There are about fifty beasts and three mounted Blackrobes leading them. Follow me to higher ground. Vas, Coles, Raskin, drop back and cover our retreat," he ordered tersely. The three men he named turned immediately and armed their bows just as horsemen burst into the meadow.

"Run!" Amray cried, and the others raced swiftly after him, back down the trail of their own making. Each listened for sounds of pursuit behind him. They heard neighing and yelling as Bani arrows drove into the Blackrobes and their horses. Evidently the enemy had been counting on surprise and had not expected resistance. Their overconfidence cost them and their animals serious injury. As Bardon dashed by giant drifts, he wondered how the tipeeke could possible have gotten so close without the sentries seeing them. *The horses are white and would be difficult to see in the new-fallen snow, but tipeeke are a dark gray, and there are fifty of them!*

Panting, the company scrambled up the boulder where Ruiina, one of the lookouts, was calling directions to Vas, Coles, and Raskin. "Lord!" he cried, turning desperately to Amray. "They are surrounded, and Vas is injured."

Amray gazed down the trail. A few of the fastest tipeeke, *white* tipeeke, had managed to get in behind the three warriors covering the Bani retreat. More were pouring into the meadow, clawing and leaping over the wounded horses. "The Blackrobes?" Amray shouted to Ruiina.

"All down," he answered.

Amray ordered nine men to bring the three warriors to the boulder. He watched as the nine plunged down the trail to their comrades and shot the tipeeke surrounding their brothers. The nine warriors slowly backed toward the rock, shooting as fast as they could put arrow to bow. The three men who had been trapped were injured but able to limp toward the boulder. The warriors did all they could to protect them. In the woods, almost beside them, ran tipeeke, now howling their high, horrible screeches. They scented weakness; it made them confident and excited. Drifts slowed and caught those tipeeke who did not stick to the trail, but the ones on the path were gaining.

Decker loosed arrows from his tree, but soon the action was out of his range, and he was left behind. The tipeeke were between him and the cliffs. He decided to stay put. He was well hidden and would have to hope that the beasts would not find him in his lofty hiding place.

Bar intently watched three tipeeke running on the north side of the trail. They had discovered an easy pathway through the snow and were racing to cut off the twelve warriors' retreat. Without stopping to think, he scrambled down the rock, ran swiftly down the trail, and broke to the right.

Above the deafening noise of tipeeke, Bar heard Amray's strident command to come back. He dismissed it, thinking the chief feared for his safety, and continued to implement his plan. His blood was singing in his veins; all his senses seemed especially acute as he fitted an arrow to his string and sighted carefully in the still air. He shot the lead animal. The tipeeke tumbled head over heels in the snow, tripping his brothers behind him. Bar could hear the men shouting, but he carefully loosed two more arrows and hit each of his targets. The animals yelped and slumped to the ground.

All Bar's concentration was on the animals coming from the west. Suddenly a high-pitched, screeching howl sliced the air right beside him. Three white tipeeke had barreled through the trees from the north and were almost on top of him! His years of daily training saved him in spite of his heart-pounding fear. In one smooth motion, Bar dropped his bow, grabbed the knife from his left boot with his left hand, and threw it at the first animal, which collapsed instantly. No sooner had the blade left his hand than he drew his long knife with his other hand. He slashed the throat of the second tipeeke, and caught the third on the blade's point, just as the creature leaped for his throat. The Bani on the rock gasped. Bar crashed down hard under the dead beast. His right arm was numb from the shattering impact of the 150-pound tipeeke. He heard screeching, yelping, and howling close—in front of him somewhere. Shoving the animal in desperation, he tried to get to his feet. His muscles were sluggish from the jarring fall and not responding properly. He couldn't budge the ugly creature.

Back on the rock, Amray had watched Bar jump into the fight in stunned amazement, fear and anger incapacitating him for a moment. He knew from past experience how the beasts fought; they never attacked from just one direction. While their enemy was focused on fighting them on one front, they would attack from the back or side. Bani had learned the hard way how to fight this cunning and vicious animal, which fought more like a man than a beast.

Amray sent Tier and Dare to help Bar while the others of their company watched the forest, both north and south. Suddenly white-coated tipeeke came from both those directions, just as he'd suspected the creatures would. Amray knew that they were in a desperate situation, and he could only pray that the sentinels on the cliff had sent for help. If it did not arrive soon, it would be too late.

He watched Bar hit the animals with arrows. The chief prayed that Dare and Tier would get there in time to save him from the tipeeke racing into the fray from the north. Bar killed the two lead animals with his knives, almost faster than the eye could see, and then went down under the third one, who was impaled on his long knife. Amray gasped in amazement at Bar's unbelievable skill. Other tipeeke were close behind the first three. Dare and Tier knelt in the snow, took aim, and killed four more tipeeke with arrows. They pulled Bar out from under the dead animal and ran, holding him between them, toward the rock. Those on the boulder covered their retreat.

The nine men on the trail also arrived safely. The three who had protected the hunting party's retreat were with them and safe for the moment. Their injuries did not appear to be life threatening, yet they were weakened from various wounds made by teeth and claw. Dare ran for his pack, but before he started to bind Coles's wound, he threw Bar the man's quiver and bow. He and Tier had left Bar's out in the snow. Bar's head and shoulder ached, but he was no longer dizzy. He caught quiver and bow and started shooting desperately at a seemingly endless pack of snarling tipeeke. The blow to his right shoulder was hurting his aim.

Amray watched from the top of the boulder and guided their shooting, but the number of tipeeke was overwhelming. He knew the fight would soon be hand to hand, and then it would be over. Voss and Sandifir, closest to the bottom on the south side, threw down their bows and drew their knives as frothing, screaming tipeeke broke through the rain of arrows. They killed the beasts, but both warriors were wounded, and more tipeeke were coming.

Silent hunters they were not. Their continual yelping and screeching created an uproar as painful to the ears as the wounds they inflicted were to the body. Amray searched behind him, hoping for rescue. He was not disappointed.

He saw band after band of silent Bani running through the trees. Relief washed through him. He shouted encouragement to his men. The cunning animals seemed to understand him. Some turned to face the trees, and all began howling and yelping to each other, as if they conversed. As reinforcements arrived, a weak cheer went up from the tired men on the boulder. The fresh Bani formed a semicircle around the beasts—the first line kneeling, the second line standing—and shot till almost all were dead. Some tipeeke managed to escape, and the cunning creatures fled north.

The hunting party collapsed where they were and thanked the Maker for their safety. Dare went to Sandifir and Voss to see what he could do for their wounds. Amray organized a retreat to the cliffs for the hunting party and half of the reinforcements.

Bar sat with an aching head on his crossed arms, catching his breath for a moment; his body was still trembling from the shock of his fall. He sensed someone in front of him and looked up quickly. Amray was glaring down at him. In a flash of memory, he heard again the order to return ... the order that he'd ignored.

"Did you hear me order you back?" Amray asked seriously.

"Aye, Lord," he answered truthfully.

"You will stay with Tier and obey his orders until we are in the vale. When I send for you, you will come to the council lodge."

"Aye, Lord."

The other half of the force stayed, at Amray's order, hopefully to bring back meat, though surely every bit of game in the valley had fled miles away, with the uproar and so many hungry tipeeke around. Amray tripled his watchers; if there were white tipeeke, he would have to place lookouts much closer to the valley floor. The lookouts in the valley had not seen the tipeeke till they were almost on top of his hunting party, and evidently, the lookouts on the cliff had seen nothing till the actual battle itself or till Ruiina had signaled them. He did not know which.

Back in the vale, Bar cleaned up as best he could with what water was in Tier's taque and changed clothes. Tier came for him at the ninth hour and told him of a change of plan. The council had discussed Bar's actions, and because he was a protected guest and not a member of their clan, they'd left his discipline in Amray's hands.

The council had also discussed the frightening attack on the hunting party. Blackrobes and tipeeke were hunting Bar and Dare very close ... too close to the vale. Had someone betrayed their hiding place? Was it just chance that had brought them so close? They had more questions than answers and knew it was important to find out what the enemy knew. They hoped that when Lavel returned he could shed some light on what the Blackrobes did and didn't know. Meanwhile, they would be very careful when they left the vale.

A Bani youth would *never* have disobeyed an order from the clan leader, in the field especially. If he did, the consequence was six months of exile for the first offense—a severe punishment to any member of this tight-knit people. Tier squeezed Bar's shoulder in sympathy but could offer him no clue about what might happen. Dare gave Bar otet before he went to the house of healing. He said nothing to his friend before he left. Bar walked to Amray's taque and waited.

Amray's anger cooled. Rarely had he been disobeyed and never when under attack. After taking the time to think, he remembered that neither Dare nor Bardon had been trained by Bani. What training they had received had been harsh and enforced with fear.

This incident is partially my fault, for giving in to their pleading and taking them on a hunt before I knew their strengths and weaknesses. But never, never did I expect such an attack and in such force! It makes me sick to think that the two marked young men might have been killed while in my care. Alati ma, Maker, for protecting them! Now, grant me wisdom.

"Were you injured?" Amray asked Bardon quietly as he took off his heavy cloak and thick, snow-covered boots.

"No, Lord. No, my head aches a little from the fall—that is all." Bar had not expected concern, and it disarmed his composure, what little of it there was. Amray sat down across from him and warmed his hands over the glowing embers. His dark eyes were thoughtful and serious, and his slanted brows and firm chin glowed in the firelight. Amray's countenance was mature, rock hard, and showed no signs of aging.

"You heard me, but you did not obey. Why?" he asked intently.

Bar hesitated and then said slowly, "I thought I knew what to do and that you did not see the problem. I saw no danger to myself—I knew I could kill them, the three tipeeke, and be back in just a few minutes."

"How could I have failed to see the problem? In fact, you thought I was not up to handling the situation, that I was an inept leader and you needed to help me."

"No! I did not! Truly, Lord, I acted on impulse. I wished to ... to impress you with my skill so that you would know I was a capable warrior—so that you would let me hunt here." Bar's cheeks flushed with embarrassment at this admission. He felt like a child and knew Amray thought him one. "I did not—do not—think you inept!" His usual poise was gone; he was appalled by the Bani chief's interpretation of his actions.

"If you disobey an order, that is what you are saying—that you know better, could do it better. Did you know that the tipeeke always attack from the sides or back after they have engaged you on one front?"

"No, Lord." Bar heard the tremor in his voice.

"I did know it. What good did my experience—my months of fighting tipeeke—do you? None. Truly, you are one of the most skilled warriors I have ever seen, but your abilities are useless if they are not under control. Your disobedience today was unworthy of a warrior. No commander has time to deal with such in a battle; it distracts him from his duty."

Bardon knew what Amray said was the truth, in spite of the denials that came quickly to mind. He bowed his head in acceptance of Amray's judgment.

Amray waited a few minutes, allowing his words to sink in, and then went on, "What would have happened if I had not sent Dare and Tier, or if they had not gotten there in time?"

"I would be dead."

"What could have happened to your friends?"

Bar closed his eyes for a moment. "They could have been killed."

Amray spared Bar nothing; he could not afford to be gentle. This hishua would hold hundreds, perhaps thousands, of lives in his hands one day. He would need control and discipline—mental cunning as well as physical skill. The chief waited patiently for a response that would indicate Bar understood.

Feeling miserable, Bar struggled to put his thoughts together. "Lord,

I was wrong. I knew it the minute I saw tipeeke running out of the north woods and realized that you feared not for my skill, as I thought, but for me." He added quickly, "Even if they hadn't been there, it was still wrong to ignore an order. I am sorry. It will not happen again."

Amray looked at the young man and was satisfied that he accepted the seriousness of what he had done. The Bani leader wondered how Bar would handle his next words.

"This is my decision: You will remain in the vale as long as you are with us. There will be no trips outside until Lavel returns for you, unless he is gone longer than two months. In that case, we will reconsider. You will spend two weeks in a hidden valley to the north of us with one of our shepherds. The purpose of this separation from the vale is to provide time for reflection. Do you accept my judgment and consider it just?"

Bar was stunned. He could not speak for a minute. *Two months! Two months without riding or hunting, stuck here in the vale like a child.* "Lord, I would rather you thrashed me," he exclaimed, stung in a vulnerable spot, his pride. Amray almost smiled, but he maintained an impassive front. He waited quietly for long moments as Bardon wrestled with his judgment.

Memory returned to Bar and displayed in living color what could have happened to Dare, to Amray's eldest *son*, to himself. Genuine regret replaced his initial shock and indignation. In the back of his mind, he caught a thought that tried to scurry out of sight, like a rabbit down its hole. *I am not just anyone. I am a prince. How dare he!* Bar hated all forms of arrogance and was appalled to find it in himself. Quickly, he nodded his acceptance.

Amray would not accept that. "Look at me and answer me."

Bar raised his pale face and said steadily, "Aye, Lord, I do accept your judgment, and it is just." And it was.

"You are not of this clan and do not have to accept discipline from me. You can wait until Lavel comes back, but truthfully, the only thing that will change is your time of separation. Even as a guest, I cannot—will not—allow you out of the vale."

"It will be as you say, Lord."

Amray stood, and Bar followed his lead. "Go now. Pack your things tonight. Kostan will show you the way to Dierald's cottage tomorrow at sunrise." He placed his hands on Bar's shoulders and shook him gently to emphasize his point. "You will obey him, as you *would* me." Amray raised his eyebrows in amused question.

"Aye, Lord." Bar was unable to smile at the chief's mild jest but was comforted by it nonetheless.

As he pulled on his boots, awkwardly because of a lingering soreness in his right shoulder, Amray said, "Go to Sureese and let him look at your shoulder. I can see that it still pains you."

Bar wanted desperately to be alone and started automatically to argue. "It is nothing, Lord. It will—" Amray raised an eyebrow in warning. Bar caught himself midsentence. "Aye, Lord! Aye, I'm going." *I am undoubtedly a fool.* He hurried down the steps.

The result of his visit to Sureese was a massage of his shoulder with oil that burned like fire and an arm bound snugly to his body with soft strips of cloth. Sureese told him to return, before he left the next morning, for another massage and for ointment to take with him.

Tier consoled him that night with a version of his fate had he been Bani: six months of isolation instead of two weeks. It put things in perspective, but it did not help much. On the other hand, Dare gave him no sympathy at all and kept his lips pressed firmly together in disapproval, which hurt more than Bar wanted to admit.

The next morning Dare was still only speaking to Bar when it was necessary and even then only briefly. Bar shook arms with both friends. He wanted to speak to Dare, to ask him what was wrong, but could find no words.

Later, when he and Kostan arrived at the healing house, a student told him that Dare and Sureese were busy with a birth. Could Karalise treat his shoulder? He agreed and waited impatiently, pacing the wood-planked floor. *Dare and I will have to talk about his healing studies more—a birth? That is, if Dare ever talks to me again.*

"Bar?" a crisp voice asked. He looked up and stopped breathing for a moment. Karalise was Amray's daughter. They'd never been in the same place at the same time and had not met. Kostan had warned Bar that she was a poor nurse and enjoyed working with elong more than people.

She was not beautiful exactly, but she was very alive, radiant. Her shining black hair was gathered with a strip of leather high on her head, and strands escaped at her neck and cheeks. Her eyes were large and gray and her brows slightly slanted, as were most Bani's. Her little nose was straight, and her full mouth was ready to smile. She was tall for a Bani woman, five feet eight inches at least. She wore a floor-length wool skirt, a beautifully tooled black leather belt, and a white tunic shirt, much like his, tied at the neck.

Bar tried to speak normally and almost succeeded. "Aye. I was told you will treat my shoulder before I leave."

She nodded. "Come this way."

This massage did not hurt nearly as much as the first. He relaxed and teased with Karalise and Kostan until she was done. He felt better than he had for many hours, but on his way out, he saw Dare rushing to get some mats. He knew he had not been forgiven. He hesitated, but one could not interrupt a birth, and he left with a heavy heart.

His time alone had not materialized yet. He put off solitude until he would be high on a hilltop, with only sheep for company.

TAL QUA

DIERALD WAS STRONG, STERN, AND DEFINITELY not Bani. Bar was not sure who his people might be. He was six feet tall and had a muscular build, curly brown hair, and a full beard. Unlike the Bani, he wore a cream-colored tunic, breeches, and a cloak that was lined with fleece, as were his boots and gloves. He appeared to be middle-aged, though it was difficult to tell. His weathered skin was tan, and his eyes were a strange, shimmering gray. His barrel chest was massive, as were his upper arms. So might one of the early shepherd prophets have looked! Rarely did he speak, and that suited Bar perfectly.

They ate a quiet dinner of cooked grain mixed with dried fruit and fresh milk. Then both went to bed early in familiar elong hammocks. They were padded with thick mats, and there were plenty of sheepskins to keep Bar warm.

For the first two days, Dierald went out into the valley with Bar to teach him to care for the sheep. Then he allowed Bar to take a part of the flock alone. Bar was still under the shepherd's careful eye, but he was apart from him, either on a different slope or down in a valley when Dierald was above. Various predators looked at the sheep longingly—it was winter, and food was difficult to find—but with staff, bow, and knife the shepherds guarded their flocks.

Four beautiful dogs worked with Dierald: a male, a female, and two of their pups, now serious two-year-olds. Without them, Dierald could never handle so many sheep alone. The dogs were wirehairs—blond, agile, and tough. Whitey, one of the two-year-olds, adopted Bar, knowing with mysterious canine wisdom that he was new at his job and needed help. In quiet moments, Bar held, petted, and talked to the animal, absorbing into his bruised spirit the dog's warm, boisterous affection. Dogs were definitely the Maker's gift to humankind.

Beneath the vast, starry sky at night or the sun and clouds by day, Bar was alone with the powerful influences of nature. The wind, trees, animals, and sky all spoke to him of his Creator. Nature's vastness, its great age, put his own life and problems into perspective. His racing mind quieted.

Dierald himself was absorbed in a brooding quiet from which he rarely surfaced. His beautiful gray eyes could be distant or warm.

Time flowed by, filled with daily tasks, fresh air, and hard work. Before Bar had thought it possible, the two weeks were up, and it was time to return to the vale.

Bar thanked Dierald for his hospitality and then took leave of him early one morning. He walked eagerly down the rough path out of the valley. It was a cold, windy day, but the sun shone brightly. Bar was glad to be on his way and looked forward to seeing his friends. He inhaled deeply air that smelled of pine, snow, and woodsmoke. Hearing the piercing cry of a hawk, he searched the sky but could not locate the bird. The hawk's cry and the song of wind were the only sounds in the morning quiet.

Suddenly, something crashed and bounced down the steep trail. It landed at the foot of a pine near him. Startled, Bar bent to pick up the small rock and saw … booted feet! His heart slammed against his rib cage in response to his instant recognition of their pattern. They were intricately designed Basca' boots. He quickly cried, "Enemy!" *Who will hear me?*

The young prince launched a ferocious kick at the boot owner's kneecap—too late! He landed only a glancing blow. He spun right, driving himself at those who had to be behind him. He was not wrong, but they were more than prepared for his charge. He drove his fist into the stomach of the attacker on his right, but a flying kick to his left thigh knocked him off balance. One of the attackers caught his right leg, raised for a kick, and twisted it. He crashed, facedown, in the pine needles and snow.

They pinned all his limbs, and he screamed again as loudly as his position would allow. They threatened to break his arm if he made another sound; then they bound his hands tightly behind him. If no one had heard his scream, he was lost. They jerked Bar to his feet and held him upright by the neck of his cloak. They spun him around to face the owner of the boots.

"Tal—Tal qua!" he choked out in shock, breathing hard. Tal's face was rock hard, his eyes bright with suppressed anger.

"Aye, my prince," his weapons master answered bitterly, bowing slightly. "Our king has sent me after you. He wishes to have his son back."

Bar forced himself to think past the pain, fear, and shock. "You will … go to the village?" he asked thickly. Tal nodded affirmation. "Dare." Again Tal nodded.

Panic hit Bar's gut. He pleaded with his old mentor and friend, his words tumbling out hurriedly. "Tal, they are good people! Do them no harm. I will go down and get him for you—bring him back—without anyone knowing. You know I will keep my word. I have never lied to you or broken a promise."

Above all things, he did not want these men in the vale. They were not needlessly cruel, but their absolute dedication to duty was legendary. They would do whatever it took to fulfill the king's command. Visions of dead and injured Bani flashed through Bar's mind, causing him to break out in a cold sweat.

Tal's hand flashed in the sunshine as he slapped Bar. Unprepared for such a blow, Bar rocked back. Only the tight grip of the warrior holding him by his cloak kept Bar on his feet. Pain exploded through his left jaw and ear and dazed his wits. Bar was stunned.

The Basca' were a rigidly controlled people who never expressed strong emotion—to do so was considered a sign of weakness. *Why would Tal do such a thing?* Bar had loved—no, idolized was a better word—Tal qua with all his heart as a child, in spite of the man's perfect loyalty to his father. He loved him still. He thought Tal held him in strong affection also. Through a haze of pain, he shook his head and tried to think of why. *What did I say or do to cause such a reaction?*

Tal qua's barely contained fury showed in his trembling hands and tightly compressed lips. Bar forced hurt from his mind. *I have always known that Tal's loyalty to the king is as certain as death. But why is he so angry? Even his men are shocked.*

Tal reached both his powerful hands for Bar's shirt. Bar flinched and braced himself for whatever was coming; the warrior behind him held him fast. His heart was beating wildly. Tal tore his shirt to the waist and then pulled the halves off his shoulders. He stared at the triangular blue-gray scar and stumbled back, his face growing rigid. The men with him stared at the mark also and looked at Tal in amazement.

"It is true then—this story of your being marked by E Clue?" he asked blankly.

"Aye," Bar said, spitting blood on the ground. Tal stared at him for long moments; his eyes were full of confusion. Bar dared to hope. Then Tal turned quickly and ordered, "Gag him. Then take elong, bind him, and hang him up in this tree till we return."

"Tal! *No!*" Bar cried as they grabbed him. "Why? Why?" he shouted. He was throttled quickly, then gagged. He fought them, but with little hope of freeing himself. A dreaded sensation began as they hauled him up. Tal told one of the men to wait and remove the gag when Bar became ill and then follow.

Disorientation, so strong it was like a blow, slammed through Bar, causing strong nausea. He tried but could not convince his dangling feet that firm ground was beneath them. Soon—very soon—he would be unable to even think clearly. As he searched the valleys and cliffs around him, he cried out to the Maker. *Where will my help come from?*

His guard lowered him after a few minutes, removed the cloth tied around his mouth, and then raised him again and left, confident Bar would be unable to cry out. He was quite right. Bar fought a battle he knew he would lose against the growing wave of queal symptoms.

———————

The Basca' made only one mistake in their careful planning. They sent a single warrior to bind Dierald. After all, what chance did a simple shepherd have against a trained Basca'? Dierald knocked the warrior's knife from his hand with one blow from his shepherd's staff. Before the amazed young man could fathom what was happening, he was quickly knocked unconscious. Dierald bound him and left him inside his cottage—a thoughtful kindness to an enemy in the winter.

The shepherd stole quietly down the trail, guided by Bar's scream and other voices. From behind a large boulder, the shepherd watched as well as heard the scene between Bar and Tal qua. He was amazed and then filled with joy at what he heard.

Wasting no time, he stealthily climbed down a far more dangerous but shorter game trail and warned Amray about the uninvited guests and their purpose. The unthinkable happened. Basca' warriors walked into a carefully laid trap. Rarely in their long history had such a thing occurred.

Amray sent his sons and Dare to rescue Bar. The Bani chief set a careful watch on the most dangerous prisoners he had ever taken, and he sent experienced warriors to retrieve Dierald's prisoner. What were they to do with four Basca' prisoners?

By the time Kostan, Tier, and Dare reached Bar, queal had taken most of his voice and the movement in his legs, arms, and hands. They quickly lowered him and cut his bonds. Dare reached for snow and gently cleaned his face. Gratitude for release, for human touch, and for speech filled Bar.

Dazed and freezing, he whispered thickly, "Basca' warriors are going to vale! Hurry!"

Kostan assured him that no one was in danger and told him what had happened to his captors, thanks to Dierald. Bar hung on his every word, struggling to understand. He closed his eyes gratefully when their assurances convinced him that all was really well. "Thank the Maker!"

His eyes flew open. "Tier, I must talk to your father, quickly."

They helped him rise on unsteady legs and mostly carried him back to the vale. They took him to where Amray and his councillors were gathered, discussing what to do with the prisoners.

"They are almost impossible to imprison," Bar explained. His voice was barely above a whisper. "It is a matter of honor with them to continually try to escape, and frequently, they do. One will die to save the others; they will risk life and limb. They will do anything to free themselves, and now their honor is damaged by this failure. They—"

Amray held up his hand to silence Bar and said dryly, "We understand."

The council gazed at the young man in front of them in consternation. He was still unable to stand by himself—Tier and Dare held him upright— and his lip was bleeding, yet he had come to warn them as soon as he'd returned. They felt his urgency but did not know what to do. To kill in battle was one thing, but to kill defenseless men was unthinkable. Yet they had no prison, no way to hold the Basca'. Old Neaom asked Bar if he had any thoughts on the subject.

Bar, his voice barely audible, said decisively, "For now, give them di'ak, the herb you gave me for queal. Keep them apart, bound and guarded at all times, even while eating, sleeping, or relieving themselves. That will give us time to think."

"A good idea. We will do so. Now go see to your injuries," Amray said.

Dare and Tier took Bar to the healing house immediately. On the way there, he slumped in exhaustion, and Dare carried him the rest of the way.

Dare and Tier helped Bar bathe and dress in clean clothing. Sureese gently probed the swelling bruise on his thigh, which he endured with gritted teeth. The healer packed it with snow but otherwise left it alone. After cleaning his cut lip, Sureese said, "Sleep now," and dropped a woven screen from the ceiling to give him some privacy. Bar knew no more until the next morning, though Sureese removed the snow pack and checked on him twice during the night.

After breakfast, Bar felt like a new human being. He found Dare, and they went to a quiet corner in the hall. "Tell me what is wrong," he said softly.

Dare frowned and looked at his hands for a few moments. "I'm not sure I understand exactly myself, but I am really angry." He sighed and sat on one of the benches. After a pause, he said, "I would like to shake you and make you listen to me, but you're always too banged up to take any more, so I don't do it or say anything. Do you realize how many times I have bandaged you and sewn up cuts? And then you run into danger, again! Against orders! I knew! I knew you were going to do it. I thought, *He wouldn't!* But you did—and I was too late to stop you."

"Since when are you my keeper?" Bar asked hotly, in spite of his good intentions to remain calm.

"Since the beginning! Since Starfire put this mark on me and I agreed to be part of the prophecy!" Dare was really angry; his eyes were blazing, and his face was flushed with color. "I think my whole job in this, whatever it is, is keeping you in one piece—and it's not easy! Who can predict the crazy things you're going to do?" Dare's voice had gradually gotten louder, and people were turning to stare at them with curiosity. Dare clenched his fists.

Hanging on to his temper, Bar made an effort to speak quietly. "Great Gant, Dare, you are not responsible for me or what I do! I am! Did Starfire say anything to indicate that you are my protector? No! I don't need a nursemaid! You are younger than I am, and I can take care of myself— well"—he grinned at this obvious untruth—"most of the time anyway." Dare's lip quirked, but he did not smile.

"Bar!" a breathless Kostan cried as he hurried up to them. "I've been looking for you. Father wants you to come immediately to the taque where they are holding Tal, the one that belongs to Akeel. I'll show you the way. He wants you too, Dare."

"What now?" Bar asked, exasperated. He and Dare looked at each other anxiously and hurried after Kostan.

———❦———

Dare and Bar looked at Amray in astonishment. "He said what?" Bar asked faintly.

"He wants to talk to you. He pleaded with his guard not to force any more of the drug down him until he had talked to both of us. From what you have told me, he is an honest man, so I agreed and sent for you. I want Dare to be with us since he is part of this thing too. Better he hear whatever Tal has to say firsthand. Do you have any idea what this is about?"

"No, Lord, none."

They entered the dark taque and saw Tal sitting on his hammock, slumped over, with his head held in his hands. His hands and feet were bound, yet a guard still stood by watching him closely. Tal tried to stand when he sensed their presence but could not and sat back down weakly. Bar could sympathize; he remembered the aftereffects of di'ak.

"We are here to listen," Amray said simply.

"Alati, Lord, for the opportunity," Tal replied with a respectful, though seated, bow. "I do not quite know how to begin. My thoughts are disordered. Please bear with me. Ask any questions you like, if I'm not making sense."

At first he spoke to Amray and Dare. "I have known the prince since he was six. I watched him grow and held him in strong affection, but I was constrained to obey the king in all things, even when they were not in Bar's best interest." For a moment Tal could not go on, but then he spoke again softly. "King Bardock holds a very important Basca' child. She's no longer a child really—she is Bar's age." Tal swallowed hard and closed his eyes.

Dare and Bar looked at each other in amazement. Amray handed a cup of water to Tal, who held it awkwardly in his bound hands and gratefully took a long drink. He said shakily, "She is important to our people because her birth was predicted long ago. We believe"—his voice grew stronger— "she will save a person's life who is important to the prophecy. When she was born, one of our elders prophesied this. The Basca' have a different heritage than the Bani, but we know of the prophecy and follow the Maker. It seems that only those tribes who long ago split away from the rest still do. Bardock knows we will do anything to preserve her life. Once a year we may see her, and then she is taken back to wherever they hide her. They do this so that we may know she is well and unharmed."

Tal's gaze shifted to Bar. "It was I, Bar, who carried you to your room that night after Bardock left you hanging in the training room. No one ever knew what I did. After knocking on your servant's door and waking him, I told him you needed help and then left quickly. It was dark, and he never saw me. When the woman, one of your personal servants named Ala, came to me, I almost did not get up and come for you. I knew what it meant if your father found out—if my own people found out! I have never been sorry for doing it, though."

He closed his eyes again for a few moments. "We have all heard the rumors of E Clue marking you—the whole city of Feisan has heard them. By now I suspect the whole island knows! When the Blackrobes' raid on the monastery failed to catch you, your father sent us after you. My confusion and guilt were—are—terrible. How could I protect Ellarann, the Basca' hostage, at your expense, if you were a part of the prophecy also? That is why I was so angry and slapped you. I was—am—betraying my people to even think of not taking you back. The king may kill her! Yet I am no longer sure he will not kill *you*. He has grown more cold and … strange. Even if he did not kill you, I could not bear to think what he might do. I was torn continually between you and El. When I saw the mark and knew beyond doubt that you are the Maker's chosen one, I knew I had to let go of

Ellarann, but I could not. I forced myself to go through with our plan. The others were as shaken as I. We did not know which part of the prophecy to protect. Then we were captured."

He looked intently at Amray. "I can no longer serve Bardock. I must leave our Basca' child in the Creator's hands and pray the king will not harm her. I do not know what you will advise, but"—he looked at Bar—"I will serve my prince if he will have me. If not, my men and I must disappear. It is my hope that if the king thinks we died in our search, he will not take revenge on the Basca' hostage. Our clan will send four more men to serve him and then mourn our deaths. I do not know why you should believe me, yet you know, Bar, that though I have done many things I am not proud of, I do not lie." Tal stopped abruptly. He was pale and looked sick.

Amray sent Naidra, Akeel's wife, for food and tea. He poked up the fire and put on more coal. "Tal, do you give me your word that you'll not try to escape if I cut your bonds?"

"Aye, Lord, I do," Tal answered steadily.

Dazed, Bar sat down near the fire and stared at his old weapons master. Dare's eyes were hard and suspicious, and he stood, feet apart, staring at Tal also. Amray's knife flashed in the fire's glow as he cut Tal's bonds. He then chafed the man's swollen hands. Tal bowed his thanks; he could not trust his voice. Amray had that effect on people. The Bani chief evidently accepted Tal's story, at least enough to free his hands and feet.

"Why was it necessary to tie Bar up in a tree?" Dare asked harshly. His eyes glittered with anger, and his tone startled both Amray and Bar. "Perhaps your 'difficult decision' might account for your other actions but not that one."

Tal nodded in understanding but did not answer; he just stared at the floor.

Amray said, "I, too, think you must tell us why you did this. You knew full well how it would affect him—by your own admission."

Tal looked away, obviously uncomfortable with either the question or the answer. He said softly, "The king ordered it. A queal-sick prince does not try to escape and is disposed to answer questions." He looked directly at Bar. "He badly wants to know who is helping you. It has finally entered his stubborn, proud brain that there is an organization out there somewhere working against him. He has realized that no individual or group of individuals could keep escaping him, as you have done, without well-organized help."

Bar willed himself not to care, not to feel the hurt. It didn't work. He realized that Tal had not wanted to tell him for that very reason.

No matter how you looked at it, this information was disturbing. The underground needed to remain an insubstantial rumor—something that sounded hopeful to the people but probably was not true. If the king believed they existed and threw all his considerable power into finding them, he would, in time, certainly find them.

After a great deal of time and discussion, the council decided to free the Basca' warriors if they each took an oath of loyalty to Bar. The Bani council now knew who he was, of course, because there was no explaining the story without revealing Bar's identity. In fact, everyone in the vale knew. Two of the Basca' warriors, Tage and Steri, asked to stay with the Bani and help them in their fight to remain hidden from the king. Both had families and did not want to go any farther from them than they already were. Neither knew when he might be able to return to his home.

The other two, Tal and Oster, elected to go with Bardon and Dare to Glidden Mountain when and if Lavel returned. Glidden Mountain, home of the underground, was on the other side of the island from Feisan, across a difficult mountain range, and therefore safer. They all needed time to plan and to reconsider. Tal had given them invaluable information concerning events in Feisan and Casterray. He'd also told them of the connection between Blalock, creator of the braith, and Draville, Choack's priest, an overwhelmingly pernicious combination.

Oster, a young man with no family of his own, and Tal asked to become Dare and Bar's bodyguards. Bar groaned inwardly. That would make three nursemaids! He knew that, in spite of their conversation, Dare would continue to look out for him.

On a snowy winter afternoon, in front of the council, Tal qua and his men knelt on one knee before Bar. They swore their oath of loyalty with such fervor that they brought tears to the young prince's eyes. He in turn promised to treat each man with fairness and respect. Bar placed his hands on Tal's head, as he had the other three Basca', in acceptance of his oath and asked the Maker's blessing on him. He noticed gray hair among the black and felt compassion for this man who had spent so many years of his adult life away from his people—forced to serve a king he watched become more and more evil.

A Rescue

Dare, Bar and everyone in the vale waited and waited. After two weeks, there was still no word from Lavel, and everyone was worried. Bar had endured the vale for about as long as he thought possible. He desperately wanted to be out in the open—hunting on a horse with the wind in his face. He had endured people. He had endured training on every conceivable subject. He had been patient. But a desperate desire to move on was growing in him.

To the prince's surprise, Dare was content in the vale. He was learning so much from Sureese and from Tal qua and his warriors that he was hardly aware of time passing. Bar realized that among the Bani, Dare was enjoying a sense of belonging—of family—for the first time in many years.

Bar caught Amray's sharp, watchful gaze resting on him many times, and he knew that the chief sensed his restlessness. He grinned at him sourly, reassuringly. Not for any reason would he break his promise to stay in the vale. Amray assigned him to watch duty with the lookouts placed on the cliffs, and it helped a little. He could see freedom, and he was alone. Bar smiled to himself as he thought of the seemingly tough Bani leader, who softened his discipline to help Bar endure it. The weather had warmed, which made the deep snow heavy and slushy.

On his fourth day of watch duty, as he slipped and slid to his high vantage point among the rocks, he heard distinctive birdcalls. Their message excited him: the scout out on Cracked Rock had seen a small group traveling northwest. The sentry on duty carried the message back to Amray, knowing he would want to hear it right away. The group was fast approaching Bar's position, and he waited for instructions. Amray and three warriors appeared thirty minutes later, breathing hard from the steep, slippery climb. Sounding like a wild snow goose, Amray told the scout who had first spotted the group to wait and not reveal himself.

After thirty long minutes, they watched two men, each leading a horse, stumble through the snow. One horse was carrying supplies and the other a huge man. This man was tied to his mount and appeared to be dazed and weak. Bar recognized Lavel and Balful, and surely the large man on the horse was Devon. Amray, Bar, and two of the warriors went down to greet them, leaving the third to watch. Amray ordered the warrior left behind to keep a sharp watch for anyone or any creatures that might be following the small party. They greeted the travelers quietly but with great relief and joy and took them back to the vale as quickly as possible in the slushy snow.

A congenial group sat around Amray's firepit that evening. Lavel and Balful looked rested after a day of sleep and good food. Devon was pale but more comfortable after spending the day in the healing house with Sureese. They ate a fine meal, and as Tier served them hot tea in pottery cups, Lavel began to tell them what had happened to him and Balful.

"After killing the two tipeeke the Blackrobes left behind, we followed their party, but not too closely. They returned directly to Saint Fauver's. The bridge across the chasm had already been repaired, and the tipeeke crossed that thing without any urging or a backward look. The monastery had been burned, its windows broken. Much of the ancient building was stone that was now scarred by fire and smoke. The Blackrobes we were following led us to a troop of the king's guard that was camped nearby. Evidently the soldiers were waiting for their return. They had put up large tents and a rope corral for their horses, which indicated to me that they were prepared to stay awhile.

"We crept close to the campfires that night and listened to their conversation. They must have expected no trouble, because the tipeeke were all piled in a mound, sound asleep, a few hundred feet away from the camp—and downwind thankfully. There were only two sentries, and they were watching the road, so we were able to get quite close.

"From their conversation, we realized that there were other search parties still out. That gave us quite a scare, as you can imagine, and we began watching our backs, which we had not done before—had not thought to do. They said many interesting things, but of main interest to us was their discussion of a troop that had left the day before. This troop was escorting all the monks of Saint Fauver's back to Feisan for questioning. We were understandably shocked by this news and withdrew to the woods to talk—to try to decide what to do. The soldiers we listened to were going to stay in their camp and wait for the other search parties to return. Though Balful and I did not want tipeeke and Blackrobes at our backs, we decided to follow the road to Feisan, in the hope that we could catch up with Devon and his brothers. We wanted to search what was left of the monastery at daylight, but it was too well guarded. We had to give up that idea and go on. The trail was easy to follow—wide and messy. Among the footprints and hoofprints, there were items in the snow—sandals and articles of clothing—that kind of thing.

"We pushed harder, fearing for their lives. Perhaps to preserve their prisoners' health and get them to Feisan faster, the soldiers commandeered some wagons from local farmers. We came on them in the middle of the third day.

"There were three wagons with about fifteen brothers in each. Twenty mounted soldiers with their captain guarded them, but little guarding was needed." Lavel's voice grew hard, and he stared into the fire as he saw the scene again. "Many had been hurt in the assault on the monastery. They had bandaged each other's wounds and burns as well as they were able. All were weak with cold, pain, hunger, and rough treatment. At first I could not find Devon, and I feared that he was not with the group. Later, we realized he was lying down in one of the wagons with the brothers gathered around him to keep him warm."

He grinned at their serious faces and said, "To make this very long story somewhat shorter, that night we stole two of the soldiers' horses and went ahead of the troop to the outskirts of Feisan. I have some, er, friends there. It took us all that day to gather men, horses, and supplies. We laid careful plans and started back down the road with our scouts far ahead of us. The scouts found their camp the next day. That night, while they slept, we overcame their sentries and captured those in the camp. While my friends bound and blindfolded the rest of the soldiers, Balful and I released the monks. They changed quickly out of their habits and into the work clothes we'd brought for them. At our urging, they mounted the soldiers' horses, and my folk took them into Feisan to hide them. Eventually they will be given new identities. Thank the Maker it is easier to get into Feisan than out of it. The soldiers, I'm sure, were able to free themselves in time and return to the city on foot. They saw none of us and will not be able to describe any of our party to the king. That is the good news. There is also bad news."

He looked at Devon painfully, but Devon shook his head and said, "You tell them."

Lavel nodded and continued, looking at Bar, "The soldiers who captured the monks carried a special drug with them. They worked Devon over, and when he still refused to answer their questions, they forced it down him." Bar had experienced that drug and knew with icy clarity what Lavel was going to say.

"They asked Devon if the two new novitiates were Dare and Bardon, and after a time, when the drug had taken full effect, he said aye. By the Maker's favor, there are some questions the captain was not informed enough to ask. That is why he was taking the whole population of the monastery back to Feisan—to the king and Draville. The captain and Blackrobes with him now know there is an underground, who I am, and that we had three Bani guides. Devon did not know the location of Glimmervale, thank heaven, but he knew it existed—and now, they know that also."

Lavel looked at Amray with distress in his eyes. "I am sorry, Amray. You were a forgotten people—an intangible myth—and now you are a reality. Surely the king will seek you with all the resources at his disposal."

Amray's face was pale but calm. He said, "It is not to be expected that our release from Bardock and his parasites will cost us nothing or that we could stay a secret forever."

Calley, who sat next to Amray, had listened intently to the whole tale. She smiled stiffly at Devon, understanding written plainly on her face. "Do not think we blame you. Do not fear for us. The Maker has always protected us because we are faithful and have kept his word. He will continue to do so." Devon was amazed; he bowed his head in grateful acknowledgment of her kindness and faith.

Bar, too, reassured him. "I have experienced re-al. If you are hungry and weakened, it works faster, but it always, *always* works in time. There is nothing you could have done to prevent what happened."

Surprised and skeptical, Devon said, "*You've* experienced re-al? How can that be?"

Bardon looked away. "It doesn't matter; just believe I know what I am saying." Devon stared at him for a few long moments but did not press the issue. Bar quickly suppressed the flooding unpleasant memories.

Lavel began making immediate plans to leave the vale. He would take Bar, Dare, Tal qua, and Oster with him. It took him some time to accept the fact that two of the dreaded Basca' were going with them. He had finally agreed to take them, but he was still uncomfortable and suspicious. The two warriors would know too many underground secrets, far too many! Lavel's superiors would be furious that he shared confidential information with them without the council's approval. Lavel did not blame the council. Lives were at stake—the underground itself was at stake—but he could not refuse the Basca', as he had been outvoted.

Devon's back was healing from the scourging the Blackrobes had inflicted to make him talk, but he was far from well. The abbot of St. Fauver's was bruised and battered as a result of his attempts to protect the monks, from both the soldiers' and tipeeke's brutal attack. Injured though he was, he wanted to go to Glidden with Lavel. The harassed leader finally agreed. He felt the whole mission was growing out of his control.

The vale was filled with activity for the next two days, and finally their party was ready to go. The two large horses that Lavel had stolen from the soldiers served as his and Devon's mounts. They were the only animals available that were large enough to carry the brothers. The Bani gave the rest of the party their own tough mountain ponies. Anything the Bani could think of that the fugitives might need was carefully packed on men or horses. They thought it crazy to travel in the winter but understood Lavel's and Bar's certainty that they must hurry and get to the safety of

Glidden. Glidden's leader needed to know what was happening in Feisan and elsewhere on their island home.

The small group left quietly early the next morning. The air was still and frigid as the small party said goodbye to their Bani friends in the darkness. Amray watched them leave with a heavy heart. Against all wisdom, against all sanity, he had allowed his firstborn to go with them.

DEVIL'S GATE

CONSCIOUS THAT THERE WERE AT LEAST TWO search parties of tipeeke and Blackrobes that could be anywhere, the fugitives traveled with extreme caution. When they needed to cross large, bare valleys or meadows, they did so at night. There was no way to hide the tracks of seven men and nine horses in the deep snow, but with their combined skills they made it as difficult as possible for anyone tracking them. They stayed among the trees and on rocky ground when possible, carefully skirting bare meadows and slopes.

Traveling north and east steadily, they headed for a pass on Mount Riinar that Lavel hoped would be open in spite of the snow. The pass was called Devil's Gate because of its shape and the red glow it framed in the sky as one approached it. Near a live volcano, it was a pass most travelers avoided, but using this pass was a necessary risk to those who chose to travel in the second month of winter. They would have to select one of the two trails up Mount Riinar: either the northern, difficult path or the northeastern trail, which was easier to climb but took longer. Both paths led to Devil's Gate.

After an uneventful three days on the trail, they developed a routine, and everyone took different responsibilities. Lavel led the group with relaxed confidence and quiet authority. He had regained his composure once they were on the trail and out of the vale. With years of experience behind him, Lavel knew it was unwise to be taking Tal or Oster, whom he did not trust. It made no more sense to take Devon, who was still weak and sick, or

Tierray, who was next in line to lead the Bani. Once he had been convinced and outvoted, he'd accepted the additions to their party with equanimity.

Devon was their cook and organized an efficient camp routine, but because of his injuries, he tired easily. They all tried to help him when they could find the time. His calm disposition and steady good humor were important assets to their company. Tal and Oster—Os, for short—were their scouts and hunters. They also tended the horses, though everyone took basic care of his own mount. Tier and Bar helped Tal and Oster, often taking night watches in trees and atop rocks. Dare did much the same but added healer to his list. Devon made sure that cook's helper, a task they all really, really hated, was shared equally.

Their fourth day out of Glimmervale was a difficult one from the beginning. The heavy overcast deepened and lowered, then blanketed them with thickly falling snow. Immense flakes fell on their morn meal fire and came close to putting the flames out. Pristine white covered their food, clothing, blankets—everything—so quickly that they were compelled to stuff down their food and break camp quickly, while they could still find their equipment. The path that day was rocky and gradually climbed up toward the base of Mount Riinar. It was difficult to find the trail, much less see all the obstacles in their way under the thick cover of snow. Sounds were muffled, and only a darkening at the end of the day told them the time. Occasionally the snow would let up for a few moments, and they could see the towering cliffs they were approaching but never the tops of the mountains, which were entirely hidden from view. They stopped at the base of a wall of perpendicular rock, which gave them some protection from the snow, and made a hurried camp. Trusting that the thick curtain of white would hide a fire from their enemies, they built a small, hot blaze against the rock face. Blackened rocks and ashes were evidence that someone before them had done the same.

They good-naturedly jostled each other to get a place close to the fire and absorb its heat. Slowly the warmth began to thaw their cold bodies and to dry their damp clothes. As they ate Devon's stew in the shifting firelight, they heard a muffled howling in the distance, a howling that sounded like a mountain cat.

The horses neighed and shifted nervously, twitching their ears. The company took particular care of their mounts, rubbing them down carefully and giving them extra grain. It had been a difficult day of climbing through deep snow, and the animals were tired. Tal and Os went among them stroking and talking softly, trying to ease their anxiety. Even after the horses settled down, talk around the fire was subdued. Each man's eyes vainly tried to penetrate the silently falling snow.

At Lavel's order, Bar and Os took the first watch. Lavel and Tal quietly sipped their tea, but their every sense was alert. They were listening and watching for trouble. Bar went south of camp, and Os went west. The young Basca' climbed a huge boulder that overlooked the trail they had just climbed and the forested slopes to the north of them, neither of which he could see very often. Bar could find no such natural observation point and ended up climbing a spruce. *An army could march through here fifty feet away, and I'd never see them. All I can see is snow!*

While Os and Bar started their watch, the rest built a lean-to against the cliff with limbs they cut from the fir and pine around them. Then they threw one of their elong-coated tarps over the top and snugged it down with rope. It made a fine, fragrant shelter. Devon said dryly, "It's worth the hard work. We will need it, if we don't want to wake up in the morning with two feet of snow on top of us."

At first, the cold and wetness of the falling snow helped Bar stay awake, but after a time, the quiet and his inability to see much made him drowsy. *This is like being in a cocoon—a cold cocoon,* he thought miserably as his head fell forward for the third time and jerked him awake. He decided to climb down and walk around rather than fall asleep at his post. The thick branches over his head broke up the falling snow. They gave him better visibility on the ground than he had from his perch in the tree, still not good but better.

Out of the corner of his eye, Bar caught movement, fleeting but swift, of something impossibly large and sleek. All traces of drowsiness vanished. Piercing fear brought his every sense awake and made his heart pound. A scream almost escaped him, but he stifled it to a small, desperate sound. The thought of a mountain cat raced through his mind as he searched the blinding snow and strained every nerve to listen for sounds that would tell him where it was. He quietly drew an arrow from his quiver and placed it on the string. Bending his bow in readiness, he turned in a cautious circle.

Bar bit back a scream. Braith! There were two giant apparitions, breathing softly, teeth bared in threatening snarls, directly in front of him. Their red eyes gleamed with malice. The one on the right slunk a few steps closer.

How can braith be here? His stunned brain tried to absorb the fact that they were real, whether it made sense or not. As he opened his mouth to scream for help, the beast approaching him snarled a low and menacing warning. He gasped in apprehension and backed slowly away from it. At a steady pace, they herded Bar where they wanted him to go. He could think of no way to outsmart them. The slightest move of his hands elicited a fierce warning. He had no doubt they would attack if he did not do as they wished. Even through his numb dread, he marveled again, as he had the first time he'd fought them, at their intelligence.

Suddenly, Bar backed out of the trees into an open meadow. Before he could think, he found himself only a few feet from Blackrobes sitting around a campfire. They jumped up in alarm when they saw him, for he was still holding his bow and arrow. They thought he was threatening them until they saw the braith behind him.

"Good work, my brothers, good work indeed!" a man said softly. Then he rose slowly to his feet. He was dressed in black, but there was no emblem on his long robe. His hood hid his face, and an oak ring glowed on his finger. He wore an air of command, of power, like a cloak. Bar instinctively shrank back from him. *This is the braith's master, the legendary Blalock! The braith would obey only their creator.*

He came slowly forward until he stood directly in front of Bar, who was ready to bolt, braith or no. As if they read his intention, two of the Blackrobes, whose faces he also could not see, grabbed him roughly by either arm. In spite of the temperature, Bar started to sweat and fought to stay calm.

"We have caught the royal hawk before we even knew the birds were in our trap. This blasted snow hides everything! We took a chance, my friend, that your party would come this way. Our other group watches the lower trail up Riinar."

With these words, Bar realized that they had not been followed. The Blackrobes and Blalock had come here and waited, who knew how long, on the chance he and the others would come this way. *How did they guess—or did they know—that we would flee over the mountains? Does he have spies everywhere watching for us?* He knew the answer was yes.

In the fire's flickering light, Bar caught glimpses of long white hair, a high forehead, and light eyes—a noble face was hidden in the hood. The voice sounded deep, reasonable, and even hypnotic. "Now, my brave hawk, you must tell us where your companions are camped and which trail they intend to use, though I think we know that now." Bar hardened his resolve and said nothing. "There are many other questions I have for you—many, many."

Bar was thinking fast. *Evidently, the braith were sent to search for us, but when they found only me, they brought me back. There is still a chance for the others if I don't talk. Blalock has not sent the beasts back out—not yet anyway.*

"Gal-re, bring me the vial in my leather case—the small green one on the bottom."

Bar stiffened. *More re-al? The stuff is expensive—hard to come by even for a sage connected to Choack.* As he looked at this man, he realized that he might be, probably was, speaking with the creator of the strange concoction.

"Well, my prince, you can take this the easy way, or we can force it down you. It is your choice." The eyes within the dark hood glittered. Bar knew that he, like Devon, would betray everything he had learned, everyone he knew, to this man, unless he could think of something, anything, to stall. Every minute he distracted Blalock gave him that much more time to be rescued.

With a disarming smile—Bar could be charming when he chose—he said, "You don't need to give me re-al. I will tell you everything you want to know without the drug."

He talked and talked, but Blalock was cunning and soon realized that it was a ruse. He was learning nothing new from his young prisoner.

"Enough!" he said harshly. Anger and the threat of violence were in his voice. As he unstopped the small green bottle, Bar clenched his jaw. "Ah, the hard way I see. Well, I suspected as much." Bar fought them with all his strength and skill, but in the end, it was useless—there were too many of them. He inflicted some damage on the Blackrobes; they inflicted only a little on him, because Blalock restrained them. Having immobilized each limb by holding him spread on the ground, they cut off his air. He struggled against their grasping hands and weight, but darkness covered his vision. As unconsciousness took him, he gasped for air, and they poured the contents of the bottle down his throat. He choked and coughed, but most of it ended up in his stomach. They carried him into their master's tent and laid him on furs near the brazier in the middle.

Dazed, he found he couldn't rise to flee. A fire began to burn in his blood, and he continued to sweat, though he felt very cold. His limbs were too heavy to lift. *Maker, keep my mouth shut—let them learn nothing from me! Warn the others.* Bar fought desperately to stay lucid, but the re-al took more and more of him. There was no real pain, but he groaned in frustration.

Later, a dark figure bent over him. "Let us begin, Gal-re. I think he's ready." Perhaps Bar's warm dinner and tea slowed down the drug's effects, or perhaps the braith's master was too eager and did not wait long enough. Whatever the reason, though Bardon talked and talked, he was able to control most of what he said. He retained a small part of his will—his mind—at first.

Then confusion started to rule. *What did I just say?* Bar was bewildered. *Who is this I'm talking to? Hang on—hang on, you're losing it. Enemy mustn't learn ... learn what? I've forgotten. Enemy! But who? So hot—need to get up and get out of here.*

"Let me go! Let me go!" he yelled desperately, but his movements were uncoordinated, slow and totally ineffective.

Meanwhile, back at camp, Tal noticed that the ponies and horses were edgy again. He stopped his companions' grumbling and building with a raised hand and ordered, "Listen!" He made a deep cry like a snow owl. Os answered him immediately, but no answer came from Bar, who was south and west of the camp. Tal tried again, and still only Os answered him. Tal sent a call to Os that meant "Stay. Possible trouble." He looked to Lavel for orders; his body language communicated tight control. He was used to giving the orders, not following them.

Lavel's dark eyes were puzzled. "Tal, take Dare and Devon and search for Bar. Do not go too far without telling me. Tier and I will stay here and guard the camp."

"Aye, sir." Tal nodded and lit a torch from their supplies by jabbing it in the fire. Dare quickly grabbed his pack and slung it over his shoulder.

The thick snow swallowed up the glow of their flickering torch as the trio disappeared into the forest. Devon and Dare had their bows strung and ready. Devon found the braith's tracks and called Tal and Dare. "Tal," Devon whispered in shock, "what cat could make tracks this size? These animals are at least seven feet long!" Tal walked to a bush nearby and found a snag of white hair. He showed it to them with a puzzled frown.

Dare remembered the braith, and as unreasonable as it seemed, he knew what creatures had left these tracks. "It's the braith," he said firmly, his eyes glittering with fear for Bardon. *One sixteen-year-old against two huge cats … very bad odds.*

Tal's frown deepened. "Are the braith real?"

"Very," Dare answered impatiently, "and I have fought them. Arrows have little or no effect on them, unless driven into their chest by a longbow. If you get close enough to use a knife, you are in range of their claws and teeth. We do not have time to make a spear, and it would take many spears to stop two braith. I have poison Sureese gave me that we can put on our arrowheads. It is fast acting and I think our best chance."

Tal nodded. "Let's give this poison a try."

They smeared the greasy substance from Dare's pack onto four arrowheads. Then Tal pushed the torch into deep snow to put it out. Bows ready, they quickly followed the tracks, watching and listening for the braith. It was dark and difficult to see in the constant fall of smothering snow, but they could not chance a torch. They smelled the campfire before they saw its glow. They needed to find the cats before the cats found them. If the animals located them first, the noise of the altercation would alert the whole camp, and they did not want that. They also might not survive the encounter.

Dare shinnied up a tree quickly. In the dense snow, he could see little: just the trees around him and the faint glow of the campfire. He almost started down again, but a sudden shift of wind whirled the snow away. For a moment, he could see the campsite. There was a large tent, dark-robed figures around a blazing wood fire, and two large cats nearby, ruddy-colored in the fire's glow. The braith had not been sent out again. *Praise the Maker! This gives us a chance.*

Dare knew they would have to move quickly and take advantage of this unbelievable opportunity. In a few minutes, the cats could be back out in the thick snow, and then they would be invisible. Their white color and their heightened sense of smell and hearing would give the braith all the advantage. He scrambled down the pine, his heart pounding with fear that they wouldn't be quick enough. The three made their plans in hurried whispers. Devon was not as good a shot as Dare or Tal, so they gave him the task of scattering the horses.

When Devon was in place near the enemies' mounts, he hooted softly like an owl. At this sign from the large monk, Tal and Dare put two poisoned arrows in each braith. Still shooting from their cover in the trees, they also shot normal arrows into the small group of men. Panic broke loose in the enemies' camp and increased when Devon freed the Blackrobes' horses. He slapped and screamed at them to make them scatter. Then he joined Dare and Tal at the campfire. His two companions still had their bows drawn, threatening both the uninjured and wounded Blackrobes, who stood in a cowed group. The large monk tied them up with their own rope and gagged them.

Only a few minutes had passed, but they had made a great deal of noise. "I do not understand why there are so few men. Where are the soldiers?" Tal asked with disquiet.

"Tal, there were many tracks near the horses, some of them tipeeke. Soldiers and tipeeke may be out searching for us. They may have missed our passing in the heavy snow. We must hurry before they return," Devon whispered.

Tal stood guard outside the large tent while Devon and Dare slipped inside. After a few heart-pounding minutes as watchman, the Basca' urged Devon and Dare to greater speed. This rescue was going too smoothly. The camp seemed virtually unguarded, and not one of their enemies had raised a weapon or strung a bow. The braith had died quickly but with furious roars as they'd tried to leap after their attackers. Those roars worried Tal qua.

Inside the tent, Bar lay in confusion. The dark figures near the fire had turned, shouted to one another, and then left. After their departure, someone burst into the tent and called his name urgently. "Bar!"

Is that someone I know? So hot. Also kind of sick feeling, truth be told.

Someone shook him. "Bar, Bar, are you all right?"

"Aye," he answered. "All right, but so hot."

Another voice said, "That would be the drug; it did that to me too. Dare, we must get him out of here. I'll carry him. Let's get back to our camp. I don't like this."

While Tal waited outside the tent, he searched for movement in the woods or from any of the bound captives around the fire. He thought he saw a shadow near the woods and whirled in that direction. At that moment, Dare and Devon came out of the tent. Thank the Maker, Devon carried a dazed and weak Bardon.

"They have used re-al on him, Tal. He is absolutely under re-al's control and making no sense. We have to assume that they could know everything he knows."

"How do you know its re-al?"

"I remember its smell—its effects." Devon spoke with conviction. They all stared at each other for a few seconds as the implications sank in.

"Were there men in the tent?"

"One at least, maybe more. They or he slashed the canvas and slipped out the back when we entered. I couldn't be sure of their number in the dim light." He eased the burden in his arms to a more comfortable position.

Tal looked at Devon and Dare intently for a few moments, then said, "Back to camp with you both. Be prepared to move when I get back. I'm going to stay for a few minutes. Go, now!"

Devon eyed Tal sternly, a stubborn look about his mouth. He was not used to taking orders any more than Tal was, and he did not want to leave the Basca' behind. However, as Bar twisted and mumbled in his arms, he realized there was no time for discussion, and he agreed.

Devon and Dare went back to their camp as swiftly as they could in the deep snow. Dare grinned, in spite of their serious situation, and chuckled at a private joke. *This expedition has far too many captains and not enough soldiers. There's likely to be one unbelievable explosion before it's all over. I hope I'm there to see it!* On this unholy note, he focused on keeping up with Devon, who was outdistancing him, burden or no.

Tal searched for tracks at the back of the tent. He found them and followed the deep indentations to the edge of the wood. *This is the spot where I saw a shadow.* Looking at the footprints longingly, he hesitated a moment but decided to go back to the fire. There were at least two sets of tracks, but there was no time to follow them. Three of the Blackrobes were injured from arrow wounds in the initial attack. None of the injuries were serious. The men were all securely bound. Devon had pulled their deep hoods down over their faces so they could not see anything. Tal took their weapons and a satchel he found and put the fire out quickly with the contents of the kettle hanging over it. He melted into the woods and stole carefully back to camp. The Basca' warrior was fully conscious of the danger represented by the men who got away.

Tal approached his own camp cautiously, whistling his presence before he went in. In spite of the signal, he faced many armed bows. Their caution pleased him greatly. When his friends recognized him, they lowered their weapons in relief. The fire was out, and they were ready to move.

"How is Bar?" he asked quietly.

Lavel answered, "Out of his head and babbling."

Tal nodded and told them what he'd discovered. Then he said, "I don't think any of the Blackrobes will find their horses and follow us before morning unless someone frees them, but the men who got away concern me. If I were them, I would go back to camp, free my companions, and then look for their their scattered horses, and the soldiers, and tipeeke." After thinking for a few minutes, Tal added, "If they find the other members of their group quickly, it is possible, even likely, that they will come for us tonight."

"What if there are soldiers waiting for us at the top?" Dare asked. They all stared at him.

Lavel said, "Bar told us that Blalock was waiting for us here, knowing that this pass is one of the few that remain open in winter."

Without torch or fire, each of them appeared to the other like a dark shadow, but they could see Tal stiffen at Lavel's words. "You have questioned him?" he asked.

"Aye. He said one group was waiting here for us, and there are evidently others who wait at the northeastern trailhead," Lavel answered. "How can we travel at night, with no moon or torches, up a steep mountain path into what may be—what probably is—a trap?" Lavel asked, mostly to himself. "If they are up there, Blalock may be able to signal them. We will be caught between the two forces!"

"Well," Tal said grimly, "there is only one way to find out. I will take Oster and go up the trail and see, while you come more slowly behind."

"Take me, sir," Tier said. "Oster has been sitting on a rock for the last few hours and is undoubtedly frozen and tired."

"No thank you, young fire-eater. Os and I know each other well, and *this* night, it may be important that we do. But I thank you for the offer." Tier could not be offended; Tal was right as well as courteous.

It seemed a poor plan, dangerous on all sides, yet no one could think of a better one. Certainly, no one wanted to go back down into the valley, where enemies might also wait. If only they knew where their enemies were, what they planned, and how much they knew.

Os and Tal disappeared into the darkness and falling snow on the trail above them. Devon wrapped the restless prince in blankets and put him in Lavel's arms. Bar could not sit a horse for any length of time or remember to be quiet. Devon led his horse and walked ahead of them, calling back soft directions. Before long, Lavel's back muscles were cramped and aching from holding Bar, so he and Devon changed places. Their progress was slow and painstaking. They rounded boulders and watched for invisible holes with burning eyes. Dare walked at the end of the line, his vision blurred from fatigue. He was cold and longed to sleep. In front of him, he could see Tier slumped in the saddle and knew he must be feeling the same.

Back at the edge of the fugitives' deserted camp, a tipeeke crept closer and closer. When he discovered that his prey had fled, he threw back his head and howled in frustration and fury. Even the thick snow could not muffle the hideous, screeching sound that only an enraged tipeeke could make. His fellows slunk out of the trees and shrieked with him till their horrible noise filled the night.

Blalock strode out of the forest and cried with restrained fury, "Silence! Silence, you filthy beasts!"

"You'll never teach them to be quiet on the scent, my lord, never. It's just not in their nature," a Blackrobe named Krasa said softly as he came out of the trees to join Blalock.

"The foolish creatures will alert them!" Blalock motioned the tipeeke to spread out with a hand signal. They soon found the scent again and started up the trail toward Devil's Gate. "Ha," Blalock exclaimed. He threw back his head and laughed softly as he noted the tipeekes' direction. "They might have escaped us if they had turned back! Now, I have them between us and my soldiers at the top."

Then Krasa saw an uncommon sight, for rarely did Blalock let anyone see his face. Krasa held a torch, and by its light, he beheld a proud, strong visage framed by thick white hair that fell in waves to Blalock's shoulders. Under prominent brow bones, strange light eyes peered out. Blalock's nose was a sharp blade, his lips were full and well carved, and his skin was fair. It was a wild but noble countenance, except for the eyes that glittered with insane desire.

"The fools are caught in my trap!"

Krasa, a hard man, pitied them.

A Legend Lives

As they followed the tipeeke, Blalock explained to Krasa what he had done after the traitors had attacked his camp. Elated by imminent success, he was unusually communicative. "I ran through the woods as fast as the knee-deep snow would allow." Krasa noticed that Blalock's robes were still wet up to his thighs. "Occasionally, I whistled softly, hoping that the horses whose tracks I followed would hear and respond. In a clearing, I saw two dim shadows that I believed might be some of our livestock. Again I whistled softly. The dark shapes materialized into two of our steeds. They walked nervously toward me, glad to see a person in that strange wood but unsure of me. I reassured them with pats and gentle talk, then mounted one and led the other. We traveled south to search for Surra's camp."

As they rode, Blalock reviewed his actions. This evaluation he did not share with Krasa. The wily sorcerer berated himself furiously. *Two of my cunning, beautiful braith are dead, my royal prisoner is stolen, and I, Blalock, was forced to sneak away in the night, like a thief!* He acknowledged to himself that he had been careless and, worse, greedy. *My brother would tell me that they are my worst faults.* He scowled at this thought, and Krasa wondered in dismay what could be troubling his master. *I should have sent the braith back out, to guard our camp, but I so badly wanted the information the prince could give me. In that, too, I erred. Bar was not truly under the drug's control when I questioned him, and I learned little.*

Blalock consoled himself with what he'd done right. *However, I did find the rest of my men and the tipeeke. I ordered Gal-re to wait until it was safe and then free the useless Blackrobes. I learned where the fugitives' camp was located and which trail they are using to reach the pass. Now, I will take back my prize and gain many others also! People are generally quite stupid; all it takes to deceive them is a little thought—a little planning.* Basking in self-satisfaction once again, he rode on, ignoring the cold and his own hunger. *It is really disappointing that they dumped our eve meal in the fire.*

Meanwhile, Lavel's tired troop struggled up a trail that wound like a writhing serpent. Gradually the snow diminished and then stopped. It was rarely deep on the narrow trail, but even now, with the bright moonlight, it was difficult to see the rocky path clearly. The trail was carved into the side of Mount Riinar. Sheer rock cliffs rose to towering heights on the right. On the left, there was a drop-off, sometimes of only a few feet, sometimes of hundreds of feet. Cold, silent hours passed in dreary, tedious riding. Each member of the group questioned, at some point during the climb, their leader's decision to travel at night and without rest. They grumbled, until they heard a frantic but familiar howling below them—tipeeke! Blalock, the cunning, tenacious sage, was already on their trail!

They looked at each other grimly, thankful they were not in their camp. Even at night, the tipeeke could find their trail easily, and this steep path was not a good place for a fight, especially if there were soldiers ahead of them. At least Tal and Oster would warn them of that.

Lavel called a halt to rest and eat quickly. They washed down dried fruit and flatbread with cold water from their skins. Each wished for something hot, but there was no time. A pine-scented wind sang among the rocks above them, making eerie music. The fruit was sweet, sticky, and very good. Bar had finally quieted, and though he still had no strength, he was more himself.

"I don't know what I told them," he said.

"It doesn't matter," Lavel said softly. "They know which trail we have taken and are following us. There may be soldiers ahead of us as well." He looked at his tired, anxious companions. "If they catch up to us, we will drop back by turns, in pairs, to shoot at them. If they are ahead of us also, we will hope for a good place on the trail to defend ourselves." He smiled fiercely. "By the Maker's favor, we'll find a way out of this yet. Now let's ride."

In spite of the circumstances, they were heartened and rode with renewed energy. Behind them, they could hear frenzied screeching on the night air. As the moon started to descend, Lavel held up his hand suddenly, and they all stopped. Their horses' hooves clattered on the hard rock. Two figures, dwarfed by the high cliff walls, were riding swiftly through dappled shadows down the trail toward them. It was Tal and Oster.

Tal told them quickly, "There are men at the top—I don't know how many. Come quickly! We have found a place that is defensible—only a large cleft in the rock, but it is high, and its entrance is narrow. We must hurry! The hounds have alerted those above us." His face, lit by the moon's light, was as hard as the rock around them.

Lavel said, "Maker help us! Lead the way!"

They rode faster, trusting to Tal and Oster's leading. Yet it was dangerous to travel this fast when one could not see well. The moon was setting behind the cliff walls. After perhaps three-quarters of an hour, Oster led them up a steep incline to a large rift in the cliff wall. They would have to climb a short ridge to reach the cave entrance. "Watch the drop-off at the back of the cave!" he called out. The horses were sweating as they clambered up loose shale that gave way beneath their hooves. Rockslides rattled to the trail below and surrounded the hooves of the horses waiting to ascend.

Tal glanced anxiously up the trail toward the pass, fearing that the soldiers above them would arrive before everyone was safely in the triangular crack.

Lavel slung Bar across his saddle in front of him, like a sack of meal, so that he could have both his hands free. The head-down position made the already nauseated hishua feel much worse. Bar prayed earnestly that he would not lose the contents of his stomach, but the pressure on this abused organ as the horse jolted and jumped upward did not help matters. The burdened steed labored mightily, his muscles bunching as he scrambled up the steep incline. At least Bar was able to wait until they pulled him off the horse in the cave. He was then violently ill.

That left only Devon and Tal down on the trail, and they quickly followed the rest. There was still no sign of their enemy, but they could hear the wild baying of the tipeeke growing more frantic. As often as he had heard the sound, it still made Dare feel the clutching terror of panic.

Lavel quickly organized them in the best defensive position. He sent Oster, their best archer, to watch from an outcrop of rock at the entrance. Os could clearly see the trail in both directions. He would have to move when the Blackrobes and their troop from below arrived, because he would be exposed to their archers, but the outcrop would protect him from arrows shot by those on the trail above him.

A clatter of hooves from above warned them that soldiers approached. Oster readied his bow, and as he shot, he whispered hoarsely, "Four, I can only see four." His first shot missed the mark, but his second wounded the lead man. The four soldiers quickly dismounted and scrambled for cover among the rocks. There was little cover to be had, so they backed farther up the trail and out of range. Oster shot again and again. His arrows managed to pin them back but not to hit them.

Tal guarded Oster's back and watched below. The hideous, screeching sounds were growing closer and closer. "I abhor, detest, and abominate these stinking beasts," he said quietly but with great vehemence as he raised his bow. The others smiled slightly at his words but agreed with him wholeheartedly.

Scuffling sounds at the back of the cave startled them all. Tal did not take his eyes off the trail below him, but he said, "Boer's bow! What now?"

"I'll go see," Devon said with his usual calm. He strode back to where their horses waited, but the horses were gone! He was just in time to see the last one being led up a wooden ramp and into an opening above the drop-off. Astounded, he started to yell, "What—" but just then a strange odor filled his nostrils. At the same time, a soft voice hissed in his ear, "Do not speak if you wish to live." A knife at his back had already sliced through his clothing and was pricking his bare skin, but he yelled weakly anyway. *I must warn them!* Pain exploded in his head, and he lost consciousness.

Pandemonium broke loose in the cave. White-haired, white-clad shapes sprang from the shadows and quickly forced all of them, at knifepoint, up the padded ramp that bridged the deep drop-off at the back of the cave and led to a dark opening on the other side. The company gasped but did not struggle in the burly grip of arms like oak trees. The sight of Devon's limp body being dragged through the opening kept them from testing the strange men's willingness to knock them out also. Tal groaned at his inability to call Os, who was still at his post, keeping a sharp eye on the soldiers.

"Tal, Tal?" Os had called worriedly as soon as he heard the commotion. Suddenly all the sounds of scuffling turned to deadly silence. He quickly turned around to look but could find no trace of any of his companions. He threw a quick glance at the enemy, who had not moved, and then he crawled backward into the cave. The howling of tipeeke and the sound of horses' hooves filled his ears. They were getting closer. *The soldiers from the peak will wait until those below us on the trail arrive, I hope. That will be soon … very soon.* He stood in the cave, eyes searching. He could find no one! Not a horse, not a pack—not anything!

Stunned, he searched the unrevealing rock floor. It told him nothing. *Where are they?* Os knew his friends would not leave him if they had a choice. That meant that someone, or something, had taken them against their will—but who and where? As he peered down the pitch-black crack, he heard men scrabbling up the incline that led to the cave. Feeling deserted and bewildered, he turned, bow drawn in defiance, to face the enemy.

Two soldiers appeared at the cave entrance, followed by two Blackrobes. "Drop your weapons, all of them," one of the Blackrobes ordered fiercely. He threw his hood back in order to see well in the dark interior of the cave. Outside, Os could hear strident voices commanding the tipeeke to sit and be still. Their dreadful din subsided slowly but with many passionate outbursts. Unable to think of anything else he could do, Os obeyed and dropped his bow. He drew his long knife from its scabbard and dropped it also.

The Blackrobe searched the depths of the cave and asked angrily, impatiently, "Where are the others? Where are your horses?" He strode up to Os, his face pale with rage, grabbed the Basca' by his beaded jacket, and shook him. "Where? Where?" he shouted.

A deep, beautiful voice said quietly, "Easy, Surra, easy. I'm sure he is, ah, dying to tell us. Just give him a moment to gather his thoughts." A tall, commanding figure walked easily toward them. The middle-aged, handsome Surra dropped his trembling hands and bowed deeply, but he was too angry to speak. "You must learn to control your temper, my friend, though, ah, it has its uses," Blalock said smoothly. Os shivered at the implication.

"Now, my young Bani—no, not Bani but Basca' warrior—how very strange. Where is the rest of your … party?"

Os looked him straight in the eye and said clearly, "I have no idea. I was guarding the entrance from that jutting rock out front and holding the soldiers on the high trail at bay. I heard some scuffling and called to my companions, but they did not answer me. I came and searched for them, but I found the cave as you see it—empty …" He trailed off, and genuine puzzlement showed on his face. He again searched the cave, as if his companions would appear at any moment and explain.

Blalock sighed and removed his hood. "Go get torches, Surra. We will search this place. Perhaps there is a tunnel."

Surra hurried to comply, but the glowing torchlight revealed nothing. They even searched the deep crack at the back of the cave—nothing. No one thought to look up. Even if they had, they would have seen only shadowy cracks and rough rock. The elusive white-clad men had pushed a large rock into the huge fissure they'd taken their prisoners through.

When it became apparent that their exhaustive search was fruitless, a less calm Blalock turned with vicious intent toward the now bound Oster. "I think it is time you told us the truth, my friend." Oster straightened to face the two. Surra cracked his knuckles and came up behind Blalock eagerly.

Fear knotted Os's stomach. *At least I don't know anything.* Small comfort.

MOOR HA CHI

DEEP WITHIN RIINAR OSTER'S COMPANIONS were resting in a small room hewn out of rock. They had been forced to run through dim tunnels and caves, at least some of them man-made, by a people out of legend—a people no one knew still existed. If any of their group were ever free again, they could attest that the Moor ha Chi lived.

Devon said with wonder, "Moor ha Chi! I can't believe it! I thought them an ancient people, long dead and almost forgotten. The Maker taught them to work in stone. They made dams, roads, beautiful buildings. Why, Saint Fauver's was made by the Moor ha Chi!" Devon's fellows smiled at his enthusiasm. He seemed to take no notice of his exhaustion, the cold, his hunger, or the tight bonds. They were all too miserable, too apprehensive to rest, though they needed it badly.

Their captors were firm and insistent but not cruel. They'd allowed them short rests and water on their flight through deep, dark places, but they had insisted on silence and threatened to gag Tal when he'd persisted in asking questions.

They all sympathized with Tal. No one knew if it was better that Os had been left behind or if he would be better off with them. Tal qua's harsh face registered the agony of his indecision. The Moor ha Chi might go back for Oster, if they knew of his predicament. He was surely in Blalock's hands by now. Surely there could be no worse fate. Tal said bleakly what they all were thinking. "Blalock will never believe that Os doesn't know where we are."

186

And he didn't. Blalock possessed a brilliant, cunning mind. He expected to reach his objectives. That his prey had escaped him again seemed ridiculous, totally unbelievable. *It is enough to cause one to believe in the Maker!* He shook his head in consternation and disbelief. Demons he believed in and avoided. He knew there was terrible risk in that direction, enough risk that he was not tempted by their undeniable power. But there was no Maker! If there were, it would be a major inconvenience. He badly wanted to run his own life, so he firmly denied that there could be a great intelligence of any kind. He told himself it insulted his reason, but actually the implications of an all-powerful being were so awful to contemplate that he didn't.

As he looked at the pale, defiant young Basca', he wished for more re-al. Unfortunately, his supply was in a case that the enemy had taken. The Basca' were notoriously stubborn. Well, one did the best one could with what one had. He sighed. He had little faith in the outcome.

Unseen gray eyes peered into the cave from a dark crack above Surra and Blalock.

Back in a dark room deep within Riinar somewhere, Os's companions shivered miserably. Their guard spoke to someone, and they all tried to prepare themselves for whatever their captors had in mind. Two strong Chi came in, followed by an older man who spoke to them kindly. "Welcome to our domain," he said softly. "Our leader would like to talk to you. Will you please follow me?"

Stunned, Lavel answered with equal courtesy, "Gl-gladly."

They stumbled to their feet; too many miles without rest or food had made them awkward. Dare and Tier supported Bar, who was at the end of his strength and barely conscious. They did not have far to go. After walking through a few wide passageways, they entered a natural cave lit by flaming torches held in brackets attached to the wall.

Many Moor ha Chi, both men and women, turned to gaze at them with serious intensity. All were dressed in flowing white with traces of color in beautiful beadwork here and there on their clothing. All had white hair, light eyes of different hues, and tan skin. They gathered around a chair of stone, a throne really but a very simple one. As they moved back, the companions could see a large Chi with harsh features and gray eyes sitting on the throne and observing them carefully.

Bar was reminded of the head of the wharvers' quarter; this man's gaze was as potent and tenacious. He wore white wool robes embroidered with blue thread and had a beautiful sword across his knees. The man who had brought them to this place said simply, "Meggatirra, king of the Moor ha Chi."

Lavel, Devon, and Tal had no trouble returning the king's gaze, and the hishua's eyes went from the king to their leaders in wonder mixed with anxiety. They followed their elders' lead and bowed respectfully to this king out of legends.

"Against our better judgment, we have shown ourselves and saved you from the Blackrobes and the evil Blalock," the king said. He spat the name out as if it made his mouth feel dirty. His voice was deep and resonant; it filled the high cavern. "Now we must determine who it is we have saved. We have watched Blalock, the Blackrobes, and the king's soldiers for many days as they waited impatiently for something or someone to appear. We wondered what could be so important that it would bring the old fox down from his mountain retreat and cause him to mix with lesser beings. What would make Blalock take an interest in the world of men again?"

His sharp eyes ranged over them as he enumerated, "We have a Basca' warrior, a large woodsman who looks to be something more, a larger monk, and three young men: one Bani, one Possan, and an Ohsan, I would guess. What could the kingdom possibly want with you?"

There was a flurry of sound at the back of the room, and the king looked up in irritation. A young Chi came in and dropped to one knee close to the throne. "Forgive me, Lord, but I have a message for you from Chea lar," he said softly, out of breath. They talked hurriedly, and the young man left quickly. The king frowned, then looked back at the captured men before him and seemed to notice their exhaustion for the first time. There were no chairs in the room, but at the king's signal servants brought them sheepskins, and they gratefully sat down. That and the steaming-hot drinks they were given revived them a little. These courtesies also made them relax—slightly.

Meanwhile, Chea lar was feeling thankful that Blalock had left Os in the cave; otherwise the young Basca's rescue would have been much more difficult. Chea was young to be a Moor ha Chi lieutenant, only twenty-two, but his cunning and quickness had been quickly recognized by his elders. What Chea lar set out to do, he did. As the sun's rosy light crept up over the eastern mountains, he and his small group organized a diversion out on the trail. They hoped it would pull Surra and Blalock to the cave's entrance long enough for them to slip Oster away. As always, it was important not to be seen.

This time, they planned to lower Silva, who was light and strong, on a rope through a fissure in the ceiling. Then, when he had freed Oster, they would pull them both back up. Chea prayed quietly in the frigid darkness above the cave that their plan would work. If it did not, he would have two men to rescue—one of them from a race no one knew still existed. The Moor ha Chi had many places like this cave that they subtly altered for their own purposes. Meggatirra insisted, as other Moor ha Chi kings had not, that his people know as much as possible about the world outside their realm.

The distraction had begun. Out on the trail, Chea heard shale and granite rain down on soldiers, Blackrobes, and animals alike. Men and beasts started screaming and yelling as they were hit by falling rock. The soldiers' frantic search of the cliffs above revealed no men, no visible cause. As the rocks tumbled faster and their size increased, the soldiers' lieutenant yelled over the thundering noise for the men to find shelter. Chaos reigned as boulders bounced down the mountain in an ever-thickening stream that was quickly turning into an avalanche. Soldiers pulled their injured companions and terrified horses either up or down the trail to get them away from the spewing rocks.

Blalock and Surra ignored the sounds at first, intent on the exhausting but so far unsuccessful task of beating information out of Oster. Finally, exasperated at the uproar, they strode angrily to the entrance of the cave and gazed first in amazement and then in fury at the chaotic scene outside.

Terrified tipeeke howled, horses neighed and tried to break away from the men holding them, and soldiers ran to help fallen comrades. Blalock raised his fist and roared in fury, "Who is responsible for this outrage?"

Not for a moment did he think that a simple act of nature had caused tons of rock to tumble down on this section of the trail at this precise moment.

With sudden, horrified insight, Blalock whirled and ran back into the depths of the cave. He was closely followed by the perplexed Surra. The crafty sage's eyes sought in vain for their prisoner. The Basca' was gone! He had disappeared without a trace, without a sound, without a single weapon being used—unless, of course, one counted the avalanche.

In a frenzy of rage, the master of Fairgrieve berated Surra for his stupidity. "This cannot be happening!" he exclaimed over and over again. All the two could do was wait in frustration until the stream of falling rock shrank to a trickle and then stopped. It would take hours to clear the pile of rubble from the trail and reunite their split forces.

<hr>

Back in the audience chamber, the Chi leader asked, "Who will be your spokesman?"

"I will," Lavel answered clearly. "What is it you wish to know?"

Meggatirra raised his eyebrows with a satirical look at this brazen question. "*Who* are you?" he asked harshly.

Lavel was tempted to give him back his own impertinent list of "a Basca' warrior, a large woodsman, a larger monk …" but thought better of it. His companions breathed a sigh of relief, knowing full well what was going through his mind. Experience had taught Lavel that under stress he tended to be both flippant and cutting. He controlled the impulse firmly, but what answer could he give? What *truthful* answer? He did not wish to lie to this powerful man who had saved them from the Blackrobes, soldiers, and Blalock. By helping them, the Chi king had broken a tradition of hundreds of years of silence and hiding by his race. Yet how could Lavel tell him the truth?

Lavel chose the middle ground. "We are fugitives from the king's justice. We have each broken his law, though in a different way, and have joined together to flee over the mountains to Tro-pay, where we hope we can hide in safety."

Meggatirra looked both skeptical and impatient but said simply, "Go on." Lavel started sweating. He had hoped his simple explanation would suffice; he should have known better. These people had given much; they deserved better answers, but could they be trusted with any part of his and his companions' story? Lavel quickly analyzed the situation and asked the Maker to guide him.

"May I come closer, Lord?" he asked with deference. Meggatirra's court moved restlessly and murmured, not liking the idea of this stranger close to their lord, but Lavel kept his eyes on the king.

"Come," Meggatirra said simply. He looked extremely capable of handling anyone, even someone of Lavel's size, with his right arm tied behind him. Two armed warriors near the throne stepped forward protectively but did not stop Lavel as he rose and walked slowly toward the king. He knelt on one knee as he had seen the messenger do; he was barely two feet from Meggatirra. He spoke softly for a few minutes. Meggatirra rose swiftly and asked his lords and ladies to leave except for four. "Cision, Senusa, Orca, and Sanera, please stay." He looked at the kneeling Lavel. "Your name?"

"Lavel."

"Rejoin your companions, Lavel," the Chi king ordered shortly.

The room quickly cleared, and servants brought camp chairs of wood and leather for those Chi who stayed and refreshments as well. As the last servant disappeared from the room, Meggatirra said, "Please start with your names and a short history of your life." The small company looked to Lavel for direction, unsure how much of the truth to tell, especially Bar, who was light-headed still from the drug, no sleep, and an empty stomach. He was sure he did not have the sense to formulate a believable lie.

"My name is Lavel. I was born in Tro-pay. I am a merchant of sorts, but also I help people who are out of favor with the regime to escape, as I am doing with this group. We planned to use Devil's Gate to reach Tro-pay and hide," Lavel said quietly. He looked at Devon. "This man is my brother."

Devon continued, "I was the abbot of Saint Fauver's Monastery. The king's men destroyed the monastery and took the brothers and me prisoner. They were taking us back to Feisan when my brother, Lavel, rescued us."

So far so good, Dare thought. Tal qua gave his name and said, "I am a Basca' warrior. Until recently I served King Bardock. I found I could no longer serve him and have fled. With Bani help, I faked my death and hope the king's soldiers will believe this lie so my people will not suffer for my actions."

Tier stated simply that he wanted to help Lavel and was accompanying the group with the permission of his father, Lord Amray of the Bani.

Dare basically told the truth. "I am a runaway serf that the Bani helped put in touch with Lavel."

Bar was last. "I served in Casterray and ran away. The Bani found me also and helped me by putting me in touch with Lavel."

No one lied, but no one told the whole truth either. Meggatirra's face hardened with intense anger. "These are half-truths at best. Why do you not trust us when we have risked a great deal for you?" he asked, perplexed.

"Lord, you have rescued us, and we thank you. It would be no way to thank or honor you to lie to you, yet we cannot tell you the whole truth," Lavel said desperately.

"Do you think my people will let you out of here? To betray us—to tell the world where we are, that we still live? It will be, perhaps, the worst day of your lives … this day that we rescued you! You will be our prisoners till you die—unless you can give us good reason to trust you with our secret … to let you go," Meggatirra replied vehemently, his eyes fierce. His harsh voice filled the large cavern.

Lavel paled visibly as the probable truth of this statement hit him. After a few moments, he asked, "May we talk among ourselves, Lord? It is not my decision alone to make."

The king nodded and ordered, "A few minutes only and then you must answer us. Before you speak to each other, I will tell you that the messenger who interrupted us informed me that we left one of your party behind. Our warriors have rescued him. It seems Blalock did not believe that he did not know where you all were."

Tal's voice trembled slightly as he said, "Thank you, Lord. He is a friend and kinsman."

The king nodded, searching Tal's face, and then suggested, "Talk now. You do not have much time."

Dare felt Bar slump against him, unconscious. He looked up quickly to see if the king or his councillors noticed. Of course, Meggatirra, who missed nothing, was watching him. The king asked quietly, "Is he injured or ill? My men told me you had to carry him." The Chi king rose and came across the room to stand directly in front of Dare.

"He ... he is not ill or injured, sir." Dare stuttered to a halt, seeing danger in saying any more.

For some reason Meggatirra did not press him but asked simply, "Does he need special care?"

"He needs food, water, rest, and mostly to be warm, Lord. He is cold to the bone," Dare answered.

"We have hot baths and healers. They will take him and care for him." Turning to the guards, the king instructed them to bring healers. They quickly ran to do his bidding. Dare looked at his friends in dismay. He had not thought what the outcome of his words might be. *If they undress him, they will see the mark. Will they know what it means? Have they heard of the prophecy?* The healers came, carefully placed Bar on a cot, and carried him away.

The small company fought against a growing fog of exhaustion as they tried to determine what to say and, more importantly, what not to say.

In the healers' hall, Bar regained consciousness slowly. He heard voices talking quietly in a strange language—well, maybe just an older form of his language, because he could understand some of the words and part of the meaning. Memory returned in partial flashes. *Moor ha Chi! Endless dark tunnels and passageways ... feeling cold and weak ... King named Megga something ... Where am I now?*

Bardon forced himself back to consciousness with an effort and struggled to sit up. *Must think ... must remember ... Lavel in danger ... they are all in danger! I must help them.*

A Chi in front of him was watching him carefully. Dressed in the habitual white, the old man greeted Bar softly, his green eyes perplexed and very intent. Bar did not stop to wonder why. "Welcome, young one. You are in our healing rooms. Rest and tell us what we may do for you," he said courteously enough, but the steel of authority was there, just below the surface. *A leader then ...*

Bar answered him cautiously, trying to pull his scattered wits together.

193

Will I ever feel like myself again? "Where are my companions?" he asked, clenching the sides of the cot in an effort to keep upright, grasping so hard that his knuckles turned white.

"They are still with the king. My name is Rus-chak," the healer answered.

"What time is it, Rus-chak?" Bar asked.

"It is early morning. You have been unconscious for only a few minutes."

Bar's head swam, but he ignored it, saying, "When—"

"Enough," Rus-chak said gruffly, pushing Bar gently back down on the cot. "Now you will do as I say. First eat some food. Then take a bath—believe me, you need it. And then sleep. After that we will see about answering more questions." Bar opened his mouth to argue but changed his mind after a good look at Rus-chak's face. It would be useless, and truthfully he felt too weak to persuade the healer.

As one of Rus-chak's cohorts fed him soup, Bar realized something with a shock that made him choke on the broth. *I am naked under these blankets! Rus-chak … perhaps the other healers also … have seen my mark. Do they know what it means? Have they sent word to their king? If so, will he know who I am, who we all are?* Bar was unsure of what to say. *How reliable is the Moor ha Chi's knowledge of the outside world?*

As if in answer to his question, the king and four of his councillors strode into the room followed by two guards. The king nodded toward Rus-chak. "My thanks, healer." Rus-chak bowed in response but said nothing. *Well, that answers one question. Rus-chak did send for the king.* The healer feeding him soup bowed to his sovereign quickly and left. Bar found himself staring into the eyes of a striking, very powerful man and wishing himself elsewhere. *I do not have the energy for this … or the wisdom.*

"My healer has told me that you bear a mark … a very distinctive mark. Will you show it to me?"

What choice do I have? Maker, help me. "Aye, Lord," Bar responded and struggled to a more upright position. The blankets fell to his lap, making the mark very apparent.

Meggatirra and his councillors gazed at him quietly. The king reached out a strong, calloused hand to touch the mark. For a second his hand trembled. Then he touched the scar, searching with eyes and cool fingertips for some sign that it had been painted on, that it wasn't real. He satisfied himself that it was quite real. Looking at Bardon with hard, fierce eyes, he said, "We must talk, but first you need rest. We are allowing your companions to eat, bathe, and rest also. They are safe, and you may see them when you wake." He continued his searching gaze for many moments, then turned and left. The others followed him with a swirl of soft fabric.

Bar swallowed hard and sank back onto the soft skins. "Alati, Maker," he sighed, "for a short reprieve."

The bath was wonderful. He felt warm and clean for the first time in days. He thought he wouldn't be able to sleep, but he did, a deep sleep without dreams. With their fears for Os's safety alleviated, his companions also were able to sleep.

Oster's face was badly swollen and his ribs sore and bruised from Surra's enthusiastic fists, but he was very grateful that was all he'd had to endure. If Chea and Silva had not come, it would have gone on and on. The healers wrapped his ribs, put a numbing salve on his face, and gave him something to drink that helped the pain and allowed him to sleep. Whoever these white-haired people with the strange eyes were, he was very grateful to them.

AUDIENCE WITH THE KING

T LEAST THIS TIME WE HAVE EACH BEEN accorded the honor of a chair, Dare thought as he gazed around the king's somber audience chamber. What a change in appearance he and his friends presented when compared with the last time! They were rested and clean; even their clothing had been washed. Black leathers and boots were polished, and each man, according to his custom, had trimmed, braided, or tied his shining hair. They were a handsome group.

The Moor ha Chi were thoughtful and kind but not friendly, certainly not warm. The small band of fugitives was unknown to them, and they were obviously withholding judgment until they knew more. In these times, Dare could not blame them for their caution.

The awesome cavern was well lit with wall torches and much warmer than the last time. This was not for the Moor ha Chi, Dare knew, but for them. A large brazier in the center of the room radiated heat. They were seated in a loose circle facing the throne, where the king sat with the same four councillors as last time.

When they entered and sat in their chairs, as Meggatirra invited them to do, the king resolved immediately any question in their minds concerning what to say. He laid waste their careful planning with one short sentence, in which he greeted Bar by name … by his whole name.

"Bardon Diona e Sacino, son of Bardock Diona e H'cram, marked by E Clue and part of the prophecy, we greet you. You are welcome in our land, if your claims be true," Meggatirra announced in his deep voice. His look and that of his councillors were grave to the point of harshness. Bar went white. *So much for secrecy.* He was not sure he could have quoted his lineage as well as the Chi king; he knew none of his group knew it or cared.

Bar returned Meggatirra's glare, but after a moment, he glanced at Lavel, seeking instruction. Lavel responded with a negative shake of his head. "You must decide now. If he knows this, there is probably little else he does not know. Though how he knows anything," he said, staring at Meggatirra, evaluating this glimpse of Chi resources, "living in this mountain is beyond my comprehension."

Bar nodded and objected in a clear voice, "I make no claims, Lord. It is as you say. I am Bardock's son, and E Clue did mark me, but beyond that I know little of what my involvement with the prophecy will mean."

"Why does your father pursue you?" Meggatirra inquired with an intense frown. Before Bar could answer, he added, "Why do you run from him?" He shifted forward in his chair. The room was very quiet except for the small sounds of torches hissing and black rock settling in the brazier. The king and his council's intensity told Bar that his answer to this question was very important to them.

Why do the Moor ha Chi, why does everyone, assume they have the right to ask personal questions? Bar wondered bitterly. *My life, my most personal feelings, my mistakes are discussed by everyone ... by anyone ... without any concern for my privacy.*

Attempting to contain his anger at Meggatirra's intrusive rudeness, Bar answered him calmly but with a sharp edge to his voice. Those who were well acquainted with him knew how close he was to losing his temper. Bar might not believe in his father's god or governing methods, but he had nonetheless inherited much of his temperament. His harsh training in Casterray had given him rigid control over all his emotions but especially over anger. A certain hauteur, never before heard by his companions, infused his voice and manner. "He pursues me to make me his prisoner. I ran from him because I do not want to study his religion, which is the worship of Choack. He would use Dare or anyone I cared for, even someone I did not, to force me to do his will in this matter or any other. I ran away from Casterray because I had enough of being controlled and manipulated and also because I knew he would win ... would force me to his will in the end."

Meggatirra and his councillors' faces were as expressionless as the dark granite walls around them and as hard. An older man named Senusa sneered, "How could he force you, against your will?"

Bar forced himself to answer calmly. "He knew those I cared for, and if I did not do as he wished, they suffered for my disobedience. It was good incentive."

"Suffered. How?" Senusa inquired with cutting skepticism.

Bar's face was a mask. Pain knotted within till he did not think he could bear it. Dare wanted to end these probing questions, but after one look at Meggatirra's face, he kept his mouth shut. The silence in the room grew uncomfortable, but no one dared to break it. Bar replied in a voice barren of emotion, "Demotion, dismissal, flogging, imprisonment, torture, and possibly death." The company felt sick. Neither the council nor the king reacted in any visible way. Suddenly, Dare wondered if they already knew the answers to these questions … if this were some kind of test.

"He did not physically harm or imprison you?" Senusa asked.

"Never. He did not touch me ever, nor was anyone else allowed to," Bardon responded.

The interrogation went on for what seemed like hours, and somehow Bar kept his temper. The king and his councillors questioned everyone until they were satisfied that they knew everything the runaways could tell them. No one held anything back.

There were a few things they did *not* ask: the location of Glimmervale and the names of those who had helped Bar and Dare, like Tar Andrew and Morin.

There is some benefit to us in all this talk, Dare thought. *So far, this expedition has been heavy on action and light on time for reflection or explanation. As people joined us, they had to jump in and gather information as best they could. We are hearing, some of us for the first time, each person's part in the whole story.*

Meggatirra demanded of Lavel, "What were the king and Draville planning that caused you to rescue Dare and Bar from Casterray so quickly?"

"A plan was overheard, by a method I won't explain, to use Dare to force Bar into submission on a number of issues, but especially the study and worship of Choack," Lavel answered, twisting uncomfortably in his chair.

"We were not sure Dare would survive the persuasion process and decided to chance pulling them both out. We knew it would cause an uproar, but we never dreamed what we were getting into. We did not realize then that both of them are part of the prophecy."

Meggatirra stared at Bardon fiercely. "You seek the throne of Ree!" It was an accusation.

Bar's heart jumped, as did his companions', and his voice stuck in his throat. When he found it, he exclaimed hotly, "I do not *seek* the throne. E Clue said that one day, if I were loyal and true, I would rule. We ... I have not thought of a throne, only of survival ... of finding a place of safety."

Everyone's nerves were raw from the tone and length of the Chi's interrogation. They were all on the edge of temper and rash outburst. Dare had not thought of a throne either, but now, he saw clearly, in spite of his weariness, what the king was seeking. When Bar had accepted E Clue's mark, he'd committed himself to things none of them had thought through.

"You are unworthy of the prophecy ... of that marking!" Meggatirra accused. He pointed at the covered mark, his eyes blazing. Bar stared in amazement at the furious king, then closed his eyes, distressed and spent. His friends gasped in fury at Meggatirra's unjustified attack. Dare, hands knotted into fists, was halfway out of his chair when Devon pulled him back down.

Bar wondered, *Why does the accusation hurt? Because it is true? Undeniably true.* Recent memories flooded him. Bar pushed them down. *Not now ... I cannot afford them now.* Anger, swift and unexpected, rose to replace guilt. It was both deep and long gathering. *For long months I have been hounded, chased, intimidated, injured, hidden, disguised, drugged ... and now this!*

Opening his dark eyes, Bar glared at Meggatirra. He declared flatly, with a fierceness that matched the king's own, "I do not *seek* or even *want* the throne of Ree. When E Clue marked me, I wanted only to do the Maker's will. I thought that might mean I would someday accept the throne but not seek it. There is a big difference!"

In the intense quiet that followed this statement, Meggatirra inquired, his voice scathing, "Did it never occur to you that you might have to fight for the kingship of Ree, even if you are *marked* by the Maker?"

Bewildered in spite of his wrath, Bar stared like one struck dumb.

The king scowled at six infuriated men whose eyes said they wanted to defend their friend and stop this interrogation that was an attack on him. Lavel raised his hand quickly to still their muttering and stop an imminent outburst. He interposed furiously, "He has had no time to think since his marking, nor has Dare, nor have any of the rest of us! We have been too busy trying to stay alive!"

Meggatirra gave his councillors a grim smile. "Well, that answers one of our concerns." The councillors nodded agreement. The tense atmosphere in the cavern deflated with this unexpected and mild remark.

What does he mean by that? Bar wondered, as did his companions.

Calm as ever, Devon injected unexpectedly, "Yet fighting is something we must take the time to consider. I'm afraid the king is right. The Maker may not hand Bardon a throne. It is something we must all fight for, if we believe in the prophecies, and … we *will* fight for it if we can ever stop running."

They all quieted for a moment as they considered the unexpected task Meggatirra had pointed out to them. It would mean overthrowing a powerful regime that possessed a well-entrenched network of spies, a powerful army, and, it appeared, some supernatural power, to say nothing of a strong king of the true blood. Hundreds of years of persecution had caused the Bani to seek anonymity, the Moor ha Chi to disappear from the face of the planet (and from many people's memories), and any followers of the Maker to keep their belief to themselves. The name Choack might be new, but darkness and oppression of anything to do with the light were old … very old.

"I have been harsh," Meggatirra stated simply, "but there is much at stake here. We all have a great deal to lose. It seems to me that someone must take the time to think, to plan."

Lavel responded passionately, "That is what I am trying to do. We are taking Bar and Dare to a place of safety and people I know who will think this through. Please do not ask me who or where. If it were not for you, I know well we would all be dead or in Blalock's hands right now. We thank you for that. Send us on our way, and we will go to those who are wise and will consider these things. The Maker knows they are above me!"

Meggatirra sighed and raised his eyes to the dark rock over their heads.

He muttered, "Great things in the hands of simple men and children. We have waited long. We can wait longer." He said to the wrung-out company, "Excuse us. We must confer with each other and our people. Please rest and stay in your rooms until we call for you. It should not be long, and then I can give you our decision."

Guards escorted them to a guest room near the healers. Bar's anger deflated like a pierced wineskin when they walked out, leaving him shaken, cold, and empty.

They sat on pallets around a glowing brazier to talk and consider their audience with Meggatirra. Tal qua prepared strong tea, sweetened with honey, and passed it around in heavy pottery cups. "I think the Maker's oldest children have gotten a little full of themselves over the years," Tier observed with a martial light in his eye as he turned his cup around and around. There were nods of agreement.

"I get the feeling that he pushed Bar and all of us very much on purpose," Devon remarked thoughtfully.

"Brother Devon, do you *ever* get riled?" Oster demanded, his swollen, black-and-blue face registering exasperation.

"Aye, young hothead, I do, but over the years I have gained mastery over my emotions and learned to use my intellect instead," he replied severely, a twinkle in his eye.

Lavel choked on his steaming tea and then laughed out loud. The rest joined in his mirth. "Would you like me to tell a few stories of this great mastery?" he challenged Devon with a wicked grin.

Devon laughed too but protested, "Please do not … my reputation as an abbot will suffer considerably. I am supposed to set the sheep a good example."

"How about the time young Brother Devon became the 'Ghost of Old Bain' and terrorized the whole monastery?" Lavel remembered.

"Lavel, please," Devon pleaded with an embarrassed flush.

"Tell us, Lavel," Tier urged, and the others joined him. It was hard to believe that self-contained and calm Brother Devon could have ever gotten into mischief.

"Well," Lavel said, "one of Devon's teachers, Brother Quarren, was a prim and proper old soul and very rigid in his interpretation of the scrolls.

He came down hard on Devon, again and again, for some of his views and questions. He made him redo assignments and even gave him extra work—gardening, if I remember correctly—as discipline for doubting traditional views. Devon became angry, and knowing of Brother Quarren's admiration for Old Bain, a long-dead abbot, he brought Bain back to haunt Quarren. He was caught, of course, but not for a number of weeks. During that time, his apparition disrupted the whole monastery, and the brothers talked of nothing else."

Devon grinned and added, "Thank heaven the abbot at that time had a sense of humor. He thought Quarren too rigid in some of his ideas also, or I might have been sent home. As it was, I did a great deal of gardening and apologizing." Laughter cleared the air. Even Bar looked less pale and burdened.

"Devon, why do you think Meggatirra was pushing Bar and us so hard?" Tal asked.

Devon explained, "I kept having the feeling that they were testing us, watching us, especially Bar, to see what we are made of … what kind of men we are. It is almost as if they are thinking of making some kind of commitment to our cause and are exasperated to find that we don't think of it as a … cause. I don't think there is any question that they have stayed true to the Maker all these years. They have probably treasured the prophecy and waited and watched for signs that the time is right, so that they can help us throw off our oppressors … and we haven't even stopped to think of it as a battle! The idea of organizing, fighting, or planning has not yet entered our heads." They looked at him in amazement.

"Of course!" Tier agreed. "Remember when Meggatirra left, he said, 'Great things in the hands of simple men and children. We have waited long. We can wait longer,' or something like that? We consider ourselves an underground. We help people hide from the king and his soldiers, but that is all we do right now. Lavel and his spies get information from all over the island on what Bardock and his men are planning. So far we have not openly fought him or interfered with what he is doing except in secret. We simply rescue folk and help them find a new life."

"The poor man is ready to back a cause, and there isn't one … yet," Devon said with feeling. For many minutes, there was only the sound of the fire and water boiling in the kettle. They all tried to digest what Devon was suggesting. Bar had endured enough; he groaned and fell back on his pallet.

"Be of good cheer, young monarch," Devon encouraged as he punched his arm. "It will all happen in time, just as it is supposed to. You cannot hasten the birth of a baby or a movement. That is the Spirit's work, and he does all things well, always."

Bar sighed and asked, "Are you sure, Big Brother?"

"Very sure. The Creator's work is done his way and in his time. You will know what you need to do and when you need to do it." Devon paused, a frown furrowing his forehead. "*What* did you call me?"

The King's Decision

UCH TO DEVON'S ANNOYANCE, "BIG Brother" stuck like freshly pressed elong sap. He complained that they were not showing proper respect for an abbot or for his dignity. The company grinned. They agreed, but they continued to use the nickname. Occasionally someone would even whisper "Old Bain," but not when they were close to Big Brother's mighty right arm.

The distant sound of bells and drums woke the anxious fugitives the next morning and filled them with a strange sense of expectancy. Not long after they dressed and ate, one of their guards announced Meggatirra. Surprisingly, the king came alone, and pulling up one of the chairs, he sat down as if he were an ordinary mortal. He motioned them to do the same. They were even more astonished when he dismissed the guard at the entrance.

Smiling faintly, he asked, "Do you think me so weak that I must depend on others to defend me?"

"Never, Lord," Lavel responded diplomatically. Not that it wasn't the truth. Meggatirra looked strong enough to handle a rock bear by himself. His upper body, even for a Chi, was extremely thick and muscled. Yet they thought it a good sign that the Moor ha Chi would trust their leader to be alone with them.

"My people have decided to free you," he stated quietly. "We ask your word that you will not tell anyone of our existence or location. When you have discussed with your leaders what you plan to do, we would like to know what you decide. We have watched for a long time for evidence that the prophecy is being fulfilled. I thank the Maker that he has allowed us to see with our own eyes the two he has marked.

"I also have eyes and ears out in the world who report back to me." He looked at Lavel and said, "You are not the only one with a network of informers. That is how I knew you. The Moor ha Chi will stay hidden for now but not always. Send someone with a message for me, when the time is right, to Devil's Gate; we always keep a watch there. Now it is enough I think—what you already know about us. But later, when trust is established, I would like you to see my kingdom, strange though it may be. Part of establishing that trust will be your keeping the Moor ha Chi a secret."

They were relieved by this statement and impressed by the king's lack of ceremony. He was proud; however, his pride did not seem to rest in himself but in his people, his heritage. He took respect for granted and would have been offended by a lack of it, but he did not seem overly impressed with himself. This raised the company's opinion of him.

Bar decided to do a little pushing of his own and asked respectfully, "Lord, we are not what you expected, are we?"

The king looked them over for a few moments, ran his fingers through his thick hair, and sighed ruefully. "No, you definitely are not."

"Is that why you were so angry yesterday?" Bar asked.

"Only partially. I was also seeing what you were made of … what kind of men you all are," he admitted. "We did not expect the Maker to choose to mark … one of Bardock's blood. It never occurred to us that you might follow the Maker. Indeed, we expected you to be as steeped in the worship of Choack as your father and his court are. If you will forgive me for saying so, your reputation was one that did not encourage us. We heard you were cold, haughty, and cruel, just like your father. Now, we can certainly understand why you acted that way." Bar nodded his understanding of their mistaken assumption.

Meggatirra reflected, "When we heard the rumor about Bardock's son being marked by E Clue, we were truly shocked and disappointed. The second shock was that you were sixteen years old. Then we learned that Dare had been chosen and was fourteen. Neither of you lead; you follow, and quite humbly, the men who have extricated you from one difficult situation after another. We did not know if you had the strength or the spirit to lead. We especially did not know if others *would* follow you or be loyal. It takes special qualities to be a good king and to be a king's friend in Dare's case, and we couldn't resist testing you a little to see if you possessed them."

A little! More than one of the company thought.

"Not that it makes any difference in the long run; we will help you because the Creator has chosen you and because you follow him. That is enough to know," he stated firmly.

They were amazed. Lavel reiterated, "You intended to help us all along, to let us go?"

"Aye, we were almost convinced even before you arrived that Bar and Dare were the chosen. After seeing their marks and talking to them, we were—are—convinced. We would have held some of you captive to ensure your silence, if we had not believed you could be trusted. My people depend on me to protect them. Our supposed extinction is important to our survival as a race."

After instructing them to get ready to leave, Meggatirra left. They looked at each other with relief, some amazement, and a great deal of irritation, but they hurriedly began to pack, before something else happened. "Since none of us are being taken hostage, I assume our hatchlings, and the rest of us, passed the test," Lavel commented to the group with a grin as he packed his saddlebags.

Bar and Dare liked this nickname about as much as Devon liked "Big Brother." They were so relieved by the king's words, though, that they overlooked the ribbing that followed Lavel's use of this undesirable label.

Bar exclaimed, "I can't believe what we went through, what he put us through … and all along they were going to let at least most of us go."

Tier said, "I really didn't know if we were ever going to get out of here." The others commented that they'd envisioned years of imprisonment and vented their various feelings about the "inquisition." As they talked over their ordeal, they could faintly hear drums and music in some distant part of the mountain.

Meggatirra met them later in a large cavern, where Chi brought them their horses. The company had been led blindfolded to this place and could not have given anyone even an approximate guess where they were.

The king had begun to explain what had been added to their supplies when they heard an imperious, little voice say, "But I wish to see them, and Father did not say that I couldn't ... well, not precisely." A young boy of about four stood at the entrance to the cave surveying them critically. An elderly Chi stood by his side. The child's white brows were drawn down in a frown. His saucer-round eyes were a light, frosty gray, and his white hair fell freely to his shoulders. It was cut in thick bangs across his forehead. Even at four, his chest and upper arms were thick and well developed.

They were tempted to smile, but this small person took his dignity so seriously that they maintained a passive front and looked back at him politely. Meggatirra's brows rose in question and displeasure, but the little one took no notice of him. The Chi who had tried to restrain him stepped back in resignation. The child walked deliberately to each one of the company, except Bar, whom he did not see, because he stood behind Lavel. He looked them over, small hands on hips, with adult seriousness. But amazement overcame him as he saw races he had never seen before, and his expression changed to wonder. He was particularly intrigued by Tal and Oster's darkness and touched their hands curiously.

When he came to the king's side, he reached up his arms in confident expectation of being picked up, but he never took his eyes off of the company. Meggatirra sighed and lifted him. Amazement shot through Bar at the child's complete confidence in his father's affection. In a like circumstance, Bar would have been terrified. No, he would never have pushed the king's authority in the first place.

"This is my son, Rafiel, who has evidently escaped his tutor ... and disobeyed his father."

Rafiel's large, expressive eyes swung to his father, and he said earnestly, "You did not say I might not see them."

"I said no one was to see them, except those who had my permission to do so, did I not?" the king queried sternly.

Unaffected, Rafiel assured him, with great patience for this lapse in royal intelligence, "But, Father, I am not just anyone! And I must know about these people, if I am to rule one day."

This time the company did laugh and did not attempt to hide it. Rafiel did not understand what was causing their mirth and looked at his father questioningly. "Why are they laughing?" Before his father could explain, Rafiel's eyes fastened on Bar, who was quietly standing next to Meggatirra, holding his horse's reins. "This is the one you spoke of, Father?"

"Aye," the king assured, but he said no more as Rafiel reached out his little hand.

"May I see your mark?" Rafiel asked seriously.

Bar was strangely moved by this child, though he was not sure why. He smiled at the boy and nodded assent. As he untied the string at the neck of his shirt, Rafiel's eyes did not leave his, and the room grew strangely quiet. Even the restless horses, who were eager to be outside, settled down. A gentle hush spread through the cave. Bardon pulled the shirt as far off his shoulder as he could without ripping it, and Rafiel pressed his hand against the scar. Bar gasped softly. Warmth spread through him and then a flooding peace … an assurance that all would be well. It quieted anxieties that circled constantly in his mind, anxieties he had not even named, and drained away his anger. Still the solemn eyes gazed into his. They did not search him, as there was no need—it seemed Rafiel knew Bar well already. Rafiel lightly pressed Bar's temples with both his chubby, very dirty, little hands and leaned forward to place a kiss on his forehead.

A woman's voice broke the quiet serenity in the cave. "So there you are, young man. He *was* very curious, my lord," she explained, looking at the king with a rueful smile.

A shaken Meggatirra put his small son down and ordered faintly, "Go to your mother and tutor now, child. I will come soon."

The king's wife looked around the cave with a puzzled expression. She realized she had interrupted something. Everyone looked very strange. She took Rafiel's hand and led him away. He chattered to her happily about the new people he had just seen.

The horses tossed their heads and neighed, anxious to be on their way after long days of rest. The men resumed their preparations—all but Bar, who stood still and dazed in the center of this busy activity. Meggatirra spoke quietly with Lavel and Tal qua about their route giving Bar time to recover himself.

After a few minutes, the marked prince came forward to shake Meggatirra's forearm. "Not an ordinary child," he said with a shaky grin. "Does he do that often?"

"Not often but … enough that we agree with your opinion," Meggatirra replied with the first real smile Bar had seen on his face. "We have blocked the other pass with an avalanche of snow and timber. They cannot follow you that way."

"Many thanks, sir," Bar said. The company expressed their gratitude for all that the Moor ha Chi had done and left the cave, Lavel in the lead.

Much to Bar's amazement, they were on the other side of the pass. Devil's Gate was behind them—they would not have to pass Blalock's sentries. Somehow the Chi had brought them through the mountain to the other side.

In front of them was a terrifying sight. A live volcano filled the sky with smoke and a pulsing red color that tinted everything around them with a flickering cherry glow. The mountain's summit had blown off in the ancient past. The ground up to the rim was black from lava that had once flowed from the top. The molten rock was now hardened in strange, tortured contours. At the base, scraggly undergrowth had reasserted itself, and farther up, a few stands of diseased trees stood forlorn. Otherwise, the mountain housed no living thing. Its heat, its violent, throbbing power overwhelmed the senses. Mesmerized, they stared until the horses' restlessness brought them back to themselves.

Lavel quickly led them down a steep and winding trail flanked by towering pine. A gusty, cold wind swept the ground clean in some places and piled snow high in others. It made their eyes water and their noses run, and its keening wail troubled their ears and made it hard to think. The pines bent under its blast, and the birds overhead screamed in delight or anger as they rode its turbulent currents. A weak winter sun shone overhead, giving little warmth, but their combination clothing protected them from the cold. Between Bani and Chi, they were undoubtedly the best-outfitted travelers in all Ree. They wore an assortment of leather, sheepskin, and wool that was unusual but effective.

Lavel pushed them hard to reach the first goal Meggatirra had set them. At the end of the day, they were exhausted and hungry but in good spirits.

A new warrior sat around their roaring campfire that night; Chea lar had joined them. His hair, eyelashes, and brows had been dyed a light brown, but there was nothing anyone could do about his light, frosty gray eyes. They hoped his eyes and tan skin would appear to any chance traveler to be the result of a mixed background. Marriage between the races was common in all of Ree's cities, if not out in more rural, isolated communities. Hopefully no one remembered what Chi looked like or, for that matter, that the race had ever existed.

Lavel accepted this addition to their company with resignation. In his care was another young, though very capable, responsibility—one whose death could harm their relations with the Moor ha Chi forever. Neither he nor Meggatirra was happy about Chea's presence, but they could both see that the lieutenant's suggestion to accompany them made good sense. Chea would be the underground's messenger back to Meggatirra.

As Lavel gazed at the faces around the fire, he acknowledged, with faltering faith, his Lord's hand. *Dear Maker, what are you doing? This company has grown to eight men and represents six races, one of which I thought lived only in history. I am a simple man, Lord. Who am I to have in my charge your marked prince, a marked healer, Lord Amray's son, and now one of King Meggatirra's officers, who is also his nephew?*

A clear, quiet thought whispered through his mind: *What I have started, I will bring to completion. Whom I have chosen, I will lead. What I set out to do … I do … always, completely, perfectly.* Lavel's knot of anxiety relaxed at this gentle reminder of who was in charge.

THE DUNGEON OF GREEN CLIFFS

T HE COMPANY HAD LITTLE FEAR OF BEING
followed, yet they were cautious. The Moor ha Chi had promised to
guard their back trail. The Chi would not openly fight Blalock, but there
were many other ways to stop him, such as another avalanche. There were
other passes, of course, but in winter few were accessible. It would take
Blalock and the king's men time to find them, time to cross to the other side
of the island. Even if Blalock or the king's men reached the western side of
Ree, they would have a large territory to search—impossibly large.

However, Bardock operated an efficient network of spies. Neither Tal
qua nor Bar knew exactly how his people communicated; it was a well-kept
secret. They could only guess at his methods: messenger birds, signal towers,
perhaps mica-stone flashes or runners? Boats traveled around the island,
and there were good roads that circled north and south of the mountain
ranges. Both means of travel would take many days, which would give the
fugitives time. They hoped. With the inventive Blalock on the king's side,
they knew anything might happen.

They rolled out of their sleeping skins the next morning to watch a
glowing rose-and-gold sunrise spread across the sky. Another fair day
dawned; it was cold but not far below freezing. They set forward with light
hearts and full stomachs. Lavel enjoyed the peace; he knew from experience
that it wouldn't last.

All eight men took turns breaking through large snowdrifts when they
could not go around them. They were making good time and easily reached

their goal that night. Everyone worked at their assigned tasks, and their camp took shape quickly. They chose a quiet spot in a valley near an ice-crusted stream.

Bar broke the thin ice with his bone knife in order to fill one of their waterskins. His thoughts strayed to the shepherd who had given the knife to him. Suddenly, he saw that man's face in the light of new knowledge.

He hurried back to the fire eagerly. Everyone was there, ready to eat whatever Devon was cooking in his black leather kettle. Looking at Chea lar, Bar said triumphantly, "Dierald! Am I right?"

"I cannot say," Chea answered, but his eyes danced.

"What do you mean, Bar?" Devon asked with a perplexed frown.

Woodsmoke blew in Bar's face, and he choked and coughed for a minute before he could answer. Holding out his wooden bowl for a big ladle of stew, he said, "Dierald is one of the Moor ha Chi informants! He has to be. He has a Chi build, and we know after the way he handled a Basca' warrior that he is more than a simple shepherd. I think he is a Chi who has either dyed his hair, as Chea has done, or is of mixed blood. I would guess the latter because his eyes are not quite Chi." The others discussed his idea for a few minutes and decided he was right. Tier especially agreed, but Chea would not say one way or the other. They talked contentedly around the fire about many things. Each enjoyed a sense of safety that they had not experienced often on this journey.

The light was fading, and one by one the stars became visible. Lavel appointed the watches for the night, and everyone turned in, except Oster and Chea, who drew first watch. They drank the bitter, scalding dregs of the tea to help them stay awake.

Both horses and men were bedded down in a small copse of aspen. Chea and Oster each walked the perimeter carefully, watching the small valley and tree-covered mountains that circled them. The night was dark. The moon had not yet risen, and even when it did, the small crescent gave little light.

Chea was having second thoughts about joining this company. It had seemed like a good idea at the time. *I sought the Maker's will and thought I found it, but now I wonder. I feel like an outsider ... These men know each other well. They know Ree well. I have never lived with any people but my own.*

I do not understand their customs, expressions ... or even their jokes. I have never been anywhere but the Moor ha Chi kingdom, which is wonderful but small compared to the wide world. Under the vast, starry sky he felt naked and lost. Longing—for his family, his people, familiar faces, and familiar ways—filled him.

Oster, too, was struggling, not so much with loneliness as guilt. His family thought he was dead. *How can I do this to them! Will I ever see them again? When? How? I should have stayed loyal to the king and returned.* Even as the idea went through his mind, he rejected it. He never could have betrayed Bar and Dare to the king. Knowing Bardock's and Draville's reputations throughout Casterray, he didn't even like to imagine what their capture might mean. But the price for doing what he hoped was right was high, very high.

The hours passed slowly but uneventfully, and Chea and Oster woke Devon and Tier to take the second watch.

Big Brother leaned against a slender aspen, which bowed under his considerable weight, and meditated on the daily devotions of his order. His eyes surveyed the valley, but his mind enjoyed majestic words from an ancient prophet. As he gazed at the blazing stars overhead, he whispered the petition that burned in his heart. "Mighty Shepherd of the stars, Shepherd of men also, watch over us, for we are each far from home and our enemies seek us relentlessly. Bring us safely to Glidden, and by your great power, may not one of us be lost. I know we are far more important to you than the stars, and the scrolls say you have never lost one of those."

On the other side of the small stand of trees, Tier felt the familiar ache of homesickness. During the day, he could forget his family, his clan, Glimmervale, and the Valley of the Cracked Rock, but at times like this, when he was alone, longing for them overcame him. He petitioned the Maker for each member of his family and clan by name as his eyes searched for enemies, and he was comforted.

Devon and Tier wakened Bar and Dare. Then they gratefully crawled into their sleeping skins. The last watch was the coldest of the night. Dare and Bar shivered uncontrollably as they stomped to their posts. Slowly their bodies adjusted to the cold and were able to build up heat under their heavy, fleece-lined cloaks. The next night, they would rotate the watches, and both hishua would sleep the full time, as Lavel and Tal were doing this night. To sleep one whole night in four was a definite advantage in having eight in their group.

As Dare searched the valley floor and then the forested slopes, he longed for a cup of strong, hot tea. He caught a glint of light, a small twinkle among the dense forest. He rubbed both eyes with his fists and looked again. Nothing. He stared at the spot for long minutes, and then … he saw it again! What could be out there? These mountains were high and wild. Could someone live up there? He whistled softly once and then again, as he had been instructed. In a few moments Tal and Lavel, still struggling into their cloaks, joined him. He pointed to the small light, high among the trees. They stared at it and then nodded. Tal left; Dare presumed he went to see if Bar saw anything on the other side.

Suddenly more pinpoints of light appeared—and then more! They seemed to be moving steadily down the mountainside. Lavel quietly woke the others and with hand signals told them to break camp and get ready to move. Tal came from speaking with Bar and reported that there were lights moving down the other side of the mountain also. They were almost surrounded, but by whom or what? They did not wait to find out.

Quietly, they stole out of the trees and headed for the pass out of the valley. Lavel petitioned heaven that whoever or whatever was out there would not cut them off. He led, and Tal and Oster brought up the rear. They all felt exposed against the white snow and went quickly from whatever cover they could find to the next. It was to their advantage that the moon was a mere sliver that gave little light.

The horses snorted, their harnesses made slapping sounds, the saddles creaked, and the thick crust on the snow crunched with each step the animals took. In the quietness of the night, the company's tightly strung nerves winced at the thunderclap loudness of these small sounds.

Dare felt close to panic as he watched the lights ahead of them and behind them multiply, pouring into the valley like a fast-running stream. They were trapped. The bouncing torches were between them and the pass. Now they could hear their enemy: faint voices, crunching in the snow, and the creak of leather. But they heard no horses; these men were on foot. Lavel called a halt.

Tal rode up to him, and they talked quickly. A voice called to them out of the darkness, "You are surrounded, my lords. Give up and no one will be hurt. I give you my word on it." Foot soldiers in dark-green livery approached them steadily, their leather armor gleaming in the flickering light of the torches. The color indicated to Lavel and Bar that they were probably Duke Oltive's men. In the midst of the soldiers was a man on horseback. It was he who had called to them. The eight of them approached within thirty feet and then stopped. There were at least fifty men in front of them and that many behind.

The small group of fugitives worked to control their restless horses that stomped, snorted, and bumped into each other in their nervous fear. The men all looked to Lavel for direction. His eyes were distressed and desperate. Devon reached out and grabbed his brother's arm gently. "It's hopeless, Lavel. There are too many of them. We cannot risk even one of the hishua in a fight."

"Can we risk letting them fall into Bardock's hands?" he retorted passionately. "Oltive's loyalty to the king is well known, and for good reason. This duke could destroy the prophecy in one blow!"

"There is nothing else we *can* do. Let us trust the Creator and be patient. He can protect his own," Devon said intently. His eyes never left Lavel's.

Lavel looked at Tal, who was still beside him. "What do you say, friend?"

Tal's face was rigid as stone. "I agree. There is nothing else we can do."

"So be it," Lavel said. His horse took exception to the closeness of Tal's pony and snorted his anger, then reared. Lavel controlled his plunging gray with an effort and spun to face the man on horseback. "Who is in charge here? What is it you want?" he shouted.

The man urged his animal a little closer and said, "I am Captain N'uer of the house of Oltive. The king has ordered me to take prisoner Lavel, Brother Devon, Prince Bardon, Dare of Ravensperch, and any other in their company. You will be escorted back to Feisan by the West Highway." The captain was young and very deferential. However, in case anyone thought to deny their identity, he added forcefully, "I have been at court and recognize Your Highness." He bowed to Bar. "And the descriptions of Lavel and Brother Devon were really very detailed. I could hardly be mistaken in my identification. You will be well treated, I promise you, if you cooperate with us."

"Well, Captain N'uer, I hardly think we have any choice in the matter, since we are overwhelmingly outnumbered. Would you care to reveal how you found us?" Lavel asked acidly.

Captain N'uer replied, "I'm afraid I am not allowed to say, sir." The "sir" was an unnecessary courtesy to a prisoner, and Lavel's estimation of the young man went up a notch. "My uncle, Duke Oltive, waits for you at Green Cliffs. Before we leave, I must search each of you. Please get down and lay all your weapons on the blanket," he ordered, gesturing to the blanket his men were laying on the snow.

What choice did they have? They did as he commanded. The search was professional; no hidden weapons escaped the captain's sharp eyes and hands. True to his promise, he remained unfailingly calm and courteous. Not even when he found hidden knives on Lavel and Tal, which they had not thrown onto the blanket, did he become angry. When Lavel shouted furiously at him for having them tied up, he answered respectfully, "You are skilled warriors, and your reputation goes before you."

Eyes flashing as a soldier bound his hands behind him, Lavel said sarcastically, "I gather you would have us take being bound like peasants as a compliment."

"Aye, sir. I would."

Lavel rolled his eyes in disgust. They mounted again, and mature, seasoned soldiers led their horses toward the pass.

After many miles, the darkness lightened in the east, and the sun rose, shedding brilliant light on the beautiful landscape. The trail led steadily down into a meadow surrounded by peaks that were lofty but not so high as the ones they had left. In the distance, they could see a tower made of gray stone that blended with the rock cliffs around it. It was to this tower that Captain N'uer led them. It took them perhaps five hours to reach it. They all began to perceive a possible method of communication. Perhaps Blalock, high on Riinar or some other peak, had sent a message to this tower, either by fire at night or by smoke or mica flashes during the day, perhaps even by pigeon. If he could do that, he might also have the ability to send messages by relay from tower to tower all the way back to Feisan. Terrible thought!

They were fed and allowed to rest before they started for Green Cliffs, Duke Oltive's home. They could hear pigeons above them in the tower cooing and flapping their wings. The birds took flight in an explosive blur when a soldier slammed the heavy wooden doors behind them. Captain N'uer asked them not to speak to one another, a command they would have given in his place and one they covertly disobeyed. He soon caught them at it and had them gagged, with no greater show of temper than a frown. They did not stop to sleep that night but traveled all through it, which was as exhausting to the captors as captives—more so perhaps, as the soldiers, except for N'uer, were on foot.

Lulled by the monotonous gate of his pony, Bar fell into a half sleep. In a dream, he saw a strange cliff wall, bright with sunshine. High on a narrow game trail he noticed small caves with smooth openings. He entered one and saw, at the very back, something reddish brown glistening in the faint light. A voice said, "Seek within." He did and was suddenly choked by blackness. He jerked fully awake in the saddle, overcome by a feeling of terror. At the same time, he knew that whatever lay in the back of that cave was important and he must find it.

Midmorning the next day, they approached Green Cliffs, a rambling structure with lofty spires. High upon a bluff, the castle overlooked a magnificent valley dotted with picturesque farms, domestic animals, and beautiful cottonwoods. A placid but pale N'uer greeted Duke Oltive and then turned his prisoners over to the castle guard. Oltive was a large man, mildly overweight, with curling white hair and a pleasant if not handsome countenance. His clothing was warm and serviceable but not at all grand. He greeted N'uer affectionately. "Well done, Nephew. Well done."

He surveyed the company with hard blue eyes and said, "One of King Bardock's captains will be here to take you to Feisan in about twelve days. Meanwhile, you are to be held in my dungeon. It is not my choice to put you there, but orders are orders." Lavel nodded. He was too exhausted to speak and prayed that he would stay on his feet until the duke dismissed them. Fainting dead away in the courtyard would be most embarrassing.

The exhausted company collapsed in a large, dank cell somewhere deep beneath Oltive's castle. There were no windows, and the single door was made of heavy wood, held tightly shut by a plank on the other side. A narrow crack at the top allowed air to circulate and light from the corridor to enter. There was fresh hay on the floor, a pail to relieve themselves in, and a pitcher containing water. That was all! There were no hammocks to get them off the cold stone floor and no blankets. They were appalled.

To take their exhausted minds off the barren cell, Devon asked Lavel, "Is there a chance Oltive will help us? He has a reputation as an honest ruler. I saw no signs of arrogance or cruelty, and he treated us with respect."

"True," Lavel replied, "but he will obey the king. He always has. Oltive is not a wicked ruler, and his people don't hate him, yet they are not fond of him either. He is simply wise enough to know that if he treats his people well, they will not rebel. He rules with an iron hand and crushes without mercy or hesitation anyone who gets in his way, yet he sees no reason to rouse the people to anger or rebellion unnecessarily. He is fair, protects them, and allows them many festivals and contests. Though he is very ambitious, he knows who holds the power in Ree. The result is a well-run province with very few uprisings or problems."

"So much for that idea," Devon said as he ran his fingers through his lengthening hair. They all had longer hair and stubbly beards as well. There had been no time for such niceties as hair trimming or shaving.

They could conceive of no plan to escape; the efficient N'uer saw to that. They were well guarded with every possible precaution taken. Minimal food, cold, and no exercise weakened them, as it was supposed to do. Elong handcuffs, hardened on them, bound their wrists with twelve inches of play between them. The dungeon cells, so far below ground, were damp, and in spite of their more than adequate clothing, it was difficult to stay warm.

Tal paced like a wild animal, but with his hands bound in front of him, and those bonds checked every watch, even simple things like eating were difficult; escaping was impossible. He knew whomever King Bardock sent would possibly recognize him and Oster. The deception of their deaths that he and Amray had so carefully arranged would be exposed. That would place the Basca' hostage the king held in great danger and give Bardock an opportunity to do … who knew what? Tal writhed inside at the thought and fought to trust the Maker with the outcome. For a few minutes, he would find peace; then some awful vision would bring fear back all over again. They rested, they talked, they waited, and they all sought to hide their anxiety.

Devon spoke words from the scrolls every day from memory, which brought comfort and peace to their burdened hearts. For a time, the sights, smells, and indignities of incarceration faded. By day five, the effects of little food, the cold, and the resulting improper rest had taken a heavy toll on all of them. The younger members of their group suffered especially.

Lavel tried to hide his impotent fury from the others. To imprison fugitives was understandable and expected, but he was at first dismayed and then made truly apprehensive by the conditions, which they would all be fortunate to survive. Why take such a chance with Bar's life, even if they cared nothing for the rest of them?

On day twelve of their imprisonment, Captain N'uer and four guards took them out of Oltive's dark, musty dungeon and into the courtyard. The captain's eyes were pained and strangely sad. The condition of the prisoners was deplorable. It was overcast, but even this soft light hurt their eyes. They stank, they were weak from inactivity and lack of food, their leathers and Chi wool were filthy, and some looked ill.

The company's future appeared grim, yet their mood lifted as they felt the clean, cold breeze. Pigeons and doves cooed on the castle walls, and servants talked cheerfully in the courtyard. The wonderful aroma of bread baking, the fresh fragrance of pine, and the strong odor of woodsmoke raised their spirits. The sweet sounds and poignant smells of life swirled around them, and like thirsty earth in the rain, their arid spirits eagerly soaked it all up.

The castle doors opened, and three men came swiftly down the steps: Lord Oltive, a Blackrobe, and one of the king's captains. The company stood taller and at attention, preparing for the worst. The captain, his cloak flapping in the breeze, walked across the courtyard and talked to his men shortly. They brought the company's own horses and ponies to them and ordered them to mount. Their saddlebags looked intact, although they had undoubtedly been thoroughly searched. That was a comfort if true. Dare would consider it a privilege to brush his teeth.

The captain said goodbye to Oltive and N'uer, then mounted his magnificent bay and led his soldiers, the Blackrobe, and the company out of the gates. He was immaculate in his beautiful gray wool uniform trimmed with gold leather. They saw neither his nor the Blackrobe's face. However,

the pity Dare saw in both N'uer's and Oltive's expressions sent shivers down
his spine. Oltive did not seem to be the kind of man who allowed himself
an emotion as tender as pity.

They rode hard and in almost total silence. Their weakness made the
ride a nightmare for the whole company. Their muscles ached and trembled,
and they became light-headed from the exertion and their ravenous hunger.
There were soldiers surrounding them, and finally, in desperation, Lavel
asked the silent soldier next to him if they could put on their gloves and hats.
They'd never been warm in Oltive's dungeon, and the wind was taking what
little body heat the exercise built up. The soldier called out to the captain,
and the company halted. Bound hands and numb fingers made their efforts
to get into their saddlebags clumsy and slow. The impatient captain ordered
his men to help them, which the soldiers quietly did. The silence was as
wearing as the cold and hunger. They tried talking to each other and were
quickly silenced.

At noon, they halted where a large stand of pine sheltered the road.
The captain ordered them to dismount. It was all they could do to remain
standing once on their feet.

Dare clung to the saddle horn and commanded his body to stay upright.
It was not listening very well. He slid to his knees in the snow as his vision
went black.

Back at Green Cliffs, Oltive sat by a roaring fire with a bowl of warm wine
by his side. He read again, with pleasure, the decree that made the Port of
Costul a part of his province.

CAPTAIN TORI AND LOTU

STRONG HANDS LIFTED DARE TO HIS FEET. *Devon*, he thought through the dark fog. When he could not stand, Big Brother carried him somewhere. Dare did not completely lose consciousness. He could hear voices, though he did not understand what they were saying, but he could not see. After a minute, Devon sat him down in the snow and pushed his head down between his legs, talking softly all the while. "There now, you'll be better in a minute, if the captain will leave us alone," he said as he rubbed cold snow on the back of Dare's neck and face.

Two of the soldiers gave each prisoner a waterskin. Devon softened a heel of hard bread, saved in his pocket, and held it to Dare's mouth. "Eat this; it will give you strength." Dare shook his head no. The thought of food made him sick; he didn't want it. "Obey me, child. You don't know it, but it is just what you need." Vaguely Dare realized he was being foolish. He did need food, and he opened his mouth. He ate some bread and drank the cold water from his waterskin thirstily. Slowly vision and consciousness returned, but his limbs were trembling. His body ached, and he felt nauseated.

"Alati, good brother."

Devon was deeply concerned. Dare had deep circles under his eyes, and his skin was pale and his face thin. He needed good food, warmth, and lots of rest. Devon sighed. Dare was not likely to get any of them.

When Dare looked up, he saw the captain pointing his riding crop toward a grove of red pine. The soldiers roughly pushed the company in that direction. Devon helped him get to his feet, and they joined the others. The

221

soldiers' animosity was palpable. The company helped each other as best they could and sat in the snow. Not the wisest choice perhaps, but standing was no longer an option because of their weakness.

The captain and the Blackrobe approached them. Dare lightly kicked Bar, who was next to him, to get his attention. Bar raised his head from his arms and gave Dare a questioning look. His face was pale, thinner, and older looking because of his dark beard, which was already an inch long. There were dark circles under his eyes, and his eyes themselves were filled with weariness. Dare nodded at the boots in the snow directly in front of them. Bar swallowed with difficulty and, gathering his courage, looked up.

Captain Tori and Lotu. Wonderful! Now we face an old enemy and Draville's toad-eating right hand. They are mature and experienced. The king chose well, Bar thought bitterly, but he said nothing.

"On your feet, my prince," Tori ordered gently, caressing the prince's face with the end of his riding crop. Loathing made Bar feel ill. Tori was the eldest son of one of his father's best friends, Krow of Ekat. Tori came from an old and noble family. The son had a reputation for being vicious as well as cunning. From firsthand experience, Bar knew his reputation was deserved. You might even call him brilliant, in his own way. Tori participated in the dark practices of Choack and was said to have mysterious powers. Even his friends were afraid of his unpredictable, vicious temper.

Lotu was Draville's assistant. Bar knew little of him, except that he was always close to his master's side, a slender, menacing shadow. The king and his priest were determined indeed. This time they'd sent powerful men close to the throne to bring the slippery fugitives back. Of course, Blalock was no unknown weakling, and they had, by the Maker's favor, escaped him. Bar took courage from this thought as he tried to rise.

His bound hands and weak knees confounded his effort, and he stumbled to one knee. Panting, he rested a moment. "How appropriate, my lord prince. Begging for mercy already, I see." Furious, Bar pushed himself up with the help of anger, but he would have fallen if Tori had not reached out a hand to steady him. He wanted to shake the arm off but was afraid he would fall without Tori's aid, which would be more embarrassing than the help. "So easy to bait, as always," Tori remarked with a condescending smile.

Bar's blood boiled, as it always had at Tori's badgering. He pressed his lips firmly together, well aware of who would suffer for his temper if he lost it.

Tori was a small, slender man, meticulously dressed and groomed. His superb fighting ability with the Gin'hana, the reddish brown sword, was legend. The Gin'hana was forbidden to any but the nobility, officers, and some special units in the guard. An old and valuable one, made by Belhas, hung sheathed in leather at Tori's side. The intricately carved handle glowed in the sunlight.

"There will be no miraculous escape this time, my prince. Lotu and I have more than enough power between us to defeat your simple Maker or his, ah ... simple followers. Remember there will be a price to pay for any ... misbehavior or attempt to escape."

In spite of his rigid effort at self-control, pain and frustration flickered across Bar's face at the old threat. Tori smiled wickedly, satisfied that he had made his point. The smile never reached his black eyes, which glittered with malice and which were so like Bar's own. They looked much alike, these two Possans. They had lithe, slim builds, brown skin, straight black hair, dark eyes, high cheekbones, sharp noses, and full lips—a haughty face of angles ... no softness anywhere. Bar was much taller and would one day be much heavier. Tori slapped him gently on the cheek with his crop and then strolled to the fire that his oppressively quiet men had built. *Why are his men so quiet anyway?*

Lotu paused a moment to look them all over. He walked deliberately to Tal, then Oster. They both paled visibly at this special attention, which was perhaps a sign of recognition. They did not personally know Lotu, but that did not mean he wouldn't recognize the king's Basca' trackers. Lotu laughed softly to himself and joined Tori at the fire. No one knew what his face looked like; his dark cowl completely hid it.

Bar sat down carefully, slowly, tying not to disturb his swimming head any further. A burden of fear he had not carried for many months descended on his heart. The weight seemed unbearable after experiencing life without it, and he groaned softly. Dare gripped his knee a moment with his bound right hand. With the soldiers so close Bar did not chance looking at him or speaking. Dare understood Bar's burden and wanted him to know that now he was not alone. Bar understood and was grateful but gave no sign. Any attempt at communication would bring a blow to one of his companions' backs, not his own.

They were given hot food and drink in large portions and a chance to relieve themselves. Then they rode again. Food helped for a time, but they were each close to the end of their endurance, particularly Dare. He seemed to have suffered more from their imprisonment than the others. By late afternoon, their weakened bodies were sagging in their saddles. The company rode in a column two abreast in the middle of a larger column of soldiers. There were eight men in front of them, eight men behind them, and four on each side. Like inseparable twins, Tori and Lotu rode side by side in front of the column, eyes searching the mountainous landscape. Another company of twenty-four rode behind them on the wide, smooth highway.

Dare thought, through a haze of exhaustion, *Fifty men guarding eight! It seems overdone, yet we have slipped out of many traps before this one, all praise to heaven. I guess it makes sense.* He rode next to Bar in their tight little row with greater and greater difficulty. Sweat rolled down his face and body, and finally, he slumped forward on his horse's neck. *Maker*, he pled silently, *I cannot …*

"Captain Tori!" Bar cried, catching Dare's heavy body as it slid off the saddle. He was deadweight, and Bar struggled to hold him on his horse. The column slowed, then stopped. Bar slid down on the right side of his pony while steadying Dare's considerable weight, but his own trembling muscles betrayed him, and he fell beneath his friend.

Two angry soldiers, cursing them under their breath, got down to help. They kicked Dare's unconscious body to waken him. Rage and then genuine fear for his friend gave Bar strength, and gripping Dare, he rolled on top of him to shield his body. He took a kick in the ribs and one on the arm before the soldiers realized whom they were kicking. They wore heavy black boots and were in a very surly mood, as they had been since the beginning. The blows were hard, but Bar clung to Dare blindly. "Captain, stop them!" Lavel cried from his dancing horse, trying to turn the animal and come to their aid. "This is shameful. They are young and have been without proper food or rest for twelve days."

Tori rode back swiftly, leaving Lotu to watch. The column split frantically before him, for his Gin'hana was drawn. In a voice of ice, he commanded the soldiers to carry Dare to the side of the road. All eight men on his left desperately pulled their horses back as he used his wildly waving sword as a pointer. "We will camp here for the night. See to it, Lieutenant Vere'na," he ordered. Frustration showed in every line of his taut body.

The king had commanded a quick return of his heir and companions with veiled threats of what would happen if Tori failed. It had been the king's own orders to keep the fugitives in Green Cliffs' cold dungeon on short rations. Bardock's growing fear of their ability to escape had prompted the decision. He wanted them too weak to think or to fight. *Well, they are too weak all right—too weak to travel! Asinine, stupid monarch,* Tori fumed, but only to himself. It would be unhealthy to say such things aloud. Sharp fear prompted him to glance covertly at Lotu, who was a very acute man— no, a very acute prelate. Tori must never forget the influence this man had with Draville ... and Draville with Bardock. Sometimes Lotu seemed able to read minds.

Bar lay on the ground with his teeth clenched against a groan, which his enemy would take great delight in hearing. Tori loved pain, *other* people's pain.

Tori's irritation was at the exploding point, and his voice registered growing hysteria. "Rise, my prince. We will stop for the night, so that you and your dirty rabble may rest. You have picked such ... unusual friends ... which is normal for you, is it not?"

Bar really tried to rise. He pushed up with his left arm and got his feet under him. He managed to stand and was feeling mildly proud of himself. Then he swayed and fell unconscious to the ground.

Lavel got down to help him and was struck by the flat of Tori's Gin'hana. Seething, Tori yelled, "Get back on your horse, peasant. When I want your help, I'll ask for it." Lavel restrained his temper and did as he was told, for fear of what the madman might do to Bar. The two soldiers who had kicked Dare and Bar were frozen with terror. "And who, might I inquire, kicked our royal lord?" Tori asked silkily, a mad light in his eyes, as he looked the soldiers over.

"It was Hein, Captain," one of the two soldiers blurted in terror.

The other man shouted, "Me? It was not me; it was you!"

"Silence!" Tori screamed. He beat them both on the back with the flat of his sword till they cried for mercy. They were punished not because they'd kicked a now unconscious fifteen-year-old but because they had inadvertently kicked nobility, in this case the king's son.

Lavel thought he understood the strange tension and quiet in Tori's men. They never knew when their captain's temper might explode. Tori was probably under the same pressure that Captain Ganshof had been under when he'd taken Bar and Dare to Feisan, with the king holding the death of his family over his head. It was probably safer to say nothing at all than to risk provoking Captain Tori.

With Tori's permission, Devon carried Bar to a fallen log. He and Tal used supplies from Dare's pack to wrap his bruised ribs. He woke slowly and in his confusion started to fight them. They finally convinced him that they were friends. "Sorry," he whispered faintly when memory returned.

Captain Tori ordered the troop to halt and prepare a camp. The soldiers quickly obeyed and soon had a meal cooking and water heating for tea. The prisoners ate as much as they could hold and then slept in a comfortably warm shelter the soldiers had built for them. They were allowed twelve long hours of rest. Tori had done what he could to revive his captives, but from now on, he would tie them to their horses if necessary to make up for lost time.

The next day, Tal poured otet into Dare and Bardon whenever they stopped long enough, but the day was still a blur of exhaustion for both of them. Their companions covertly helped them all day, and the soldiers tolerated it, as long as no word was spoken. After all, it helped them toward their goal. Speed was the only thing that placated the captain's temper.

The soldiers who had kicked Bar and Dare were reduced in rank and put in the rear of the company. There was no sympathy for them from their rough companions, just derision.

When they stopped that evening to set up camp, glorious color streamed over the mountain peaks as the sun sank behind them. Golden light filtered through the trees and made the softly falling snow sparkle. They camped in a small valley near the road, circled on three sides by cliff walls over two hundred feet high. The walls went straight up and were honeycombed with shallow caves and fissures. Confident that there would be no attack from the steep cliffs, Tori set guards only on the open side. The cold wind that had lashed them all day could not reach inside the valley, and they were grateful to be free of its icy sting.

Devon helped Dare down from his pony, and Tal helped Bar. They rolled the hishua in warm sheepskins with packs for pillows and let them rest until Tori's cooks had prepared the eve meal. The hishua whispered to each other amid the activity and were not silenced. "Would you think me a weakling if I told you that I would like to weep like a child?" Bar asked, his face white with exhaustion and pain from aching ribs.

"I'm shocked, my lord. I'm sure princes are not allowed to cry. Do you know that I forget, until something reminds me, that you are one ... a prince, I mean," Dare mumbled and closed his eyes.

Bar replied, "I am crushed ... deeply offended."

As he drifted off to sleep, Bar felt a sudden weight on his neck. He jerked against it in shock but could not move his head. "Relax, my friend," Tori purred. "It is only I." Bar could not turn his head to look at him because of a well-placed boot. "Do you have any idea what awaits you and your humble friend when we get to Feisan? Poor Dare—the king has most unpleasant plans for him. Soon, you will know about them yourselves of course, in only twelve days." Then he released Bar's neck and walked away. Neither Bar nor Dare was upset by Tori's threat. They were too tired, and their trust in the Maker had grown greatly. His will would be done.

Snow drifted down on them more heavily, and soon clouds hid the stars that were just appearing in the night sky. Tori instructed his cooks to make a substantial meal; the food was hot and good. As they sat to eat, wolves howled on the mountain.

Shelters were put up quickly, and the camp settled down to sleep in the steadily falling snow. The soldiers made the shelters by stringing elong between two trees, throwing tarps over the rope, and tacking the tarps down every few feet with stakes. They then cut boughs from the trees, laid them on the ground, put tarps on top of the fragrant branches, and covered themselves in animal skins. They blocked each end of the makeshift tent with another tarp. Tori and Lotu's tent was a little more elaborate but not much.

The fugitive company slept together in one such shelter. Their guards would not let them talk even at night, and they were developing the ability

227

to communicate with expressions and with their hands and eyes when they were not being observed. They slept undisturbed and warm until a sound woke them during the night. It was pitch black in their shelter, and they had no idea what the time might be. They raised their heads cautiously, listening. There was no sign of their guards.

The tarps on both ends of their shelter slipped quietly to the ground. The elong ties had been cut! Lavel pushed himself to a kneeling position and faced the opening closest to him so that he might defend them from whoever was out there. Devon did the same at the other opening. Cold air flooded into their shelter. There was no sound. As their eyes adjusted to the gloom, they could see that it was still snowing. They tensed at the sound of a scuffle … then a thud. A large man, finger raised to his lips to caution them to silence, appeared at Lavel's opening. He motioned them out with the other hand. They recognized the man as Meggatirra!

Chea lar grinned in relief at his companions. He had shared with his new friends his belief that the Chi might yet rescue them. Meggatirra would have watched their progress closely and would thus know they'd been taken. Chea had known the rescue would have to take place before they were out of the mountains, so that the Chi could take advantage of their domain's natural terrain. They used tunnels, caves, streams, valleys, and fissures in the mountains as other people used trails and roads. His people used the gifts their rugged terrain gave them: a thousand places to hide.

The Chi had infiltrated Tori's camp right after the last watch changed. The sentries were unconscious, because of a special herb-soaked cloth the Chi had held over their faces. The Chi had bound the soldiers securely while the rest of the camp slept. The Chi now hurried their friends through a large fissure in the cliff wall that had been invisible yesterday and would be again. Dare paused at the opening to look back at the valley. The Chi had left a welter of footprints leading in many directions all over the valley floor to muddle their trail. The snow was deep, and there was no way to hide their tracks, other than to confuse the enemy by a profusion of contradictory trails.

A small group of Chi, mounted on Chi horses and towing the fugitive company's eight horses, fled south down the king's road. Hopefully, Tori would think that the fugitives had escaped by stealing their horses and would dash off in pursuit of them. This would lead him away from the campsite and prohibit any reasoning that could lead him to the correct solution. Then the three Chi who were leading the king's men in a false direction would disappear and return by a devious route to their people. It was the Chi's hope that Tori would never suspect what had really happened. A hidden entrance in a cave or rock wall worked well as an escape route only so long as the enemy did not suspect its existence. This method of escape would not work nearly so well the next time if the trick were discovered this time.

Meggatirra looked over the valley thoroughly and then gave the signal to close the fissure. It took six men to slide the huge section of rock back into place. The Chi used cleverly carved handholds, spaced evenly along the rock's length, to push it back in place. When someone lit a torch, the company gazed at the wall. Even though they knew the section was there, they found it difficult to find the seams. Quickly, Meggatirra led them down a dark, tight tunnel—so tight that Devon's and Lavel's massive shoulders, like Meggatirra's, scraped the sides. The ceiling was so low they were forced to bend over. Dare started sweating and battling to keep his fear of being shut in under control. Bar was behind him and kept up a quiet stream of encouraging small talk.

Bar thought, *We are free, rescued again! Bardock will surely go mad! But ... we are free only to continue our journey. I wonder if I, if any of us, will ever be truly free again.*

THE VALLEY OF LACIDEM

ONE OF MEGGATIRRA'S WARRIORS HAD RESCUED their weapons, which he'd found tumbled together in a blanket with their other gear. For the most part, they were unbroken, though they were tangled and mixed with the contents of their saddlebags. There was a good chance that even their horses would be returned to them if the Chi acting as decoys managed to escape Tori. Yesterday, all looked hopeless—they'd prepared themselves for the worst. Today, they were not only free but had also recovered many of their belongings.

This new hope helped carry them ever up a fissure that was sometimes natural and sometimes widened by human device. The higher they climbed, the colder and the steeper the passageway became. As they rounded a sharp turn, they saw the golden light of dawn far ahead. The crooked tunnel became a huge cavern, whose exit framed a spectacular view of the surrounding mountains. The wonderful beauty of towering, snow-covered peaks awed them. A wild wind swirled pristine white crystals around the pinnacles. In pine-choked valleys, mighty geysers spewed water hundreds of feet into the air. The frigid wind whipped the water spray onto the surrounding rock and trees and shaped it into fantastic ice sculptures. However, a huge, bubbling field of lacidem, a mud-like substance, dominated the whole scene and the company's senses. The lacidem lake lay on the valley floor like a possessed thing: shifting, hissing, and exploding into fountains of thick ooze. The whole field was shrouded in drifting, contorted steam.

Dare knew of the substance but had never seen it in its raw form. There were only three such fields in all of Ree. Lacidem was used for hundreds of purposes: from waterproofing tents to forming pliant, heat-resistant shields on leather. Lacidem was one of Ree's most important resources, perhaps the most important. *The reddish brown field is as big as three orchards; it must be extremely valuable. Surely this place, close as it is to the king's highway, is well known! There will be roads, merchants, and their wagons to carry the precious stuff back to cities and towns.* The security Dare felt evaporated.

The Chi king leaned against one side of the rocky archway and explained to them where they were going next. His eyes betrayed fatigue. Dare suspected the Chi had pushed themselves unmercifully in their attempt to anticipate the enemy and plan a rescue. Meggatirra explained, "There are elong vines of enormous size that crisscross down into the valley. Perhaps it is the lacidem-laden steam that makes them grow unusually large here. We will use them to lower ourselves to the valley floor. So far as we know, this valley is a secret to any but the Moor ha Chi. We come here occasionally to gather lacidem, and always we have a yureq, a small scouting party, in this mountain to watch the king's road. Those who travel the highway frequently camp in the shelter of the same cliffs Captain Tori chose. We listen to what they are saying; it is one of the ways we gather information." Meggatirra gave Lavel a weary smile. "Now we will all rest and eat before we descend into the valley." The Chi as well as the fugitives were ready to take a break. Because of his queal, Bar knew he could not join his companions for their brief meal. His stomach growled in protest.

After a short time, Meggatirra said, "I know we are all still tired, but we must keep moving." He raised his voice for emphasis. "You *must* stay close behind our guide once we are on the valley floor. The ground is rough and pocked with depressions where the lacidem is hidden below a thick crust. A man's weight will easily break through. Even if we managed to pull you out before you disappeared from sight, you would be fatally burned. The heat and fumes are disorienting. Keep your wits about you. If you feel faint, ask for help."

Bar had explained to Meggatirra, in the Chi's first long questioning, about his problem with queal. He trusted that the king had planned a way to get him down from this dizzy height.

As it turned out, he would know nothing about the trip down.

Meggatirra approached him with a cloth in his hand that smelled vaguely familiar. "Do you remember the otog-soaked cloth we placed over the sentries' noses and mouths, the one that made them lose consciousness?"

"Aye, Lord," Bar answered, seeing clearly how he would be taken down the cliffs and accepting it, with less embarrassment than usual. Perhaps he was getting used to being hauled up or lowered down heights, perhaps after all they had been through, it seemed a small thing.

"We will lower you very carefully, I promise," Meggatirra assured with a twinkle in his eye. "Aye, like a sack of grain," Bar said.

The company harassed him about taking the easy way down while they toiled and sweated. He listened to their jibes with humor and responded in kind. "Finally, I am being treated with proper respect for my position," he declared with mock dignity. This was greeted by shouts of disagreement and laughter.

Lavel asked, "What position is that?"

Unable to think of a good comeback, Bar refrained from answering as Meggatirra placed the cloth over his mouth.

The Chi gave the fugitives sturdy gloves but very few instructions. Mostly, the group imitated Meggatirra and his men's descent. With a Chi placed between each of them, they slid down vines from ledge to shelf to rock. Evidently the Chi never considered safety ropes, for they used none, except to lower Bar and much of their gear. At first the height was numbing, but they each took the Chi's advice and concentrated on the rock in front of them and did not look down. Once they had started, they realized that the cliff walls were not so steep as they had appeared from the top. As their confidence grew, they even enjoyed the experience.

The valley was filling with light as the sun rose higher, its bright rays warming them and the air. Soon they were sweating. Angry birds of many kinds screamed at them as they passed close to their nests. Others hung in the air above the cliffs, riding the thermals and watching them with sharp eyes. When they reached the ground, they walked carefully behind their guides, each one putting his feet where the man before him had walked. The air was full of strange mists and scents. The sound of the bubbling lacidem was continually in their ears.

Because it was humid and warm, they wished they could remove their layers of warm clothing, but no one wanted to stop long enough to do it. The good-natured banter they'd shared while clambering down the cliff dissolved into tense silence as they worked their way across the extraordinary valley. Bar was beginning to wake up and groggily requested to be put down. Meggatirra himself carried him. He told him patiently, quietly, as one would talk to a fretful child, to wait until he was more fully awake and stronger.

When they reached the other side, they stopped to rest and have a drink. Meggatirra looked as if he needed it; Bar was no light burden. A strange look came over the king's face, and he sniffed the air tentatively. He wrinkled his nose as if he smelled something unpleasant. "By the burning rock, have none of you had a bath since you left us?" he asked indignantly. The company laughed at him and the other Chi, who were trying not to notice their odor. The humid, warm air betrayed the fragrance of bodies not washed for weeks. It was unbearably strong.

Lavel jested, "Oltive's dungeon lacked bathing facilities, my lord. We shall have to talk to him about that sometime in the future ... in the very distant future, I hope."

Meggatirra was clearly offended by their filthy condition and grumbled as they started again, "As soon as possible, we will find a place to bathe."

Tal qua threw back his head and searched the cliffs above them thoroughly. "How are we going to get out of here?" he asked.

Meggatirra smiled and said, "Follow me." They worked their way up a narrow trail where the spoor of an animal, perhaps the beautiful mountain goats the Chi admired, was scattered on the trail. Many hundreds of feet up, there were small caves peppering the cliff wall that had not been apparent from below. From the valley floor, the caves appeared to be shadows on the craggy wall. They looked as if they had been carved by water that had, at one time, rinsed away some deposit in the earth's composition. The hard granite had hardly been affected. Some were man height, some much smaller. The goats had been in them and probably other animals as well.

Bar stood still, staring at the caves. *Caves I have seen before ... but I can't have! I have never been here.* He frowned, trying to recall the occasion of this clear memory. *The caves were in my dream, the compeling vision ... or whatever it was. These are the exact caves.*

Dare put his hand on Bar's shoulder and shook him. "Bar, what's wrong with you? Are you ill?"

"No, no. Dare, I dreamed about this place. There is something important that we must do here." His eyes glittered darkly in his strained face. "I can't remember," he said with frustration, closing his eyes. The others stopped and watched Dare and Bar quietly.

"Tell me what you saw," Dare suggested. "Start at the beginning."

"I saw these small caves that looked like decay in the cliff face, and in one of them something reddish brown glittered. A voice ordered, 'Seek within.' I went in and was choked with a terrible darkness, but at the back of the cave was something ... something we are to find. Does that sound crazy?" he asked Dare in confusion.

"No crazier than any of the other things that have happened." Dare grinned. "I don't much like the sound of 'choking darkness,' but lead the way, and let's see what this glittering object is."

Bar relaxed a little because of Dare's casual attitude. "Aye," he agreed shakily. They looked at their many leaders for permission.

"I'll go first," Tal said with no expression but a strange light in his eyes. "Which cave?" he asked as he searched the many that lined the narrow animal trail.

"I'm not sure," Bar said. He walked slowly up the path, searching. Nothing looked quite right. Then he came to a narrow opening of man height that really appeared no different than the others, except the shape of the opening was familiar. "This one I think," he said, feeling foolish. Did the Maker really lead his children this way ... with waking dreams? At the time he had felt sure that the vision was important, but now ... he didn't know.

Tal lit a torch that Meggatirra gave him and entered the cave slowly, motioning Dare and Bar to wait. They watched the fiery glow grow dimmer. The cave was deeper than Dare had thought possible, and he grew worried about Tal. The Basca' was too far away for them to reach him quickly if he should need help. Panic gripped him, and he started in, orders or no. "No, Dare," Lavel protested, right behind him.

"Tal!" Dare called out clearly but not very loud. "Are you all right?" For some reason, he hated to make any sound.

Tal answered faintly, "Aye. Come ... carefully."

Meggatirra left his men to guard the entrance, and they all filed in, one after the other. A terrible screeching noise exploded in their ears, and dark forms erupted past them into the bright sky. "Bats," Meggatirra called out quickly, to quiet their fear. Dare's heart was pounding like a rock smith's hammer. As they approached Tal's flickering torch, they could see faint light above them. There was a chimney in the rock that reached all the way to the top of the cliffs. They passed under it and joined Tal, who stood by a wall of solid rock. It was clear that when it rained, water flooded down the chimney and rushed out to the cliff wall, where it poured over the edge. During rainstorms, the opening to the cave must make a beautiful waterfall. Some of the water had found its way deeper into the cliff, wearing a wide, open space beyond the chimney.

There was nothing there. Bar pushed down his rising frustration and his fear that he was leading them on a worthless, time-consuming search. He touched the wall of solid rock and stretched his hands up as far as he could reach. Tal moved his torch closer. "There is a crack a few feet above your hand, Bar," Meggatirra said with suppressed excitement. Devon came up and with his mighty strength pushed at the too-straight crack. A piece of rectangular rock moved inward grudgingly, forced by his fingers. He continued to push the ponderous thing until it fell inward with a dull crash. The cut stone was at least two feet thick and three feet wide. Devon swallowed heavily and looked at his companions in astonishment.

Suddenly the torches went out, and they all retched and gagged. Bad air! They staggered down the narrow tunnel, pushing and helping each other toward daylight and fresh air. The Chi at the entrance helped them. After a time, they recovered. "So that was the 'choking darkness,'" Dare gasped.

"What a fool I was," Meggatirra said with disgust. "I know better. But there must be quite a space behind that opening to have so much stagnant air."

They reentered the cave cautiously, throwing lit torches in front of them. The torches continued to burn, so they advanced, picked them up, and threw them again. They gently tossed two lit torches through the opening. The torches burned steadily, but the strange window in the rock wall was too high for the tallest of them to see over. The stench, however, was still awful.

235

Thinking that no living thing could exist in the poisonous air, Lavel allowed Bar to go first. It had been his dream, after all. Devon lifted him on his shoulders, and Bar pulled himself up to the ledge. Before he could look into the room or whatever lay behind the wall, he was suddenly thrown back, violently. Thanks to Devon's quick instincts, Bar landed in the monk's outstretched arms. Then they both crashed to the floor. Bar thrashed wildly in Devon's grasp. The stunned company could see no enemy and stood frozen and confused.

Something was choking Bar fiercely. He heard a roaring in his ears, and his consciousness started to fade. Someone—no, *something* threw him on the floor. Bar's frantically searching arms could find nothing to fight, to throw off of him. He could hear his friends yelling conflicting ideas at each other. Their fear was evident.

Dare was thrown against the wall when he tried to help Bar, and he sat dazed on the floor. When any member of the company tried to help their marked prince, they were attacked by something entirely invisible. Groans and screams filled the small space. Worse than the pain was the confusion. Despair settled around their minds like a thick fog.

A horrible, oppressive fear came over each of them. They felt an overwhelming desire to flee whatever ancient evil had been set to guard this place. Only with enormous effort did they manage to hold their ground and try to defeat … whatever this was. Their remaining torches had been knocked from their hands and lay on the ground, still burning. Bar was writhing, in the grip of something, and weakly fought his unseen adversary. He arched his back to throw the adversary off, to no avail. Any who tried to help him were thrown off easily, including Devon and Lavel.

Devon stood, as if transfixed, in the middle of this chaos. He suddenly began to speak in a loud but shaky voice. "In the Maker's … ho-holy name, I command you, evil spirit, to depart this place, for you have no authority here. We are under his wings. Go! In the Maker of all's name, go!" The evil presence screamed and retreated somewhat, and the stench increased. "Fill your minds with words from the holy scrolls … Sing a hymn of praise to the Maker … Resist this evil spirit in your hearts and minds by the Maker's power," Devon commanded them in a voice filled with authority.

They tried to obey him. Even Bar had heard. He whispered only one word—"Maker!"—and the stranglehold on his neck broke. They heard an audible wail, and all sense of evil was gone. They felt as if darkest night had suddenly turned to day. They almost doubted their senses. Had they imagined the whole thing?

Devon was panting as if he had run a race. The rest of the company collapsed where they were to rest and to give the pain from their injuries a chance to lessen. Unseen by any of the company, Oster picked up his knife from the floor and placed it back in its sheath. Dare had to crawl to reach Bardon and help him sit up.

"What," Meggatirra asked in a shaken, sick voice, "was that?"

Devon slid down the wall behind him to a crouch. "Whatever is in there"—he pointed to the faintly lit opening—"was guarded by an evil spirit, perhaps more than one; I don't know. I have read of such things in the scrolls. It was common at one time, but I have never come in contact with this before. It took me a moment to remember the scrolls' instructions. All believers have the authority to order demons away in the Maker's name, but I did not recognize the enemy for what it was. Forgive me. Bar, are you all right?" he asked, struggling to rise.

"No," Bar croaked through a bruised, sore throat, "but I'll live. Could that thing have killed me? I have never felt such hatred from any living thing. It wanted to … destroy me."

"It could not have actually killed you. Evil spirits do not have permission to go that far, but it could have tried to keep you from its prize … to discourage you from trying again. It also could have tried to use one of us against you. We have not had to fight this kind of overt evil for centuries, not since early times."

Whatever the evil spirit's powers included, they were grateful it was gone. Dare was too shaken to treat their injuries and sat with his head in his hands. Some of the Chi had come quickly at their shouting to see what was wrong. They had seen bodies struggling in the flickering light but little else. At Meggatirra's order, one of the men ran to get his pack. Their injuries were minor: bruises, scrapes, and swelling bumps. The Chi who had retrieved Meggatirra's pack patched them up hurriedly and gave them water. Though he said nothing, his eyes burned with curiosity.

Feeling better after a few minutes of rest, Bar looked around him and noticed Devon's bowed head. Bar raised his hand for silence. When he had their attention, he bowed his own head and spoke halting words, through an aching throat. His words were of thanksgiving and praise to their protector, who had carefully placed in their company warriors of all kinds.

At the end of this short prayer, Tal's and Meggatirra's eyes met as they shared the same thought: sometimes their future sovereign acted like one, though not very often of course.

Marked Weapons

THE GROUP STARED SOBERLY AT THE OPENING
to the hidden room. The glow of the torches thrown inside faintly
illuminated the room's rectangular shape. "Well," Meggatirra said, "I
suppose it is time to try again. This time let either Oster or Tier go first. The
opening is too small for any of the rest of us. There may be other dangers,
besides the evil spirit, but I can think of no way to prepare for them, except
caution. Can anyone else?" He gazed at the company.

Lavel shook his head no with the others and then added, "Who could
have anticipated an evil spirit?"

A solemn, pale Oster said dryly, "Tie a rope around me, and I will go
first. If the floor drops out from under me, you can haul me up."

They grinned appreciatively at his suggestion, but Devon placed his
hand on Oster's shoulder and said gently, "No, Oster. There is a reason you
cannot be the one." Oster stared at him; a quick look of pain passed over his
face, and he nodded. Tal qua's gaze sharpened, and he looked questioningly
at them both. "Later," Devon said quietly.

"That leaves me," Tier said. The young Bani heaved himself up on
the ledge with Devon's help and crawled through the opening. When he
dropped to the ground on the other side, the floor did not drop out from
under him. However, a pervasive sense of evil did fill the room. Meggatirra
pushed another torch through the opening and asked what Tier saw. As
he took the torch, Tier cleared his tightening throat and answered, with a
voice that pleased him with its steadiness, for he did not feel at all steady, "I

see a room about ten by thirty feet. It has no visible ceiling, just a shadowy space that goes up and up beyond the reach of my torch. There are strange symbols on the walls ... very faded but still visible ... painted, I think, and there is an altar with dark stains on it."

Devon's face was tight with anxiety, as was everyone else's. "Do not touch anything without talking to us first."

That at least will be easy, Tier thought grimly.

"I don't like the sound of this," Devon continued. "In ancient times, people worshipped an evil being, much like they do Choack today. They practiced human sacrifice. It sounds as if you are in one of those places. Describe some of the symbols to me."

"There is an upside-down triangle with three parallel, vertical lines that are broken. The lines are in the middle of the triangle. There is a ..." His voice broke. Then he went on steadily, "A knife ..."

"That's enough, Tier. I get the picture," Devon said.

I wish I hadn't, Tier thought, looking away from the explicit images of sacrifices.

"Search the room carefully for any reddish-brown object and then—"

Tier's excited voice interrupted Devon. "There are two Gin'hana in an alcove behind the altar. Should I pick them up?"

Devon looked at his companions in anxious inquiry. "If only I could be the one in there!" he exclaimed in frustration.

Bar said, "Devon, let me go in now. I feel fine—well, almost—and perhaps my dream will help in some way."

They could think of no better plan. Tal took Bar by the shoulders and examined him carefully. His color was better, and his eyes were clear and steady. "He seems well enough," he said gruffly. The four chiefs of this single expedition—Tal, Lavel, Meggatirra, and Devon—gazed at each other. They nodded reluctant acceptance.

With Devon's help, Bar hauled himself up and dropped softly into the room. Tier waited behind the grim altar and pointed to the swords, which gleamed softly in the light of the torches. As Bar walked over to him, he reviewed the dream in his mind. There had been no warning other than the choking darkness. He spoke a silent petition and picked up the two ancient Gin'hana. They were covered with grime but seemed to be sound. No new terrible thing happened. He and Tier grinned at each other triumphantly. Then Bar said with a nervous look around, "Let's get out of here before something else happens."

Tier agreed. "Good idea."

They ran to the high opening and realized they had a problem. Tier grinned and suggested, "Stand on my shoulders, and I'll give you the swords. Hand them to Devon and then climb out. You can throw a rope to me, and I'll climb out."

Bar was too exhausted to protest and just nodded. His strength was gone, and he was barely able to pull himself to the small ledge. He quickly pushed the swords through to their companions' waiting hands. "Devon. Help!" He didn't have to say more. Devon pulled him through the opening and laid him on the ground. Chea threw a rope in to Tier and then held it fast so that Tier could climb out.

Elated, the company escaped through the tunnel to the sunshine, carrying with them their ancient treasure. Filled with anticipation and curiosity, they made haste to discover the nature of their prizes.

Devon and Lavel carefully cleaned the Gin'hana with soft cloths from their packs. The Gin'hana were more translucent than modern swords yet otherwise looked much the same. Created from lacidem poured into carefully carved molds, they retained the reddish-brown color of the original material. Not even the oldest of them recognized the master craftsman's signature on the hilt, but the carving was beautiful and intricate. After many splashes of water and a few minutes of rubbing, they were able to see what each hilt depicted.

To their amazement, on one hilt was carved, in intricate detail, an Uriisis. On the other was a beautiful wolf, which could only be Starfire or perhaps one of her ancestors. For a few shocked seconds, everyone stared at the luminous Gin'hana. Lavel smiled and handed Bar the Gin'hana he held, the one with the Uriisis. As Bar gazed, first at one hilt, then at the other, his hand trembled. He laid the sword down quickly, as if it had burned him. His mind was numb.

Devon's face was filled with wonder as he handled the other. "I think someone, long ago, tried to prevent anyone from ever finding these. For hundreds of years no one did. Yet they have come into our hands marked with familiar symbols."

Looking at Dare, he said, "I do not know who carved these or who the evil person was who hid them, but I do know who is meant to carry this one." He handed it to Dare, his eyes full of pleasure for the marked healer, who once had been a drudge. Dare automatically accepted it, but his eyes were glazed and uncomprehending.

Brother Devon, he stammered, "I just learned to use a bow. I have never even held a s ... sword, much less been taught to use one!" he objected.

"You will learn," Big Brother assured him confidently. Dare felt no such confidence.

"Would the Maker forget who ... what I am? No! I cannot legally carry a Gin'hana; it is against the royal codes. It cannot be meant for me," he said strongly, fear in his voice.

Devon started to speak, but Bar came out of his reverie at that moment and pointed out, "It has your mark, Dare. Look! It is on the blade, up high near the hilt." They all looked and saw the same four pale scratches on the blade that were plain to see on Dare's shoulder. Dare touched them. They were deep and evenly spaced; they were certainly not accidental scuff marks. Still, he was unconvinced.

However, there was no doubt in any of his companions' minds; they were confident that the marked were meant to wield the ancient weapons. The wearied fugitives' confidence that they were on the right track increased. In spite of the tangle their lives had been these last few months, they were evidently where they were supposed to be. There was a plan; someone was in charge.

Bar reached out slowly, as if he were afraid the sword would disappear, and put his hand around the hilt. He tested the weapon's weight and length. *It has been a long time since I handled a Gin'hana. Carrying a sword would have marked me as one of the nobility or a high-ranking officer ... or a thief. That kind of attention I didn't need. Do I need it now?* He looked at Devon. "It seems they are meant for Dare and me, yet there is nothing in the prophecy about them ... Wait! I am forgetting ... 'Uriisis and wolf marked, this pair, shining, like-marked swords will bear.'" The company was awed and full of joy. "Should we carry them openly? They will draw attention to us. Why—"

Devon held up his hands to halt the flow and said with a laugh, "I do not know the answers to any of your questions, but for now let us carefully hide them from view and get out of this strange place. If that creature back there has any friends around, I don't wish to meet them, especially after dark." Meggatirra strongly agreed. After wrapping both swords in sheepskin, they tied them securely with elong. One of the Chi would carry them along with the marked ones' packs and saddlebags. Both young warriors were at the end of their endurance. It would be all they could do to put one foot in front of the other.

After a quick meal, the rest of their party picked up their share of gear and entered another narrow cave that, with much climbing and twisting, took them to the surface. Everyone was too tired to admire the beautiful view from the top of the cliff. Neither Dare nor Bar had started this escape in good shape; they were exhausted now.

They trudged wearily after Meggatirra into a thick forest of pine, spruce, and fir. The sun was setting; its slanting rays reached through the trees in a golden haze that patterned the forest floor. Even after it was truly dark and the stars were blazing overhead, they kept walking. The Chi were laughing quietly about something. Dare wondered what, but he was too tired to ask. None of their company had started this journey in good shape. His head and body ached from the battering he had received. He had seen Bar stumble and knew he was at the end of his strength also. If Meggatirra did not stop soon, he would ask for a break and give Bar some more otet.

Chea had noticed Dare assessing Bar's condition and assured him that their destination was not much farther. "We lost time today searching for the swords, but we could have stopped earlier. The king is intent on getting to a certain camping place."

"A safer one?" Dare responded with fatigue.

"No ..." Chea retorted with a grin. "He seeks a site with lots of hot water and a place to bathe."

"All these miles for a bath?" Dare almost shouted, thinking angrily how tired and sore all of them were from their treatment in Oltive's dungeon and the battle in the cave.

Yet later, as he sat immersed in a pool of steaming water, he forgave Meggatirra all those hard miles. It was wonderful to soak away the soreness and the filth of weeks. They washed clothes as well as bodies with areean leaves, whose spicy scent drifted on the steam that snaked through their camp. Devon and Lavel trimmed the group's hair and beards as best they could with their sharp knives. In the flickering firelight, they noticed that the hishua's youthfulness seemed to have disappeared, replaced by bristling beards, thinned faces, and gaunt bodies. There were dark circles below their eyes and a wariness in them that spoke of negative experiences.

As he fell asleep, Dare whispered anxiously to Bar, "Our clothes will never dry by morning, will they?"

"At least they are clean. I think ol' Megga might desert us else …" Bar's voice trailed off as he fell asleep.

The next day they did no traveling. Meggatirra allowed the battered company to rest. After that, they traveled for three days in a generally southern and then western direction. On the fourth day, Meggatirra called a halt in a heavily forested valley. This place was a prearranged site, to meet the warriors he had sent to mislead Tori. The men took time to rest and repair their weapons and gear. The missing warriors did not arrive that day or the next, and the king grew grim, his temper brittle.

On the second morning of waiting, Tal qua found Devon sitting by the fire alone, working on a boot whose seams had ripped open. He sat on the log next to him in order to talk privately about Oster. Devon told him what had happened.

"In the fight in the cave with the evil spirit or spirits, Oster drew his knife and came close to injuring Bardon. In the confusion, I don't think anyone else observed him. At least, they have not mentioned it if they did. I knocked the blade from his hand. He seemed dazed then and stayed back out of the action."

Devon looked thoughtfully at the boot and chose his next words carefully. "It greatly concerns me that Oster drew a weapon. The only person it could have injured was one of us. It would have had no effect on demons … who do not have bodies. I think the evil spirit made the suggestion that he use it. For whatever reason, Oster was open to its leading." He looked at Tal regretfully. "That's why I couldn't let him enter the hidden cave. If he is not a follower of the Maker, he has little protection against the evil ones, especially in direct conflict. He is a good lad, Tal, and I've nothing against him, but it would have been foolish to send him against such … such evil without the Maker's protection."

Tal stared thoughtfully into the fire. "With our people, belief in the Maker is something taken for granted. It is a part of the children's teaching … a part of our lives, but there are probably many who do not really know him themselves. To invoke his name is, to them, part of being Basca' … yet they have no firsthand knowledge of his power."

Tal mused, "Os is young to have been sent to Feisan, but they try to send those without families of their own. He joined me along with the others about a year ago. We have worked well together; he is an excellent tracker as well as a skilled warrior. Yet I cannot think that we have ever discussed the Maker, except in a historical way. I will speak to him about this, and if he is willing, I would like him to come talk to you. He is probably feeling confused and guilty about the whole incident."

"A good idea," Devon agreed.

A shadow fell on them both, and they looked up. Oster had seen them together and knew they were probably talking about him. He came hoping to join their conversation. The turmoil inside him had grown to alarming proportions.

"Sit down," Devon invited as he bit off the strand of thin leather he'd used to mend the boot. Oster held his hands out to the flames to warm them; the day was cold in spite of the bright sunshine. Devon explained to Oster why he had not let him go into the hidden room, just as he had explained it to Tal. Then he said, "You cannot fight in spiritual battles unless the Spirit of the Creator is in you, or you will certainly lose."

As if the memory oppressed him, Os uttered shakily, "I have never known such … fear. I wanted to run." He dropped his head at this shameful admission.

"So did the rest of us," Tal said flatly, "yet you did not run."

Oster looked up with haunted eyes. "But no one else drew a weapon! In my mind, at that moment, I thought I could kill it … I felt safer with a knife in my hand. Something whispered, 'Kill it!' over and over again. I don't know what I might have done if you had not knocked the knife from my hand! I remember you saying that evil spirits will try to use one person to hurt another … to do what they *cannot* do." He closed his eyes and shook his head at the possibilities. "After you knocked the knife away, I came to myself. I knew what I had done was stupid and could have been fatal for Bar or someone else, but I could not seem to think clearly. I couldn't remember a single hymn or saying from the scrolls, yet I learned many as a child. All I could do was say the Maker's name over and over again."

Devon considered a moment and then asked Oster if he had ever participated in or seen a ceremony honoring Choack while in the royal capital. "Aye, sir," he answered grimly, flushing.

"Tell me about it," Devon said.

"There is little to tell, sir. One of the soldiers invited me to go to a Mirg Rorroh, a service honoring Choack, with him. I said no, but he taunted me and said, among other things, that I was afraid. Furious, I accepted … and then immediately regretted my impulsive words. But I was too proud to back down, so I went." There was bitterness in his voice. "The Mirg was in the palace itself. I managed to hide where I was going from Tal. That I didn't want him to know should have told me something, but this man's remarks about me and my people stung. I wanted to prove him wrong, so I didn't let myself analyze what I was doing too deeply. At first, the service was mostly chanting and seemed foolish; then everyone seemed to enter a kind of trance. Draville and Lotu started to talk to their god. I hate to call it prayer, but I guess that's what it was. They praised his … cunning lies and deceptions, the strength of his boiling hatred, the mighty power he wielded for them, and the terror it inflicted on their enemies. They asked him to defeat their foes, and then … they asked for his presence and a show of power. Up to that point, I was sickened but not really afraid."

Oster shook his head, as if still unable to believe what happened next. "Their request was answered! A strong sense of evil filled the room. It was so strong that I felt weighed down, and numbness began to steal over me. Strange things began to happen, like objects floating through the air. The chanting grew louder and frenzied.

"Men, who wore long cloaks and stood in a group by themselves, suddenly threw back their hoods in a kind of ecstasy. Their heads were shaved, and their eyes were closed. Then they started to moan in unison … the same sound over and over again … 'Uh … uh … uh.' I know it sounds silly … foolish even, but it wasn't! Perspiration ran down my face and back with my effort to break loose, but I could not move my body. Inside my mind, I cried for help desperately. I called on the Maker's name, and the men's hold on me was broken."

Os met their eyes for the first time since he started his story. "I knew I had to leave quickly or I would not be able to leave at all. I stumbled and pushed through the crowd ... knocked down a guard at the door who was too far gone in a trance to put up much of a fight and ran till I reached our barracks. I lay shaking and sick in my hammock for hours before I could sleep and then only fitfully."

Again lost in memory, he continued, "The soldier who had made fun of me laughed scornfully at me the next time we met. He continued his sneering remarks, but I no longer cared. I never went back with him again, yet once was enough to ... to disturb my peace. To this day, I have terrible dreams of that night."

Devon asked, "Did you participate in the chanting?"

Oster hesitated and then admitted, "Aye, Brother. At first I joined them to prove how silly it was ... how strong I was, but as my fear grew, I stopped. It no longer seemed ... silly."

Devon said, "Look at me." Oster raised his eyes, which were full of a growing comprehension of what that night might have cost him ... had cost him. He found both Tal's and Devon's expressions compassionate but searching. They did not have to say what they thought; it was written on their faces. Speaking of his actions for the first time made that night clearer in his own mind. Tal and Devon's response was important to him, for of all the men he knew, he respected and valued these two the most.

Tal rose and, squeezing Oster's shoulder encouragingly, said, "I will leave you to Brother Devon now. If you wish, we will speak of this later." Then he left. Oster's heart ached so that he felt his chest would break open.

"Let's go for a walk in the wood," Devon suggested. Oster nodded and got up. "When you voluntarily went with this soldier to scoff at not only a false god but an evil one, you put yourself where no child of the Maker should ever be. When you raised your voice in worship—" At Oster's quick objection, he said, "I know. You did not mean it as worship ... yet the dark one took it as such. You willingly placed yourself on evil's ground and participated in its service. Evil does have power, not power such as the

Creator, who is without limit, but more than a godless man. Choack and those like him are created beings, after all, and on a tether. Their time to meddle and destroy on our planet is limited. We are, all of us, involved in a spiritual battle as well as a physical one. You were in enemy territory, and even though you ran, a part of you was taken captive. That's the way it is in war. It is as if you opened a door to the evil one. Now you must close it. Do you understand?"

Oster stopped walking and thought hard, not seeing the beautiful snow-covered forest or its chattering inhabitants. "It's not fair! It's not what I meant to happen," he cried out with anger and grief both.

"Our enemy is *never* fair, nor does he care what you meant," Devon replied grimly. "He gladly pounces on every slip we make. Only the Maker is fair and, thanks to him, more than fair. He is also merciful and compassionate. He loves you very much, and it grieves him to see you turn to a being of pure evil who means you only harm … as you have experienced."

After a few minutes of reflection, Oster asked quietly, "Can you show me how to close that door?"

"Aye," Devon answered. He told Oster what to do: "Acknowledge your faith breaking to the Maker and ask him to pardon you. Then ask him to close the door you opened. Do this, that your armor against evil will be whole. In the past, if your belief was based on others' views and not your own, consider making it personal, between him and you. He offers you a love based on a relationship with him not just rules, though the rules are important too." Oster nodded, and Devon left.

The young Basca' sat on a fallen log and leaned back against a huge rock. His thoughts were slow at first. *Forgive me, Maker. I thought I was strong enough to … break your law and not be touched or hurt. I knew I was breaking it … that we are to give worship to no one and nothing but you. In the process, the enemy took a part of me prisoner. Please throw him out and close the door I opened. May no part of me be under his control or influence. I reprove him in your name … and order him to leave.* Forgotten words came back to him. *Be my armor. Be my strength, for I do not have strength enough of my own to defeat this enemy.*

An attitude that was a part of his life became apparent to him. He wondered why he had never seen it before; it was so clear to him now.

After only a second's hesitation, he acknowledged it as faith breaking and made his choice. *I have followed you in name only. I kept you at arm's length because … well, because I desired … to live my way … to choose my own path. The last thing I wanted was to know what you wanted for my life! You see, then I would be obligated to do it. A part of me still feels that way. I trusted in my own ability and strength and got into … deep trouble. I thank you for Devon's hand that knocked the knife away … that I harmed no one, and I thank you for saving me that awful night from … Choack. Now, I seek to follow you with all my being.*

He experienced a grief and sorrow too deep for tears as he looked back, and not just because he'd attended the Mirg. Os could see the arrogant attitude of many years that had led to his acceptance of the soldier's invitation. He groaned as memories and images passed before his eyes. *Forgive me this too.* Then tears came, healing in their release.

After a time, Oster became aware of snow glistening in the sunshine and birds chattering in the branches above him. The lingering oppression that he had lived with so long, an oppression that had seemed a part of him, disappeared. Peace, such as he had never experienced, flooded his being. He murmured in amazed gratitude, "Alati."

A sense of well-being followed and an awareness that he was clean, that the darkness that had shadowed him was gone. *I will no longer look over my shoulder in fear or have terrible nightmares*, he realized with relief. He closed his eyes, leaned his head back against the rough bark, and was content to do nothing but rest and enjoy the tranquil sounds around him.

After a time, he rose with renewed energy and walked back to camp. He felt light and full of vigor. *I want to hunt, to run, and to ride. Right now, I think I could beat even Bar at kuni wrestling, but first I want something to eat.* He started to whistle and stopped in embarrassment; Basca' did not display their emotions for all to see. He grinned, then walked indifferently back to camp, as befitted a warrior.

Big Brother, who was cooking venison stew for midmeal, was getting ready to go look for Oster because he had been gone so long. Then the young man walked out of the trees. Devon was relieved and pleased when he saw Oster's shining eyes and merry face.

"Big Brother, please tell me there's something to eat in that pot you're stirring," Oster said with a grin he could not contain.

Devon smiled back and replied, "There is! Have a seat, and I'll give you a bowl. When you have ... settled down a little, I would like to talk more about this Mirg."

"When I have settled down!" Os exclaimed indignantly. He gave Devon a quelling stare and said with a raised eyebrow, "Basca' are always grave and stern, as befits a warrior." Then he destroyed the effect by laughing. Devon joined him.

A DIFFICULT JOURNEY

FOR THREE LONG DAYS, THE COMPANY WAITED for the Chi who had led Tori and his soldiers away from their camp. During morn meal on the fourth day, a scout high on the cliff started chattering like an angry squirrel. The Chi stopped to listen. Chea interpreted the message for the company. "Party returns, some injuries." In spite of the bad news, Meggatirra looked relieved. Injured warriors were better than dead or captured warriors. Some men were quickly assigned to help the three Chi reach the valley.

After the warriors had eaten and their wounds had been tended, they told their story. Tori and Lotu, with their soldiers, had pushed the three decoy warriors hard, both day and night, and had not been deceived by any of their tricks.

"We tried, Lord," a warrior named Ta'en explained with distress, "but they backtracked each time and figured out what we had done. We left no sign. We were as careful as I know how to be, yet time after time, they discovered our ruse." As the young man continued his tale, Meggatirra and the other Chi were at first amazed and then alarmed. The volatile captain and his venomous cohort's ability to see through the Chi's best deceptions, strategies that had worked in the past, was frightening.

"A part of Tori's troop took the high mountainous trail in Kolrowa Valley and got in front of us. We were on the low trail, the one that goes through a broad meadow and then passes between high cliffs. They ambushed us from the top of the cliffs. That's when we received our injuries.

Thanks to Delur's sharp eyes, we knew they were there. We hid ourselves by clinging to the sides of our steeds and staying in the midst of the horses. We set them at the fastest pace they could make after so many days of travel."

He sighed wearily. "They, the soldiers, know now that there were only three of us. We survived their attack, but our mounts were tiring. The other part of Tori's troop was still pushing us hard from behind, and they were gaining. When we came to another pass, we were out of their sight for a few minutes, behind a stand of pine. I sent the horses on, hoping they would pursue them. We hid ourselves among the rock and trees. They swept by us and followed the horses into the pass. Immediately, we scrambled up the mountain and hid ourselves in"—he remembered the non-Chi among them and revised what he was going to say—"in the place you know of that is near there. In a short time, they figured out what we'd done and tracked us, but they could not find our hiding place. Finally, after a full day of searching, they gave up."

Ta'en finished, "If it had not been for that hiding place, they would have been on our trail again. It was a near thing. We have been making our way, very carefully, to this valley ever since."

Meggatirra gazed at the ground, a frown on his face. The young lieutenant waited anxiously for his lord's reply to this perplexing report. Finally the king looked up. "You have done well, Ta'en, Delur, Teh'sa. Thank the Creator you are safe and back with us. Go now and rest. We have much to think about and also planning to do," he said, his frown deepening with distraction.

Worried that he had not done all he could, Ta'en said with troubled regret, "I am sorry we lost the horses, Lord. Perhaps, if—"

Meggatirra's brows came down as he interrupted, "And I am glad. You are much more important than horses. Their loss saved your lives. Now off with you, and no more regrets. You did what you could; that's all any of us can do." Ta'en bowed gratefully and left with his two companions.

Meggatirra observed with suppressed anger, "I am disturbed and, aye, surprised at Tori and Lotu's abilities. It is perhaps injured pride on my part, yet our hiding places, our methods, have always worked before this time. And they have worked without exception. I fear we must travel even more carefully."

Lavel was staring at the fire, his forehead wrinkled in concentration. He looked up at Meggatirra and said sincerely, "Sire, we have so much to thank you for. We are truly grateful for all you have done. I have had time to consider our position and seek the Maker these last few days. I strongly feel that we must leave now and head for Glidden ... *alone*. You are far from home, and I would see you safely back in your mountains."

He sighed and ran his fingers through his dark hair. "I am pleased that you also think we must all use extra caution. Oster's experiences with these ... these Choack worshippers has warned us that they are a force to be taken seriously. I am sure watchers have been carefully placed to find us, and I do not think that they are all human. Lotu may be receiving help from this evil spirit he worships, though I cannot guess how or of what nature."

Analyzing Ta'en's report, Lavel continued, "I do not know how the king's soldiers on the cliff interpreted your three warriors' appearance: their hair, eyes, and skin color. Surely they reported it to their captain. Lotu and Tori, at least, would be versed in Ree's history and suspect the warriors they saw were Chi. If so, one of your defenses has already been breached. They will speculate that the Moor ha Chi still exist. It will not take them long to conclude that our amazing escapes were organized by people who know these mountains well. I fear for you. I fear they may start to hunt you also."

Bar added forcefully, "Tori is acute; I assure you that this is true. It is why my ... King Bardock values him so highly. If they all get together and compare their experiences—I mean Tori, Lotu, Blalock, and the Blackrobe captains—they might figure out many things. Then they will hunt relentlessly with all their enormous resources the Moor ha Chi as well as the Bani."

All those present looked as if they had been struck an unexpected blow. The clearing around the fire was quiet, except for the sighing of the wind in the pines. His face pale, Tier spoke his thoughts aloud. "My father said that the Bani could not expect to stay hidden forever, nor could we expect the crowning of the marked one to cost us nothing. Perhaps it is time for the Bani, at least, to be known again."

Meggatirra looked at him for long seconds. No one spoke. Tier became aware that, in spite of his attempt at diplomacy, his words suggested that the Chi should do the same. He swallowed hard, embarrassed that he had spoken. Meggatirra broke the tense silence. "Out of the mouths of youth. Perhaps the time for the Chi to be known approaches also, but," he said, smiling to put Tier at ease, "we will choose the day ... and this is *not* it. We must prepare to leave quickly."

The king gave orders, as did Tal and Lavel, which meant, of course, that the "youth" worked steadily for the next few hours, dividing and packing their gear. The men ate a midmeal together and then took regretful leave of each other.

As the two groups separated under the lofty trees, to go their different ways, Bar realized how much he would miss the Chi and especially Meggatirra. His respect and affection for the man had grown over the last few days. He had come to admire his strength, his cunning, and his steady calm in all situations.

Chea lar went to Meggatirra and asked for his blessing by pressing both hands together, palm to palm, and touching them to his forehead. The king placed both his hands on Chea's head and spoke. The others did not hear his words. Chea touched the area over his heart, a gesture common to all peoples that meant "heartfelt thanks" or "thank the Maker," and turned quickly to join their company.

As was his way, to do whatever he did with his whole heart, Bar crossed the clearing before Meggatirra could leave. He dropped to one knee before him, as was proper to a king or one of high rank. They had all treated Meggatirra as the captain of their company, not as the king of an ancient and proud people. This sovereign was descended from the "first ones," those the Maker himself had walked with and taught.

It was in Bar's heart to do Meggatirra honor, for he had twice saved their lives, at great risk to himself and his people. Bar touched his heart as Chea had, hoping the king would understand, for he did not know Chi customs well. A calloused, weathered hand raised his bowed head. The king's luminous eyes were fierce, but he said gently enough, "Our hope is in the Maker. May he protect you, marked one, you and yours from your enemies. I pity those who oppose you; they have already lost." He raised Bar to his feet and embraced him. The Chi warriors were greatly touched and did not forget Bardon's reverence to their king.

For the next few weeks, Bar and the others made their way toward

Glidden. Lavel used every strategy he could think of to keep them hidden. They traveled at night, when the moon gave enough light. They stayed hidden among the trees and avoided barren places, even if it meant a loss of time or going miles out of their way. If they had no choice in the passes between valleys, as they often did not, they traveled early or late or at night. In spite of the time it took, Lavel confused their trail. In spite of the cold, he marched them through streams and up flooding hillsides to hide their tracks. Because spring was coming, the snow thawed during the warmer afternoons, and everywhere, they could hear the sound of running, dripping water.

Lavel, whose leadership had always been relaxed, was stern to the point of fierceness. His brother did not know him and was puzzled at the change. He enforced strict discipline: there would be no talking, no noise, and no trace of their passage left anywhere. They did not cut wood, they did not leave holes in the ground, and they did not bend twigs. Their fires were small, hidden, smokeless, and scattered when they were finished, then covered.

Lavel had not told them of his dreams—dreams that constantly warned him of danger. In these dreams the rocks, the birds, even the cliffs—all high places—had eyes that searched for them to report their location to the enemy. The weight of his responsibility was always heavily on him.

Almost, Devon spoke to him about trusting and relaxing a little, but he decided against it. The situation *was* grave; the measures, though uncomfortable, made sense. The hishua gave Lavel no argument, for they, too, understood the danger. Imprisonment in Green Cliffs' dungeon, the evil spirit in the cave, and the king's men's uncanny ability to find them had all had their effect on the young men. They could not seem to shake their enemy, no matter what they tried. Occasionally they grumbled under their breath but not often and not very seriously. Lavel did not realize they knew about his dreams, but they all were aware of his disturbed sleep, for his restlessness and murmuring frequently woke them.

After waiting many hours for the sun to go down, Chea took the lead as they approached a pass one quiet evening. They were moving carefully through a meadow that offered them little cover, yet it seemed a safe enough thing to do in the mellow twilight. With a gesture that was barely visible, a mere flick of his fingers, Chea motioned them to get down behind whatever cover they could find in the growing shadows. They were so used to stealth, to observing the smallest signal, that they immediately melted into shadow and stopped, to a man. Birds, whom their quiet passage had not disturbed, sang their evening songs. Darkness deepened, and still Chea did not move a muscle. Whatever he had seen, no one else had observed, nor could they see it now, though they searched with keen eyes.

High on a rocky promontory above them, a dark hooded figure stood, stretched, slipped away, and was replaced by another who had a dark, bristly shape the size of a tipeeke beside him. The two shadowlike figures settled into the same spot and became invisible.

Dare had excellent vision, but he could no longer see them, though he knew they were there. Darkness came, and still they did not move. Colder air, smelling of melted snow, drifted in shifting currents around them, and somewhere, a wolf howled. Their muscles cramped, and the cold penetrated their limbs, in spite of their warm clothing. Tipeeke had excellent night vision. Some said the creatures used to be creatures of the night, though now they also hunted in the day. Dare could no longer see Chea. He saw those closest to him only as dark, lumpy blotches. They could not stay here forever. The moon would rise later. Yet so thorough had been Lavel's training that not one of them thought of moving. A cricket chirped, the Bani signal for "wait." They waited, till they were so cold and numb that they didn't know if they could move.

It is a little cold for a cricket. Lavel hoped their watcher wouldn't find the sound suspicious. Chea was forced to use signals they all understood, a difficulty they would have to work on at a better time. They needed audible signs that they all could recognize. *Mighty Maker, guide me!* Lavel's brain searched for a solution but found none. If they moved now, the sharp-eyed tipeeke would see them. If they waited, the moon would rise, and the tipeeke would still see them, even if they didn't move. If they survived that possibility somehow, daylight would come and then ... *sure* capture. The longer they waited, the worse the situation would become.

Lavel was ready to take a chance and move his company. Suddenly, wolves started howling and snarling on the cliff opposite the watcher. The tipeeke screeched indignantly, furious that other animals were in his territory. They could see the beast clearly and also the hooded shape that tried to control him. The tipeeke was so agitated that it seemed he would leap off the cliff in his frenzied attempt to drive the usurpers away. The animal yapped, screeched, and wailed incessantly. Throwing their heads up to the night sky, the angry wolves howled more fiercely and paced to the very edge of the cliff and back.

Lavel commanded urgently in the deafening noise, "Move ... now, but do not run! Slip steadily through the pass while we have the chance." With pounding hearts, they complied. Each man recognized how important it was not to panic. Still, it was difficult to move slowly.

Lavel talked softly but steadily as each one of them walked by him into the narrow gorge. "Drift from shadow to shadow ... slowly, slowly," he cautioned. Lavel followed the last man with a sigh of relief. As the company passed deeper into the gorge and out of sight, the tipeeke and wolves were still noisily contesting territorial rights. The fugitives traveled swiftly all night; fear gave them new energy.

By the time the eastern sky was growing light, they had found shelter in a dense grove of red and doro pine. They were close—very close—to Glidden. No one complained again, even in his own thoughts, about Lavel's detailed, careful precautions.

They rested all through the day. That night, Lavel led them cautiously to a familiar shepherd's cottage where they would wait for the Glidden folk to find them. He knew it would not take long, yet he paced anxiously, his thoughts in turmoil.

Bardock's scouts cannot watch the whole western half of the island! Why then is an unimportant pass in a deserted area guarded? Have they found Glidden while I have been away? Who will come for us? How much do they know? The peace of the shepherd's cottage began to feel like a baited trap. He decided they would leave. Then he heard a noise outside. *Too late!*

Hoping he would see well-known friends, Lavel faced the only door grimly. He motioned the others behind him, a gesture that Tal and Devon ignored without hesitation. They took their places by his side with bow and arrow ready. The door opened softly, stealthily, and a figure slipped in. "Identify yourself, quickly!" Lavel commanded.

A familiar badgering voice replied, "Peace, my large friend. Don't attack!

It is only Sher. There are a few too many of you, and Lock wants me to check the situation out. May I come in?"

"Come," Lavel said with relief. "Give us a minute, and we will light the lamp for you." In the soft glow of lamplight, Sher looked the company over. He nodded to Dare with a friendly smile of recognition.

Lavel introduced his party with a hint of a smile. *Poor Sher*, he thought. *This is going to take some getting used to.* "This is Prince Bardon, son of Bardock; Tierray, son of the Bani chief; Oster and Tal qua of the Basca'; Devon, abbot of Saint Fauver's *and* my brother; and Chea, nephew of Meggatirra, who is king of the Moor ha Chi."

Sher looked thunderstruck. "Who? Would you repeat that? Surely I have heard you wrong."

Lavel laughed softly for the first time in many days. "Aye, it *is* a lot to take in. I had trouble myself, and it happened over a period of time, so I could get used to things slowly." He repeated, at a more leisurely pace, all he had said before. Sher looked little better the second time around. "It is a long story, Sher. Go tell Lock all is well and get us safely into the mountain. I warn you: we are dangerous fugitives to give sanctuary. We are being hunted and perhaps followed or watched, right this moment. By the grace of the Maker have we made it safely this far. Hurry … and be invisible."

Sher took one last stunned look at Chea lar and turned on his heel to slip quietly out the door. Bar found himself in second place as a personage of interest. A living Chi, straight out of legend, was difficult competition. He was glad that for once he was not the center of attention. Lavel paced nervously, but in a very few minutes, four Glidden men came in followed by Lock. They must have been waiting in the woods. Lavel gave much away to sharp eyes in his deferential bow to his chief. Both respect and trepidation were apparent.

No one was prepared for Bardon's reaction. He gasped, "You!" and backed away as far as he could in the small cabin. He drew his knife and took a defensive stance. His brain was in turmoil. Dare looked at him with confusion but knew his duty and stepped in front of Bar, knife drawn. The others followed his lead, all but Lavel, who was mystified.

"What is it, Bar?" Lavel asked.

Bar shouted in confusion and anger, "I know him. He was once my father's battle commander. His name is not Lock but Duke Ecuder Rael of Possan, a loyal subject of Bardock." Bar felt betrayed, yet Lavel seemed sincerely baffled, and the rest of the company appeared loyal. He tried to calm himself and think rationally.

Lock's men were bewildered but remained steadfast and ready to defend him. Lock sighed and said softly, as if talking mostly to himself, "This I did not anticipate." He raised his voice and spoke directly to his accuser. "Bardon, you have nothing to fear from me. It is true that I was ... am ... Ecuder Rael, but I disappeared with my family from Ree's society many years ago. My family planned an accident that would convince the king we were all dead. I have hidden here ever since, in self-imposed exile. I did not realize you had ever seen me, or I would have tried to prepare you before we met."

Bar's intense stare never left Lock's face, but his body relaxed a little. He asked Lavel, "Is this your chief? Have you known him long?"

"Aye to both, Bar."

"Bar, we must get out of here while it is still dark. The sky will soon begin to lighten with the coming dawn. Trust me. Trust Lavel, until I can explain more fully," Lock requested urgently.

Bar looked at Lavel, distrust plain on his face, but after a few moments he said, "All right, I will ... trust. Let's go."

As they hurried through the trees, a distinctive howl filled the quiet night. Lock turned to look back, his face shocked. "What was that?"

Lavel pushed his chief gently onward. "I'll explain later. Let's get out of here!"

GLIDDEN

At Lavel's advice, Lock sent out an immediate warning to all his people that king's men, Blackrobes, and a strange, very dangerous animal called a tipeeke were in their area. He also decided to send scouts and patrols to strategic places, and he pulled in all his hunting parties. Glidden men were sent to warn shepherds as well as local villagers to be alert and careful. It was all they could do ... for now.

Later the next day, Bar looked around him and sighed. *More explanations. How many times have we been through this? Many.* His gaze rested on Lock, who was explaining his past, a past unknown to many of Glidden's residents. Memory stirred, and a thought came to him that seemed, at first, absurd but no more so than any of the other strange things he now accepted as fact.

As Dare sat listening to the same council that had questioned him many seasons ago, he marveled, *I have come full circle. I am back where I started, but life has changed ... I have changed! For a drudge, who had never stepped one foot outside of Rave, I have now seen much of Ree.* He grinned as he thought of the Chi and their caverns. *In fact, I have seen parts of Ree few living men know exist!*

They sat around a fire in the same warm cavern Dare had been questioned in before, with the same stern guards at each entrance. It had taken hours to explain who each man was and his part in the story. Dare was tired of sitting but even more tired of talking. He moved restlessly, stretching aching muscles as unobtrusively as possible, while he thought his own thoughts. He quickly lost the thread of the council's conversation. Dare felt a gaze and looked up with guilt. Shonar gave his former apprentice a look of mock censure for his restlessness. Dare grinned back and tried to pay attention, but his thoughts wandered to his and Shonar's meeting that morning.

The old healer had been present when they'd burst into the council room. A pang of anxiety had shot through Dare the minute he saw Shonar, who seemed frailer and looked thinner than he had last summer. Dare dipped his chin in a hurried bow of respect, then embraced the old man in response to his welcoming grin, but he did this before Shonar had spoken. "Are these the manners I taught you?" Shonar said sternly, but the twinkle in his eye belied the firm words. Dare came to proper respect with his head bowed, hands clasped behind his back, and feet slightly apart. He did not wipe the grin from his face, however. Shonar walked around him as if he were a mountain and said with mock anger, "You have grown. In six short seasons, you have gained weight and grown! We shall run out of supplies trying to feed you."

Since he had been spoken to, Dare could now lift his head. "Aye, sir."

"I suppose you have forgotten all I taught you?"

"No, sir. I've learned even more. You will likely be amazed at my new skills and knowledge."

Shonar laughed and said, "I'm sure I will. I am already very pleased with all I've heard about you since you left us."

The company looked on their reunion with gladness, eager to meet the venerable healer that Dare referred to all the time. He introduced Shonar to the rest of the company. The old healer held Bardon's forearm a fraction of a second longer than the others. With a smile, he'd touched Bar's forehead with his left palm in blessing. It had signified acceptance as well.

Dare's thoughts returned to the current meeting. The council was not nearly as accepting. They mistrusted Bar instinctively, and it showed. He was Bardock's son! Surely the Maker had made a mistake in marking this one. He had been raised in Feisan, in their minds an ungodly and evil city. He had a reputation for coldness and cruelty. Worst of all, he had been exposed to the cult of Choack.

They, of course, had supported Lavel and the alliance's efforts to save both Bar and Dare. However, that had been when Bar was out there on the other side of the mountains. It was quite a different thing to have Bardock's son here in their safe haven, to say nothing of a Moor ha Chi and a Bani, who should not exist; two of the Basca', whom everyone knew had always been loyal to the king; and an abbot whose monastery had been burned to the ground. To give this young man, this prince, shelter was as foolish as attempting to steal a rock bear cub from its mother. Already the desperate, ragtag fugitives had brought them trouble. There were now Blackrobes and tipeeke on *this* side of the mountains.

It is an uncomfortable time for all of us, Dare thought with empathy, *a time to risk … to come out of hiding and fight for what we believe. Or not.*

The underground had an efficient system of communication that involved runners, boats, pigeons, and many other methods. The mountains, however, slowed this system considerably. All the underground's routes involved going around the mountains, which took time. Somehow, Bardock had overcome this difficulty, for his messages went over them. The council had known by Lavel's handwritten code, which had come to them through many different messengers, that Dare and Bar were coming. However, that knowledge had not prepared them for the rush of tangled feelings they were experiencing. Any man or woman who was a part of Glidden had already experienced tragedy, or they would not be here in the first place. Their fears were realistic, based on the facts of their lives.

The story they were hearing was so strange, so fantastic, so frustrating, and … so true. They saw Bar's mark. They saw Dare's mark. They were convinced that the hishua were the marked ones the prophecy had foretold. Yet the presence of these two young men created many problems. They were not happy about any of it, not happy at all. The talking was taking the better part of a day. Everyone had more information to sort than they could handle. It was time to eat, to sleep, and to let their new knowledge rest for a time. But that was not to be.

Lock's head jerked up in irritation as the sounds of men's voices, raised in anger, filled the corridor. "Who is it, Laicos?" he asked the guard at the west entrance.

"It is Evitis and Sutol, Lord. They say they must speak to you, now."

Lock knew these two men; they were mature and trustworthy scouts. Whatever was wrong, it must be important. "Tell them to come in." He turned to his guests. "Please excuse this disturbance." They started to rise, and he said, "No, do not leave. Whatever this is, we are in it together now." Two men came in, both middle-aged, one tall and slender, the other of medium height. They were out of breath and obviously distressed but forcing themselves to remain calm.

"It's Tnasaelp, Lock!" Evitis said. The scouts looked uncomfortably at Lavel and Devon. "We went to warn them, but we were too late. These Blackrobes, along with the king's soldiers, have surrounded it and taken the people captive. They've whipped the two men on the village council to scare the others into talking. They think the villagers know where Lavel and Devon might be. Thank the Maker the poor folk know nothing to tell."

Lavel and Devon paled. Long ago, they'd lived with their parents in little Tnasaelp. Devon had left years ago, but Lavel still knew and visited with the people when he was in the area. They knew him as a broker of various wares—one who found new goods for merchants to sell. This profession gave him an excuse to travel freely all over Ree. How quickly Bardock's spies had made the connection! Lavel understood immediately why an insignificant pass had been watched. Perhaps they did not know about Glidden, but they had discovered, somehow, where his and Devon's home was located. Their village would be a natural place to look for the fleeing fugitives. Lavel's stomach knotted in anger and grief. The common people of Tnasaelp had committed no crime. They simply shared his and Devon's birthplace.

Evitis added, "Also there are men searching all the woods and the mountain. Someone told the soldiers somethin' about us, and they sure know where to look now. We're surrounded and not so safe, I'm thinkin', for they're close, Lock, close to looking in the right places!"

Soon reports started coming in from other sentries that king's men were all around. Lavel reevaluated. *Perhaps they do know about Glidden!*

Glidden became an anthill of activity as Lock gave terse orders—orders he had hoped never to give. He was both dismayed and angry. *I, who know the king's soldiers so well, know their tactics and their leader ... and I am unprepared! Our patrols have picked up no unusual activity. Or have they?*

Has someone within the Glidden community betrayed us? It is possible … even probable given the unscrupulous methods that have ever been arrows in Bardock's quiver. Bribes, imprisonment, loss of lands, and death of loved ones—all are tools he uses to reach his goals. Lock hurried up stone stairs to one of the northern lookouts, where he could observe the king's men, who were close to finding an entrance on that side.

Lock sent the company to rest and eat, since they could not help with the present problem. They were unfamiliar with Glidden and its defenses, all except Lavel. Guilt dogged Bar, though he tried hard to dismiss it. Morin would have been shocked to learn that his wise words, concerning giving in to despair, remained firmly in Bar's memory. Wise words or no, Bar was losing a familiar battle. He tossed and turned on his pallet while trying to push unbidden thoughts back where they belonged, to no avail.

Wherever I go, it seems disaster follows: Morin's ship, the monastery, the Bani, the Chi, the village of Tnasaelp, and now Glidden! The last stronghold of the underground is under attack! My passage is certainly eventful. I leave a trail of trouble behind me. Maker, let me cause no more grief. His petition seemed to bounce off the low, undressed rock of the ceiling and add to the already crushing weight of his guilt.

Bar did not see that his travels had brought into the open and joined together many peoples who were either part of the prophecy or necessary to its fulfillment. In a short time, amazing things had been accomplished. Bar had found Dare, and they both had been marked. They were both free—no longer enslaved to lives of misery and coercion. Amazingly, the marked ones had found important allies who were now also friends. Through his and Dare's flight, the few clans who still believed in the Maker and were watching for the fulfillment of the prophecy had been informed of Bardon's and Dare's marking. They were ready to help them. None of this had been accomplished without pain. There had been joy also, but now he could see only the grief. Unable to sleep, Bar rose quietly, so he wouldn't disturb the others, and grabbed his pack. He went to the baths. Perhaps hot water would relax him, would wash him clean of guilt. He knew better, but it was preferable to tossing and turning.

The bathing pools were deserted because of the emergency, except for one very old man: Shonar. "Join me," the healer said. Bar groaned inwardly as he slipped out of his filthy clothing and into the hot water. *I hope the old man does not want conversation. I am in no mood for it.* The steaming water eased away soreness and dirt and gave some comfort to his tired body. It even eased the distress in his mind.

Shonar started talking, and before Bardon knew how it happened, he began to unburden his mind and heart with quite a lot of conversation. Shonar was a sympathetic listener. His occasional questions and comments gave Bar a new view of his circumstances. Bar said ruefully, "Do you have this effect on everyone? I have never talked so much to anyone of … of the things that trouble me, not even to Dare, who knows more than most. I am distressed that—"

"Do not be," Shonar interrupted gently. "Sixteen is not old enough to bear such burdens alone … nor is any age. Even with my advanced years," he said, his eyes twinkling, "I need someone to talk to so that I may hear my thoughts out loud. It helps me to sort them. You especially will need this as you grow older, for your responsibilities will be heavier than most."

"And I was starting to feel better," Bar said with a groan. Then he laughed reluctantly.

Shonar smiled also. Then his gaze became unfocused. "There is always a plan. That is why he gave us the prophecy, so that we would be watchful and recognize his plan when events started to happen. We can be unafraid and confident because he is in charge. We are usually woefully aware of our own lack of power to control or change events. They roll over us without our permission. He knows the future and designs his strategy accordingly. In the end, all things serve him."

After a pause, Bar said, "Shonar, I have something I would like to discuss with you. You may think I'm crazy, but I suspect it is part of the plan. It has been on my mind ever since I met Lock, who I know is your son, and heard his history."

After listening to Bar's idea, Shonar laughed softly. "I think you have judged rightly. He's not going to like it, though, not at all."

Bar was puzzled. He had no idea why Shonar thought the idea amusing, but he did not question him about it. "Will you tell me how it is done? I have never seen anyone do it … though I've heard of it before, of course."

"Aye," Shonar said reassuringly, "I will."

LOCK

EVEN THOUGH KING'S MEN WERE STILL COMBING the area, the council met again the next day. Fortunately, the enemy had found no entrances, but it was disconcerting as well as frightening to the Glidden folk to have strange beasts, Blackrobes, and soldiers searching their lands. If Glidden warriors attacked the royal search parties, the attack would confirm the existence of a fugitive people. It would invite just what they didn't want: more troops, more searching. So they waited. Lock had scouts everywhere, but they were under strict orders to do nothing but watch.

Lock and the council arranged for a diversion that they hoped would lead the king's soldiers to an area farther north and deeper into the range. Unfortunately, it would take time for a decoy company that looked like the real one to travel to the deserted area they chose. Meanwhile, Glidden folk would plant stories of the fugitive company and their location among the local population. Until this plan pulled the search away, they would be forced to endure the enemy presence and to hope they found nothing.

Lock also placed a watch on the townsfolk that the Blackrobes had imprisoned. It was the council's desire to free the prisoners, but they knew it would be wiser to wait. Liberating the citizens of Tnasaelp would be like knocking down a wasp nest. They could not risk such an action, unless there was more violence against the people. They thought the soldiers would decide, after their fruitless search of the village, that the poor people knew nothing. Hopefully, they would set them free without further coercion.

Having set these plans in motion, Lock and the council called everyone together again in the late afternoon. They badly wanted to finish talking to the company. Lock knew that they must decide what to do with their valuable but troublesome guests.

Lavel finished telling their story, which had been interrupted the day before by the scouts. The cave remained quiet for many minutes as the council pondered. Bar realized that the time was right to speak to Lock, but a sudden nervousness came over him. He couldn't seem to speak. Lock was an intimidating man with a lot on his mind at the moment. Bar had no idea how Lock would respond to his request to become tsurtne.

Roughly, to become tsurtne meant to bind for learning. It was an old word that came from the time before the "leaving," (a time when tribal groups like the Bani hid themselves) and it named a tradition that was almost dead. In tsurtne, young men and women, particularly hishua, bound themselves to an experienced person in a craft or profession for a period of two years to learn that trade. In return for learning and room and board, the young individuals committed themselves to serve their lieges without pay. There were rules that determined all aspects of the relationship. In most cases the young person was treated as a respected relative; he or she became a part of their liege's household. After talking with Shonar, Bar was sure that Lock was the person E Clue had identified in his instructions.

He reviewed again in his mind the phrase that he thought applied: "Tsurtne he shall become to the hidden man, he who has lost all, except his family and new clan." Lock had been the leader of the king's armies; now he was a fugitive, a tribal chieftain with no wealth. He'd given up everything the king could offer him to become an exile. Ecuder Rael had gotten out of Possan with his family, and that was all. Now, as Lock, he seemed to think it more than enough.

Shonar cleared his throat and stared at Bar, urging him to speak with a slight motion of his hand. Bar took a deep breath and blurted, "Lock, I need to speak to you about something."

The words landed in the quiet room like a thunderclap. Lavel looked at him in amazement. The council members responded with suspicion, intensive scrutiny, and some, with anger. It offended them that he would speak to their leader before being addressed. What actually offended them was something quite different. He had brought danger to their sanctuary.

Aware of his prickly councillors' defensive stares, Lock smiled a swift apology. "Speak. I am listening."

Bar struggled with his voice and a strange surge of emotion. Shonar's quick smile reassured him. "Remember when I told you of E Clue's instructions?" Lock nodded. Bar went on, "I believe you are the man referred to in the instructions E Clue gave me. The phrase that I think applies says, 'Tsurtne he shall become to the hidden man, he who has lost all, except his family and new clan.'" Bar paused and then said, "I respectfully request to pledge tsurtne and learn your profession. I request this because I am convinced that you are the 'hidden man.'"

Lock's face became thoughtful but displayed no shock or surprise. On the other hand, the council members were very shocked and murmured among themselves.

Bar continued, "I have spoken with Shonar to test my reasoning, and he agrees with me, but even … even if he did not, I would have to ask you. I accepted the Maker's mark and owe him obedience. You fit the criteria …" Bar stumbled to a halt.

Lock, formerly Ecuder, rose slowly, his serious gaze on Bar's face. "Child, I do not want this. My old life and my title are gone."

"I know, sir, but remember that the prophecy says that one day I will rule. I have learned how *not* to govern from my father. Who will teach me to rule fairly with sense and justice? Would you have your future ruler know nothing of governing, except what I learned from Bardock and his ministers?" Those in the council cavern moved uncomfortably at the mention of the sovereign's name, not liking the sound of it spoken aloud in their refuge. "Would you have me learn everything the hard way?"

Lock's face became a little less stern. "One thing you will not have to learn is to speak persuasively." He sighed, gazing at something unseen, and asked soberly, "Are you sure, child?"

"Aye, sir. I'm very sure."

"Brother Devon, will you be our witness?" Lock asked.

Even Shonar was surprised. They had all expected Lock to take time to think about the request and to confer with his council. It was not like him to make an important decision so quickly, and they were astonished. Devon rose instantly to stand beside Glidden's chief, his face as calm and undisturbed as ever. Bar rose also and crossed the room to stand facing Lock.

Lock looked around the room and said in a low but easily heard voice, "Long ago I helped place Bardock on the throne. I fought other houses whose armies tried to displace him, and I defeated the brigands who wanted chaos in our land. He was the only true heir of Hector's lineage, and many of us risked our lives to make sure that the rightful king ruled. After a few years of efficient rule and long-desired peace, Bardock began to change. He was always ambitious and rather cold, but he became greedy. He used his influence to gather personal wealth. Gradually he got rid of anyone who disagreed with his policies or stood in his way. I knew that one day he would ask me to do something I could not do, so I chose to disappear rather than die in prison. He was not a truly wicked ruler until he came under the influence of the Choack cult. I have helped others escape Bardock's tyranny. We have lived here quietly waiting on the prophecy. Today this young man will promise to serve me for two years, but one day I will promise to serve him. I will help place him on the throne that Bardock, though he is of the true blood, no longer merits."

Lock put both his strong brown hands in front of him, palms up. According to Shonar's instructions, Bardon placed his hands on Lock's; they were trembling. Lock said in a low, clear voice, "I will instruct and teach all that I know. I will protect and provide for Bardon according to all the agreements of tsurtne. This I pledge to do faithfully before the Creator." His unreadable dark eyes never left Bardon's face.

Bar responded slowly, "I will study diligently and serve faithfully and loyally Lock, also known as Ecuder Rael, according to the agreements of tsurtne. This I pledge to do faithfully before the Creator."

Devon placed a hand on the shoulder of each and said, "I witness this agreement and declare Bardon tsurtne to his liege, Lock of Glidden, on this day, the twenty-first of the first month of planting season. This tsurtne will last for the next two years."

Bar pressed the back of Lock's hands to his forehead and then lips, signifying devotion and loyalty. Lock enfolded Bar's young, smooth hands between his battered, aging ones, a gesture that was a promise of protection and welcome into his household. Bardon knelt to receive his new lord's blessing, which poured gentle peace over him like warm oil. The short ceremony was over, but its effects would be far reaching.

Both Bar and Lock were more than a little overwhelmed by what they had done. Strangely, the hostile council seemed deeply moved and suddenly more accepting of the marked prince. Truth to tell, a few were ashamed of their lukewarm response to the appearance of Bar and Dare in their safe refuge. Some were awed and realized the full import of the young men's presence for the first time. Most were truly pleased but more frightened than ever about what their commitment to these two might involve. Before they left the torchlit chamber, each one stopped to speak to both Bardon and Lock, as custom demanded. In doing this they confirmed their witness and, perhaps more important, their approval. Not one failed to speak to them both, an amazing change in attitude, considering their coldness before the simple ceremony.

Bar and Lock walked the labyrinth of torchlit tunnels to the chapel to meditate. The young prince had grown enough in self-knowledge that the sense of panic and despair welling up in him did not surprise him—well, not much anyway. The old fears of being trapped and of not being in control of his life attacked fiercely.

They entered Glidden's uniquely beautiful chapel together. It was completely dark in the towering cavern, except for a swirling golden column of pure light hundreds of feet high. Bar gasped at its splendor. It took him a few minutes to realize that the light was sunshine. It streamed down from an angular rent far above them to spill onto the cavern floor. Bar was deeply moved at the sight, as was everyone who saw it, for either the first or hundredth time. *How easy to honor him here … to be still here*, he thought as he sat on one of the scattered furs.

Near him, Lock sought the Maker's strength, for he had glimpsed, during the short pledging, the path before him. He had taken the first step down a new road. The simple life he had known in Glidden was irrevocably gone. A battle had begun the day Lavel had freed Bar and Dare from Casterray. The underground just hadn't realized it. By their aid and through their efforts, two young men had been set free to become the marked.

Maker, I have been through one such conflict with this child's father. It turned brother against brother! I hate war. Please, choose someone else.

"That conflict prepared you for this one. I have chosen you. Will you leave me?"

No! No. I will not ... ever.

The weight of what he saw still crushed him.

His God reminded him that he did not bear the weight alone and that he never would. He also reminded Lock that he was in charge and there was a plan. With a bowed head, Glidden's leader acknowledged the truth of these reminders and accepted his commission. Gradually trust came and, with it, peace.

Lock lifted his head and straightened his shoulders. He turned to look at Bar and found the young man gazing at him anxiously. He smiled reassurance, and they left together.

The battle to stop an evil ruler and his regime had begun. The underground would become the Resistence.

Printed in the United States
By Bookmasters